ANOTHER OCEAN TO CROSS

A Novel

by

ANN GRIFFIN

Georgic Publishing

Dedication

This book is dedicated to the women of World War II. The mothers, the lovers, the wives, the daughters, the loners, who fought, in their own ways, for their loved ones, and their lives.

"We carry oceans inside of us, in our blood and our sweat. And we are crying the oceans, in our tears."

Gregory David Roberts, *Shantaram*

Acknowledgements

As a debut author, I have many people to thank. So many people have been involved in bringing this story of a lesser-known part of World War II, to life. My thanks to Carol Schmidt, whose fascinating account of her mother's life, propelled me to begin writing. To Michael Neff of Algonkian Writers Retreats, thank you for your encouragement and guidance to a rank amateur. To Charles Finch, author of the Charles Lennox Victorian Mystery series, thank you for convincing me that I did, perhaps, have some small smidgen of talent. To Judith Starkston: thank you for inviting me to join the Arizona Historical Writers Association, where I found my tribe. To my dear friend, Joanne Warner-Lowenthal, thank you for permission to use the name of your father, a Jew who escaped from Germany prior to World War II, as a main character. I hope this book honors him.

To my first readers, Rebecca Guevera, Dianne Hughes, Nancy Browne, and daughter Michelle Deines: thank you for your feedback and encouragement. To Caitlin Alexander, the first editor who looked at my raw pages: thank you for believing in me and telling me to do more. A huge shout-out to my editor, Kathryn Craft, author of *The Far End of Happy* and *The Art of Falling*. You took my early effort and guided me to a higher level of skill than I could ever have accomplished on my own. To Beth Deveny, my copy editor: thank you for cleaning up the script so beautifully.

To all those writers on a dozen social media sites: thank you for being there. You will never know how much help it was to see others, like me, struggling to give birth to an idea.

And last but certainly never least, my husband, Art, who has always encouraged in any way he could. Thank you, thank you.

Part I: Europe and Africa

Chapter One

The young woman drew rapidly, sketching the old man on his knees in the street, with blood running down his face. A group of five young thugs wearing Nazi uniforms kicked and beat him, cheering each blow, their taunts mingling with the old man's screams. An angry cluster of civilians urged them on, stamping and shouting.

"Jewish shit!" "*Judenschwein!*"

The blows and kicks rained down on the helpless man until his cries stopped and he moved no more. The crowd began smashing the windows of the dead man's family bakery.

"Here." Renata handed her sketchbook to the young man at her side who was also sketching, and walked deliberately, slowly, toward the body.

The crowd paused to stare at her.

She was quaking, but kept walking.

One leering youth slapped a thick stick in the palm of his hand.

Unwinding the scarf from around her neck, she knelt and carefully placed it over the dead man's face, stood and glared at the crowd, then turned her back on them and returned to her companion, ignoring the catcalls and jeers behind her.

As soon as she was no longer visible to the crowd, her friend grabbed her by the arm and pulled her close.

She realized she had been holding her breath.

He steered her briskly, back into the labyrinth of alleys and narrow streets until the crowd noise faded behind them. "What the hell were you doing out there? You could have gotten us both killed!"

"I know. But I'm not sorry. Those people are beasts! Let's get out of here, Hans." She was shivering.

"You're braver than me. But we have good sketches for Switzerland tonight. I put you in the last one."

"You did? Let me see."

Pausing behind a row of dustbins, Hans handed her the sketchbook.

He had perfectly captured the rage of the crowd, their brutality, and Renata's courage. She swallowed the lump in her throat and shuddered. "Those bastards! He could have been my father." She squeezed his hand.

Noises behind them started them running.

Arriving at Hans' back door, Renata Lowenthal tore a page from her book, handed him the sketch, then leaned up to kiss him lightly on the lips. Both eighteen, in the first flush of love, they stole moments together whenever they could, despite laws that forbade relationships between Jews and Gentiles.

He was so handsome—tall, blond, blue-eyed, a true Aryan, but without Nazi poison flowing through his veins. She and Hans had attended art school together before she was banned from classes. Hans had a friend, an employee of the railway system, who smuggled their sketches of Nazi atrocities out of Germany, and into the hands of foreign journalists willing to use them.

Hans slipped his hand around Renata's neck and drew her to him again. He nuzzled her curly hair and lifted her chin for another kiss. She threw her arms around him.

"Oh, Hans, it's getting worse every day. We have to keep believing that what we do matters."

"It does. But it's getting so dangerous, I'm not sure how long we can continue."

"If I can ever convince my parents, we'll leave, but until then, I'll keep working. We must get our real Germany back. But what about you?"

"I'll be drafted into the Army any day, God help me. I won't go. I'll leave the country first. Come on, let me walk you home."

"Not yet. The gallery sent me a letter. They won't show or sell my paintings any longer, so I have to pick up the two still there."

She frowned and kicked at a loose brick on the pavement.

Hans swore softly. "They are closing everything to Jews. I don't know how you will even eat, the way things are going. I'll get the sketches to our friend. Be careful and remember—you're stronger than you know."

Renata squeezed his arm and trudged away toward the gallery.

"Good afternoon, Herr Bauer. What's this letter you sent me?" She waved it and leaned on the counter, scowling. Tall at five feet nine inches, and with an enormous mop of curly dark hair, Renata towered over the hapless gallery owner.

His immaculate white shirt, tie, and gray vest, intended to convey an air of confidence and authority, belied his hand-wringing and nervous glances to the street outside. He stared at the wall through tortoise-shell-rimmed glasses. "I have been ordered to cease showing or selling paintings by Jews. You must remove your paintings immediately, or I may…I mean my family…they will arrest me." He looked up.

Renata noticed beads of perspiration on his brow and upper lip.

He licked his lips. His eyes pleaded with her to understand.

"And how do you expect any Jewish artists to survive if no one will sell their works? Of course, that is exactly the plan, isn't it? They don't want us around and will do whatever they must to dispose of their 'Jewish problem.'" She slammed her hand on the counter.

Herr Bauer jumped.

"Very well," she continued, her voice a growl. "Bring me my paintings. But cowards like you are the reason Hitler can get away with the horrible things he does."

Herr Bauer's glasses steamed from her acidic speech.

She wanted to throttle him.

He disappeared into the back room and returned minutes later with two paintings, wrapped in brown paper and string. His hands shook as he laid them on the counter.

"*Bitte, Fraulein…*" he began, but Renata scooped up the

paintings and left, slamming the door behind her.

She stormed up the street, until the presence of soldiers forced her to slow, to avoid drawing attention. She pulled her scarf around her head against the chilly wind. Sullen clouds threatened snow. *A dreary day, a dreary heart*, she thought. Her throat tightened at the memory of the dead baker, who in better times had given her the occasional bagel when she stopped by his shop with her mother.

She had watched the rise of Nazi brutality, seen many Jews beaten and their shops destroyed, yet her parents ignored her insistence that they leave the country. Renata was furious at what the Nazis had already done to her family. Her father, Dr. Karl Lowenthal, had been a respected physician and researcher at the medical school until he was banned from teaching. Now he treated other Jews in their homes and was paid with whatever barter the patients could manage. Renata had seen her budding career of art shows and reviews, in which she was fêted, crumble. She was still steaming at the insult when she arrived home.

Her parents believed in the basic goodness of humanity and were sure the German government would not take things too much further. Her hand tightened on the paintings as she swore she would try once more, this evening, to convince them to leave.

"*Guten Abend*, Mama."

She set the paintings down while she removed her boots and hung her coat and scarf on a rack near the door.

"*Guten Abend*, Renata," her mother replied from somewhere inside. "Your Tante Adele is here for coffee and cakes. Please join us."

Lea Lowenthal was a wiry woman in her late forties, her face etched with suffering that had slid into chronic depression. She had never recovered from the birth of her stillborn son, Solomon, fifteen years earlier. She visited the tiny grave weekly, swept it, added flowers in the summer, and wept over the dream that he would have been her perfect son. Her sister, Adele, begged her to let the little one go and focus on her living daughter, but Lea could not. Unable to provide the warmth and affection Renata needed, Lea turned instead to art and became Renata's teacher, albeit a harsh and demanding one.

Art ran deep in their family history. The walls of their home were covered with masterpieces that went back generations, including some of her own. When she married Karl, he had insisted she stop painting, believing that the husband was to be the breadwinner and the wife to be the *hausfrau*. But he did not stop her from teaching their daughter.

The little girl hated the stern lessons for years, until at some point, she found her own style and began pouring her feelings onto canvas. Four years ago, the gallery held a show of her paintings. Many sold immediately. But that was then. Now, no one would dare say anything good about a Jew, or worse yet, pay one for anything.

"Ah, there you are, my dear. So good to see you." Tante Adele swept into the hallway trailing scents of lavender and rose. She kissed Renata on the cheek and stood back to look at her flushed face. "What's wrong, Renata? You're upset. Come sit down and tell us what's happened."

They walked into the parlor and sat on overstuffed antique chairs.

Lea placed coffee and biscuits on a table beside them. She poured, and Adele helped herself to a biscuit, but Renata could not eat.

"The gallery made me bring my paintings home. They won't show them any longer, nor any other Jews' works. And old Herr Nussbaum was just beaten to death outside his shop. It's getting worse every day, Mama. We need to leave!" She thumped a fist on her thigh.

"Renata, I won't have you talking like that. I'm tired of hearing it. I'm so sorry about Herr Nussbaum, but he must have done something wrong. Tante Adele is here to look at your paintings, and since you have the two you brought, why don't you put them up on the mantel so we can look at them?" She took a sip of coffee.

Her daughter pressed her lips together at her mother's willful ignorance.

Tante Adele added, "I can't imagine Hitler will go much further. But I would like to see the paintings, my dear."

"Oh, very well." Renata swallowed her anger. She fetched

the paintings, unwrapped them, and set them out.

One was a gloomy street scene, redolent with snow, ice, and darkness illuminated only by a waning moon and one weak streetlamp. Bundled figures, hunched against the cold, hurried to unknown destinations. Hints of uniformed men with guns hid in shadows. The foreboding in the painting was unmistakable. The other, completely different in style, featured wild reds and oranges, and mouths open in screams. Tiny dots of black suggested tears, or perhaps bullets.

"I can see why the gallery told you to take them home," said Lea. "And after all I taught you about form and style."

"Mama, I'm developing my own style. Isn't that part of being a great artist?" Resentment smoldered in her belly.

"Oh, listen to her, Adele. 'A great artist.' Talk about being puffed with pride." Lea stood and walked toward the opposite wall, on which hung paintings by her father and grandmother. She gestured grandly. "These are great artists. You are still a child."

Adele attempted to derail the percolating argument. "Lea, Renata is no longer a child and while she is not yet a great artist, thanks in part to your instruction, she may well become one. Isn't that your dream, Renata?"

"Yes. I'm going to succeed, no matter what Hitler and his bullies may do." Renata squeezed her aunt's hand and gave her a wispy smile. "Someday my paintings will hang in galleries again, and I will teach at universities."

Lea rolled her eyes and poured more tea for herself, ignoring her daughter, who had learned to absorb her mother's insults as she absorbed rain on a blustery day.

Adele rose to examine Renata's paintings more closely. She took her time, thoughtfully assessing each, tilting her head this way and that, while Lea gave the paintings a cursory look.

"I believe I like the abstract better," Adele finally announced. "It allows one to bring one's own interpretation to it. Certainly, it expresses fear, but there could be many other emotions: anger and lust, for example. The other one..."

Loud knocks interrupted her. The women froze.

"Open! Open the door for the *polizei*!"

Renata could only think of the sketches she and Hans had

made. Her insides turned to jelly.

"Open now, in the name of the Führer, or we will break the door down!" The knocking became violent.

Renata moved toward the door. "I'm coming! Don't break the door, I am coming!"

She flipped the bolt and five policemen burst into the room, pushed Renata backwards and took up positions in a semicircle, where Lea and Aunt Adele stood quaking. The shiny black boots, spotless gray uniforms, and large guns seemed to fill the entire room.

Renata felt sweat trickle down her armpits.

"*Heil,* Hitler!" snapped the leader. The other men saluted. "*Heil,* Hitler!"

"We hear reports of corruption in this house." The leader paced the room and slapped a riding crop in the palm of his gloved hand. He spotted the paintings on the mantel and stopped.

"I see the reports were correct!" He pointed his crop at the abstract work. "This painting is decadent, corrupt, and has no place in the Third Reich!" He gestured to one of the men, who marched up to the painting and slashed it to ribbons with a knife.

"No!" screamed Renata. Adele and Lea clung to each other, mouths agape. Lea was weeping.

In one step, the captain reached Lea and slapped her across the face, knocking her to the floor.

"So, you are the so-called artist producing this filthy anti-Reich work?"

Renata took two steps toward him, shaking but determined. "No, she is not. She is my mother. I am the artist. Leave her alone!"

"Get up!" He hauled Lea to her feet and pushed her away, then grabbed Renata and slammed her against the wall, knocking over an antique vase which shattered when it hit the floor. "I'll show you how we treat Jews like you." With a nod of his head, he sent two of his staff to guard Lea and Adele, who were sobbing in terror. The other men grabbed Renata by the arms and held her facing the wall.

"Stop it! I'm just an artist! Don't hurt me!" Her arms hurt, they had stretched them so wide. Her mind was blank. From the corner of her eye, she could see her mother and aunt, white-faced, behind guards with drawn pistols.

The captain raised his crop and brought it down with all his strength on her back. She screamed. Stickiness oozed from the welt. She had no idea pain like this existed. Again, and again, he whipped her, until her back was crisscrossed with blood. Her screams ceased and she hung limp in the arms of the two men.

At a signal from their leader, they dropped her to the floor.

"Now, perhaps you will listen. No more of this filth, or you will be arrested and shot. Understood?" He poked Renata with the toe of his boot. Groaning, she managed to nod her head.

He turned to the other women. "If we arrest her, we'll arrest you all. And isn't your husband Karl Lowenthal, the doctor?"

Lea nodded, blubbering.

"Where is he?"

"I-I don't know. He-he-goes out for long walks in the afternoons."

The officer pushed his face into Lea's. "We have a warrant for his arrest, for making critical statements about the Führer. We'll be back for him."

He gave a curt command to the men. They left, banging the door shut behind them.

Lea and Adele rushed to Renata, who was conscious again, gasping in agony. She managed to raise her head and groaned. "Now do you believe me?"

When she opened her eyes, Renata was lying face-down on the divan, and although in terrible pain, she knew someone had cleaned and bandaged her wounds. The dress was gone and a thin sheet was her only covering.

Papa, looking ten years older, sat beside her, holding her hand. "You poor, poor darling. How are you feeling?"

"Like hell, of course." She didn't care about swearing at a time like this. Papa didn't even flinch.

Lea offered her a glass of water. "Would you like something to drink?"

Renata was desperately thirsty, but movement was excruciating, even with Papa's help. She managed a few sips, then pushed the glass aside.

She suddenly remembered what the *polizei* had said. "Papa, Mama, we have to leave."

"Shhhh, don't worry about it now," said Lea. "You need to rest."

"No, we must leave now!" Grimacing, she pushed herself up. "Papa, they will arrest you! And they don't know about everything I've been doing. If they find out, I'll be shot."

"What else have you been doing, Renata?" Karl asked quietly.

She told them of the sketches she had sent to Switzerland, but left Hans out of it. Lea gasped. Karl looked dumbfounded. Aunt Adele sat back with her mouth open.

"Tonight is our last chance. Here, help me get up."

The room circled around her. When she reached for the mantel to steady herself, her back screamed. But there was no time to think about the pain now.

"Mama, get a satchel for each of us. Papa, your medical bag and our passports. Aunt Adele, you'll come too, won't you? They'll find an excuse to arrest you, too, maybe not today, but soon."

Aunt Adele backed away slowly. "But I've done nothing wrong. They can't arrest us all, can they?" She laughed, a nervous, fluttery sound.

Renata fixed a steely glare on her dear aunt. "I've done nothing wrong, either, Tante Adele. At least nothing wrong in the free Germany we used to have. I tell you, they will find a way to arrest us all."

"But how much worse can things get? They are just trying to make a point, and when war comes, they will need us."

"No, Tante, please! Come tonight!"

But she shook her head.

Karl cleared his throat. "Lea, Renata is right. I will not risk our lives another day. Let's pack what we can and leave. Adele, you would be wise to come with us."

"But I can't leave Solomon, Karl." Lea wrung her hands. Tears welled in her eyes. "There's no one to look after him. Visit him. Pray for him."

"Mama, for God's sake."

Karl put his hands on Lea's shoulders. "Now my dear, I know this will be difficult for you, but we cannot remain here to tend one dead child only to create another. Look what they did to our Renata."

Lea averted her gaze.

Karl spoke again. "Adele, if you are determined to stay, will you watch little Solomon's grave for us?"

"Of course I will." Adele put her arms around her sister. "Go in peace, my dear. Don't worry, all will be well, and the babe has angels watching him, too, remember."

Lea's shoulders sagged. "Is there no other option?"

"No, Lea. We have tried all the others."

"Then I'll see you out, Adele, and thank you." Lea walked her to the door.

The sisters embraced and kissed. Renata's throat tightened. She sensed she would never see her aunt again.

"Hans will drive us to the *Hauptbahnhof*, I'm sure." She cranked the phone and in minutes was speaking with him.

"We've been invited to visit our family in Venice, and we would be grateful if you could drive us to the railway station... *Ja*... just me and my parents... *Danke*." When she hung up, she wondered who besides the operator was listening. Surely the call sounded innocuous? No matter. It was time to pack.

Chapter Two

The Escape, 1938

Lea heaped the family jewelry on the kitchen table as Renata hacked away at the pages of a book. She'd seen the trick in a movie, in which the heroine hid jewels and money inside a hollowed-out Bible, and she hoped it would work in the real world.

The heavy paper dulled the kitchen knife. Torn scraps fluttered to the floor as Renata chopped and cut. She scooped up the jewels and dropped them inside, but the cover would not close. She dumped them back on the table and went at the book again, tempted to rip, forcing herself to be careful, as perspiration trickled down her face and stung her back. Dropping the knife for a moment, she wiped her forehead with the back of her hand. It had to work. Again, she picked up the jewelry, including Mama's sapphire-and-diamond necklace and a pile of Reichsmarks, and dropped them into the book. Finally, it closed without any telltale gaps. If only she had some glue...but this would have to do.

Her father tramped downstairs carrying one satchel for himself and one for Lea.

"Hurry." He set the luggage by the front door.

"*Ich komme*, Papa." Renata shoved the book into her satchel, taking care that it stayed closed by cramming it beside her only change of clothing. At the last moment, she grabbed a sketchbook and some pencils and stuffed them into her bag.

"Mama, are you ready?"

"*Ja.*" Lea had hardly spoken since Adele left. Her face was gray, her eyes red.

Renata tied her headscarf, shading as much of her face as possible. The threadbare gray coat and scuffed boots were hideous, the coat stretched over three sets of clothing, but she no longer cared. Her pulse raced and her back throbbed, but they were getting away.

The women waited inside while Karl opened the door and looked right and left into the darkness, listening for the crack of jackboots or the rumble of autos. Wet snow sifted from the clouds, hiding dirt and fear.

"It's clear, come." Karl waved them outside.

Tears slid down Lea's face when her husband closed the door behind them for the last time, leaving behind their home of five generations. And Solomon.

Karl patted her back, then locked the door and dropped the key into his pocket.

Renata squeezed her mother's hand, then let go, the heavy satchel requiring all her attention on the pavement, slushy with spring snow. The few other people out in the night kept their heads down into the wind, avoiding eye contact, not wanting to know who else was outside.

Sirens wailed in the distance, coming closer.

"Here, here!" hissed Renata.

Spotting an alleyway with a recessed doorway, she pulled Lea and Karl off the sidewalk as a huge black car and truck screamed past. The little family hardly dared breathe until the sound faded into the distance. Finally, as one, they exhaled, their breath clouding the frigid air.

Karl peered around the corner.

"All right now, quickly!"

One block. Renata glanced with revulsion at new signs in several shop windows: "Aryan business." "*Juden hier nicht Wilkommen.*"

Two blocks. Lea's breathing was ragged and loud. Renata was sweating despite the cold, and she felt blood on her back. Karl had offered her morphine for her pain, but she dared not risk drowsiness.

His eyes were everywhere, scanning the last block for any sign of danger.

Lea shrieked as her legs skidded on a patch of black ice.

She came down heavily on the sidewalk, hit her head, and lay there, whimpering. Karl and Renata helped her to her feet. She was wet from the slush, and there was blood on her head.

"We're nearly there, Mama. We'll get you dried out on the train." Renata wiped the worst of the slush off her mother's coat.

Lea pulled away. "I hate this— all of it!"

Karl held his wife's arm. They could not risk another fall.

At last, they reached Hans' home. The door opened silently before them and they stepped inside.

"The car is around the back. This way." They followed Hans through the house, leaving icy piles that his mother wiped up behind them. Minutes later, she would scrape the sidewalk clear of telltale footprints.

Lea, Karl, and Renata crawled into the back of the car, shoved the suitcases onto the backseat, and hid on the floor. Lea moaned softly, her head in her hands. It occurred to Renata that her mother had no idea what real pain was like—at least the physical kind. Hans clicked the door shut, climbed into the driver's seat, and allowed the car to coast down the alley to the closest intersection.

Finally, he pushed the starter button. The motor revved smoothly. He flicked the headlamps on, and they were on their way.

Hans spoke over his shoulder. "Why the sudden decision?"

"They beat me, Hans. For degenerate art. My back is shredded. And they have a warrant to arrest Papa."

"*Mein Gott!*" He gripped the steering wheel and barely avoided swerving the car out of the lane. Cursing under his breath, he refocused on driving, but his expression was grim. "They are not stopping Jews from buying tickets at the station, but the chance to escape is disappearing quickly, now that Hitler plans to annex Austria. Most are heading for Switzerland. They've started house-to-house searches, and rumor has it that there's to be a registry of Jewish property. I'll go back to your house to collect some of your art, if I can, and store it until this is over."

Karl flashed him a grateful look and dropped his house key on the car's dashboard.

"Thank you. I only wish I had listened to my daughter, and left sooner."

Hans parked the car around the corner from the railway

station's main entrance. After they clambered out, Karl turned to Hans.

"*Danke*, dear friend, and God reward you. Terrible times are coming. I will pray for your safety."

"You are most welcome. I, too, will pray for your safety. And Renata…"

She went to him and he embraced her gently, avoiding her savaged back.

"Hans, I will miss you so much. I love you."

Hans wiped away her tears with his thumb. He cradled her face in his hands and kissed her.

"Get well. Never let them defeat you. We will meet again, I promise, when things are better." Then his Teutonic reserve deserted him. Emotion clouded his face. He backed away, touched his fingers to his hat, and was gone.

Armed soldiers with Alsatian dogs stood around the square outside the Munich *Hauptbahnhof*, where travelers flooded under stone arches into the lobby. People shoved; parents called to children. Elderly couples gripped each other, struggling to stay upright. Porters wheeled bulky suitcases and trunks through the doors and disappeared into the melee. Officers barked commands, but the size of the crowd made keeping order difficult—even for the Nazis.

Lea and Karl stared at the scene, while Renata urged them forward, grimacing in pain with each step. A torrent of desperate people beat against the wickets, asking to pay fares, holding children high above the throng. Clerks sold tickets with the enthusiasm of jailers exercising prisoners. Ticket-holders then fought their way forward to the control gate, where they were interrogated before being allowed through to the train platform.

"Three tickets to Venice, *bitte*," shouted Papa above the noise, once the family arrived at the head of the line. He pushed cash under the wicket. "The ten o'clock train."

"Papers!" demanded the clerk, accepting the cash with one hand and holding out the other. Papa fumbled with their papers and stumbled as a hysterical, buxom woman crashed into him and

Renata from behind. Renata yelped, her back aflame. The woman disappeared with a quick apology and Papa shoved the papers under the bar to the clerk.

The clerk glanced at the papers and saw the Jewish surname, Lowenthal. He spat into the corner.

"They don't like Jews any better in Italy," he growled, as he stamped the papers and handed over the tickets.

Papa took the papers and tickets, turned to Renata and Mama, and nodded his head in the direction of the trains. Maneuvering the satchels in the jam of bodies was so difficult that Renata was sure her shoulders would be torn from their sockets. She lost track of the number of times her feet were stepped on, and her back was bleeding. The gate control officer, impeccable in his Nazi uniform, sat behind a small portable wooden table, on which were several wooden stamps, an inkwell, and a blotter. Behind him, two burly armed guards stared at the family with undisguised loathing.

"Papers." The officer snapped his fingers.

Renata took the papers from Papa, glided forward, and leaned her fingertips on the table, smiling at the officer.

"Here they are, Officer."

"Why should we give you an exit visa, Jew?"

"Oh, Officer," she cooed, "we're visiting relatives in Italy." She pouted at him and fluttered her eyelashes.

"When do you return?" the officer demanded, his voice raspy as an iron file.

"Two weeks, sir. I must say, you do look handsome in that uniform." She reached out to touch his arm, but he pushed her hand away, his face crimson. Behind him, the soldiers cradling machine guns leered at her. Renata twisted a lock of hair in her finger and winked at the soldiers, who grinned back, but snapped to attention the moment the officer glared at them.

"One week only and you must be back. If you overstay, you will be subject to arrest anywhere you are found in Germany or Italy." He stamped their passports with the exit visa and returned the papers and tickets, muttering under his breath.

Papa and Mama, arms interlocked, and tense as hunted deer facing wolves, followed Renata through the barrier onto the platform. They were far from safe. Soldiers and SS officers in spotless uniforms swaggered up to terrified passengers and demanded to see papers again and again. Where were they going? Why? When were they returning? Lea gasped as they watched an old man being dragged to a corner and beaten senseless with truncheons. Something clamped inside Renata, but intervening on the old man's behalf would be suicidal, she decided. They were herded into lines according to which train they were taking. The seconds ticked by so loudly that Renata was sure someone behind the large wall clock had an enormous drum and was beating it, louder, louder, slower— driving them all mad.

The train rumbled into the station, hissed to a stop, and doors opened for a few well-dressed travelers disembarking. Porters rushed to assist with their bags. One woman, an aristocratic German with a fox fur draped over her shoulder and a lengthy cigarette holder in hand, swept a haughty glance over the people around her as she exhaled a cloud of smoke. She brushed past, caught Renata's eye for a fleeting second, then looked away. *I was one of you*, Renata thought, *before it was a crime to be me. How would it feel, to have your beauty, your assurance, and most of all, your safety?*

They scrambled up the stairs into the nearest coach and found seats in the second compartment. Renata and Papa shoved the suitcases onto the ledge above their seats, while others filled the compartment. A baby opposite them was crying, so its mother put it to her breast, and a moment of peace descended. Their travel companions included a hungry-looking girl about four years old with a runny nose and her thumb in her mouth, who huddled against the nursing mother; a haggard middle-aged man, probably the father of the two children; a bearded rabbi in his seventies and his plump wife; and a lone young man of around twenty. They all glanced briefly at each other, fear in every set of eyes, strangers together for whatever this journey might bring.

Within minutes, the doors closed, the guard blew his whistle, and the train lurched out of the station, belching smoke. Papa leaned his head on the back of the seat and exhaled. Renata used her handkerchief to dab at her mother's head, cleaning up the minor scrape as best she could.

"Let me look at your back, Renata," said Papa, once the train had settled into a steady rhythm.

Blood had soaked through the two layers of clothing stuck to her wounds. Removing it caused more bleeding, despite her father's tender touch. Apologizing to the others, she faced a corner and turned her back. While her father cleaned the tortured flesh with gauze and alcohol, Renata clamped her teeth on the handle of her satchel to avoid crying out. Soon it was done. She leaned on him, trying unsuccessfully to find a comfortable position for sleep.

Lea wept quietly, murmuring, "Solomon! Solomon!"

The train rocked and clattered on, lulling the exhausted passengers into a fitful sleep.

Chapter Three

The Train to Italy, 1938

"Border-crossing, ten minutes," bellowed the train conductor again and again, his voice fading as he strode toward the back of the train. Renata awakened, groggy and sore, and looked around. Passengers stirred and rummaged for papers. They were entering Austria, and didn't know what to expect, but, from the looks on every face and the smell of sweat, no one thought it would be easy.

The train's brakes squealed as the chugging rhythm slowed. The adults looked out the window. The youth, who was closest, said, "I see soldiers, and lots of tanks and trucks."

Renata could see a long line of headlights. The grind and rattle of tanks was enough to cause a small earthquake, and she thought she could see soldiers marching. Surely, they didn't need all this equipment to handle one train. Then she realized: Austria was about to be invaded.

The train stopped, and the engine hissed a cloud of steam. Cinders rained on the pristine snow in a meadow where armed guards ordered passengers off the train without luggage, and organized them into lines: one for Jews, one for Germans and Austrians, and a third for anyone else. Barbed wire stretched around the bleak field. The wind whipped Renata's headscarf. The cold needled her face and legs. Even the soldiers were red-faced with the frost, despite a few fires scattered around.

The line of Germans and Austrians moved quickly

forward, the guards unsmiling but respectful, documents receiving only cursory examination. The passengers were allowed to re-board the train, which was chuffing slowly to keep its steam. Foreigners, too, had a relatively easy time of it. Two young women, apparently American, judging from their flashy clothing and careless self-assurance, flirted with the guards. The guards enjoyed it, and waved the women through with a laugh.

The line of Jews moved much more slowly. The guards cuffed passengers when responses were not quick enough or not to their liking. Several in the line were pulled away, families pleading for them to be returned. The unfortunates were taken into the darkness by a few guards, and shortly, shots were heard in the distance. Terrified weeping expanded into screams of horror.

Karl gripped the hands of his wife and daughter as they shuffled forward.

He handed their papers to the young guard, who looked them over, then asked for the ticket stubs. Karl produced them.

"Why are you going to Venice?" The guard used a tone of voice suitable for arresting a serial killer.

"To visit family, sir." Karl shifted his weight from one foot to the other, trying to keep warm, frost building on his beard.

"Do you think you'll have a warm welcome from the Italians, Jew?" the guard sneered. "I should save them the trouble and shoot you now." He drew out his pistol and motioned Papa to one side. Karl was shaking, but he looked the guard straight in the eye, clenched his jaw, and took one deliberate step to the right.

"No!" screamed Renata, lunging toward her father. The guard turned, trained his pistol on her chest, and shoved Karl back into the line with his wife.

"Is this your daughter? A Jewish whore? Watch what we do with whores!"

He grasped Renata by the arm and jerked her to him. One hand held the gun to her temple while the other fumbled through the thick clothing for her breasts and her thighs. The other soldiers laughed.

She dug her nails deeply into her palms, willing herself not to scream.

"Leave her alone!"

She looked up into her father's ashen face, shame heating her cheeks. He stepped from the line, fists clenched, even though he had never been in a fight in his life.

"No, Karl!" Lea pulled at his sleeve, but he tore away.

The guard holding Renata jeered. "You think you can stop us from taking her, old man?" He pushed her back into line.

She stumbled and nearly fell. It was all in slow motion... slow, all too slow.

The guard lifted his pistol and clouted her father across the jaw.

Papa—who had built her a dollhouse, who stayed up all night holding Frau Werner's dying son—fell to his knees. Lea screamed again, and the guard shoved Karl to the ground.

"Take your wife and whore daughter out of my sight." He tossed the precious papers onto the snow.

Renata scrambled to retrieve them before the ink could run.

"Come, Papa," she whispered, crouching beside him.

She and Mama each took one arm around their shoulders, supporting him, partially dragging him to the train door. Blood dripped onto his coat. His breathing was erratic, his face pale. They stumbled into their compartment where Papa slumped onto a seat, groaning.

Renata lifted one of their suitcases down, gasping when she felt the lacerations on her back ooze again. The first suitable thing she could find—one of Papa's undershirts—she wet in the tiny lavatory sink, and dabbed at her father's face. A huge bruise purpled one cheek; his lips were swollen and cut, and a front tooth was missing.

Lea sobbed as she replaced the suitcase.

"Why do they hate us so much? What have we done?" She wrung her hands. "I hate them! I hate them! I hate them!"

Renata put an arm around her mother's shoulder and spoke softly. "We are here. Still alive. Mama, can you find some schnapps?"

Mama found the schnapps and handed it to Renata, who urged her father to drink. He managed only one swallow, then put a hand on her shoulder and squeezed twice, his grateful eyes saying what his mouth could not.

Renata took a brief swig, then handed it back to Lea, who

drank before hiding the flask again.

With a clank and bump, the train began to move, but of their original companions in the compartment, only the elderly couple and the mother with two children had returned. The mother sobbed, cradling her infant, and crushing the little girl, now shaking, to her bosom.

"Your husband?" Renata's question hung in the air, but the mother's sobbing only intensified, and she shook her head. Renata started to say she was sorry, but it seemed hopelessly trivial under the circumstances. Instead, she found a piece of cheese in her bag, broke off a bit and offered it to the little girl, who wiped the snot from her nose and ate the cheese in a flash. The sobs in the compartment subsided, and everyone finally dozed, exhausted and broken, as they rode through Austria—famous for Mozart and the Alps and Viennese waltzes, and, if stories were to be believed, was begging Hitler to come in and clean up its "Jewish problem."

Papa, speaking with difficulty through his injured mouth, addressed his daughter.

"My darling, we don't know what is facing us. If we are separated, I want you to promise me you will fight with everything you have, to get to Palestine. If God grants, we will meet again there, and if not, make a life for yourself. Marry! Have children! Never give up! Promise me! And if I am taken from you, do your best to protect your mother. Do you promise?" His lips shook.

Renata clung desperately to composure, her eyes wet.

Lea's chin quivered, and she wept, glancing at the daughter she was unwilling to defend.

Renata held Papa's hands and clasped them tightly. "Papa, I will not let these pigs harm Mama, I swear. But we will not be separated. I will not allow it."

He folded her to him in a long embrace.

Several stops and another border later, the conductor walked through the train calling, "*Venizia! Venizia!*"

The hungry, disheveled travelers were met by warm air, the musical cadence of the Italian language, and hostile glares from the local people. It was March twelfth, and the newspapers blazed headlines no one could miss: Hitler had rolled into Austria, unopposed; cheered, in fact. The Lowenthals knew no Italian, but the photos required no interpretation: Italy now bordered the bloated German Reich. The swastika was everywhere. Il Duce was everywhere. Banners and posters were glued on walls and poles. Flags flew from windows. Small clutches of jubilant troops marched through the square.

The little family shambled along the rough, cobbled streets, staring at everything, looking for a friendly face or business.

"Local Jews, if we can connect with them, are our best chance of help to get out of Italy," said Papa.

They could not find a café that would serve them, but one shopkeeper, speaking rapid Italian, pointed vaguely east, in the direction of the docks. Renata grasped for meaning.

"He could be showing us the way to the Jewish quarter! Let's go that way."

"How do you know?" asked Mama.

"I don't, but we may as well try."

They lifted their satchels and walked in the direction the man indicated.

Venice was the most confusing city they had ever seen. Streets and canals curled in an endless Möbius loop. Everything looked the same after a while. Even the famous gondoliers appeared to be brothers.

Two hours later, hopelessly lost, Mama slumped onto the pavement. Renata's back was screaming, and Papa's face was a swollen mess.

"What now, Karl?" Lea's tone was sharp.

"We need help, my dear." He turned to his daughter. "Perhaps the shopkeepers will be kinder to a young woman, Renata. Please go see what you can learn."

With a sigh, Renata headed toward a cluster of shops on the street, unsure of what to do. She removed her headscarf and attempted to straighten her hair with her fingers. The first shop was a bakery, with smells so enticing she was ready to climb over the counter and devour the entire display.

The baker raised his eyebrows at the disheveled young

woman. He spoke politely enough, although Renata knew no Italian. She decided to try Yiddish.

"We need help. Do you know any Jewish families here?"

The man's attitude darkened. He pointed to the door, his next words far from polite. She left, and tried the next shop, and the next, with similar results, and then, miraculously, she was in a Kosher bakery, where an orthodox rabbi was purchasing bread.

She cleared her throat. "Excuse me, Rabbi…"

He turned around. "Yes?"

Renata's story tumbled out, and minutes later, the man followed her to where Mama and Papa sat leaning against a wall.

"Mama! Papa! Look, I found a rabbi who can help us! This is Rabbi Pontecorvo. Rabbi, here are my parents, Karl and Lea Lowenthal."

Rabbi Pontecorvo wore a black hat, coat, and scruffy boots. His bushy beard and earlocks bobbed as he talked. His brown eyes crinkled at the corners and his mouth broke into a kindly smile.

"Come with me. It is not safe here. May I help you with your bags?"

He took Lea's satchel and strode away. Papa followed, wincing when he tried to smile at Renata, settling for a solemn wink instead.

The rabbi's home was a modest apartment, three flights above another Kosher bakery, the windows of which were broken and partially boarded over. Signora Pontecorvo was a round, beaming woman with olive skin and graying hair drawn up into a bun. Used to taking strangers in with no notice, she bustled around the visitors, her Yiddish strange with an Italian accent.

"Come from Munich, have you? *Oy*, there's a journey, likely a long tale to tell. Well, you'll be wanting a wash-up and something to eat. Toilet facilities are out the back, washing up is this way." She led them to a tiny room with a basin, a sliver of soap, and a threadbare-but-clean towel.

"My husband's mouth is injured so he cannot talk very well," said Lea.

The Signora tut-tutted her disapproval. "Ah, here are some rags for you."

Lea cleaned Karl's mouth and gave him cold cloths to hold

on the bruises. She scowled at the missing tooth, the cuts.

"Those bastards!" She called down all the curses of heaven and hell on the German guards. Finished, she washed her own face and hands.

About twenty minutes later, the trio felt tolerably clean, the water in the basin bloody. Signora Pontecorvo tossed it out the window and drew fresh water for Renata.

"Papa..." Renata indicated her back, bloody and tender under the layers of clothing.

"Clean what you can, then I will tend to your back in the kitchen, if the Signora permits."

Renata nodded and closed the washroom door, then removed all but one of her skirts, hitched up the remaining one, and rolled down her stockings. Water only, soap just for the private parts and those most dirty. She cleaned what she could, rinsed the cloth, and threw out the dirty water a second time. Then she went to the kitchen where her father was waiting.

Signora Pontecorvo nearly fainted at the sight of Renata's raw back, yet Karl detected signs of improvement.

"Much of it is scabbing over now, so you shouldn't have as much bleeding. And no sign of infection yet. You're doing well."

She gritted her teeth as he dabbed the wounds. "Thank you, Papa."

Lea took the bloody clothes and rinsed them, while Renata put on her one spare dress.

"You can hang them on the line on the balcony." Signora indicated the back of the apartment. "The clothes will be dry by morning, if it hasn't rained."

"Thank you, Signora. You are so kind."

"Come eat now." She offered them fish, ciabatta bread, tomatoes sprinkled with basil, and coffee, but did not eat herself. She kept glancing at Renata's back.

Karl sipped on chicken broth while the women made sandwiches. Once they had eaten, Renata collected the dishes and cleaned them in the kitchen.

Karl, in pain from the broken tooth, decided rest and a glass of liqueur were the best medicine. Once he was asleep, Renata approached Rabbi Pontecorvo, to discuss their plans.

The rabbi looked up from the book he was reading and smiled. "Where are you heading, Daughter?"

"Palestine. I have promised my father that no matter what, I will get Mama and me there, even if we are separated."

The rabbi nodded. "You have courage. That is good. You will need it. Do you know the way?"

"We were planning to go over land at first, but with Bulgaria occupied, and the Germans threatening Yugoslavia and Greece, I think a boat will be safer."

"How is it that a young girl like you is so well-informed?"

"I am eighteen. I have been watching the news carefully since I was fifteen, even the one-sided news of the Reich. We listened to forbidden broadcasts late at night, and I believe Hitler will not stop until he has conquered all of Europe."

"I agree. But I prefer to discuss this with your father."

"Please, Rabbi! He is sleeping, and we don't want to lose time."

"I'm sorry, Daughter. Tomorrow." He lit his pipe and picked up a newspaper.

Renata, biting her tongue, headed for the kitchen. Perhaps the signora, chatting in the kitchen with her mother as they cleaned the dishes, would have some ideas.

"Mama, what are we going to do now, with Papa injured?"

"Really, Renata, your injuries are worse. We're going to wait."

"I am already healing. The rabbi will only talk with Papa. I don't see why he can't talk with me."

The two older women glanced at each other.

Lea said, "You are barely more than a child, and he wants to speak with the head of the household. You know this, Renata. Why are you complaining?"

"Because it's wrong! Who insisted we had to leave Germany? Who said we should go to Palestine? Me, so I think I deserve a say in our decisions."

Signora Pontecorvo put down her dishrag and laid a hand on Renata's shoulder. "I know it is difficult for you, but things must be done the right way. Why don't you get some sleep now, and we'll talk in the morning?"

Renata snorted, defeated for the moment. "*Ja*, I am tired. Thank you for the food and bed, Signora." Her smile was weak. She returned to the living room and laid on the sofa, the drone of the women's voices in her ears. Just for a minute...

"Wake up, *cara mia*." Renata woke with a jerk to Signora Pontecorvo shaking her shoulder. She grimaced with the sudden movement. Confused, wondering where she was, she glanced around, then recognized the apartment. She heard Mama in the kitchen cooking, but Papa was nowhere to be seen, and street noises indicated she had slept far beyond her usual waking time.

"I am sorry to put you to all this trouble, Signora." She hoped her rusty Yiddish was comprehensible.

"No need, my dear, you had a terrible journey. Your mother and father told us about it. Now come, have something to eat. Do you like coffee? It is ersatz, but better than nothing." She handed Renata a steaming mug of dark liquid.

Renata munched on some Italian bread and sipped the hot drink.

"Where is my father?"

"My husband, he takes your father to talk with some men. He gets help for you, so you can escape from here."

"But what about you and the rabbi, Signora? Aren't you in danger, too?"

"Of course, *cara*. We are all in danger these days. Someday we will be the ones who have to leave." She shrugged and raised her hands. "But in the meantime, we help those whom God brings to us."

"But, Signora, soon it will be too late! Leave now, while you still can!"

"Mussolini and Hitler hate the Jews, it is true, but how far can they go? They can't put all of us in jail." She chuckled at the idea.

Renata clenched her jaw. "I think they can, and they will."

"How do you know more than your elders about this?" She turned to Lea.

The two women chatted about chicken soup recipes, child-rearing hints, and opinions of the Nazi regimes they faced. Renata fretted at the obtuseness of her elders.

The sound of male voices and feet on stairs interrupted them. Karl and Rabbi Pontecorvo tramped into the kitchen.

Karl hung his coat on the back of a chair and attempted a smile. "Lea, Renata, we have a plan. The rabbi knows of a fisherman willing to take us to Yugoslavia. From there we must find a train to take us to Greece. We must dress as a fisherman and his family, not as German Jews."

Lea, Karl, and Renata spent the rest of the day finding suitable clothing.

Scratching his beard, the rabbi eventually admitted, "I am sorry, but your satchels may be too heavy. There is room on the boat, no doubt, but if you have to carry them through water..."

Renata's throat constricted. "Did you say, through water? Papa, are you mad? Mama cannot swim, and we have already left so much behind. How can we part with more?"

"Renata, watch your tongue," muttered Mama.

Papa's eyes were somber. "Yet we must. We will leave some clothing with the Pontecorvos, who will share it with others in need."

Renata and Lea were stunned, but they complied, sorting their possessions and keeping only the most vital. They retained Renata's paintbrushes, the precious book with its hidden secret, and one change of clothing each. Looking at her parents, Renata, for the first time, had doubts about her father's ability to get them to Palestine. Walking through water? With Mama unable to swim? This journey was forcing them to do things beyond their ability. She hoped Hans was right about her strength.

The streets were quiet the next day. They declined to tempt fate, and remained indoors. Karl's face and Renata's back improved, but the coming journey would be arduous. Renata mentioned her family in her prayers to Yahweh, if He was listening.

Chapter Four

The Da Vinci, 1938

Dusk flowed through the streets, a cool gray blanket of anonymity. Soldiers marched up and down, barking orders, and the residents dissolved into the gloom.

"I cannot accompany you, obviously," said the rabbi, handing a paper to Karl. "Here are directions to the dock and a description of the boat. Memorize it. You cannot take it with you."

"My daughter has a better memory than me." Papa handed the paper to Renata, which she scanned, then returned.

"I cannot thank you enough for your help, Rabbi and Signora. I only hope we are worthy of your effort. We will pray for your safety." Karl and the rabbi shook hands.

Lea and Signora Pontecorvo wept as they said their good-byes. "Next year, in Jerusalem," they promised each other.

In their fishing garb, the Lowenthals exited onto the street, trying not to look as odd as they felt. Karl's missing tooth gave him the rakish look of a fisherman living a rough life. They avoided speech. Whenever soldiers approached, they followed the rabbi's advice, smiling and saluting as the battalion passed. It worked. The soldiers ignored them.

They wound through labyrinthine streets to the docks, where row upon row of fishing boats bobbed and swayed. The place reeked of seaweed, creosote, and fish. Seagulls, perched on barnacled pilings, ruffled their feathers and competed for sleeping space.

Up and down the wharf the family searched while darkness encroached.

"There it is!" Renata pointed to a red-and-green-striped boat, bumping the scruffy blue boat beside it. She caught the eye of a man on board who spoke before she could say anything.

"You my new crew?" The swarthy fellow was dressed in a stained undershirt and filthy red pants held up with a piece of rope. To their surprise, he spoke heavily accented German. "I'm Guido, and welcome to my lovely lady, *The Da Vinci*. Come aboard!"

Guido broke into a ferocious coughing spell, produced a gob of phlegm he spat overboard, then wiped his mouth with the back of his hand.

"Pfah! Goddamn tobacco! Someday they'll tell us the stuff makes us sick. Here, *gutte Frau*, take my hand and step this way."

Lea stared at Guido with distaste. She reluctantly accepted his oil-smeared hand, and stepped over the gunwale. Karl helped Renata aboard. Guido showed them down into a tiny cabin, sour with the smell of bilges. Renata and her mother covered their noses, trying vainly to keep the stench at bay.

"Thank you for taking us," began Karl, but Guido shook his head.

"You're not the first, nor will you be the last, I suspect. Anything to help someone away from them Nazi *bosch*. C'mon now, put your things in that corner. Sorry accommodations isn't that fancy. Young lady, you come with me and I'll show you how we cast off. You ready t' help?"

He climbed to the bridge with a reluctant Renata following. She had no idea why he wanted her up there and wasn't interested in the boat's operation.

"This here's the throttle, and here's the gear shift. The motor's in neutral right now. Hold on while I cast off." He moved to the deck and loosened three thick ropes. The boat rolled gently in its berth.

When Guido returned, wiping oily hands on the sides of his red pants, he grinned. "We're ready. I'll take her out into the channel, then you want a turn?"

"Well," she said uncertainly, "perhaps it will be fun."

The motor burped and grumbled into gear, enveloping them with oily smoke fumes. The boat rolled away from the quay, while Renata hung onto a rail. Once the dockyard was behind them, Guido shifted into forward gear, cranked on the wheel, and turned the bow towards the Adriatic Sea. When he opened the throttle, the boat surged forward, slicing through the inky water, sending spray flying over the bridge.

He stepped to one side. "Your turn." He smiled, kindness in his rough face. "Don't be afraid. It's not hard when the weather's decent."

Renata had never been on a boat before. She felt dubious, but accepted the wheel anyway. It was silly to be afraid of something new.

The boat twisted to one side. "Oh, it's pulling!"

"*Ja*, you must keep her going straight. The waves will try to pull the rudder this way and that. Stand with feet apart like this." He demonstrated. "You'll have more control."

Feet planted wide, Renata gripped the wheel with all her strength and brought the vessel under control. She shouted above the spray drenching the window. "I can't see where we're going. How do you steer it?"

"Her, *Fraulein*. A boat's always a *her*. Look here at the compass. See the needle, moving from side to side?"

Renata nodded.

"We want to keep it at 110 degrees, roughly southeast. Understand? Now try again."

Watching the compass instead of the black ocean, she kept the craft heading toward the Yugoslavian coast. *I can do this,* she thought, exultant. *I'm steering a boat!* She grinned at Guido.

He nodded his approval, then called Karl and Lea upstairs. Once they gathered near the wheel, he lit a cigarette.

"Now listen close. We're heading around this peninsula that's part of Italy. We will see two towns when we get to the Yugoslav coast." He pointed to a nautical map spread on a table and drew lines on it with his finger.

"The river in between is the Rječina. Sušak, on the southeast, is mostly Croats who hate the Italians. Rijeka, on the northwest, is mostly Italians, who can't stand the Croats. The railway station is in Rijeka, but there's a long breakwater around it that I can't get into, so I'll drop you off near Sušak. Once you're ashore, get into some dry clothing and find something to eat. Then it won't be too hard to get train tickets."

"Which dock will we land at?" Karl sounded confused.

"Dock? I can't dock, so you'll have to wade in. Don't worry, it's not that far at high tide."

Renata glanced at Lea, who was white with fear. "My mother can't swim."

Guido waved his hand. "No need."

Lea gave him a withering look. "I hope you are right."

"How long will it take?" asked Renata.

"With fair weather, about six hours in this slow boat. Bad weather, could be twice that if we're going into the wind. Once we get past the peninsula, we turn due east, to Sǔsak. Now I suggest you get some rest."

Lea and Karl, shivering, headed back to the cabin but Renata still had the wheel.

"You want to stay there awhile?" asked Guido, tapping ash overboard and stubbing out his cigarette on the deck. He lit up again, tossed a match into the murk.

"A little longer, if that's all right. It's more fun than I thought." She grinned at him. "How did you come to be taking Jews out of Italy, Guido?"

He leaned against the bridge railing and exhaled a large cloud of smoke. A shadow crossed his face. "I had a sister. Her legs were withered from polio, and she could only walk with crutches."

"What was her name?"

"Carlina. She couldn't get out much, but she knitted sweaters and caps for all the fishermen and their wives. She was a sweet thing."

Guido paused.

Renata glanced at him. He was struggling to keep his emotions in check.

"What happened to her?" She turned the wheel slightly to adjust their course.

"The *Fascisti* don't want cripples. One day, soldiers arrived and took her for some new treatment, they said. We got a letter a few months later saying she had died of pneumonia, but I'm damned sure they killed her. This is why I help you."

"How awful. It's not just Jews they hate, then. You are a good man, Guido."

"Not really. This is my revenge."

They lapsed into companionable silence. An hour later, glancing at his chronometer, a rusty old instrument of dubious reliability, Guido took back the bridge.

"Good job, you learn fast. You never know when you might need to pilot a boat. Now, try to sleep before we get there."

Renata headed below, pleased with herself. Her smile faded when she entered the cabin. Lea, a stickler for cleanliness, stood holding onto the doorknob, having searched in vain for any clean space in a room full of oily old rags, fishnets, and tools. A wooden bench built into the wall had not been cleaned in several years.

"This place is disgusting, Renata. There's nowhere clean to sit."

Renata pushed the tools into a corner and used some rags to wipe the bench.

"Mama, this is the best we can do. Sit here and try to rest."

Lea sat down, frowning, so Renata said nothing more and joined her mother.

Over the next hour, the rocking and pitching grew. Queasiness burbled up Renata's throat until she staggered outside and vomited into the ocean. Her parents followed. They stared at each other with pallid faces and silently prayed for the voyage to be over.

Without warning, a massive storm broke, drenching them to the skin. Papa shepherded the women back into the cabin, which bucked like a wild horse. They found something to hang onto, but were slammed and tossed about like chaff while Guido, Renata hoped, was keeping them from drowning. They vomited again, this time with nowhere to dispose of the stinky mess. The floor and their clothes were soon slimy. Renata swore to herself that she would never go on a boat again. Water flowed under the cabin door when the boat dipped into the trough of a wave. Inches of water, oil, and vomit soon soaked everything they owned, except the bag of books, stowed in a high cupboard.

Karl looked around for something they could use to bail out the mess, but there was nothing. Renata hung on to the arm of the bench with all her strength, desperate to avoid falling on the floor.

During an especially wild pitch, Mama lost her grip and fell into the filth.

"I'll get her! You stay there!" Karl yelled above the howling tempest.

Renata wondered how they would manage if they were all hurt.

He reached Lea, got an arm under her, and dragged her onto the bench above the swirling mess.

She groaned. "My God, Karl, when will this be over?"

"Stay here. We're all filthy. You can't get any dirtier than you are now." He raised his eyes and cocked his head.

Renata noticed it too. "Papa, we changed direction, didn't we?"

"*Ja*, I wonder why. Why don't you go and ask Guido?"

Renata frowned. Couldn't her father at least do this much?

"I need to see to your mother, Renata, and I know nothing about boats."

Still frowning, she pulled open the door. The ferocious storm threw her back, but she pulled herself to the bridge, one step at a time, half-blinded by the stinging rain.

"Guido, why did we change course?" she hollered.

But no one was on the bridge, even though the throttle was wide open. The boat raced helter-skelter across the sea, the wheel spinning back and forth.

"Guido!" She screamed. "Guido! Where are you?" The rain lashed her face; the wind tore her clothing.

"Papa," she yelled, "Guido is missing!"

She grabbed the wheel. Rain plastered her hair to her face. She swept it behind her ears, grunting with the effort of holding the wheel, and eased the throttle to quarter speed. The heading should have been one hundred ten, but they were at forty degrees. She braced one foot against the side of the bridge and cranked the wheel inch by painful inch. Fifty degrees. Back to sixty. Now seventy. She was sweating, despite the frigid storm.

A huge wave washed over her, and she nearly lost her grip. *That's what happened to Guido*, she thought, clutching the wheel.

"Renata, what on earth?" Karl materialized behind her.

"Guido washed overboard! It nearly happened to me, too." Her voice shook. "We need to find him!" *But we need to get to Yugoslavia.*

What if the Italian patrol boats find us? Ashamed of her selfish thoughts, she imagined Guido trying to stay afloat in the angry sea.

Karl stared at her. "Dear God, we are lost." He peered into the darkness and shook his head. "We must try to find him."

Her father's words pulled her thinking around. "Of course."

"I think the storm is fading. The motion isn't quite so terrible. Let me get your mother." He clumped back downstairs.

Renata held the boat steady on her best guess of the heading back to Venice, with the throttle on dead slow. Visions of Guido drowning filled her. She was his only hope, if he was still alive.

The wind and rain, tired of their terrible game, slowed and finally stopped altogether. She heard Mama's wailing as she climbed to the deck.

"What will we do? We are going to die!" cried Lea, clinging to Karl. "Where are we? I wish to God we had never come!" She broke into loud sobs.

Renata snapped. "Calm down, Mama! We are still alive and I'm going to keep us that way, so stop your hysterics!"

The rebuff silenced Lea, but she refused to leave the bridge.

"I think we're retracing our steps, but we may be way off course by now. Watch the water for any sign of Guido. I'm going as slowly as possible."

Karl spotted a piece of wood, but no one clung to it. After an hour, they conceded defeat. Surviving that long in the stormy ocean with no life jacket did not seem remotely possible.

Karl covered his eyes and began the Kaddish, the mourning prayer. Renata brought the boat to a stop while they sang. Guido, dirty and coarse, but with a heart of gold. He would help no more Jews escape from Hitler. She added a prayer of thanks for him.

"Poor Guido, he gave his life to get us this far. Now we must survive on our own," said Karl. "Renata, where is our destination?"

"We must get back to heading one ten." She turned the wheel and eased the throttle forward, watching the compass needle swing around. When it reached the right heading, she held it steady and opened the throttle. The boat surged forward into the waning night.

She and her father reviewed the chart.

"We're going in the right direction for now. I think we

should turn at dawn, and look for the towns Guido told us about. We could get close to the shore and keep going until we see them, but we mustn't go into Italian territory."

Karl glanced at the chronometer. "Two hours until decent light."

"I just want to get off this boat," muttered Lea, shivering.

"Lea, we all want to get off. Try to be patient. You can stay here or in the cabin."

"I'm waiting here. That cabin is nasty."

All possibility of sleep gone, teeth chattering, Renata focused on the controls while Karl and Lea sat propped against the wall of the bridge, waiting for hope to rise in the east.

The drone of the motor lulled Lea into a fitful sleep leaning against her husband.

He remained awake for Renata's sake.

When the darkness began to dissolve, she turned the boat due east. Pale light spread and grew, silhouetting land in the distance.

"Look, Papa! Land!"

"Well done, my dear. Now if only we can find the towns."

Rolling hills and a hint of buildings appeared as the stars winked out, one by one. Renata slowed the boat to half speed and concentrated on the looming shore.

"Papa, Mama, you'd better get our things. We're getting close and I don't know how far in to take this boat." As they stood, she added, "Would you get my book bag? It's in one of the cupboards."

Karl headed to the cabin and returned minutes later with her satchel, which was not entirely dry.

"Thank you, Papa. Look over there. See the lights? I'll take us in closer; they look bright enough to be a town."

"But we don't know if we are out of Italy."

"No. I bet Guido kept binoculars here, though. See if you can find some, would you?"

Karl searched through cupboards until he found a pair. He fiddled with the focusing rings, adjusting them to his satisfaction. "Yes, that's a town." He scanned the shore carefully. "I can see buildings, but it's still early."

"Keep looking, Papa. We're getting closer all the time." It dawned on Renata that she was taking over as the leader of the family. And although annoyed at her mother's weakness, she felt a twinge of sympathy for her, sheltered as her life had been.

Ten minutes later, Karl let out a cry. "There! I saw a flag. Italian! Head south, quickly!"

Renata hauled the wheel to starboard and the boat tilted into a sharp curve, then settled into its new course at full speed. Half an hour later, the shoreline curved away steeply to the east, passing the peninsula that marked the end of Italian territory. The sun glinted off distant roofs and waves.

Mama, too, strained her eyes to see.

Renata watched the water, looking for a dock, other boats, debris. Consulting the chart, she steered them due east past several small islands.

"I see the towns!" Karl said. "Just as Guido said, a river in the middle, and a town on each side. It's not too far."

The town seemed to emerge from the water. White buildings and red roofs focused and diverged: a green space here, shops there. A few old vehicles drove along a shore road.

The water color changed from black to indigo to light blue.

"I see the bottom, now, Renata. Go slowly."

Renata pulled back the throttle to the slowest speed and the motor subsided into a bass rumble. "How deep?"

"I can't tell, but less than three meters, I would guess."

"We'll have to abandon this old hulk. Mama, we have to wade through the water."

"Perhaps it will help wash the stink out of our clothes." Lea managed a weak smile.

"We're going to hit bottom. Hang on." Renata accelerated the boat slightly. Seconds later the hull scraped rocks. Renata turned off the motor while Papa looked for a way to lower them into the water. He returned with a rope ladder and a pike from the fishing supplies.

"Guido was prepared. Thank goodness."

Renata squared her shoulders and pressed her lips together. "If we survived that storm, we can survive this. Let's get it over with."

"I agree," said Karl. "Come on, Lea."

But Lea's face was white with terror.

He heaved the ladder over the side and elected to go down first. The water reached his chest.

Renata lowered his satchel of clothes and the pike which he would use for balance. Then she helped her shaking mother turn around to face the ship, and guided her foot onto the first rung.

Lea whimpered and screwed her eyes shut. "I can't do this, Karl, I'm so afraid!"

"Yes, you can, my dear. Our lives depend on it. Take another step down. That's it, come on." She took another tentative step out of Renata's reach, should something go wrong.

"The water is at the next rung. Your feet will get wet." Karl calmly talked her down the flimsy ladder while balancing a bundle on his head in over a meter of water.

Step by step, Lea whimpered the whole way, but finally she was down, pushing her billowing skirt, clinging to her husband.

"I will hold your hand, but don't grab me, or we will both go down. Use the pike."

Lea took the pike, and stretched her head to clear the water.

Next it was Renata's turn. Her skirt billowed as Mama's had, and she struggled to get the air out of it. She gasped, but the cold was bearable. The water lapped near the top of her chest, forcing her to balance the satchel on her head. She struggled for a footing while mentally blessing her parents for insisting on swimming lessons all those years ago. She noted with surprise that the cold water eased the pain of her back.

They gazed one last time at the battered boat.

"*Da Vinci*, thank you. Guido, rest in peace," said Renata.

Facing the beach, they felt for each slippery step before committing to it. Improving light winked on the stony shore. A whiff of smoke promised food and warmth. Renata picked up her pace but seaweed caught around her legs like tentacles, pulling her down. Brine filled her mouth. She spewed it out, choking and coughing. The bag slipped off her head a few times and she struggled to keep it out of the water.

Buildings and the Rječina river came into focus. They saw

people, cars, and horses pulling carts. Shingle stones rattled and clattered down the slope of the beach with each wave that receded back into itself. On their left, the concrete breakwater arched into the ocean, away from them to the north, toward Rijeka. Masts of a score or more vessels swayed inside the breakwater, and a wet sheen from the storm covered every surface.

At last, water streaming from hair and clothing and bits of seaweed stuck here and there, they emerged from the shallow surf. Separating the beach from the road was a seawall, with a stairwell leading up to the road, where they sat on top of the wall to take stock.

"Our clothing is wet," said Karl. "But it's nothing a little sunshine won't fix." He smiled. "How is the book, Renata?"

Renata peered into her bag and drew out the volume. "Wet. We'll have to dry it somewhere with the pages spread open, if we're not to lose it." She looked over the others. "I think the rest will be all right."

"Good. Thank you." He turned to his wife. "Lea, how are you managing?"

She pursed her mouth in disgust, as she emptied sand from her shoes and wrung seawater from her hair. "I'm alive."

"We need to find the train station." Renata lifted the bag onto her shoulder, and tramped up the steps to the road. "And get dry. I'm freezing. When was the last time we ate anything?"

Lea said, "The bread Signora Pontecorvo gave us is soggy. There's a bit of cheese here, if you don't mind some sand and a fishy smell." At the top of the steps she offered it to Papa, who sniffed and shook his head. Renata broke off a piece and bit into it, but when her teeth grated on grains of sand, she spat it on the ground, then instantly regretted it, not knowing where they would find their next meal.

"Come on," Renata urged. "We can't stop here." She helped Papa and Mama to their feet, and they started up the street.

Locals gave the soggy trio a wide berth. Papa removed his cap, ran his hands through his wet hair, and smiled at two passing women, who ignored him.

Now, to find the train station.

Chapter Five

Athens, 1938

A scruffier, dirtier, sorrier little family had not been seen in recent memory by the Athenians, judging from the stares they received and the number of people who sidestepped around them when they exited the train station in Athens a day later.

Renata scratched her arms. Salt ground into every inch of her body. With skin this raw she could only imagine how bad the hidden parts looked, and if her odor was unpleasant to her, she wondered how repulsive it was for strangers. Mouthwatering smells drifted out of the cafés, making the growling in her empty stomach more uncomfortable. She glanced at her mother, who had become very quiet since Yugoslavia. Papa's hand under her elbow kept her moving forward, but his mouth had not fully healed, and Renata was worried about them both.

"Papa, Mama, the smell from these cafés is maddening. Can we buy some food?"

Without waiting for an answer, she dashed inside a bakery and tried to buy some gyros, but the proprietor ordered her out with shouts and gestures.

"We look so filthy they don't want to serve us." Karl paused to sit on a bench.

"I'm not giving up." Renata squinted at the Greek lettering above the shops. Learning the Greek alphabet in school years ago was not much help, but slowly she began to make sense of the letters by looking at the shops' contents. *Αρτοποιείο*—a bakery. *Χρυσό και ασήμι*—a jewelry store.

Wait. I wonder, thought Renata. *Gold and silver. Could they be Jewish?* She hurried into the tiny shop.

With one look, the jeweler charged at her, yelling, gesticulating toward the door, his meaning clear: "Get out!"

Renata approached, palms extended, speaking in Yiddish. "We are Jews who just escaped from Germany. I'm so sorry for our appearance, but we mean you no harm. We need help. Please."

The jeweler gaped for a long moment before recovering his manners and replying rapidly in Greek-accented Yiddish.

"My God, you escaped those pigs? We are so afraid of them. But how did you…? Forgive me, I am so rude. My name is Ketzis. What can I do for you?"

She introduced herself and her parents. "Please, if you know someone who will help us…"

An exhausting hour's walk later, the jeweler introduced them to Mrs. Moustaki, whose family assisted refugees on their way to Palestine. A round, red-faced, smiling woman in a long skirt and a white apron, wore her hair tied back with a triangular scarf. She had rough red hands but warm, friendly eyes. She opened the door and stood to one side as they entered. She, too, spoke Yiddish.

"In here, in here and we get you food and drink. You'd like to bathe soon, no?" She bustled about, beaming, face shiny with perspiration.

"Gina! Roza! Water, right now!" She clapped her hands to get her daughters' attention, then invited her guests to sit down.

They collapsed gratefully on a cushioned divan.

Roza, who looked about sixteen, disappeared and returned minutes later with an enormous vat of water, which she manhandled onto the stove.

Renata tried her rusty Yiddish. "Are you always lifting such heavy loads?"

Roza laughed and slapped her thighs in merriment. "We do this every day! How you think we such strong women?" She grinned at Renata and stoked the stove with wood, then slid her pot to one side, making room for Gina's equally massive pot.

"The wine, girls," said Mrs. Moustaki, who appeared with a tray of flat bread, and a pale brownish-yellow paste of some kind. She placed it in front of her guests. "Eat, eat! Fresh pita, I make this morning. And hummus. Water will be hot soon."

Gina returned with a bottle of wine and six chipped glasses. She poured, and the Lowenthals and the Moustakis toasted freedom and Palestine.

Renata hesitated over the unfamiliar food despite her hunger, watching to see how their hosts ate it. She copied them, tearing off a piece of the bread, dipping it in the hummus, and tasting. Strange, she decided, but good. She helped herself to more. Everyone tucked in, and soon the small platter was empty.

Mrs. Moustaki gathered the glasses and noticed the water simmering. "Such lazy girls! I apologize for them. Gina! That water is hot enough now. You fill the tub, and Roza, where are your manners? Find towels and soap. Get some spare clothes—Pater's, too. Go!"

Gina and Roza giggled, and left to do her bidding. The girls obviously adored their noisy mother.

Renata decided she was kind beyond belief, despite her loudness.

Lea disappeared into the bathroom, appearing twenty minutes later with a smile on her face. "Now you, Renata," she said, toweling her damp hair.

Renata moaned with pleasure as she sank into the deep tub. Her back no longer stung, but she tried not to dislodge the scabs. The indescribable luxury of hot water and soap, followed by clean clothes, albeit ill-fitting and strange, left her weepy with fatigue and relief. When clean and dressed, she emerged.

"Your turn, Papa."

Karl's face looked much better when he returned from the bathroom clean shaven and in pants at least three inches too short.

"Papa, you look like a rascal with that missing tooth! I almost like it." Renata gave him a hug.

Mrs. Moustaki breezed into the room. "Ah, you better now. Come. Dinner is ready. Afterwards we wash your clothes."

Karl approached her. "We would like to pay you for your kindness, *Frau* Moustaki."

Throwing up her hands in mock horror, Mrs. Moustaki laughed. "Pay? Of course not! We do this to help our fellow Jews. Don't be silly."

Despite—or maybe because of—their friendliness, Renata wondered why she and her family deserved such generosity. And why she deserved to live when Guido and his sister had died. Perhaps there would come a time when she would need to be equally generous, toward strangers or perhaps even people she disliked. She pushed aside the thought and followed her parents into the courtyard, surrounded by white stucco walls punctuated with cobalt blue tile. Large red tiles covered the floor and a multicolored, striped umbrella shaded the table.

"Gina! Roza! Get the souvlaki! Where are the dolmades I made this morning? Hurry!" Mrs. Moustaki spoke a mangle of Greek and Yiddish at the top of her capable lungs.

The daughters returned with platters of lamb, rice, grape leaves, and olives—unfamiliar, but with a smell Renata would forever associate with heaven. The Lowenthals enjoyed their first taste of real food in three days. Renata and Lea glanced at one another. Both took small portions, but Mrs. Moustaki would not have it.

"Eat, eat! I prepare for you. We have plenty!"

Gina and Roza snickered and nudged each other.

All the family could do was thank her, and follow her bidding.

After the main course, Mrs. Moustaki served a delicate pastry drizzled with honey, called baklava.

It was the most delicious thing Renata had ever tasted. She wished she could stay and learn how to make their food. She wondered how they managed to feed their own family this way, let alone refugees whom they sheltered whenever the need arose.

"Avraam returns in a few hours," Mrs. Moustaki said, when the meal was over. "Better you rest now while it is still light. You may have to leave in darkness. We don't know tonight or another night. Go sleep, I will call you. Follow me."

She led them to a room upstairs, cleanly furnished with six cots. No one needed to be encouraged to lie down. Renata, savoring the unfamiliar sensation of safety, fell asleep in seconds.

It was dark when Mrs. Moustaki awakened them. Her husband, who owned a Kosher butcher shop, was home, and wanted to meet the guests.

So that is how they can afford the lamb, deduced Renata.

Avraam Moustaki sported the largest moustache she had ever seen. He was short and stocky, with a thatch of thick black hair, leathery skin, and hands that were used to rough work. If not for the twinkle in his eyes and the fondness he showed for his family, he would be intimidating, but Renata warmed to him at once.

"Welcome to our home," he said. "Would you care to join me for a glass of wine?"

Karl, Lea, and Renata joined him in the courtyard, where Avraam pulled out a pipe and offered a spare to Papa, which he accepted. They tamped down the tobacco and lit up together, leaning back in the comfortable cool of the evening. The sweet tobacco aroma drifted around the courtyard, and inside where Gina, Roza, and Mrs. Moustaki were playing a card game.

"So, you wish to go to Palestine." Avraam leaned back in his chair. He spoke fluent Yiddish.

"Yes," said Karl.

"We prefer Palestine," added Renata, "but anywhere we are away from the Nazis is a good start."

"The British are not letting any more Jews into Palestine, because they can't guarantee their ability to defend the country. Personally, I think they are a little afraid of so many Jews in one place."

Karl nodded. "One wonders why they would be afraid, when they see how easily we are cowed by Hitler."

"Where can we go, then?" asked Renata.

Avraam sent a smoke ring into the air. "The most popular place right now for Jewish and other refugees is Alexandria, Egypt."

Lea and Renata looked at each other, eyes wide.

"Do we need visas?" asked Karl.

"With passports, the British will let you in. There is a sizable Jewish community in Alexandria, and I'm told the climate is most pleasant. There is a British base there, and the Jewish community lives unmolested, as far as I know. The sea is the safest, most reliable route."

Lea shrugged. "So long as we are out of Germany, and with

other Jews, what does it matter?"

"Is there no other way, *Herr* Moustaki? That last boat ride was so terrible," Renata pleaded.

"Overland is too far and dangerous, some of it in enemy territory. The passenger ships have waiting lists for tickets, but there are other ways."

"Let us take the passenger boat." Lea folded her arms and gave her husband that look she had when her mind was made up.

"Very well. Renata?" Karl turned to his daughter.

Renata was shaking at the mere thought of another boat ride. "I'm not spending the rest of my life in Egypt, but if that's where we have to go for now, so be it. But *Herr* Moustaki, why don't you and your family come with us? Greece will not be not safe for long."

Avraam raised his eyebrows. "The British have promised to protect us, and our own army will fight to the death."

"In Germany, Austria, and Italy, Jews live worse than cattle. I was beaten for daring to paint anti-Nazi art. Look!"

She turned her back to him and lowered the back of her dress.

Avraam's jaw dropped. "My God!"

"We took a boat from Venice, owned by a man whose sister was killed by the *Fascisti* because she was a cripple. Do not think you are safe. You are not." She pulled her dress back into place and sat down.

Lea interrupted. "Renata, they must make up their own minds."

"Guido, the boat owner, died getting us to safety," Renata ignored her mother. "You don't want your wife and daughters to be killed, do you?"

Avraam cleared his throat. A vein stood out on his neck and his face blazed. "These are difficult times, but we must all choose our own paths. Miss Lowenthal, thank you for your opinion, but I have heard enough."

Renata stifled a sigh and sagged, drumming her fingers on the arm of the chair.

Karl turned to his family. "Tomorrow, Avraam will take me to the passenger docks where, with any luck, I can buy tickets.

Renata, we'll take some of the jewelry to Mr. Ketzis and have it changed into cash. In the meantime, get what sleep you can."

Karl and Lea headed to bed, but Renata wanted to talk to Gina and Roza. She found them hanging up her family's freshly laundered clothing. They smiled at her.

"Thank you," she said. "Clean clothing will feel so good after all the sand we collected in the ocean."

"Did you really wade from boat?" asked Roza, a dreamy expression on her face. "I'd like that."

"No, you wouldn't. It was terrifying, and our pilot lost his life. And now we must take another boat to Egypt."

"You go to Egypt? I come with you!" Gina jumped up and did a little dance.

"I tried to convince your father that you should come with us. Do you know how dangerous the world is now?" She thought that perhaps if the daughters were brave enough, they might try escaping on their own.

Gina and Roza looked at each other, slight creases on their brows.

Roza spoke, twisting her apron tie around one finger. "Mother and Father keep unhappy news from us, but we know, we hear some. Is true Hitler now in Austria?"

"Yes. We saw the soldiers and tanks from our train. I think Hungary or Czechoslovakia will be next. And then Greece."

Two pairs of eyed widened.

"But Father say Britain save us," said Gina. "They promised."

"Maybe, but I would not risk staying here. You have no idea how determined Hitler is."

"We talk Mother and Father again." Roza twisted her fingers. "Why not you stay here for a few months?"

Renata sighed and hugged her. "You are so sweet. Will you write to me when we find a home somewhere?"

"Of course! I give our address." Gina disappeared and returned with a scrap of paper and pencil stub. She scribbled on it and handed it to Renata.

"Thank you." Renata hugged each of them. "I'll never forget you, and I hope someday we'll meet again.

Lying on her cot later that evening, Renata mulled over the

new plan. *Egypt? Pyramids and mummies and Arabs? What could be there for me?*

But they could not get on a boat the next day, or even the next week, despite daily trips to the dock. A flood of humanity clamored to board each ship. If it floated and was heading across the Mediterranean, the captains got outrageous sums from the desperate passengers. Lea and Karl, used to following rules, waited uselessly at the ticket wickets, until finally, Renata had had enough.

"Mama and Papa, if we want to get on a boat, we must walk to the ship we want to board and haggle with the captain for space. We must pay all we can, or we won't get on."

"I won't do that!" snapped Lea. "Why should we pay all we have to be squeezed onto some overcrowded tub that might sink halfway?"

"Because we have to, Mama. Unless you want to stay in Greece." Her voice rose in frustration.

Papa twisted his mouth and ran his fingers through his thinning hair. "Lea, I regret to say I believe Renata is right."

"I'm not taking another stinking ship!" Lea shouted.

"Now, Lea, I doubt it will be stinking." He tried to put an arm around his wife's shoulder, but she shrugged him off and crossed her arms in defiance, eyes smoldering.

Renata lowered her voice with some effort.

"Mama, it might be even worse than *The Da Vinci*, but the alternative is to stay in Greece and wait for the Nazi invasion. For the love of God, let me do it."

"You don't have to scare her," said Karl, "but, here, take the money and do what you can."

"All right. Once we pay the fare, we'll board immediately."

Karl's face drooped.

He's depending on me, Renata thought. *My strong father, not so strong anymore.* She hid the money in her pockets. "Papa, we can do this today, or come back early tomorrow morning and stay here until we get on board. Your choice."

"Today," said Karl, a tone of doom in his voice.

Lea hunched her shoulders. Her face was a tight mask.

"Let's go, then." Renata hoisted her satchel onto her shoulder.

At the harbor, they joined thousands equally determined to find a ship. A rusty tanker sat at the dock. People were streaming up the gangplank, taking seats on any horizontal surface. In minutes, the ship disappeared under an ant-like swarm of bodies. The gangplank was raised, and the ship chugged away, wallowing under its heavy load.

Four smaller fishing boats took on a few dozen people each. Renata kept her parents moving closer to the wharf. She encountered a few elbows. It was like the train station in Munich, minus the guards. The crowds, however, were thousands, not hundreds, pressing closer and closer until it was hard to breathe.

"Mama, are you there?" she shouted, unable to turn around for a look.

"*Ja*, we are still here!"

Renata felt the crowd surge, lift her off her feet, and carry her toward an ancient freighter just docking. She screamed, women screamed, and men yelled. Babies wailed. The men did their best to stop the crush. Voices shouted their fear.

"Hold on!"

"Be careful before someone gets hurt!"

"For God's sake, stop!"

Renata's feet found the ground again but she was forced to keep walking to avoid being trampled. She had no idea where her parents were.

Port Authority workers moved in, blowing whistles and raising batons. Some were on horseback, and one with a megaphone shouted something in Greek.

Renata was pushed this way and that, always closer to the wharf and the now-docked freighter.

The instant the gangplank was set up, people pressed their way up it, heedless of danger or each other. The ship's captain stood at the top, taking money, armed guards on either side of him.

The sun beat down on the packed mob. Aggression turned to alarm and pleas for help when several people fainted, although Renata could not see where they were. She looked behind her.

Her parents were nowhere in sight.

She was tantalizingly close to the gangplank. She tried to turn around, but it was impossible. Bodies shoved her forward. At last her feet touched the gangplank and she climbed up, turning around and shouting as she went. "Mama! Papa! Where are you?"

But three dozen others were shouting the same thing. She thought she saw them about ten meters back, too far to gain the gangplank, and then the captain was there with his hand out.

"My parents! They must come, too. I have all the money. Will you pick them up on your next trip?" She was out of breath.

"Sorry, Miss, our next trip will be four days from now. Someone else will have them by then. Two hundred drachmas. Pay up quickly, others are behind you."

Quivering with rage at the extortionate sum, she handed it over and stepped onto the deck. Managing to find a wedge of railing not occupied, she strained her eyes over the crowd, and spotted Karl waving at her frantically.

"I see you, Papa! I'm sorry. Please try to get on here!"

But his reply was lost in the noise.

"I'll find you, I promise!" she shouted, but the wind carried her voice seaward.

Minutes later, the gangplank lifted, and the boat eased away.

Chapter Six

Alexandria, 1938

The boat disgorged its sweaty cargo two days later at Alexandria, Egypt. Mercifully, the weather had been mild, but there was no food and little water. Toilets had overflowed. Tempers had flared, forcing Renata to huddle in a tiny alcove behind firefighting equipment, on the second deck. To walk outside into fresh air and sunshine was a relief.

Renata was worried sick about her parents, ravenous, and terrifyingly alone in a strange country. Clutching the satchel containing her paintbrushes and a single change of clothing, she stumbled down the gangplank with the rest of the passengers.

Local officials, all British, herded them into lines.

The copper African sun, barely softened by the offshore breeze, forced those without hats to cover their heads with anything they could. Female volunteers circulated with glasses of water, but still people fainted, and first aid workers were kept busy, occasionally calling for stretchers.

Renata drank all the water she was offered, but her throat felt like sandpaper, and her feet and back ached from hours of standing. It didn't bear to think about what she would do after she was through customs. She had the money her parents should have had for their passage, but knew they would need it when—she clung to faith it would happen—the three of them were reunited.

Several hours later, it was her turn to speak with an exhausted Red Cross volunteer sitting behind a makeshift desk.

"Greek? *Italiano? Français? Deutsches?*" His voice was hoarse.

He sipped at the glass of water on his desk.

Renata replied in German, her own voice husky. "I'm Jewish, from Germany." She tried unsuccessfully to clear her throat.

Sticking with German, he asked for her name, birthdate, birthplace, and parents' names.

"I lost my parents in Greece. Can you help me find out where they are?"

He looked over his glasses, his mouth pursed.

"My dear girl, you see how overwhelmed we are. Once you are settled, see the Red Cross central administration."

Renata nodded, but her mind was back on that crowded dock.

"...I said, do you have a passport?"

"Oh, sorry, yes, here it is."

He picked up the German passport as if it were contaminated, opened it, stamped it, and put it in a box at his side.

"Can't I have that back?"

"You are a stateless person now. You cannot travel from Egypt on an enemy nation's passport. You are here, either until danger of hostilities ceases, or until you obtain other citizenship. Instead, you will receive a displaced person ID card." He wrote her information on a blank card, blotted it, and handed it to her, advising her to keep it on her person at all times.

He gestured her on and focused on the person behind her. She looked at the ID card, her new reality. She was officially no longer German, like one of her canvasses that she decided to wipe clean. A nothing. Suddenly, she felt chilly, despite the heat.

At the next table, a Red Cross volunteer handed her a blanket, a towel, and a change of clothes, then another volunteer took her and several other single women to a gymnasium that was to serve as housing. It held rows and rows of Army cots and nothing else. Renata felt numb, but the other women selected a cot each, and placed their possessions on it, so she did the same, choosing a cot next to them. She sat down. They stared at each other.

"Thank God for somewhere to sit," began Renata, speaking in German.

Two of the women chuckled and sat on their cots. The others followed their example, two stretched out on the cots, sighed, and closed their eyes. No one else spoke. They looked at one another.

Renata decided to break the silence again. Speaking first in German, she then repeated herself in rusty English.

"It looks like we'll be roommates. I'm Renata, a Jew from Germany."

A petite blonde who had laughed, spoke next. "Rachel. Another Jew from Germany."

"Alicia Suarez. Spain."

"Sofia. A Greek Jew."

They found ways to communicate, finally settling on English as the language they had most in common. Within half an hour, they knew a bit of each others' stories. Sofia, too, had been separated from her parents. Renata began to relax a little.

Alicia asked, "Where can we get something to eat? I'm starving."

"No idea," answered Sofia, "but let's find out." They were directed to a mess hall. Food was flatbread, olives, and fish that wasn't entirely fresh. Renata ate as much flatbread as she could, but the smell of the fish made her queasy.

After the meal, she and Sofia approached a Red Cross worker about finding their parents.

The worker looked at them dubiously. "You'll have to talk to the Red Cross senior administrator. Come along, I'll take you to her office."

Around a corner was a tent with an enormous red cross stitched onto each side. A queue extended outside and wound around several buildings. Renata groaned. Probably an hour or two at least to get inside. Still, what choice did they have?

Stumbling with a mangle of English and Yiddish, Sofia and Renata talked. Sofia was the daughter of a carpenter, who knew the Allies in Egypt would be looking for tradesmen. Renata thought that surely, as a doctor, her father's services would be welcomed. But first she had to find him and her mother.

The sun was tilting over the edge of the sky when Renata reached the front of the line. A tired but friendly woman in a Red Cross uniform gave her a polite smile. Her nameplate said "Jeannette Thoroughgood."

"ID card, please."

Renata handed it over.

"Thank you. Now, Miss Lowenthal, what can I do for you?"

"Help me find my parents. We were separated at the dock in Greece."

"Here, fill out this form. Their names, birthdates, et cetera. Usually in this kind of case, they turn up in a few days, so keep your chin up."

Relief tiptoed around Renata, but she still felt jumpy as a rabbit in a roomful of terriers. She filled out the form and returned it.

Miss Thoroughgood gave her a sympathetic smile. "I know how desperate you must feel, but please trust us. We want to reunite you with your family, too." She placed one hand over Renata's.

Renata gulped a "thank you" and left the tent, swallowing the lump that took up residence in her throat. When Sofia was finished, the two returned to the gymnasium together, arms linked.

Sofia's parents appeared three days later.

Renata felt a twinge of jealousy as Sofia left the gymnasium to join her parents in a tiny apartment in Alexandria, thanks to their Greek passports. She wondered how her parents would pay for their passage. Perhaps the Moustakis would lend them the money.

She had to do something to keep from losing her mind, so she asked Miss Thoroughgood if she had any unlined paper.

"Not usually, but today you are in luck. We had a shipment of identity cards, only they weren't printed properly and one side is blank. I think I could spare you a dozen sheets or so."

"Marvelous, that would be just right!" Renata accepted them reverently and headed for her pencils. She would sketch the gymnasium, her mates, and later perhaps, she could paint them.

With a few deft strokes, a little smudging and shading, she captured their faces, managing to imbue each portrait with strength and confidence. Yes, and hope.

"Where did you learn to do that? You're amazing!" said Rachel.

"It's more like the real me." Alicia laughed, and the others quickly agreed.

"I look…" Sofia paused, looking for the right word. "… powerful!"

"Yes, that's it, exactly. Me, as I wish I was right now," agreed Rachel. She looked at Alicia with awe.

The girls hugged Renata.

"That's my first bit of fun since we left home," said Alicia, and the others nodded. They secured the group sketch on a wall with a bit of wire.

That night, Renata slept well. Somehow, she would find her parents.

Two days later, volunteers and British soldiers marched into the gymnasium. The head matron stepped onto a box provided by one of the soldiers, then tapped a cane for silence. Renata's heart was racing, thinking of her experiences with German soldiers and police.

"Ladies, your attention please." Her voice boomed in the large wooden gym. "As you are aware, we are receiving shiploads of displaced persons every day. We have done our best to house you in the facilities we have at hand, but that is now impossible. Therefore, we are removing you to a camp west of here, called Tolumbat."

The room erupted with chatter. The matron whacked the box again.

"Silence! Silence, please!"

The chatter subsided.

"The move will occur immediately. Please wait for assignment to the trucks that will take you there. Canvas sacks will be distributed for your belongings. Miss Thoroughgood, whom you know, will take it from here. That is all." She stepped down and marched outside, ignoring the shouted questions.

Miss Thoroughgood stepped onto the box.

"I'm sorry, ladies. I know you were beginning to settle in here, poor as accommodations are, but we have had three thousand people arrive in the past two weeks. Soldiers, please distribute the sacks."

The soldiers headed down one aisle and up another, dropping a sack on each cot.

Renata watched them cautiously.

"Now, ladies, I'm sure you have many questions. Men and

families are already being moved. You will be in a section reserved for single women. There will be ten people to each tent. There are washing, cooking, and toilet facilities, although they are a little rough."

Thoroughgood paused to let the murmurs fade. "The Red Cross on-site will assist you with reconnecting with your loved ones, any health concerns, and distribution of food. Trucks are lined up outside." She gestured to the large main doors. "You will be called to board by name. Any questions?"

Noise erupted.

Thoroughgood rapped on the box. "I'm sorry. I can't understand when you all talk at once. Here," she pointed at a woman close to her, "what is your question?"

"How will we store our things in tents?"

"You will each have a foot locker. Next." She pointed to someone else.

"How will we get our letters?"

"Your mail will be redirected to Tolumbat. No one should lose any mail."

A murmur of relief rippled through the room.

While questions continued, Renata stuffed her few clothes, her art supplies, and some food into the canvas sack, which smelled like the tent she'd stayed in as a Girl Guide, years ago. She could only think about neighbors in Germany, hauled away in trucks like the ones standing outside in the street.

An hour later they stared at their new home. An ocean of canvas flapped gently in the breeze, surrounded by a fence topped with barbed wire.

"That doesn't look overly friendly, does it?" murmured Rachel as she and Renata walked toward the main gate staffed with soldiers.

"No, it doesn't. We'll have to work on softening up those soldiers, so we can get out now and then."

"Renata, you are so naughty!" Rachel stifled her smile when they reached the control gate.

A soldier checked their ID cards, consulted a list, and directed them to the right.

"Tent 134 in the Women's section, if you please. Pick up

supplies on your way."

More volunteers handed out a small cooking pot, dishes, and a towel to each woman, then sent them on. They wound through the camp, noticing overlapping guy wires and tent poles.

"They didn't waste any space," Renata muttered to Rachel and Alicia, who had just joined them.

"At least we're not in one room with a hundred people," Alicia added. "Let's look on the positive side, shall we?"

Life in Tolumbat quickly fell into a predictable, through tedious, routine. Men skilled with wood and metal were soon turning out stools and tables. Women took over the cooking. Musicians made primitive instruments from oil cans, string, empty boxes, bits of wood, and the resultant sound got everyone's toes tapping. Anyone who had a talent offered to teach others, from singing to pottery to accounting. Schools popped up, thanks to the Red Cross, complete with chalkboards and stiff walls on which the teachers hung lessons or artwork. Nurses and doctors tended to the many refugees who were ill or injured, but there was never enough staff to address the need. Renata was in demand to teach drawing, using only scraps of paper and pencil stubs.

She wrote to Hans, describing the camp and her new friends. In a letter to Gina and Roza, she begged them again to leave, and asked if they had any news of her parents. She enclosed a small sketch of her own tent and cot.

Daily, Renata checked the list of "found persons" posted outside the Red Cross administration tent. Finally, near the bottom, she read "Dr. Karl Lowenthal. Mrs. Lea Lowenthal." She had to read it twice, then ran inside, waving and shouting at the volunteer.

Chapter Seven

Reunion, 1938

"My parents, they're here! Where do I find them?" Her skin burned with anticipation.

Miss Thoroughgood checked her list. "They're coming from Moses Wells, northeast of here."

"When?"

"Tomorrow, I should think. Check here in the afternoon and I'll take you to them."

Renata reached across the table and hugged the woman. "You're an angel!"

She danced outside, singing, and ran to tell her friends. They gathered around, hugging and laughing with her, except Rachel, who stood to one side.

Rachel's chin wobbled. "You're so lucky, Renata. I have no idea where any of my family are, or if any of them made it out of Germany."

Renata wrapped her arms around her. "We are your new family. Right?" She peered into her eyes.

Rachel nodded. "I should go now." She walked away, head down. Renata and Alicia looked at each other.

"Some people here will never find their loved ones." Renata stared at Rachel's back.

"We're lucky, we have to remember that."

"You're right." She clasped Alicia's hands. "I'll see you back in the tent, then."

Renata did not know what to do with herself until the next day. She tried drawing but could not concentrate. She bit her nails, an old habit she thought she had conquered. She paced outside her tent for hours, until sleep finally claimed her in the early morning hours.

"Renata, are you all right?" asked Rachel while they were attempting to do something with their hair, using one ancient brush. "Your hands are shaking."

"I'm so nervous! I never had a good relationship with my mother. Being away from her has been a relief, awful as that sounds. But I've missed her, too, which to be honest, surprises me. I would have been devastated to lose her forever."

Rachel sighed. "I have lost mine forever, I think. And how about your father?"

"He and I were always close. He's a darling." *But not as strong as he used to be.* She gave up on her hair and handed the brush to her friend. "I'm sorry, Rachel. It must be so hard, seeing Sofia and me with our families. I don't know what I'd do."

Rachel's eyes reddened, but she brought herself under control. "There's really no choice. You just keep going, otherwise you would go mad."

Renata rubbed her arms. It was hard, being excited yet knowing others were so sad. She wondered how her parents would greet her. It was time.

Inside a small inner office, her mother and father, looking haggard but relieved, opened their arms to her.

"Mama! Papa!" She threw herself into their arms, content to be their little girl once more. "I'm so sorry I left you behind," she murmured, her head on her father's shoulder.

"Shhh, my dear, you could not help it. We saw what happened. It doesn't matter." He kissed the top of her head. The three of them clung together, weeping with joy.

Lea, tears in her eyes, held Renata at arm's length. "I thought I would never see you again. I-I spent so many years missing Solomon, I neglected you, my daughter. Can you forgive me?" Her voice wobbled.

Renata noticed something else in her eyes. Was that fear? "Oh, Mama, of course I forgive you, and I hope you can forgive me, too."

Mother and daughter held each other tightly.

That night, Renata slept well beside her parents, able to breathe at last.

Karl and Renata were up with the sun, seeking latrines and washing huts. The stench of the latrines permeated the air well before they were in view. Lines of men, women, and children waited their turn, holding their noses.

"I must say something about this to the authorities." Karl frowned. "This is not sanitary."

Renata had observed the same thing. Finally, they reached the front of the line. No one dawdled over the necessary bodily functions. They left for the wash huts to scrub their hands thoroughly.

The gray towels in the wash hut had Karl shaking his head again. "Don't use those towels, Renata, just let your hands air dry."

"But Papa, what about showers? We are allowed one per week, with a small sliver of soap and one thin towel. How else can we keep clean?"

"We must do our best. This is a recipe for disaster. Come, let's find your mother and get something to eat."

They collected Lea and headed to the mess tent for breakfast, which consisted of pita bread, olives, and fresh oranges.

Lea spoke quietly, her hand on Karl's arm. "Karl, we must get out of here before we catch typhoid or cholera or something worse."

Renata was amazed at the lack of stridency she heard. Her mother had learned something. She hoped it would last.

Karl agreed. "I'm going to meet the commander today to complain. You can best help by keeping our own space clean, and scrounging some clean towels, if that's possible. Surely some of the other women are doing this also."

"You know I'm not very good at that sort of thing…." Lea hesitated.

Renata held her breath, waiting for her mother's refusal.

"…but I will do my best."

Renata hardly knew how to relate to this new mother. The improvement was breathtaking.

She shared her own plans. "I'm teaching art at the school tents. And Alicia, Rachel, and I are trying to find a way out of here."

"Be careful! I can't lose you again." This was a bit of the old Lea.

"Don't worry, Mama, I will not let that happen."

The weeks dragged a reluctant summer into fall and winter. "Rainy season" aptly described the constant wind and rain that arrived in December and stayed through January.

Thanks to Karl's complaints, more latrines were dug, and liberal use of lime reduced the stench. He taught first aid and practical nursing when not treating patients.

"I'm off, then," he said after breakfast, giving Lea a quick kiss on the cheek. He picked up his black bag and disappeared to battle whooping cough, tuberculosis, and malnutrition.

"He loves the children, don't you think?" Renata asked her mother as she scooped up remains of tasteless mush with the last scrap of pita bread.

"No question." Lea stacked the cups in preparation for a trip to the communal sinks. A brief shadow passed over her face. She seldom mentioned Solomon now.

Renata decided not to comment.

"And now I'm working with children, too." She handed her plate to her mother. "They enjoy their art lessons, so long as we have paper and pencils. What I wouldn't give for some paints, though."

Alicia popped her head into the tent. "Ready?"

"Yes, let me get my things." She dug under her cot for her satchel, filled with supplies she'd obtained the day before. "Did you get the glue?"

Alicia leaned against a tent pole while Renata ran the brush through her hair.

"No. Instead, we're collecting candle stubs, and next week I'm going to show them how to make candles in the sand."

As they walked toward the school, Renata scowled and kicked aside some pebbles.

"Much as I see the importance of teaching, Alicia, I'm going crazy in this camp. I'd give a lot to get out for a while."

"Me, too." Alicia lowered her voice. "Do you know I have over fifty candles made? They're in a crate behind my cot, waiting to be sold."

Renata raised her eyebrows. "Clever girl! I've done sketches of the camp." Thoughts of the sketches she and Hans made flitted through her mind. "I could do portraits for cash, too. What if we could get permission to sell in the Alexandria market?"

Alicia sighed. "Even one day a week outside, meeting other people, seeing shops and cafés, would be heaven."

"I bet we could find a way. Maybe a hole in the fence. Or we could flirt with a guard."

"Sure, Renata. That wouldn't work." Alicia made a face.

They separated to their classrooms. All day, while Renata taught children about perspective with one half of her mind, the other half was concocting ways of escaping. The day dragged.

Finally, she picked up the pencils and papers, and collected Alicia.

"Let's talk to Matron Tompkins and see if she'll give you, me, and Rachel a pass—No, wait," she said as Alicia started to interrupt. "I know it's about as easy as finding a gold nugget in a sandstorm. But let's try."

Marjorie Tompkins, Red Cross matron, had a reputation as fair, but hard on those flouting regulations. She looked up from her desk at Renata and Alicia.

"Miss Lowenthal, isn't it? And Miss Suarez?" she waved her hand. "Come in, then, dears. What can I do for you?"

Renata cleared her throat. "Mrs. Tompkins, there are three of us who want to go to the market in Alexandria to sell things we have made. You have seen some of my sketches in the school, haven't you?"

The matron nodded.

"Alicia makes candles, and Rachel remakes old clothes into babies' clothing. We're asking that we be permitted out of camp one day a week to go to market. We're desperate to see buildings made of brick instead of canvas. Please!" She put on her best supplicant face.

"Hmm." Mrs. Tompkins cupped her chin with one hand and chewed on a pencil. "Really, the menfolk are supposed to support you. Why are you girls worrying about this at all?"

"Times are changing, ma'am. Alicia and Rachel have no father or husband to support them. My parents need whatever I can earn."

"The problem is, if we allow you, we must allow anyone.

We can't have you disappearing into the city. The locals wouldn't stand for it."

"Couldn't someone escort us?"

Matron Tompkins gave Renata her official smile. "Tell you what, let me think it over and I'll let you know tomorrow. Fair?"

"Yes, ma'am, thank you." Renata turned, then said over her shoulder, "It would give the newspapers something good to print about life in Tolumbat."

Renata left to queue at the mail tent, but Alicia and Rachel headed home.

When an envelope with Swiss stamps was deposited into her hands, she yelped with joy and raced to her tent.

Alicia and Lea were setting out the meal of rice, beans, and pita bread. Rachel began serving portions onto tin plates. Renata slid onto a bench beside her father, who was munching pita and reading a book.

She wondered where he found books in this place.

"How was your day, Renata?" asked Lea.

"We've asked Mrs. Tompkins for permission to sell my sketches in the market in Alexandria one day a week."

Papa looked up. "And..?"

"We asked for all three of us." She glanced at Rachel. "We could earn some money. I'm to return tomorrow for her answer."

"If you don't break any rules, you should be fine," commented Papa. He returned to his book.

Mama's eyes glinted. "Karl, how can we get out of here?"

He folded the book and set it aside. "The camp commander says we must pay fifty pounds per person, then they will allow us to move into Alexandria."

"How soon can you earn that much, Papa?" Renata spooned another mouthful of beans.

He sighed and spread his hands. "I can't imagine saving that much on the pittance they pay me for medical work. I think we're stuck here for the duration. I'm sorry."

Stunned, Renata turned away, her heart beating a little faster. Had her father abdicated his leadership role so completely? She clenched her fists and promised herself that if her father couldn't earn the money to free them, she would do it herself.

Rachel and Alicia were staring at her. Gesturing for them to come closer, she spoke softly. "We have to save ourselves. You are without parents; I'm without resourceful parents." She squeezed their hands.

They cleared the dishes and Alicia brought out a pack of cards she had found. Lea put a bowl of dates in the middle of the table.

"Wait," said Renata, "I have more to tell you. I received a letter from Hans." She held up the still-sealed envelope.

Alicia and Rachel squealed. "What does it say?"

With agonizing slowness, Renata inserted her thumb under the tab and opened the envelope, then slid out the thin piece of paper inside. "Give me a minute, will you?"

She went outside to read it.

June 17, 1938
Dear Renata,

I was so happy to hear that you are safely in Egypt. As expected, I was ordered to report to the Army two days after you left, so that afternoon I took the first train I could get to Geneva. Regretfully, I had no time to retrieve any of your artwork, but my parents have the key to your home and will keep an eye on it. You may have heard that Jewish property must be registered, but because we have the key, we're claiming it as ours for the time being to protect it, so long as we can. Sorry I can't do more.

I am safe here, although I have plans that will take me into danger. I won't be here long enough to receive letters and have no forwarding address. Do not write to my parents because your letters could get them in trouble. I will write to you when I am able.

Saying good-bye was the hardest thing I've ever done. I miss you every day, and pray that someday we can be reunited.

I love you.
Hans

Renata did not know whether to laugh or cry. He loved her!

How could she not write back? She squeezed the letter to her breast and suppressed a squeal.

She went inside again, unable to remove the smile from her face.

"He was in Switzerland in June, but I don't know where he is now. I'm not to write back."

"Come on, Renata, we can tell by that glow on your face that he said something else." Alicia sidled up to Renata and put an arm around her shoulder. "Tell."

Renata curled away, grinning. "Not on your life. Some things are private!"

"Ooo, that sounds a little spicy! Let me read it!"

Renata shrieked when Alicia chased her around the table reaching unsuccessfully for the letter. The two collapsed, giggling, on the floor.

Karl looked over his glasses, smiling. "I'm glad you heard from him." Then he returned to his book. He tamped tobacco into his pipe, and soon the fragrant smoke curled around their heads.

Lea sat down beside Renata. "I'm glad you got the letter, but how likely is it that you and Hans will meet again?"

Renata's stomach lurched. A taut string inside her began to thrum. *Just like Mother to ruin my excitement.*

"Have you given up your idea of marrying him?" Mama selected a date from the bowl and chewed thoughtfully, eyes on her daughter.

The others studied their fingernails.

Renata put down her cutlery and touched her fingertips to her forehead. Neither of her parents had any idea how much she loved Hans. She swallowed her sadness, kept her voice level. "He wants to meet with me after this is all over. And he will."

"Renata, think! War, when it comes, will cause terrible changes. We can count on nothing being as it was before. You would be much wiser to consider the soldiers and sailors in the city."

"Oh, Mama, I just can't." She got up, appetite gone. Dear, brave Hans. Her own life devoid of meaning, stuck in the camp. She shook her head, put the letter in her pocket, and headed out for a walk. She had to get out now.

Chapter Eight

Frustration, 1939

Mrs. Tompkins said no. "Too much risk of favoritism, dear. I'm sure you understand."

Renata was not deterred. She talked to Rachel and Alicia later that day.

The next morning, she announced that she and her friends were going to help move food boxes to the kitchen tents. Lea nodded, barely listening, while Karl headed out to the clinic.

"Papa!" she whispered urgently, pulling him outside. "I'm trying to get out on the supply truck with Alicia and Rachel. We'll go into the city to sell our wares, then come back tomorrow. Let Mama know tonight, please?"

"Be careful." He hugged her and disappeared.

His mild reaction was confusing, but she had no time to think it through.

She and her two friends met near the supply trucks with overstuffed bags they hid in a corner.

"Are you sure about this?" Rachel whispered.

"No, but what other choice do we have?"

An olive-green truck rumbled in, churning dust and grinding gears. The driver parked with practiced expertise, jumped out, and lifted the tarp from the back.

The three joined the volunteers swarming to unload the crates. As the work wound down, the volunteers drifted away.

Renata lagged, pretending to check inside for anything they might have missed. Rachel and Alicia picked up their bags, then they jumped inside and pulled a tarp over themselves. Barely breathing, they heard someone flip the large tarp down. Minutes later, the truck began moving.

It was ridiculously easy. Once in Alexandria, the driver disappeared. Rachel crept to the edge and peeked out at a deserted compound.

"It's clear."

A jump and a sprint to the gate, and they were in the city.

Renata laughed and lifted her face to the sun. "We did it!" she cried. "Come on, let's find the market."

But after an hour of walking, they knew they were lost.

"Hallo there, sorry, didn't mean to bump into you," said a male voice.

Renata looked up, flustered, at a smiling young man with flaming curls visible below his sailor's cap, and a small galaxy of freckles across his nose and cheeks. His green eyes twinkled.

"No, I'm the one to apologize." She gripped her satchel across her chest. "I'm quite all right, thank you."

"White women don't usually come to this part of town." His brows knit together.

She hesitated, but he looked so friendly and sweet. "Truth is, we're lost. We're trying to get to the market, so we can sell things. Could you help us find it?"

He beamed. "It's not far. I'd be happy to walk you there. This way."

A shabby, narrow street expanded into a large courtyard, off which spurted small alleys and alcoves crammed with stalls selling everything imaginable. Brilliant colors and the scents of nutmeg, tobacco, and coffee competed for attention with bleating donkeys, the gentle music of camel bells, and shouts of those hawking their wares. Renata looked around, dazzled.

Their guide said, "I'll take you for a tour. It's rather a lot the first time, but you'll get used to it."

They followed him through the maze.

"Thank you, you've been so kind. By the way, my name is Renata."

"Everyone calls me Mickey."

"Mickey, these are my friends, Alicia and Rachel."

Mickey tipped his hat and bowed to each of them.

He took on the tones of a tour guide. "This section is clothing and textiles. Local linens and cotton, and silk from India. Brassware and woodenware are to the left. It grew like this over time, and it's been here for donkey's years. Look at the jewelry over there."

Alicia paused to examine the finely tooled gold and silver necklaces and bracelets, more ornate than anything she had seen. A veiled female vendor looked at her hopefully, but Alicia, without money, shrugged apologetically and moved on.

Rachel examined the clothing with a practiced eye. "I hope my things will sell here. The styles are completely different."

"You said you have art to sell, Renata. Would you like to see the art section?" Mickey asked.

"Of course. How will they feel about me selling and sketching, though? I hope I won't cause any problems."

"If you remember to avoid eye contact with the men, you should be all right. They can't stand our forward Western women." Renata's brow creased. For her plan to work, she needed to be accepted.

They turned into another alcove. On the walls hung landscapes of the desert, the Nile, Egypt's famous ancient landmarks. Oil lamps and some unremarkable pottery took up one table.

She noticed an empty table and bench. Approaching one of the men, her eyes low, she showed her sketches to him, gestured at the table, then at her friends.

He nodded.

Alicia gave him a candle, which he accepted with a gap-toothed smile. Rachel brought out her baby clothes and was instantly surrounded by women eager to look, feel, and buy.

Once she had set up her sketches and an easel, Renata asked Mickey if she could sketch him.

"Me? Why?"

"Because I want people to see me at work. Please?"

Twenty minutes later, a small crowd had gathered to watch her. She captured perfectly his curls, the freckles, and, of course, the uniform.

"Wow, it's great!" exclaimed Mickey when he saw the

finished product. "Could I buy it from you? It would make my mother so happy."

"Mickey, it's yours. You've done me a big favor today. Let's just call us even, all right?" She gave him the portrait.

"I must get back to the base. Are you sure you'll be okay here?"

"Actually, I think we'll need help to find the trucks that brought us here from Tolumbat. Do you know where they park for the night?"

He lowered his eyebrows. "I think so. Do you know the name of the street?"

The women looked at each other.

"Oh, no," said Rachel. "We weren't paying attention."

"It was a large compound on a street that had trees on the other side. We couldn't see the water and it was not downtown. Is that any help at all?" Renata crossed her fingers.

"Let me work on it. I'll be back in a couple of hours." Mickey dissolved into the crowd.

"You think we'll ever see him again?" asked Alicia. "Nice looker, isn't he?"

"Very handsome. I hope he comes back," said Rachel, between customers.

A European woman, expensively dressed, approached Renata's table and requested a portrait.

Two hours later, all three women were sold out. Renata had no more pages in her sketchbook and had made three pounds; Rachel, two; and Alicia, two pounds six.

Mickey had not returned. They decided to leave, and look for the compound themselves, but as they exited the market, there was Mickey, leaning against a pillar on the opposite side of the street.

As soon as he saw them, he trotted across.

"I found the trucks, but are you sure that's where you want to spend the night? Sorry I don't have a warm place to take you. I'd welcome you in the barracks, but our sergeant would take a dim view."

The women blushed.

"Here are our choices." Renata enumerated them on her fingers when the group arrived at the deserted truck compound. "We can sleep in the truck, but we'll have to leave before they start to load it, then walk home. Find somewhere else to spend the night. Find someone to help us. Or walk back to the camp."

Alicia and Rachel shifted uneasily, shivering in the evening chill.

"The camp's too far to walk. At least ten kilometers." Alicia was not one for exercise.

"We have no idea who we can trust. Except Mickey." Rachel grinned at him and slapped her arms to keep warm.

"Then we spend the night or we walk. Who wants to spend the night?"

Alicia and Renata put up their hands. Rachel glowered.

"That's it, then. We'll stay in the truck. Mickey, thanks for your help. I hope we see you again." Renata climbed into the truck. "We still have the tarpaulins. They're better than nothing."

Huddling together for warmth, they rotated spaces periodically so everyone had a turn in the middle. Sleep eventually claimed them for a few restless hours.

They awoke unrested, hungry, and cold. The delicate aroma of shawarma drifted into the alley.

"Do you smell that?" asked Rachel. "If I could eat it, I'd feel a lot better."

Alicia yawned and stretched. "Oh, God, that smells fantastic. Let's go find it. Renata?"

Renata was around a corner relieving herself. She called, "Give me a second, then we'll go."

The vendor had fresh sticks of shawarma that the women bought and devoured.

"Just as good as the smell, wasn't it, girls?" Alicia patted her tummy and wiped her hands on the side of her dress.

"Mmmm, loved it. Why don't we get that food in the camp?"

"Seriously?" asked Renata. "They don't want to give us good food, because we'll get used to the place and won't want to leave."

They collapsed, laughing.

Renata continued. "When we find the coast road, maybe we can get a lift to the camp."

"Another of your brilliant ideas." Rachel, sucking the last of the juice out of the shawarma stick, shoved Renata on the shoulder.

Using the sun as a compass, they walked east-northeast, zigzagging through city blocks until they were on the coast road.

The truck came up behind them an hour later, but despite their frantic waving and shouting, it roared past, belching smoke.

"Well, damn him!" grumbled Alicia. "You'd think three pretty women would stop a train, let alone that broken-down wreck."

"Come on, you two, only another five or so miles to go."

The others groaned, but began moving again.

Sneaking into the camp proved harder than getting out. They wriggled under the edge of the deserted supply tent, brushed off the sand, and left for their separate tents.

"We were terrified that you had been arrested, or worse!" Mama gripped her daughter fiercely.

Karl held her to him. "Thank God, you are back," he whispered. "When I said good-bye yesterday, it didn't register what you were planning to do. Sorry."

"Look what we did," said Renata, pulling three pounds out of her dress and thrusting it into her mother's hands. "Rachel and Alicia did well, too. Now tell me if it was worth the risk."

Lea and Karl eyed each other. Karl finally shrugged. "Very impressive. If you can continue, it will not take long to save enough money to buy our way out."

Renata looked from one to the other in disbelief. "So, you don't mind what I'm doing?"

Lea folded her arms. "If you want out of here permanently, find a British lad to marry. A husband is a ticket out of here, for all of us."

Renata sighed. "Any letters?" she asked.

"This one from Aunt Adele." Mama held it out.

Renata took it to her cot to read.

January 4, 1939
My Dear Sister,
When I last wrote to you, I truly thought things for Jews had become as bad as they could be, but I was wrong. Now, in addition to registering all our property, we must have "Juif" stamped on our passports. Anyone who disobeys is arrested and sent to a concentration camp for "reeducation." The one-billion-mark fine on Jews for the damage done at Kristallnacht has given the police an open hand to seize anything we own.

Remember Herr Shoenberg, the shoemaker? He disappeared last week, and his shop is boarded up. His family lives with anyone who will take them in, a few days at a time, but no one has enough food to feed four extra mouths. Even that friendly Lutheran pastor at the church near your house has been imprisoned for speaking out.

It is an evil time. I regret terribly not coming with you when I had the chance, but my chance has passed. Many of my jewels are sold for food, the rest hidden. My dear chauffeur will not leave me, although I can no longer pay him. We are so thin, you would not recognize us. At least the cat is fat, feeding on rats that come looking for scraps....

Renata could not read any more. She ground her teeth in despair. Tante Adele was trapped. Her mother had that hollow look of desolation she had had after Solomon's death. Renata got up and held her close, stroking her back.

"I won't say it will be all right because we know it won't. All we can do is survive here, Mama. And paint. And help anyone we can."

Sniffling, Mama nodded and leaned on her shoulder. Renata pressed a handkerchief into her hands. Mama blew her nose and wiped her eyes.

"I miss her so much. I don't know what I will do if anything happens to her."

"We must just keep going, Mama. It's what she would want, if she were here."

Mama squeezed Renata's arm and turned to the mindless

task of peeling potatoes. "It's time to make dinner."

Renata wrote to Hans, and hid the letter under her bedding. She had quite a collection, that she intended to show him whenever they met again.

Chapter Nine

War, September 1939

Renata and Alicia headed to their tents after a day of teaching.

"We need to hear the BBC news tonight. It's been two days." Alicia hugged the pile of workbooks she would be marking later in the evening.

Renata nodded. "If England doesn't come in now, Hitler has already won." She smiled absently as some of her art students walked by, but her heavy thoughts were focused on the invasion of Poland. She felt as if a metal band was squeezing her chest so she could hardly breathe.

Rachel materialized in front of them, along with Lea and Karl.

"We're wanted in the main square for an announcement!" She gulped for breath "Come on!"

They joined the flow of people rushing toward the rapidly filling square. Someone had set up a high platform at one end, and a soldier was adjusting a microphone, which howled and squealed intermittently until he was finished.

A few minutes later, Marjorie Tompkins appeared, accompanied by a British Army officer Renata did not recognize.

"Silence, please!" Marjorie's authoritative voice carried well, and the chatter died down instantly. "Major Richland has an important announcement for us. Major."

Richland took the podium. He had one slim folder in his hand.

Karl took Renata's hand and squeezed. She glanced down

and saw he held her mother's hand, too. She thought her chest would burst open.

"Ladies and gentlemen, boys and girls," Major Richland began, "it is my duty to inform you that effective immediately, the United Kingdom of Great Britain and Northern Ireland is in a state of war with Nazi Germany. France, Australia, and New Zealand have joined us in this declaration, and we expect other countries to join in the days ahead."

Two seconds of stunned silence were broken by a wave of excited talk, questions, and a few cheers.

Richland extended his hand for silence. The crowd hushed.

"No doubt, you have many questions. We do not have many answers for you yet, but we will provide news as it becomes available. In the meantime, a few rules will be implemented immediately." He cleared his throat.

"First, a total blackout of the camp from sunset to sunrise will be enforced. Torches modified to provide limited light will be issued to allow safe movement after dark, but no lanterns, no fires.

"Secondly, should any able-bodied men wish to enlist with the British Army or Navy, you may do so. However, enlistment is not required at this time.

"Outgoing mail will be censored. It is vital to keep information from the enemy, information he could use to his advantage. Therefore, consider what you are writing. Keep it to personal or general comments, and you are less likely to have your letters more blacked out than not. Otherwise, carry on as usual. God Save the King."

The British present replied, "God Save the King!"

Richland stepped down and disappeared.

Marjorie took the podium again. "Everyone, we have been expecting the worst for some time. Now the worst has happened, and we must all do our best to manage."

"Eh, what's that mean?" came an angry voice from across the square.

Marjorie gripped the podium and pressed her lips together. "A good question. First, we expect many more refugees, and a number of them will be placed here. I ask for your patience and cooperation as we fit in new residents."

Renata and those around her groaned. Tolumbat was already crowded.

Marjorie was not finished, though. "The Mediterranean Sea has just become a vastly more dangerous place. I have not been told, but I'm assuming all shipping will go by convoy. The numbers of troops and sailors in Alexandria will rise."

A female voice with a heavy Greek accent called out, "Will we have enough food to feed our families?"

"I don't expect we will be reduced to food rations in this fertile part of the world," replied Marjorie, "but we must all do everything we can to avoid waste."

A low murmur of agreement ran through the crowd.

A young man spoke out next. "Are we going to be bombed? We're sitting ducks here."

Marjorie gave the slightest shake of her head. "I sincerely hope not, but I can't promise you that. We must trust our Army and Navy to keep us safe. That's all for tonight, everyone. Thank you for coming."

The crowd began to break apart. Renata, Karl, Lea, and Rachel drifted back to their tents.

The tightness around Renata's chest eased. At least Hitler could no longer rampage unhindered across the continent.

With her family and a cluster of her friends, they offered prayers in their own languages, Jews and Christians united in worry. Renata prayed she would be equal to whatever this war required of her.

The borders of Tolumbat expanded several times. More tents, more people, more tempers flaring over a few inches of space or a piece of pita.

Renata shared her misery with Alicia and Rachel at the wash tent.

"I can't stand the crowds. There's no place to be alone for even a few minutes."

"And the food is worse," added Rachel. "We're hungry most of the time."

The others murmured agreement.

"There's no hope for any Jew in Europe, so who can blame them?" Rachel wrung out her washing and hung it on the tent guy lines. "I haven't heard anything from my family since before Kristallnacht." Her voice wobbled. "I miss Sofia, too," she added.

Sofia and her parents were in Alexandria, where Spiros was so busy working at the docks, he was turning down jobs. Their life seemed a golden dream to the camp residents.

Renata gave Rachel a sympathetic squeeze.

"Are you going to the market today?"

"Yes, Alicia, too."

As they approached the market, they heard angry voices. Two groups of men, Arab and British were in an escalating shouting match.

"You British use our country! You protect evil Jews who kill children!" shouted one Egyptian with an effusive beard.

"We're protecting your lot from Hitler, can't you see that?" a British sailor shouted back. "And Jews don't kill children!"

The women moved cautiously around the closest building to avoid being seen.

Rachel hissed, "That Egyptian said what Hitler says about us! How can they know that?"

Renata spotted a poster on a telephone pole, which she ripped down. "Look at this! It's identical to what the Nazis were passing around in Germany! I'll bet the Nazis are sending them money." She crumpled the poster and stamped it underfoot.

"Do you think it's safe to go to the market?" Alicia's fine face was crimped.

"I'm not sure it's a good idea," said Rachel.

But Renata was determined. "It *is* a good idea. We'll show them we're not afraid of them! Come on, let's go."

She started walking. Rachel and Alicia had little choice but to follow.

Usually patrons and vendors ignored the women, or nodded politely. But not anymore. They were jostled, elbowed, spat upon, taunted.

"What are you white women doing here?"

"Jews, go away!"

The further they got into the market, the rougher the crowd became. Renata was trying not to panic, but Rachel's eyes were glassy with fear. Alicia, defiant, spat and elbowed back. Renata joined her.

She shouted, "Get out of my way, you louts! We've been here for months, and you've bought my sketches, bought our wares. You are listening to lies!"

One burly man tried to block her way.

"Move, you! Now!" With all her strength, Renata kneed him in his privates.

He folded to the ground and crawled away, groaning.

When they reached their stall, a veiled woman selling pots reached over and patted Rachel's arm.

But sales were slow, and they left with half their usual take. Discouragement made the walk home longer than ever.

"We're never going to earn our way out of here," lamented Alicia.

Rachel nodded. "We have to do something else."

Renata picked up a stone and threw it as hard as she could. "Maybe we can get permission to sell outside the camp more often."

The other two glanced at one another.

Alicia broke the silence. "We could sell more. I'm ready. How about you, Rachel?"

Rachel sighed, then agreed.

Marjorie Tompkins sat at her desk the next morning, assessing the three.

"You want permission to go to the Alexandria market four days a week?"

Alicia and Rachel had appointed Renata as spokeswoman.

"Yes, Mrs. Tompkins."

"And you remember me turning you down for one day a week?"

"Yes, but we have things to sell, and when we earn money, we can buy things that are hard to get in camp, or buy our way out altogether." Renata looked at her friends, who nodded.

"How can I be sure you'll return at night?"

The three glanced at each other. Renata cleared her throat. "Because we've been doing it for months."

"What?"

"We found a way out of the camp, and we've been at the market selling things for ages, one day a week. We've always returned. We have nowhere else to go."

Mrs. Tompkins' face was a study in conflicting emotions. Initial anger was slowly replaced by grudging admiration, and finally, she burst out laughing.

"Well, I'll be! You little terrors!" She lowered her voice to a conspiratorial whisper. "Just between you and me, well done!" She folded her hands on her desk. "I've been telling the CO that we're much too tight, and we need to allow people into town now and again. You've just proven yourselves. Permission granted!" With a flourish, she stamped exit passes and handed one to each of them. "Now, don't let me down."

"We won't. Thank you, Mrs. Tompkins," said Alicia.

They left, huge grins on each face.

Despite the tense atmosphere at the market, the women did well enough, and gave their money to Renata's father for safekeeping. The fifty pounds per person exit fee was no longer an impossible dream.

Rachel was the first to present the full amount to a dumbfounded Mrs. Tompkins. The other two made her promise to keep in touch, and two weeks later, Alicia left to share Rachel's flat.

The three girls met regularly at the market. Rachel expanded into clothing repairs and dress design. Within a few months, she had a treadle sewing machine. Her time at the market decreased as she worked at home, where there was more room and less noise.

Alicia began making jewelry from copper wire and polished stones that she bought from another vendor. Two other jewelry-makers encouraged her and shared their tricks.

For Renata, sketching at the market had become a tedious chore, no matter how the audience gushed over her talent. When business was slow, she sketched ideas she had for paintings she would create once she had a studio, and wrote letters to Hans.

The day arrived when she and her parents left Tolumbat, thanks to her hundred fifty pounds. Money tucked in Papa's medical bag paid for rent on a scruffy little apartment near the Alexandria docks.

Renata held her breath, waiting for her mother's reaction.

Lea looked around the place with its single bedroom and shabby furniture. Her smile was forced. "It's not Munich, is it? But it is also not a tent. Let us be grateful for what we have."

Relieved, Renata agreed. "We can improve it. Soon we can buy better furniture, now that Papa will be permitted to work."

"I hope so," he answered. "Thanks to you, Renata, we have a home now."

That night, Lea lit one of Alicia's candles for their prayers. Shabbat was a makeshift affair with the wrong candles and the wrong food, but at least the prayers were the same. Something about the ancient songs and words soothed her. The beds were lumpy and damp, but they were not kept awake by old Mr. Gussman's snoring, or the sounds of sex from the next tent. Renata slept deeply and contentedly.

A week later, Renata came through the door in time to see her mother, hands on hips, ready to spew lava.

"What's wrong?" she asked, looking cautiously from her mother to her father, while she set her sketchbook on the table. Karl was sitting at the table, his head in his hands.

Lea gripped Renata's shoulders. "Papa is not allowed to work as a doctor. I don't know what we are going to do."

Renata removed her mother's hands. "What? Papa, is this true?"

Karl's head hung, his eyes avoided hers. He spoke barely above a whisper. "The Egyptian government refuses to give me a license."

"Do they know you taught in the medical school in Munich?"

"Yes, they know. It did not move them. Once again, I am punished for being Jewish." Karl sighed and spread his hands. "I can practice medicine if we go back to Tolumbat, but there I am paid a pittance, and we would be living in a tent again."

"I absolutely refuse to go back there," declared Lea, hands on her hips. "I'm glad to be out, but I want a better home than this."

Renata put an arm around her father. "Mama, this is ridiculous! How can Papa provide you with the impossible?"

"You're our only hope, Renata. I will not live in poverty. Papa cannot help."

Renata saw her father wince at her mother's thoughtless comment. He must feel terrible. Someday, she expected to find a husband, but she was not in a rush, even though she guessed her mother expected her to marry as soon as possible. Thoughts of Hans tormented her, but she pushed them away. Her only other option was to become a successful painter again, and quickly. She wondered about the market for fine art here, if there was one.

Karl pulled out the chair next to him, scraping it on the floor. "Sit down, Lea. You're making me nervous."

Lea sat with a thump.

Renata was unable to keep resentment out of her voice. "I'm only nineteen, Mama. Most girls my age, are not planning how to support their parents."

Karl's cheeks turned scarlet.

Renata touched his arm. "I'm so sorry, Papa. The Egyptian government is stupid not to use you." She curled her lips in disgust. "But I'm making as much money as possible at the market, and I don't know how to make more."

Karl shifted in his chair. "We can manage here, if you find some other work, but finding a better apartment, I don't see how."

Lea, frowning, tapped her fingers on her folded arms. "My job is looking after the home, and that's plenty for me. Renata, you need a husband. You're our ticket out of this Arabian nightmare."

"That's what I was afraid you would say, Mama." Renata walked to the window. She didn't know whether to be angry or sad.

"You are thinking about Hans again, aren't you?" Lea was getting worked up. "Forget him! Find a British officer! I'm sure they have Jews in the British Navy! Then you'll have his pay, and a British passport, and a better apartment, and so will we."

Renata whirled on her mother, hands clenched into fists.

"How dare you! Do you know what Hans and I did in Munich?"

Her mother blanched.

Renata continued. "No, not what you are thinking. We sketched the beatings and vandalism, and he smuggled them to journalists in Switzerland. He is on our side, and he loves me!"

Her parents gasped.

When Lea spoke again, she dialed the volume down.

"No matter how good a man he was, he is gone, Renata. The chances of finding him again are nonexistent, and in any case, he was a gentile. You must accept it."

Renata backed off, nettled, although she was coming to the same conclusion.

"Even if I met a man to marry tomorrow, we would still be here for a few months. It's not fair!"

Karl tried to refocus the women on the main problem. "Life is not fair, Renata. You know this. If you don't wish to marry, we will not force you, but we need more money from somewhere."

"Mama, why don't *you* get a job?" asked Renata pointedly. "You could clean houses, you could look after children."

"I will not clean anyone else's house!" Lea's face turned crimson. "How dare you suggest it! We paid others to do those jobs in Munich. I will not become a servant!"

Unsurprised at her mother's reaction, Renata addressed her father, her voice even.

"Papa, perhaps you could do medical work under the table."

"That's true, but if I get caught, I could go to prison."

"I took chances getting out of Tolumbat to earn money for exit passes. Is it really any different?"

Karl bowed his head.

Renata sat down, head in her hands, eyes closed. Her sympathy for her father was tempered by her resentment at his defeatist attitude. *I can't do this! I'm tired and I'm only nineteen and I don't want to be the family breadwinner.*

An uncomfortable silence shrouded the trio for ten eternal minutes. Renata sighed. There was only one option that she could live with. She looked at her father.

"Paintings will fetch more money than sketches. I know I

can do well. Maybe well enough to sell to the galleries here."

"But you'll need canvases, paint, a studio. All that costs money."

Renata nodded and looked out the window, biting her lip.

Lea paced the room, a scowl on her face.

Karl cleared his throat. "I will not sell the sapphire-and-diamond set unless we are destitute. But I can pawn them, and lend you money for your supplies and studio, provided you pay me back with your earnings."

"You have that much faith in me?"

He nodded. "I'm just going on the success you've already had."

"Papa, I'll find a studio space somehow. I won't let you down." She hugged her father, hoping his trust was not misplaced.

Next Shabbat, Renata had time to think after the mid-afternoon meal of cholent Mama had made the day before. The paintbrushes from Munich were unusable, thanks to their dunking in the Adriatic Sea. Everything needed for a studio—paints, thinner, brushes, canvases, easel, smock, not to mention the studio itself— would equal a month's rent in the shoddy apartment. Sighing, she wondered if her father meant what he said. Monday, they would go shopping, and she would find out. She also needed to learn what type of art sold in Alexandria.

Mid-afternoon knocking interrupted the quiet, if not entirely peaceful, day.

Renata opened the door and broke into a massive smile.

"Sofia! Rachel! Alicia! How marvelous to see you!"

The four young women embraced in a circle.

"It's Shabbat, so what are you doing here? But come in, come in!"

"Rachel and Alicia are spending Shabbat with my family. We pressed my father and he let us walk to see you," Sofia explained.

They all greeted Dr. and Mrs. Lowenthal, who hugged them each in turn.

"Papa, may we walk to the Corniche?"

She was desperate to tell her friends her latest predicament.

Karl frowned, then shrugged. "All right, but be back before sundown. Then if you wish to go out after Havdalah, you may."

Renata kissed his cheek and ran outside with her friends.

Although the normally pristine beach was blemished with barbed wire, mine warning signs, and several large manned guns behind sandbagged enclosures, the young women enjoyed wiggling their toes in the sand closest to the seawall.

Renata closed her eyes and leaned back, enjoying the beneficent sun on her face. Alicia offered everyone small cups of wine from a flask in her bag.

Sofia took a sip and sighed with pleasure. "Damn, that's good! Now Renata, it's ages since I saw you. What are you up to since you moved out of Tolumbat?"

Renata's sigh was not a happy one. She recounted the story, the big argument with her mother, and her father's offer to fund a studio and supplies. "I know I can paint, and I'm pretty sure I can make good money, but it's bloody awful to be the sole support of my own parents."

She looked at her friends. "Am I being selfish? Mama says so."

Sofia and Alicia began shaking their heads, but Rachel interrupted them. "My parents are gone. If supporting them would bring them back to life, I'd do it in a heartbeat. What other choice do you have?"

"She could get married. Then her husband would have to support them." Sofia grinned and held out her cup for a refill. "What do you think, Alicia?"

"I think Mrs. Lowenthal has no idea what she's asking of her own daughter, and it's a bloody shame Dr. Lowenthal isn't allowed to practice. You could always run away, Renata. Or start drinking."

Everyone laughed, but Renata caught the undertone in Alicia's comment. "Running away sounds more practical than drinking," she replied thoughtfully.

"Yes, but drinking is easier. More?" Alicia refilled everyone's cup with the last of the wine.

"I know how we can do both at the same time," said Sofia. "There's a cabaret in town. Drinks, dancing, sailors and soldiers, and a tarty singer. Let's go, tonight!"

"I'm in!" Alicia jumped up and began a mock waltz in the sand.

Rachel backed off, saying she had sewing to do, but Renata grasped the opportunity for a bit of escape. She invited Alicia and Sofia to her home for Havdalah, the ritual that officially ended Shabbat.

A tram ride dropped them in front of a busy café completely blacked-out like all the other buildings except the King's palace, emblazoned with lights, on the hill.

Renata pointed it out. "Does he think because he's King, that he's immune to bombs?"

Alicia shook her head. "Who knows? He must be some kind of idiot, but don't tell the locals I said that."

Renata grinned. She noticed with pleasure, dozens of young, well-dressed European men lined at the door, mostly in uniform.

A host in a white tuxedo greeted them.

"Good evening, ladies. Dinner? Or are you here for the cabaret?"

"Cabaret, please, and drinks," said Sofia.

They followed him into a room so dim that Renata was afraid she would trip on something. The host seated them at a round table a row from a stage swathed in maroon velvet curtains. Musicians in the orchestra pit tuned their instruments, running up and down scales. The murmur of speech was punctuated by laughter, the clink of glasses, and loud greetings as the tables filled.

Renata was excited and a little nervous. Her first evening at a cabaret. She hoped her inexperience would not embarrass her somehow.

"Do you know anyone here, Sofia?" Renata had to lean over the table to make herself heard above the chatter.

Sofia looked around the room and pointed. "There's one, over there. Monsieur Pécard runs an art gallery, and with him is Stefan Muratore, a local artist. My father did some work at Pécard's gallery."

"Really! I'd love to meet them." Renata scrutinized the

angular man with a razor-sharp mustache, impeccable white suit, and cigarette in a long holder.

"Sure! I'll introduce you later."

The waiter arrived to take their orders. Sofia ordered a gin and tonic, Alicia requested red wine, so Renata opted for red wine, too.

It was fun, looking around at the gathering audience and trying to imagine how she would paint each person. A table of young sailors, already flushed and noisy, across the floor, would require a lot of black and white, with darker neutrals in the background. A stunning young woman in a turquoise gown, and a headpiece of rhinestones (or were they diamonds?) and ostrich feathers, would require immensely detailed work to recreate the glitter of her outfit. A few couples holding hands, with eyes for each other only, begged for the reds and pinks of romance.

At the appointed time, with a burst of fanfare, a man in a pinstriped suit and a jaunty fedora stepped out from behind the curtain.

"Ladies and gentlemen! I hope you're gentlemen, anyway." The audience laughed. "Tonight, we have the great pleasure of presenting to you the one, the only, Madame LaChance!"

Loud applause, wolf whistles, and cheers erupted. The curtains parted to reveal a scantily clad blonde, one net stockinged leg perched on a stool, gold sequins everywhere. Two massive breasts were barely contained by her costume. Renata gasped, then cheered and clapped with everyone else. She wished she had her sketchbook.

Madame LaChance slithered to the microphone and cooed into it, "*Mesdames et Messieurs,* welcome. Tonight, we forget about nasty men with mustaches."

Laughter.

"We forget about our sorrows and worries, and instead, we will think about..." she curled herself around the microphone and whispered, "love."

The audience sighed.

The orchestra plunged into "Begin the Beguine." Madame LaChance's voice was husky, seductive, hypnotic. The crowd quieted, men put their arms around their dates' shoulders. Renata noticed couples kissing and felt a twinge of jealousy, wondering where Hans was and if he was thinking of her. She sipped more of her wine.

When the song ended, the theater erupted in cheers and applause. Someone threw a bouquet of flowers onstage. Madame bowed gracefully and launched into "Alexander's Ragtime Band," managing to make it sound sexy as well as energetic. When she invited the crowd to join her on the chorus, Renata and her friends stood with everyone else and clapped along to the melody. Couples on the dance floor twisted and gyrated in ways Renata had never seen before. Men removed their jackets and ladies unfolded fans.

She felt dizzy. Everything seemed far away, and she could not talk properly.

"Alicia, I feel funny. Am I drunk?"

"A little bit. Want to get really drunk? I'll show you how." Alicia signaled the waiter and two drinks arrived in moments.

"Not really," said Renata, pushing the drink away.

"Aw, come on, can't you keep up with me?" Alicia gulped a third drink and grinned lopsidedly at Renata, who stared at this Alicia she had never seen.

"Alicia, how can you like this feeling?"

"It blots out the others I don't want."

Of course. Alicia had lost her family. Who wouldn't want to drown out those feelings? Renata felt a rush of sympathy, but worried about her friend. After Madame LaChance's next song, there was a break. Renata turned to Sofia.

"Can you introduce me to the gallery owner?"

They picked their way through the tables to the two men, whose heads were bent in serious conversation. As soon as they noticed the ladies, they jumped to their feet, bowed, and smiled.

"*Quelle honneur, Mesdemoiselles!* Do we have the pleasure of knowing you?"

"*Non, M'sieur Pécard,*" replied Renata, switching to French. "I'm a friend of Sofia Christopoulos."

Sofia came forward and offered her hand. The men bowed over it.

"Ah, yes, *mademoiselle,* your father created some lovely display spaces in our gallery."

Sofia nodded, then touched Renata's shoulder. "This is my friend Renata Lowenthal. I told her about your art gallery."

He nodded, fingering his pencil mustache. "A pleasure, indeed. You are fond of art, *m'selle? Mon ami* here, Stefan Muratore, is one of our local artists."

"What kind of art do you do?" Renata inquired.

"Oils. Landscapes mostly. There's no lack of subject matter in this fascinating country."

"I am just beginning to discover that, having spent most of my time in Egypt in Tolumbat."

The men's faces showed instant sympathy.

Renata continued, "I and my parents left Germany for reasons you can guess, since we are Jewish. *M'sieur* Pécard, I am an artist, looking to restart my career. Any advice you might have?"

Pécard and Muratore shared skeptical glances.

"I would be delighted, but I warn you, *mademoiselle*, my gallery accepts only the most talented artists."

"I understand." She offered her hand, determined to overcome his resistance. "May I call at your gallery on Monday afternoon?"

"*Certainement, m'selle.*" Pécard bowed good-bye while the women returned to their table.

"Thanks, Sofia. He's a dear."

"I knew you would like him."

As they maneuvered between the tables, two Navy officers sitting at one caught Renata's eye. They rose to their feet.

"May we buy you lovely ladies a drink?" said the first, in an unusual accent that Renata decided was American. He was not tall, but ruggedly handsome with nearly black hair and hazel eyes. The tall, burly man at his right had flaming red hair and a mischievous grin.

"We would accept," answered Sofia, "but we have a friend in a bit of trouble over there." She gestured toward Alicia.

The men nodded. "Perhaps later," said the dark-haired one.

Renata looked across the room.

Alicia was on the dance floor with three sailors. Her hair was askew, her dress hung off one shoulder, and she flopped around like a rag doll, shrieking with laughter.

Renata was horrified. "Should we try to get her home?"

Sofia murmured a negative. "Best to just tell her we're

leaving, unless you want to hear more of the performance. She always finds her way somehow."

Renata was dubious. "I'd stay longer if I didn't have to see this."

She approached the dance floor and shook Alicia gently by the shoulders. "Alicia! Alicia, honey, are you there?"

Alicia took a few seconds to focus. "Oh...Renata..."

"Sofia and I are leaving. Why don't you come with us?"

One of the men dancing with Alicia interrupted. "We'll take care of her, babe, don't you worry."

Renata had never been called "babe" before. She scowled. "She's my friend, and I'm not your babe."

She took Alicia's arm and tried to lead her to her seat. "Come on, honey. You're going to have a terrible headache tomorrow if you keep this up."

Alicia shook off Renata's hand and pulled away, pouting like a child. "No, I wanna stay here. You go home. I'll come later."

"But how are you going to get home?"

She leered at the sailors, who stood on either side of her. "They'll get me home, wontcha, boys?"

"'Course we will," said one.

"You heard her," said the other. "Now leave us alone."

One sailor sidled up to Renata and put an arm around her, pulling her close. "C'mon, sweetheart, loosen up! I can show you a good time. A really good time!" He tried to kiss her, running his hands over as much of her body as he could.

The two officers who had offered Renata and Sofia drinks, materialized at Renata's elbow and pried the drunk off her.

"All right, now, lads, enough of this. The lady isn't interested."

"Don't get your knickers in a knot, sir. We were just leaving."

The sailor, realizing he was talking to an officer, released Renata, straightened his uniform briefly, and turned his attention back to Alicia, who was sitting on another sailor's lap, his hat on her head.

The good-looking officer at her elbow spoke. "Are you all right, miss?"

He was a junior officer, judging from his uniform.

"Yes, thanks. I've never been to a place like this. The singing was fun, but my friend…" She trailed off, unaccountably close to tears.

"I'm Ray Stern. May I walk you and your friend outside?"

"Yes, I'd appreciate it." She turned to Sofia. "This is my friend, Sofia. We were leaving anyway."

Ray's buddy introduced himself as Hamish. He bowed to Sofia and offered her his arm.

As the four walked to the door, Renata shouted back to the drunken sailors, "If you hurt her, I will tell the Military Police!"

Their eyes widened in mock terror. "Ooo, hear that, she's dangerous!" They guffawed and whooped, then returned to dancing, each with a bottle of beer in hand.

"It's all right. Let's go outside for some fresh air." Ray put an arm around Renata's waist, and she couldn't help noticing the protective gesture.

Outdoors, she took a few deep breaths, leaning against the building.

"Sofia, I thought I knew Alicia."

Sofia nodded. "It's rather shocking what she's gotten into since she moved out. My parents wouldn't allow her in the house if they knew."

"Mine either. But I feel sorry for her with no family. It's hard to judge. I probably can't trust that Pécard either."

"Oh no, you're wrong, Pécard is quite different."

Hamish touched Sofia's elbow. "Now that we're oot of the bacchanalia in there, can we offer you lovely ladies a quiet drink and desert elsewhere?"

Renata smothered a grin at his thick Scottish accent.

She and Sofia exchanged glances and shrugged. Sofia answered for them. "That's very nice of you. We accept."

Renata slipped her hand through Ray's arm and the four walked a few blocks to a quiet café where they enjoyed a liqueur and a slice of scrumptious spice cake.

Ray offered cigarettes to the others. Sofia and Hamish accepted, but Renata hesitated.

He smiled. "Go on. Everyone smokes nowadays. It's considered very chic, and it's good for your chest, I hear."

"All right." She accepted the cigarette gingerly, but the first lungful choked her. She coughed, her face red.

The others laughed.

"You'll be able to inhale when you get used to it," said Ray.

The conversation was light. They exchanged names, and casually discussed the possibility of getting together again.

Sofia glanced at her watch. "It's getting late and my tram will be here in a minute." She and Renata hugged briefly, then Sofia ran across the street and disappeared onto the lumbering vehicle.

"Would you like me to see you home, Renata?" Ray pulled her chair out, while Hamish settled the bill.

"That's kind of you, but I'll be all right. Perhaps just walk me to my tram stop." She had no idea how he would behave if she was alone with him, and didn't have any intention of finding out.

After Ray and Hamish had left, a voice behind her said, "*M'selle*, may I see you home?"

It was Pécard.

"*M'sieur*, how do I know you are no better than the fellows inside?"

"I assure you, you are perfectly safe. My interest is not in women."

Renata stared at him, open-mouthed. She had heard of men who loved other men, but had never met one. Then she realized. Pécard and Muratore.

"I...uh...excuse me, I don't know what to say."

"Nothing is necessary." He offered her his arm. "Come, show me where you live."

They climbed onto the tram.

"May I call you Renata?"

"You may. And what is your first name?"

"Louis."

"Louis, then." She smiled, tentatively. "Louis, I have no portfolio to show you, because we lost everything when we escaped from Germany, but perhaps knowing that I had two art shows, and a Berlin gallery sold my paintings, tells you that I am not a beginner."

Louis raised his eyebrows. "Indeed, it does. You surprise me, Renata. How old are you?"

"Nineteen."

"So accomplished, yet so young! Your family must be artistic, *non?*"

"*Oui*, my mother's parents and grandparents were all artists." Her voice caught. "We left all our paintings behind."

Louis murmured sympathetically. "What is your medium?" he asked as the tram clanked along.

"Oils and ink. I do portraits and landscapes. I will paint again, when I have studio space and supplies. Do you know where I might find a studio?"

"As a matter of fact, I do. There's an old warehouse called 'L'Atelier des Beaux Arts.' The rent is low, and the companionship is incomparable."

Renata patted his hand and smiled. "Here's my stop. Louis, I'm glad I found you. We'll talk Monday. Will Stefan be annoyed?"

"Ah, clever girl, we cannot hide from you." He chuckled. "Don't worry. He knows you are no threat."

Chapter Ten

New Year's Eve, 1940

The Monday meeting with Pécard was short. He showed Renata his gallery, which housed a collection of high-priced oils, sculptures, and a few watercolors.

She tipped her head at one riotous contemporary work in vivid oranges and yellows.

"You have a market for this style? It's similar to mine."

"Yes, indeed. It's extremely popular. This artist's works are gone within a week, and we have an offer on this one."

"How interesting. You mentioned you would give me directions to the studio warehouse."

"*Oui, absolument. 'L'Atelier des Beaux Arts.'*" He took a scrap of paper, wrote the address and a crude map on it.

Thanking him, she left to meet her father at a nearby café. After coffee, they purchased art supplies and then, at the warehouse, found a tiny studio space to rent.

Later, she walked along the Corniche and sketched ideas, smiling to herself. Her sketches would become paintings soon.

She began selling ink-drawn postcards of local sights: Casino San Stefano, Pompey's Pillar, and the Mahmoudieh canal, despite its revolting smell. The markets, Arabs with camels, the trams. Fast and easy, they brought in enough that she repaid her father's loan more quickly than she'd expected.

It was a momentous day when she prepped a canvas and brushed color onto it. Had it been nearly two years already? Every cell in her body tingled with excitement. Her art was bold, flooded with color, emotional. The dark escape from Berlin, the people who helped along the way, and of course, Tolumbat.

Movie Tone News clips generated ideas for her paintings. The war's tentacles curled slowly around the world, strangling more of Europe and Africa each day. Italians fought their way through Abyssinia, guns and death crawling over the sand, trailing petrol cans, blown tires, and shell casings. Allied shipping casualties were frighteningly high. Commanders kept the sea churning and desert dust blowing as they honed their men to a pitch of battle-readiness, with the Italians a short distance away in Libya.

Renata captured on canvas the horror of battle, the parched beauty of the desert, and the forced cheer of the population.

Entranced by her paintings, Louis Pécard hung them in his gallery. And they sold.

The Royal Navy Social Coordinator Lieutenant Brock Thompson— short, gap-toothed, and the most sought-after man in the city— cruised through parties and shows, dropping invitations, smiling in his wilted uniform with stains at the armpits. He arrived at the *Gallérie Française* in early December, looking for Renata.

"*Mais oui, Monsieur*, come and see the Lowenthals," Pécard gushed, ushering Thompson toward Renata's paintings. "They are marvelous, the best of the year."

At the back of the Gallérie, Renata was speaking with an elderly French couple who had decided to purchase one of her paintings. Seeing the two men approach, she directed the couple to Pécard, extended her hand to the officer, and put on her business smile.

"Brock Thompson, His Majesty's Navy," he said.

"Renata Lowenthal." She replied in English. "Do you like art?"

Thompson put a finger in his collar and tried to loosen it, grimacing in discomfort.

"Sorry, Miss, this climate is not what I'm used to. England is rainy, but it never stays this warm in winter. I like paintings, but my artistic education was sadly neglected. My parents insisted I study law." He tucked his cap under one arm.

She gestured toward the display area. They walked side by side, up and down the two rows of paintings. She noticed him perspiring, and suggested they sit in the anteroom, where she offered him a glass of water.

"Thanks, Miss." He shook his head. "Don't know how you do them."

He looked pasted into his uniform. Renata wondered why the Navy made them wear such awful clothes.

Thompson coughed. "The base is holding a dance for New Year's Eve in three weeks' time for the officers, and they've got me in charge of finding suitable young ladies to attend. We'd consider it an honor if you'd grace us with your presence. Are you by chance available?"

A tingling in her spine. A Navy ball? "I'd be honored to accept. Formal dress?"

"Yes, Miss. If you'll be so kind as to give me your address, I'll have a car sent around for you at eight o'clock in the evening." He stood, turned to leave, then looked back.

"Would your parents like to go, by any chance? It's just, well, the older officers want someone more their age to talk to."

"I think they'd love it."

"Here's my card, if you would telephone the base and let my secretary know for certain. Thank you, Miss Lowenthal." He replaced his cap, touched the rim, and departed.

She smiled to herself, thinking ahead to the ball. Time to find a smashing dress. Thanks to her rocketing sales, she and her parents would be into their new, larger apartment by then.

As Renata watched from the window, her pulse fluttering, a long black automobile glided to a stop outside their apartment.

"Mama, Papa, the car is here!" She collected her bead-encrusted evening bag and headed to the door. She wore a gown borrowed from a friend of Sofia's, a sheer golden silk with cap sleeves, piped with the thinnest imaginable black velvet. The gold lamé gathered from the waist and tied around her neck, halter-style, with a wide black velvet ribbon. A camisole of gold silk lining, cleverly inserted by Rachel, hid the scars on her back. She felt like a film star for an evening. She imagined stardust swirling around her as she twirled the gold skirt sprinkled with black flocking in the shape of bows. Borrowed gold drop earrings and black elbow-length gloves completed her ensemble.

Her jaw dropped at her father's entrance. She had not seen him formally dressed since she was a small child. Now he was resplendent in a tuxedo with tails, waistcoat, even a top hat he found at the black market.

Lea, beaming, wore a borrowed French evening dress in red silk velvet. The square neckline and ruching suited her mature figure, as did the diamond-and-sapphire necklace, recently redeemed from the pawnshop.

The chauffeur held the door open and they slid along the thick leather seats, three abreast.

"I wish I had my furs," said Lea wistfully.

Renata frowned and looked out the window.

"Never mind, dear, you look ravishing." Karl patted his wife's arm with a white-gloved hand.

Renata slipped into the fairy-tale promise of the evening. Perhaps a prince would be present, perhaps a coach with horses. The image of Hans wearing princely attire made her smile. Silly dreams, girlish dreams, but still, her heart beat a little faster and her tummy felt the beating of a thousand butterfly wings.

Soon they approached the Cecil Hotel, commandeered by the Navy as its base for the duration of the war. Renata saw neither horses nor princes, but Alexandrian society was there, eager to mingle with the wealthy, the famous, the infamous. Torches illuminated the palm-tree-lined path to the ballroom. Round tables with linen tablecloths, china, and crystal replaced the utilitarian benches used during the week, and swaths of bunting and large Union Jacks covered the walls, along with requisite photographs of King George VI and Queen Elizabeth. Clusters of gleaming candles on each table brought life to Renata's dreams of magic. On stage, the orchestra played hits by Count Basie, Glenn Miller, and Guy Lombardo.

The receiving line included the head of the British Mediterranean Fleet, Admiral Sir Andrew Cunningham, RN; his wife, Lady Cecily Cunningham; Rear Admiral and Chief of Staff A. Willis; and Flag Captain V.A. Crutchley.

"Doctor and Mrs. Karl Lowenthal, and their daughter, Miss Renata Lowenthal."

"Pleased to meet you."

Another staffer led them to their tables. "Dr. and Mrs. Lowenthal, Sir Andrew has requested you join him at his table. If you'd be so kind as to come with me. Miss Lowenthal, you will be seated at another table."

A waiter hovered at her elbow. "May I offer you something to drink, Miss? A glass of sherry? Tea?"

"Sherry would be lovely, thank you."

He disappeared.

She tried to suppress her jitters.

The room filled with the hubbub of voices and laughter. Women in shimmering gowns chatted with uniformed officers and civilians.

The staffer returned with her sherry. She ventured a sip, made a face. It was revolting, but she sipped again, then glided toward a cluster of young officers and women on the dance floor.

One Army officer, a lieutenant, who was blond with a tanned face and strong features, not handsome but attractive somehow, smiled and extended his hand.

"Good evening, Miss, or is it Ma'am?"

"Miss, thank you. Miss Renata Lowenthal."

"The artist? Phillip Mercer. Such a pleasure to meet you." He bowed over her hand, then gestured to the others.

"This is Miss Renata Lowenthal. She's the one all the artsy types are raving about. Her show is on right now at Pécard's Gallérie."

Renata, pleased and embarrassed at the compliment, gave the group a shy smile. Then she spotted Alicia on the arm of Mickey, their savior that first day at the market.

"Why, Alicia, how nice to see you! And Mickey, a pleasure." She and Alicia embraced briefly, but Renata wondered if Alicia was still drinking as much.

Phillip carried on with the introductions.

Renata couldn't help noticing how young he was.

"Sofia Christopoulos. Her father does a great deal of work for the base." Phillip took Sofia's hand briefly.

Renata laughed and hugged her friend. "Of course, darling! Who invited you here?"

"What, you think I don't deserve an invitation?" She put on an exaggerated pout, her bosom threatening to breach the confines of her snug emerald green gown. Everyone laughed.

"Captain Wilbur Kingsmith." Had to be English but the accent she couldn't place. Muscular, powerful-looking man, angles in all the right places.

"Isabella Angotti." Not an especially Jewish name, but one never knew. A bit haughty, diamonds everywhere, coral dress heavy with sequins.

"Ray Stern." She did a double-take. The man who had rescued her and Sofia at the cabaret! A decidedly Jewish name, as well.

"Nice to see you again, Ray. We met at a cabaret a few months ago, if you recall."

"Yes, indeed." He bowed and pulled Isabella a little closer.

Sofia, sidling close to Renata, confided, "I saw your paintings, doll. I will buy one when I can convince my father to pay for it. You know how he is with money."

They giggled at the thought of Spiros spending money on fine art, and promised to spend time catching up later in the evening. Sofia glided away.

Renata addressed the men. "I'm guessing you are all British, except this chap." She pointed at Ray. "You're American, I bet."

Ray demurred. "Actually, I'm a Canadian who joined the Royal Navy." His voice was deep and gravelly. It was easy to imagine him ordering others.

Someone tapped the microphone and announced that it was time to stand for "God Save the King," and the invocation, so Phillip escorted her to their shared table.

A Navy chaplain intoned the blessing, which was something like "Thank you for the food, God, bless this food, God, protect our troops, God, Amen." The German troops doubtless uttered a similar prayer over their food, their uniform belts proclaiming, "*Gott mitt uns.*" Renata wondered if there was a different god for each army.

The first course arrived, a seafood bisque, which Renata, sure it was not kosher, pretended to taste, then set aside.

Phillip chatted with a woman and her husband on his right.

On her left was her other savior from the cabaret, who re-introduced himself as Hamish McCubbin, his Scottish brogue thick as the bisque. His red hair reminded her of wild highland cattle and was nearly as untamed.

"How do you like Alexandria, Captain McCubbin?"

"Aye, very well, thank ye, but it's no' like Glasgow, where I grew up. I came here wi' the Merchant Marine, joined the Navy side as a shipping logistics coordinator. Think I'll stay with the Navy until Herr Hitler is done for. And you, Miss Lowenthal? Have ye been here long?"

"We escaped from Germany in '38, but this year, we managed to get into the city from Tolumbat."

His eyes widened. "Did ye leave family behind?"

She fought down the curdling in her stomach. "We've had some terrible letters. Jews are reduced to begging and stealing. They can't own businesses, Jewish children aren't allowed to go to school, and the government fined Jews a billion marks for damage the Nazis did themselves during Kristallnacht!" Unaware, she had raised her voice.

Others stared at her.

She stopped talking, and heat spread up her face.

Servers removed the bowls and replaced them with small salads.

Hamish looked at her, his face troubled. "God's love, what can it be like there?" He laid a giant paw on Renata's gloved hand. "I'm terribly sorry. We Jews in Scotland have heard stories, but no-one knows what to believe. I know that isn't saying much, but stories like yours remind me why we're fighting this bloody war."

She gave him a tiny smile, and speared a piece of cucumber. "McCubbin is hardly a Jewish name."

Hamish shrugged. "My mother is Jewish. I confuse everyone."

They laughed.

The menu was very British: roast lamb, mint sauce,

overcooked vegetables. As talk of her in Germany faded into discussion of the merits of the Navy Band, crooning out soft music in the background, Renata relaxed. Dessert was a plum pudding with brandy sauce flambé. Murmurs of appreciation rose from the crowd at the flaming trays.

While coffee and tea were served, the Master of Ceremonies introduced the Admiral, who adjusted the microphone and cleared his throat.

"Vice-Admirals, Officers, ladies and gentlemen, welcome to Fleet HQ as we celebrate the arrival of Nineteen-Forty."

A ripple of polite applause. He sipped water as chatter subsided.

"However, this year there is little to celebrate. A dark storm cloud is engulfing Europe, and indeed, Africa. Germany's power is growing. There has been relatively little engagement with the enemy in the Mediterranean Theatre since war was declared, but I tell you with utmost certainty: this state of affairs is coming to an end. Soon. Tonight, we have feasted, we are dressed for a party, but this will be the last New Year's Eve of celebration until the Nazi menace is wiped from the face of the Earth."

Silence filled the room. Someone coughed.

"Hitler is like a lion crouched behind a bush, hungry again after last week's hunt and gathering his limbs. He is angry about the loss of the *Graf Spee*. His armies will attack us within months, perhaps weeks, and on this continent. His U-boats and warships harry our convoys, determined to break our supply lines and our spirit, readying for an invasion of Britain. Above all else, this must not be allowed to happen. I call every military man here to pledge his life in defense of what we hold dear, and I call on all civilians to stand fast, have courage, and do all you can to support the war effort, so that in the future, you can tell your children and your grandchildren that you did your duty to defeat this evil regime. Now, please stand with me, and let us toast this coming terrible year."

Chairs scraped. Everyone stood, glass in hand.

"To 1940. To freedom, love of country, honor, and right. God Save the Royal Navy, and God Save the King!"

"God save the King," everyone repeated, clinking glasses, sipping the remains of the sherry.

The sobering speech dampened any cheer. Hamish lit Renata's cigarette and his own. They stared soberly at one another.

The master of ceremonies leapt onto the platform. "Well, folks, we know we have a rough time ahead of us, but tonight, let's dance!"

The orchestra leader raised his baton and brought it down with energy, sending the orchestra into loud, cheerful jazz, breaking the gloomy spell.

Hamish invited Renata to dance.

She accepted. "I should warn you, Hamish, I don't know the new dances."

"Och, doon't worry, I'll show ye." And he did. First the jitterbug and then the swing.

After two dances, she was overheated and begged for a rest.

Hamish headed to the next table, cruising the women.

A moment later, Phillip touched her lightly on the shoulder, and took the seat beside her. "I wanted to talk with you over dinner, but it was impossible over the din. What did you think of the Admiral's speech?"

"Not very encouraging, was it? I hope the Nazis don't invade Egypt."

"They may, they may, but we'll be ready for 'em. Right now, I'm more worried about Malta, stuck there off the south of Italy. Going to be a devil of a time to keep that island supplied, especially once Italy dips its toe in the war."

"When will you be leaving, any idea?"

"The Navy has a lot of escort duty right now. We Army rats may be heading to Libya. Mussolini wants the Suez Canal, and we can't have that." He grinned and ran a hand through his blond hair. "Well, enough doom and gloom. How about a dance? Fancy one with me?" He offered his hand.

"Can we pick a slow one?"

"Certainly. Care for a drink first?" He led her to the bar at the back of the hall, and ordered a gin and tonic for each of them.

Ray approached on her other side with Isabella on his arm. He inclined his head in her direction.

"Miss Lowenthal. Mercer. I trust you're enjoying the festivities. Looks like the last we'll have for a long time."

"Can we please stop talking about the Admiral's speech, and the war?" Renata snapped, a frown on her face. "Let's enjoy this one night, and think about the war tomorrow."

The men apologized.

Phillip steered her onto the dance floor for a waltz, slid his arm around her, pulled her close. She liked the feel of him, manly, firm, but a hint of gentleness. He reminded her of a puppy, with big floppy ears. And, a little, of Hans.

He whispered in her ear, "All the other gents here are jealous of me, because I have the most beautiful woman in the room in my arms right now."

She laughed. "You silly thing! It's the dress. If you saw me in my everyday clothes, you'd not say that."

He appraised her with mock severity, then pulled her close again. "You're right, that dress is a stunner. But you are the most beautiful woman. No, don't argue," he said, as she protested. "Just enjoy."

She relaxed in his arms, the waltz perfect for showing off the dress with its velvet bow appliques and shimmering gold silk. As the music ended, he bent her over backwards, and kissed her on the lips.

Without thinking she kissed him back, then allowed him to walk her to the bar. Lieutenant Stern had fresh drinks for them.

"Miss Lowenthal, after your drink, it is my turn to dance with you," he drawled in that nasal Canadian accent.

Flushed, fluttery with all the male attention, Renata nodded, and swallowed half her drink.

"Oi, take it easy, girl", said Phillip. "That'll catch up to you right quick if you drink it that fast."

After setting her drink down, she looked at Lieutenant Stern, who leaned his elbows backwards on the bar.

"Ray, how did a Canadian come to be in the British Navy?"

Exhaling the last of his cigarette and stubbing it out in the ashtray, he paused before responding. "I needed to get out of my dusty home town. Three years ago, the Canadian Navy was a sleepy little service, not doing much, so I chose the Royal Navy."

"And have you seen places?" Renata asked.

"Yep. Spain, Portugal, Norway, even Venezuela once."

"How do you like it here?"

"Plenty of nightlife, lots of pretty women, and work so far has been pretty easy." He appraised her. "But you're the prettiest woman I've seen so far."

That cockeyed grin. So many men, she reminded herself, don't get hooked, don't forget Hans. "Don't say that where Isabella can hear you," she reminded him.

His smile faded momentarily.

"Come on, the music is starting." He was a good dancer. A waltz was next. Crushing her to him, he whirled around, humming the tune in her ear.

After the dance was over, she thanked him and went to find her parents.

Two officers and the admiral's wife were chatting with them at their table. Lea did her best to pretend she was not interested in dancing, but Renata could tell it was just an act.

She whispered to her father, "Papa, you must dance with Mama. I know she wants to, but she won't admit it."

Karl led Lea to the dance floor as soon as a waltz started.

Renata held her breath.

Her mother remembered the steps and held herself erect. Her hands touched Karl lightly, his left hand on her waist. They flowed over the floor, beaming.

Renata felt a lump in her throat.

When the dance ended, the crowd applauded and cheered.

"I never knew you could dance so well, Mama! That was marvelous. Do you two have any other secrets you shouldn't be keeping?" She propped a hand on her hips and wagged a finger.

Karl, still out of breath, wrapped his daughter in his arms. "Darling, thank you," he said. He held her at arms' length, hands on her shoulders. "And you, my dear, are you meeting some people your own age?"

"Oh, Papa." She sighed. "Well, yes, three men. Hamish, Phillip, and Ray. They all seem very nice, polite, and they are all good dancers. Hamish and Ray are Jewish, too."

Papa raised his eyebrows. "So, dancing is important in a husband, is it?"

She pursed her lips, glaring at him. "Of course not, but it

doesn't hurt."

Even Lea joined in the laughter.

She wandered back to her cluster of new friends, preoccupied. The close of the evening approached. Phillip asked for another dance, and she accepted. It was another jitterbug. Breathless, they retired to the bar when the dance ended.

Hamish and Sofia, Ray and Isabella were there with Alicia and Mickey.

"The day after tomorrow, we're going for a sail," said Hamish. "Would you ladies care to join us?"

"No thanks," said Alicia. "I don't enjoy boats at all."

"I'm not sure," said Sofia, as she slouched on the bar, sipping her third drink.

"Oh, do come," urged Isabella. "I'd love to! I used to sail in France all the time. Do you have a boat?"

Hamish laughed. "This is the Navy, lassie, we have ships and boats, every kind ye can imagine, rowboats to battleships. Come on, we'll have some fun before the Huns get here."

Ray, Phillip, Renata, Sofia, and Isabella agreed to come. Renata had bad memories of Guido's boat, but she told herself this would be different. Two sailors and a soldier. What could possibly go wrong?

At midnight, the MC asked everyone to join hands for "Auld Lang Syne." The song made no sense to Renata, but she joined in, watching everyone link arms crossed in front, forming a large circle. "Should auld acquaintance be forgot, and never brought to mind… and days of Auld Lang Syne."

Then it was over. Everyone shouted Happy New Year.

Phillip kissed Renata long and hard. When he released her, she smiled, and caressed his cheek lightly.

A few minutes later, her parents were at her elbow. "Are you ready to go home, Renata?"

Their car was waiting. The new year, 1940, had arrived.

Chapter Eleven

The Sail, 1940

Foam splashed over the prow of the little runabout as Phillip expertly brought it about, tacking across a stiff wind. Sofia, Renata, and Isabella squealed as the spray hit them again and again, until they were soaked and laughing. An inch of water sloshed in the bottom of the boat, which bothered no one— all were barefoot— and they tried not to spill their drinks, without much success, as the boat bobbed and smashed through the waves. Hamish occasionally used a child's seaside bucket as a bailer.

"How'd ye like sailin', then?" he asked Renata with a nudge and a wink.

"Better than other boats I've been on." She tossed her hair, stringy from blowing in the salty wind, and grabbed the gunwale when another wave crashed into the bow, threatening to knock her off her feet. She admitted to herself that she was tense, waiting for something to go wrong as it had on *The Da Vinci.* Guido appeared sometimes in her dreams, screaming for help, but he always drowned before she could reach him. She forced herself to focus on Phillip.

"What other boats? What happened?" He looked at her with sudden concern.

"Never mind. I don't want to ruin our afternoon by telling gruesome stories."

Phillip lowered his eyebrows, then nodded and changed the subject, addressing the group: "Would you like a turn at the tiller, ladies?"

Isabella headed aft.

Phillip moved aside with a grin.

She took them to the next tack, came about expertly, then looked at the men, who applauded.

"Renata, you want to try the tiller for a bit?"

She swallowed and forced a smile. She replaced Isabella at the tiller, and under Phillip's tutelage, found that sailing meant using the wind, not battling against it. To her surprise, she enjoyed herself.

"There's our destination, that little promontory." He pointed over her shoulder. "Now see where the wind's coming from and where we're heading. I'll let you know when it's time to tack again."

"This is actually...I mean, I'm not scared, thanks to you." Their eyes met. Ray gave her a thumbs-up. She smiled and nodded.

Two tacks later, Phillip took over and guided them expertly to the tiny dock. Ray moored boat and they clambered out, Sofia carrying the picnic basket.

The sandy beach was perfect: gentle winter sun, warm water, mild breeze.

Isabella and Ray walked hand-in-hand along the shore, sharing a bottle of wine.

Hamish and Sofia could not stop talking and laughing. They wandered behind a sand dune, but Renata could hear Sofia's suggestive giggles.

Phillip persuaded her to try wading, until a large wave drenched them in brine, sand, and seaweed. Phillip started splashing Renata. She splashed him in return, and soon they were laughing so hard, they stumbled into one another's arms, drenched to the skin. Phillip moved a strand of wet hair away from her face, and kissed her. Without thinking, she kissed him back. To feel his body tight against hers, and his lips moving over hers, was delicious, heavenly, and safe. She suddenly realized that as much as she loved Hans, her parents were probably right; she would never see him again. It was time to let herself live a bit.

"Let's go join the others, Phillip."

"Race you!" he yelled, and they sprinted over the sand and collapsed, giggling, on the blanket. He rolled on top of her and tickled her until she screamed for mercy.

"Let me go, you silly!" she laughed, trying to push him off.

"Kiss me, then I'll let you go."

"All right, here you go." She grasped his hair and pulled his face in for a kiss.

The giggling stopped. A hunger for something besides food spread from her groin to her breasts and made her entire body tingle. They kissed again, then looked at each other in wonder, and she blushed, imagining him naked.

"Time to eat." She pushed him away, rolled over, and opened the picnic basket.

Renata and Phillip spread out sandwiches, pickles, and oranges. Avoiding his gaze was like avoiding the sun in the middle of the Sahara. Her nerves were twitching.

She raised her voice. "Who's hungry? Hey, Ray and Isabella, food's ready!"

The two returned and joined them.

Sofia and Hamish emerged from behind their rock, rearranging clothing and smoothing their hair.

Phillip draped his jacket around Renata's shoulders and sat so close she could feel his breathing, as rough as her own.

Everyone piled a plate high with the tasty, if sand-speckled, sandwiches.

"Who's thirsty?" Hamish handed out the beer with a grin.

Over food, lighthearted talk gradually turned serious. Where would Hitler attack next? Why didn't the Americans join? Where would their ships be deployed next? No one had answers, only worries and guesses.

As the shadows lengthened, Ray and Hamish collected driftwood and started a campfire. Isabella began a wistful song about friendship. The others slowly joined in, couples together, arms around shoulders and fingers interlaced. The evening star shone brightly when the song ended, and no one wanted to break the spell.

A log broke, sending a flurry of sparks into the indigo sky. It was Renata's cue to unwrap herself from Phillip. She was uncomfortably aroused, and wanted a little space to cool down.

"I brought my sketchbook. If you're interested, I can sketch you."

"That would be great! Could you do one of me and

Hamish?" Sofia asked.

"Sure, Sofia. Anyone else?"

"Don't do me," said Ray, "but if you sketch Isabella, I'll buy it from you."

When the sketches were finished, the men were astounded.

"But you did it so quickly! And it looks just like them." Phillip's astonishment made Renata laugh.

"You're marvelous, Renata! Here, Hamish, let's keep this, shall we?" Sofia and Hamish poured over the sketch in wonder.

"Bloody good. Here's a fiver for Isabella." Ray handed Renata money, and presented the sketch to his lady friend.

Embers glowed in the dying fire when the drone of aircraft intruded. Suddenly alert, they scanned the skies, and Ray spotted the "friendlies" first. But enemy aircraft could be around next, and it was time to go.

They packed up hurriedly and sailed with a following wind back to port.

Phillip asked Renata if he could take her dancing the next weekend. She said yes, then wrote about him in another pretend letter to Hans, hoping he had met some other young women and that he didn't mind her meeting other young men.

Phillip knocked at the door a week later, holding a bouquet of flowers. Removing his hat, he shook Lea's hand. "Good day, Mrs. Lowenthal, nice to see you again."

"Renata!" called Lea, with unnecessary loudness, "Phillip is here for you."

Renata coaxed one reluctant curl into place, and walked into the living room. She wore a polka dot dress with a wide red belt, red gloves, and a small black hat with an attempt at a veil.

Phillip's eyebrows shot up. "Aren't you a treat? I brought you some flowers."

"How sweet. They're lovely." She immersed her nose in the bouquet of oleander, sage, and roses.

"Does your mother have a vase?"

Mama produced a tall empty jar which worked admirably,

and set the bouquet in the center of the table.

The flowers sorted, Phillip and Renata left, hand in hand, for her favorite café on the Corniche, where they ordered baklava and coffee. Reliving the sail and picnic, they laughed about the amount of sand they were still shaking out of their clothing. Renata said that Sofia and Hamish were quite besotted with each other. Phillip mentioned that the sketch of the two of them had garnered high praise in the barracks that night. He casually draped his hand over hers, and she did not pull away.

Although she was enjoying herself, Renata was confused about Phillip. Mentally, she ticked off the list: good dancer, good soldier, polite, brought flowers, seemed nice. But despite the security a husband would bring, she wasn't sure she knew him well enough to consider him her boyfriend. And her parents had made clear their thoughts on her dating a gentile.

Her mind had wandered. Phillip was speaking.

He paused and cleared his throat. "There's something else I need to tell you, Renata. Our battalion's been ordered to Somaliland in two days."

Her mind cleared instantly. "So soon?"

"'Fraid so. But we'll be back in a month or two, at least that's what we've been told. I'd love to take you out for a bang-up dinner then."

"I'll hold you to that." But his news had settled as a hard, hot lump of fear somewhere below her breastbone. She was pondering whether she could love him, and here he was going to battle. She gripped his hand and squeezed.

"I know it's short notice, but we all knew this was coming. My only worry is leaving you behind. I want to know you'll be here when I come back."

A tiny frown creased her forehead. "Of course, I'll be here."

"No, I mean, I want more than just a girlfriend." He cleared his throat. "What I'm trying to say, Renata, is will you marry me?"

She gasped, at a loss for words. She left her hand in his, not wanting to hurt his feelings. Time stopped for a few heartbeats.

"My goodness, Phillip, you do know how to surprise a girl, don't you?" She managed a weak smile, playing for time to sort out her thoughts. "We barely know each other."

"That's true, but many of the others are getting married so they won't…" he stopped abruptly.

"…be alone? Die without making love?" she finished quietly, and squeezed his hand again in sympathy.

His crestfallen, red face told her she had hit the mark. Slowly, she withdrew her hand.

"Phillip, you are a sweet boy, and I'm fond of you, but I can't marry you. Perhaps in time. But I will be here waiting for you. I promise you a marvelous kiss. In fact, you can have one tonight, if you like."

"I'm sorry I embarrassed you." He looked away, his cheeks flushed, shoulders slumped. "Thanks for understanding."

He stood to pull out her chair, and they walked back, holding hands. Outside the apartment, she gave him a long, slow kiss that stirred urgent feelings she still didn't want to deal with. But he was a gentleman, and did not press her for more.

"Thanks, Renata. You're a great girl. I'll see you when we get home."

"Come back safely, Phillip, and the others, too. When you see the Italians, give them hell from me."

For a moment, she saw fear in his eyes, but he shuttered the look, and departed with a mock salute.

Two days later, his platoon headed into Somaliland.

Chapter Twelve

Battles, 1940

Renata and Sofia, their friendship rekindled since the ball, went regularly to the cinema. Film clips brought to life events of the war, something which had not been possible in the last war. England introduced rationing, and everyone, even infants, had gas masks. Renata gagged at the thought of the claustrophobic devices. How the photographers got footage of battleships engaging U-boats and torpedo bombers, she did not want to think.

Horrified, they watched the swastika surging through Belgium, Luxembourg, Holland, Norway, and Denmark, and the gut-churning evacuation of what remained of the British and French armies from Dunkirk on May twenty-sixth.

At least there was one scrap of good news. Winston Churchill was the new Prime Minister of England.

At home that evening, Renata looked up from the newspaper at her father.

"Why are they so happy about Mr. Churchill, Papa?"

Papa removed his glasses and peered over the paper. "He was the head of their Navy in the last war. He looks like a bulldog and apparently is just as stubborn, so the British think he will lead them to victory."

"I hope to high heaven they are right. Britain is surrounded, isn't it?"

"Yes. If only the Americans would join in." Papa turned to his paper again.

"Something truly dreadful will have to happen to get them

in," murmured Renata. She picked up the section her father had finished.

Over the next few weeks, while France was being pounded into submission, Italy declared war on June tenth and attacked Malta the next day. Suddenly, on June thirteenth, the war was in their own backyard, when three British submarines were torpedoed not far from their base in Alexandria harbor.

Renata or her father ran out each morning to get the early edition newspaper, and the family huddled around the radio for BBC news each night. It was not good.

Britain had her back to the wall. France breathed her last on June twenty-fifth. Phillip was still in the desert, situation unknown.

Hamish, Ray, and senior officers were locked in secret negotiations with the French, according to Sofia.

Needing some respite, Renata headed to her art studio the next morning. She put on her smock, selected a blank canvas, and started sketching, allowing the terrible images of war to guide her hand. Hours slipped away. When she stepped back, her progress pleased her, and the wretched tightness in her chest had gone away. On impulse, she headed toward Sofia's with the afternoon sun warming her face.

The two women embraced.

"I'm so glad to see you, Renata. It's just awful waiting and wondering."

"We know our boys are in for more fighting. It's all so surreal. Sofia…they won't all survive, will they?"

Sofia twisted her mouth and shook her head slowly. "We have to hope they will. We need something sweet, don't you agree? I picked up a few pastries from Pâttiserie Délices this morning."

Unsmiling, Renata nodded. "The world seems so sour right now."

She sat at Sofia's tiny kitchen table while her friend produced a plate of delectable goodies and a glass of wine each."

The slightly sweet wine was exactly what Renata needed. She selected a *petit-four* and bit into the delicate, crusty icing. "Mmm, Sofia, this is delicious. Thank you."

Sofia bit into an éclair and picked up the thread of conversation.

"The war is about to get real for me. I'm volunteering as a nurse."

"You are?" Renata nearly dropped her wine glass. "Have you any training?"

"No, but you can get training for basic nursing. And I'd feel better knowing I was doing something, not just sitting here wondering whether or not our lads are blown to bits!"

"Don't talk like that." Renata sipped her wine. "You're brave, I must say. Gives me the heebie-jeebies just thinking about it."

"Training starts next week."

"Well, you amaze me, girl. You're going to be out there in the thick of it, helping our men survive. What do your parents think?"

"My mother is wringing her hands, sure I'll be killed. My father is nervous, but he's glad someone in our family will be in the fight."

"What does Hamish think?" Renata stole a sideways glance at Sofia, whose cheeks flared suddenly.

"I think he's proud of me." She blushed even more. "Stop it, Renata! We're just dating!"

"Of course, you are," Renata replied without conviction.

She wrapped her arm around Sofia's waist and kissed her on the cheek once the pastries and wine disappeared.

"You come back in one piece, now." She tried to control the wobble in her voice. "I won't accept anything less. You hear me?"

"I will. I promise.

On her way home, newsies were shouting something about French ships. Curious, she gave the closest boy a coin and took a paper. "French Ships in Alexandria Demilitarized," said the headline. Skimming the story, she realized this was what Ray and Hamish had been working on. No one wanted the ships of former allies to be allowed out of the harbor where the Germans would take control of them. Admiral Cunningham and his French counterpart, Admiral Godfrey, agreed that the French ships would no longer be military.

"Thank heavens," Renata murmured. She felt pride for the men's involvement in such a key piece of diplomacy.

The telephone rang as she arrived home. It was Isabella.

"Ray and Hamish want to take me and Sofia out for dinner,

darling. Would you like to join us?"

Dinner was a joyous affair, celebrating the diplomatic victory and reduction in risk to the harbor. Once they were enjoying an espresso, Hamish tapped his glass for silence.

"Convoys to Malta start again shortly, and we're going."

There was an awkward silence.

"Right, here's to our Navy lads, then." Sofia raised her tiny cup in a caffeine toast.

"And to Phillip, with the Army," added Renata.

"To our lads," replied Isabella and Renata in unison. Their smiles were forced.

"Please come back safely. We'll never forgive you if you don't." Sofia's eyes were suspiciously moist.

"Not to worry," said Ray. "I'll shoot the first Italian I see."

"You won't see a soul, you eejit." Hamish shoved him on the shoulder. "You'll be in the officers' planning rooms, far from the action."

"Well, I hope they don't let Hamish near the guns," retorted Ray. "He'd likely shoot one of our own, his aim is so bad."

Everyone laughed.

"Enough teasing." Renata's mind was on Phillip, fighting out in the desert, and that lump was back somewhere behind her breastbone. She knew they were trying to cover their fear with humor, but it wasn't helping her. She'd seen the Nazis face-to-face. She drained the espresso, and got to her feet.

"Thanks for the invitation, Isabella. Good night, everyone."

It was August before Hamish and Ray left for Malta with "Operation Hurry," a three-day sprint to relieve the besieged island. They arrived home to news that Italians and British were engaged in heavy fighting in Somaliland.

Renata's worries for Phillip turned to gut-churning fear when on August nineteenth, Somaliland fell to Italy.

The next day, she scanned the list of casualties in the paper, and there, under "Killed in Action," was "Mercer, Phillip, Sergeant."

"Papa, Mama, Phillip's dead!" She shoved her fist into her

mouth. Her father wrapped one of her hands in his.

"Oh, no," cried Lea. She rushed from the kitchen and draped damp arms around Renata, who felt as though she had been punched in the stomach.

Her breath came in ragged gulps. "He was so nice, Mama. He even wanted to marry me!"

"What? A gentile? But, you barely knew him."

Renata instantly regretted sharing such a detail. "I know, but now that he's gone, I'll never get a chance to tell him how much I liked him."

Karl handed her his handkerchief and she blew her nose loudly.

"Surely you could not have been in love after such a short time?" Lea said.

"Lea, dear, I seem to recall you agreeing to marry me after a three-week courtship." Karl kept his voice even, but the wry smile gave him away.

"But that was different. We were so much older. I was twenty…" Lea stopped mid-sentence, a blush stealing up her cheeks. "Oh, dear, I do sound foolish, don't I? Renata, did you love him?"

"I don't think so. I mean, I love Hans. Or, I loved him. I don't know what I think anymore." She twisted the handkerchief and dabbed her eyes.

"Then Phillip was not the man intended for you. Dry your eyes and keep going, no matter what, is my advice."

"Mama, how can you be so unfeeling? He was a friend, a sweet boy, and he's gone, like so many others in this stupid war."

"I'm sorry Phillip is dead, Renata, but we must carry on," Lea said.

Karl cleared his throat. "The best we can hope for in war is that most of the men return. Your mother is merely being practical."

He walked to the sideboard and poured brandy into three glasses, handed one to Lea, one to Renata, and swirled the amber liquid in his glass before speaking. "I pray that all these deaths will not be in vain against such a bestial enemy."

He raised his glass. "To Phillip."

"To Phillip."

Her parents sipped their brandy, but Renata gulped hers.

The warmth filled her belly and soothed her distress.

She needed to talk to Sofia. She gathered her handbag and kissed her parents.

"I may be gone a little late tonight. Don't wait up for me."

She stepped onto a tram, her mind racing. Would she have married Phillip? Or was she merely following her mother's advice—well, more than advice, let's face it—her mother's *scheme*. Where was Hans in all this? Her memory of him had dimmed, yet she recollected his kisses with perfect, delicious clarity. Why was life so confusing? Was happiness something that found you, or something you chose?

The mournful wail of air-raid sirens obliterated her thoughts. The tram clanked to a halt, and the driver announced in Arabic and English that all passengers must get off and seek shelter. Their exit was orderly, if rushed.

Renata looked around anxiously. They were close to the Ramleh train station. She ran there as fast as she could. Inside, panicked people scrambled around benches and under tables, looking for shelter.

A staircase to the basement was clogged with several hundred others trying to get downstairs, so Renata opted for the ladies' bathroom. It was crammed with at least two dozen women and children plus one little dog that had found its way inside. The children were hysterical; the mothers unable to quiet them. The dog shook and panted heavily until Renata picked him up and held him.

Large, crumpling thuds began in the distance, and rapidly grew closer. Suddenly, the earth heaved, as a deafening blast cracked the air. People screamed as the floor tilted crazily, doors to the stalls popped off their hinges, and water sloshed out of toilets. Mirrors shattered, broadcasting shards of glass. Terrified children clung to sobbing mothers.

Renata held onto the dog, thinking irrationally that if she could only save it, she would save herself. A piece of falling plaster hit her on the head, knocking her to the ground. The dog wriggled out of her arms, yipping frantically, and when she looked for him, she noticed a spreading pool of blood on the floor.

"Someone's hurt!" she yelled, pulling herself to her feet.

A small circle cleared around a young woman on the floor. An enormous piece of glass had punctured her neck, and blood was everywhere. Two small children at her side were screaming.

Renata checked for a pulse and could find none. "Get those children away from her! No child should have to see this."

Renata had taken charge without thinking. Other women took the children away so they could no longer see their mother's body. Someone handed the dog back to her.

She took stock. Some had minor cuts from the glass. Anyone with a handkerchief offered it to stanch wounds. The sound of shells faded gradually, followed by the all-clear siren.

"Now, let's find a way out, carefully," Renata ordered. "We don't know what else is damaged. I need someone without children here to help me, and another two to bring up the rear. Those with children, stay in the middle."

She pushed at the door, but it would only open a fraction. She and the woman who had offered to help, pushed mightily, and finally it scraped open far enough so they could crawl out, except for one large woman. They'd worry about her later.

Outside the bathroom was bedlam. The ceiling had caved in; rafters hung at insane angles. Through a cloud of dust, Renata could see people moving over bodies on the floor.

"Hi! Over here! We need some help!" She waved at anyone moving, while women and children gathered around her.

A man with a flashlight approached. "What's your situation?"

"We have one woman probably dead, and another trapped inside. The rest of us, all women and children, are all right, with a few minor injuries."

"Follow me, then, but be careful. There are holes in the floor, and the entire building is about as safe as a rowboat in a hurricane. This way."

They picked their way out of the rubble, emerging onto the street a few minutes later. Renata, covered in gray dust, looked at the equally dusty dog in her arms. She wondered what color it really was, and who would look after the dead woman's children.

Now that everyone was out, she began to shake

uncontrollably. Sitting on a piece of broken concrete, she cried, holding the dog, and trying vainly to remember what she was doing before the air raid.

A Red Cross worker materialized in front of her, offering a blanket and a cup of tea. "Here you are, Miss. This'll perk you up a bit. Rather a dodgy afternoon it's been, eh?"

Renata nodded, irritated by the British capacity to pretend nothing much had happened.

"Does your dog need a drink?"

Renata nodded again.

"'Alf a mo', I'll bring him some."

Still dazed, Renata gazed at the animal cowering in her arms. He seemed a little less terrified. Where had he come from? Should she find the owner and return him?

The worker offered water to the dog, who lapped eagerly.

What would Mama and Papa think of him? She hadn't the heart to abandon him.

"We need a name for you," she whispered. "How about Dusty?" She brushed his coat. Short, light brown hair began to appear. He had a narrow snout, a long wiry tail, and pointed ears. He licked Renata's neck and chin and wagged his tail enthusiastically. She put him on the ground and began walking. Dusty followed her all the way home.

She took note of the damage. The tram was inoperable. Rail lines were twisted and gnarled like old oak roots. In the distance, massive fires from the oil refineries spewed ugly black clouds miles into the sky.

Renata arrived at her apartment, where her frantic parents held her tightly, sobbing with relief. A sharp bark got their attention.

"Where did this little creature come from?" asked Lea, stooping to pet him, then backing off as the dog jumped up to lick her face.

"He found me in the railway station, and he decided to stay. The station was bombed, by the way, as you can tell from all the dust on me. I didn't know what else to do with him."

"We were scared to death that you were gone. The radio said not everyone survived."

Renata thought of the woman on the bathroom floor. "No,

they didn't. But Dusty can stay, can't he?"

"We'll find a way, dear." Her father picked up the dog, who dispensed another dose of wet kisses.

Mama put down a bowl of water and a small dish of leftovers, which he tackled immediately.

"Renata, did you make it to Sofia's house?" asked Mama.

Suddenly, the memory of Phillip's death came crashing back. The dust, the explosions, the dead woman and her frantic children…She put her hand over her mouth, rushed to the bathroom and vomited.

Lea sponged her face and neck with a cool, damp towel. Karl offered her brandy, then led her to bed, where she fell asleep in minutes.

She awakened to Lea sitting beside her, holding her hand, and Dusty curled on the bed beside her. She reached out and stroked his back.

"That little dog hasn't left your side." Lea kissed her on the forehead. "Now, do you think you could eat something?"

Renata considered. "Yes, I think I could. Not too much, though." She scratched Dusty behind the ears.

Her mother went to the kitchen and reappeared with a plate of pita, some hummus, and a sliced orange.

"*Liebschen*, I have something else to tell you." Lea sat on the edge of the bed. "The men will be out on convoys again very soon."

Renata buried her nose in Dusty's soft coat, getting several eager licks and a thumping tail in return, trying to ignore the hard lump in her stomach at the thought of the men facing German guns.

Dipping the pita in hummus, Renata pondered her situation. Two days ago, she was relatively satisfied with her life, even here in Egypt. She had her studio, her family had an apartment, there was enough to eat, and she had friends. But now the war had arrived in all its ugliness. Phillip was dead. The god-awful dust, the heat—she wanted to leave, anywhere away from bombs.

She had gotten her family out of Germany. Then out of Tolumbat. Then out of poverty. Now she had to get out of Egypt. *Was it even possible?*

Renata pushed the hummus around the plate. Her mother believed marriage to a foreigner, preferably Jewish, was the answer to their problems. Renata was not enthusiastic, but she forced herself to be realistic. Look at dear old Phillip, wanting just one night with a woman before he died, a night he didn't get. She thought about how awful it would be to die, never having had made love with anyone. That one deep kiss from Phillip had given her some inkling of why people wrote poetry and songs about sex. She didn't want to die without experiencing it, either. And she wanted to continue painting, and selling her art in peace.

Mama took Renata's plate away and handed her a mug of tea. Renata sipped thoughtfully. The three goals—getting out of Egypt, having sex, and painting in peace—could be solved by marrying a Canadian or an Australian. Even an American, if they ever joined in. Very well. Let it be marriage. And perhaps love would come along, too.

Chapter Thirteen

Ray, 1940

Sofia and Hamish stopped by three days later, to find Renata still feeling fragile and not ready to return to her studio. Grateful for company, she hugged her friends.

"I was on my way to tell you about Phillip." She clenched her jaw and swallowed. "I got stuck at the railway station. And look what I got for my troubles. Here, Dusty!" Dusty raced over and jumped into her arms, licking the tears off her face until she laughed.

Sofia squealed and reached to scratch his ears and rub his tummy, then plopped him back in Renata's lap.

"Dusty is adorable." Her eyes turned somber. "I'm so sorry about Phillip. He was a dear man, and a great loss."

"Thanks."

"But the other reason we came here, is that we're getting together for dinner tonight and we want you to come. Isabella and Ray will be there, too. Say yes, won't you?"

Renata set Dusty on the floor, buying time before responding, wondering if it was all right so soon after a friend's death. But life in wartime could be very short, and this was no time to be fussy about manners and convention. And she absolutely refused to cry.

"I might not be the life of the party, but yes, I'll come."

They met at their favorite café on the Corniche as the sun was painting the sky glorious oranges, fuchsias, maroons, and pinks. It was amazing that despite a terrible war killing thousands of people, maybe even millions, and despite Phillip's untimely death,

Mother Nature still put on a display of beauty. Almost as though She wanted everyone to know it will all be over someday, and things will get better.

Slightly cheered, Renata accepted a menu. Ray and Isabella seemed cozy, she noticed, and Sofia and Hamish were intently pouring over the menu, giggling occasionally. Renata wondered what they had up their sleeves. Alone, her mood faded with the sunset.

While the others ordered entrees with wine, Renata ordered soup and bread.

Isabella sipped her wine. "Renata, darling, we were so crushed to hear about Phillip. Such ghastly news. How are you managing?" The others murmured condolences.

Renata forced a tight smile while gripping her napkin and thinking how insincere Isabella sounded. "You're so kind. I feel terrible about Phillip. He was such a nice man. His parents must be devastated."

She sounded phony even to herself. She cleared her throat and tried again.

"He and I went out a couple of times together."

Nods around the table.

"What you may not know, is he asked me to marry him the night before he left." She was aware of her eyes getting full. *Must not cry*, she ordered herself silently. She swallowed madly and gritted her teeth.

Everyone gasped.

Sofia broke the stunned silence. "Oh, no, that's awful! I mean, it's not awful that he asked, but awful that he...I mean..." she paused awkwardly.

It was Ray who smoothed the group's discomfort. "Phillip was a gentleman and a brave soldier. He would have been a good husband to any woman he chose to marry. That he asked you, says a lot about you, Renata." He raised his glass. "Let's toast Phillip, his dead comrades, and those lost in the desert. To absent friends, may they never be forgotten."

They raised their glasses together. "To absent friends." The silence that settled over them felt more comfortable than the conversation.

Renata glanced at Ray, grateful for his thoughtful words.

Such a diplomat, yet Isabella was very artificial. What did he see in her?

The food arrived, and chatter resumed. Looking at the heaped plates of the others, Renata was glad she had ordered a small meal. Her stomach was still touchy.

"Dessert, anyone?" asked Isabella. "They make fabulous baklava here."

Remembering the lovable Moustaki family, Renata decided she could handle baklava. She hoped they were out of Greece by now, and wondered why Gina and Roza had never replied to her letters.

Hamish tapped on a glass with his fork.

"Sofia and I have an announcement." He took Sofia's hand and lifted it high, where a small diamond ring perched on her third finger. "We are engaged to be married!"

The table erupted in cheers, to looks from other diners.

"That's wonderful, congratulations!" said Isabella. "And when is the big day, may we know?"

"Yes," answered Sofia, coloring. "In two weeks, so we can get married quarters before Hamish ships out again."

Ray shook Hamish's hand. "Well done, sir. I wish you the best."

Renata gaped, then closed her mouth abruptly. It was so close to what had almost happened to her and Phillip. Did they know each other well enough? Could Sofia be pregnant? Were they in love? She hoped so.

She gave Sofia a hug and murmured, "Let me know if I can help, won't you?"

"Thanks, Renata. My mother is moving into high gear, so I'm probably fine. But would you be my bridesmaid? I hope it's not too hard for you."

"I would love to." It occurred to her that if she had truly loved Phillip, she would be unable to accept Sofia's request.

Isabella began talking weddings with the enthusiasm of a caterer at an exclusive hotel. The dress, the location, the food, the rings.

Hamish interrupted her gently. "Isabella, it's so thoughtful of ye to share your ideas, but this is going to be a modest wedding.

Shall I have Sofia's mother contact ye if she wants some help?"

Isabella nodded and frowned a little. She asked Ray for a cigarette, which he lit. She blew a cloud of smoke skyward and leaned back, one arm draped around his shoulder.

Watching this little interplay, Renata wondered again what Ray saw in her. She was pretty enough, and perhaps wealthy, judging from the clothes and jewelry she wore. But something about her didn't fit. She glanced at Ray, who was blowing smoke rings into the evening sky. He tipped his chair back, ignoring the female chatter, while Isabella pursued her discussion of wedding plans with Sofia.

Seizing the opportunity, Renata touched Ray's sleeve. "When are you coming to see my paintings? Or have you already seen them?"

He blew another smoke ring. "I saw the first ones you did, but I hear they've all sold."

"All but one. Now I have new ones there. Why don't you come by tomorrow afternoon for a look?"

Stubbing out the cigarette in the ashtray, Ray gave her a curious look.

"I'm busy tomorrow, but Isabella and I could come on Thursday."

Keeping a neutral smile on her face, Renata said, "That would be wonderful! See you Thursday."

"What do you think of this one?" Renata, dressed in her gallery clothes—black suit, black shoes, white blouse—stood in front of the painting she had finished after Phillip died.

Ray and Isabella, holding hands, gazed intently at the painting.

Isabella wore a frothy white dress and a floppy beribboned hat tilted to one side. She pursed her pretty mouth and frowned.

"It looks unhappy. Could that be why it hasn't sold?" Ray replied. "What do you think, Isabella?"

Isabella shrugged and pouted. "I'm not an artist, so honestly, I have no idea." She leaned on Ray, chest to chest, and pushed up the peak of his uniform cap. "But you promised me lunch afterwards, if

I was a good girl." She smiled wickedly and licked her lips.

Detaching himself, Ray said, "Yes, I did, but being a good girl means looking at Renata's paintings and pretending to enjoy yourself, even if you're not."

Renata watched the exchange, smiling inwardly. Ray was irritated. Isabella was bored. *How perfect.* "You know, Isabella, it's all right if you aren't interested. The café outside has a lovely view and they make the best martinis, so if you'd rather wait, I won't be offended."

Isabella looked from Renata to Ray. "Would that be all right, Ray? I'm really not an artsy person."

"Sure, doll. I won't be too long, so go ahead and I'll be there when we're done."

Kissing Ray on the cheek, Isabella smiled and pirouetted, making her dress swirl, and headed to the exit.

"Sorry about that," said Ray. "Show me your other paintings?"

Renata steered him to the next painting, an abstract rendition of the Corniche with plenty of light-blues, aquas, and whites. "I was in a good mood when I did this one. The weather was perfect, and it wasn't long after we were released from Tolumbat. I think it's my most optimistic work in this show."

"It's very nice. Makes me feel like I'm lying on the beach, getting a suntan." He grinned at her and laid a hand tentatively around her waist. She pulled away gently.

"Aren't you and Isabella a steady pair?" she asked, then looked at him sideways and paused. "Although I wouldn't mind if you weren't."

She held her breath for his response. A brief image of Phillip asking her to marry him flitted into her mind and out again.

"We've dated for six months, but to tell you the truth, it's wearing a little thin. She loves to party, party, party and doesn't give much thought to anything except what she will wear."

He replaced his arm on her waist and this time she did not pull away.

"I like intelligent women," he said. "Perhaps you and I could meet for lunch sometime?"

Renata replied in even tones, "That would be nice. I'd love

to hear more of your opinions on my art."

"How about Monday, after Shabbat?"

"Yes, that's perfect."

It was awkward.

Isabella moaned to Alicia and Sofia about Ray dumping her. Even Sofia rather pointedly questioned Renata about dating too soon after Phillip's death, until Renata reminded her that she and Hamish were engaged after a courtship of mere weeks.

At a modest café, Ray and Renata lunched on sandwiches, pomegranates, and almonds which they washed down with strong Turkish coffee. Renata felt tongue-tied and jittery. She glanced at him and smiled, desperate for a topic of conversation. Luckily, he began speaking after the coffee cups were refilled.

"Like a cigarette?"

She accepted one which he lit first, then his own. The ritual of smoking had become as soothing as a lullaby. His smoke rings wobbled above their heads, and Renata laughed.

"Thanks! I love your smoke rings."

He chuckled quietly. "Just a small challenge to forget larger troubles for a while. Back home in Canada, I used them to entertain some of the local kids, like my Dad did when we were small."

"Really? I feel the same way, you know." She paused, tapping the ash into the metal ashtray. "What troubles are you forgetting tonight?"

He wobbled his head a little. "I'll tell, if you tell me yours too. Deal?"

"Deal. You first."

He stubbed out his cigarette and interlaced his fingers on top of the table. "I haven't heard from my brother in a long time. He's in Europe, but I don't know where. My mother is beside herself." He raised his eyebrows. "Now your turn."

She took a deep breath and stared at the empty cup in front of her. "I'm supporting my parents because my father isn't allowed to practice medicine here. My mother wants the posh lifestyle we had in Munich, and guess who is tasked with making that possible?"

She ground the butt of her cigarette into the ashtray. "Me."

"But you're how old?"

"Nineteen."

Ray scratched his head. "How are you making enough money for your apartment?"

"Selling art. Not just those hanging in the gallery. I do sketches and sell them in the market."

He looked at her in amazement. "And I thought you were a good artist making a few extra bucks. I had no idea you were the family breadwinner." He paused. "How does your father feel about it?"

She turned the cup around and around in its saucer. "He feels terrible, but he's afraid to try black-market work. If he were caught, it would mean prison. Also, his health is deteriorating. I think it's something serious."

Saying it out loud, she realized how true it was. She swallowed madly to push back threatening tears.

He slid his hand across the table and took one of hers. "You should be going to parties, dancing, not worrying about money." He kissed the back of her hand gently.

She enjoyed the feel of her hand in his. "But in wartime, we all do what we must, isn't that what the Admiral said? This is what I must do to save my family. I'm sure you'd do as much for your brother."

"Of course. Every family has its sad stories, it seems." He glanced at his watch. "I hate to interrupt, but I must get back to the office. "How about dinner next week?"

"Lovely, thank you. I've enjoyed lunch very much."

Renata left the restaurant on his arm before departing for her studio. Ray walked away whistling. Renata noticed an unfamiliar feeling of lightness. The air seemed brighter. She felt like singing a song. Then she realized what it was. Happiness. She was happy.

The Lowenthal family morning ritual included reading the newspaper and listening to the radio's doleful news about "The Blitz," as the papers called it.

Renata finished the front page. "How can Britain win now, Papa?"

"I don't know. But they must."

Lea looked up. "Is there any hope for us?"

Renata and Karl glanced at each other.

A knock at the door startled them. Dusty barked and pranced with excitement, now that he was used to a certain frequent visitor.

"Come in, Ray." Karl gestured toward the kitchen chairs. "We saw the headlines. Can you tell us anymore?"

"Things are about to get hopping. Not sure how much I'll be ashore until this bloody mess ends." Ray pressed his palms down on the table. "I'm being re-mustered to *Illustrious*, one of the new carriers, and Hamish will be on *Valiant*. My guess is we'll be sent to Malta again before long. The poor sods there must be eating grass, now that Italy's blockading every British port in the Mediterranean."

Dusty jumped onto Renata's lap. She frowned, absently scratching the dog's ears. "All the news is bad."

"You don't know the half of it. Hitler and Stalin are playing footsie to see who can get the biggest slice of territory in Eastern Europe. Stalin managed to scoop up the poor bloody Estonians and Latvians." Ray shook his head in disgust, thumped one fist into the other. "But we lads are chomping at the bit and can't wait to get a few Huns in our sights. We need to protect supply routes, and things are going to heat up in Africa with Italian control of Libya and Abyssinia."

His nostrils flared, his face flushed. "My apologies for my language."

"No need," said Karl. "Should we be worried? About the Italians, I mean?"

"The official line is, don't worry. But, frankly, we're vastly outnumbered in both men and equipment. Anyone can see the Italians want control of Suez. Be prepared for another attack."

Lea gasped. Renata moved to her father's side and gripped his hand. She had noticed the pallor of his skin getting worse, which he brushed off as worry and fatigue.

"Ray," said Renata, "if you're leaving soon, would you like to take me to that dinner you promised before you go?"

With her parents watching, he drew her hand to his mouth and brushed it with his lips. "Marvelous idea. Tonight?"

"Why not? Can we eat at La Verandah? I've always wanted to go there, and that's the perfect place for a send-off."

"I'll come at six." He touched the brim of his cap and was gone.

Karl looked at his daughter. "It looks like Ray is in your sights now."

"He's smart, he works hard, and he likes my art. He's Jewish, too, Papa. He and Isabella were about to break up anyway, so it isn't as if I did anything wrong." Her cheeks pinked.

"Everyone's emotions are running high these days." Her father reached for his pipe and picked up the newspaper. "Be careful yours don't run away with you."

He shuffled to the chair on the balcony, lit his pipe, and read.

Renata watched her father for a minute, thinking of his words. Was Ray worth pursuing? She planned to find out at dinner tonight.

Her wardrobe was her first priority. "Mama, what shall I wear? La Verandah is a swanky place." Her eyes sparkled.

Her mother considered, her arms folded. "How about this one? The red suits you, it's very smart. Or the brown silk, more subdued but classy."

"This one, I think." Renata fingered the delicate silk. "Understated elegance. Let me try it on."

She slipped into it, twirled around toward Lea, who appraised her with a critical eye.

"Those buttons are wrong for evening wear. Let me check my button box." Lea headed for her sewing supplies.

While her mother searched, Renata lifted the skirt at the sides and let it fall. The sheer cocoa brown outer layer and a taffeta silk lining felt like molten milk chocolate. She agreed about the buttons, though.

Lea returned triumphantly, holding up two rectangular rhinestone buttons set in imitation gold.

"Perfect, thank you, Mama!" She lifted the dress over her head, handed it over, and put on her day dress. By the time she was finished, her mother was nearly done.

"What an improvement! Thank goodness you have a button box again." She pecked Lea lightly on the cheek, not without noticing the cloud that hovered over her mother's face with yet another memory of all they had lost.

"I'd be grateful if you'd find a nice Jewish boy to marry, so we can get out of here." Her mother had lost her waspish tone, but the wistfulness was harder to bear. Lea was more often melancholy than cheerful, and her moods pressed on Renata and Karl like humidity before a storm that never breaks.

Renata winced inwardly, then hung the dresses back in the closet.

She must think about how to do her hair.

Chapter Fourteen

Dinner, 1940

Promptly at six, Ray arrived, resplendent in dress whites. Karl invited him to sit in the living room.

Renata looked at herself once more in the mirror, and made an entrance worthy of a film star. Ray shot to his feet, and Dusty circled around his legs, whining, begging to be picked up.

"Wow, you look fabulous! Come here, turn around, let me see." He turned her in a slow pirouette, then drew her closer and brushed her gloved hand with his lips. "Very, very lovely. Miss Lowenthal, it is my privilege to escort you to dinner tonight."

"My pleasure, Lieutenant."

He helped her into the waiting car and directed the driver to Pompey's Pillar. A memorial to the Emperor Diocletian, Ray explained, the pillar, which towered over everything nearby, was one of the few remaining signs of the Roman occupation many centuries ago.

They got out. Ray took her hand and led her over the rough ground.

The low hill offered a view of a small sphinx, ruins of an old colonnade, and the city. The setting sun threw its last desperate, magnificent colors across desert and sea, and above, the velvet night stole in.

Ray, holding her hand, pointed out other details visible in the dying light. He stood behind Renata and put his arms around her.

Her hair brushed his face and she felt the lumps of his

uniform ribbons and buttons pressing into her back. She liked the feel of him there.

"This is a special place, isn't it?" she said. "Strange to think of Romans riding around in chariots on this very ground."

He brushed her hair out of his eyes with one hand. "Yes, very strange. I wonder what they'd think of our airplanes and submarines." He looked around again. "I've always loved history, and this part of the world is where it began. I'm glad you like it, too."

They returned to the car, and a short drive later, they were seated at La Verandah, one of Alexandria's famous old restaurants. There since the 1920s, it was the formal dining half of Pâtisserie Délices.

The vaulted ceilings and walls were covered in mahogany paneling and decorative molding. Renata took in the monstrous chandeliers, a few carefully placed sculptures, and armloads of fresh flowers in enormous vases. Unctuous waiters in tuxedos, and customers smoking cigars reminded Renata of the expensive Munich restaurants to which her father had taken her on her birthday each year, another world ago.

"I haven't been here before, but I've wanted to for quite some time." She smiled, cradling the leather-bound menu. "Thanks for being the one to invite me."

Ray's smile was restrained. "Shall we order a bottle of wine to start, or do you prefer sherry?"

Renata leaned over the table conspiratorially. "The truth? I hate sherry! Why do the Brits drink the stuff?"

He tipped back his head and laughed. "You're the first one I've heard say that, and I agree with you! My parents serve it at Christmas, and the British drink it before dinner, but it's like crankcase oil."

"Exactly! We must be the only two people in the country who can't stand it."

They both chuckled. Other diners frowned.

"Oops, pardon us," whispered Renata, partially covering her mouth with one hand, eyes twinkling. It started them snickering all over again.

The waiter approached. "Would you care for something to drink, Sir? Miss?"

Ray ordered a bottle of Cabernet Sauvignon. They reviewed the menu with studied seriousness, chuckling whenever their eyes met. The evening was already going better than Renata could have expected.

The menu featured Greek and Arab food, with some Western choices. Renata, remembering Mrs. Moustaki's cooking, ordered rack of lamb and dolmades, while Ray ordered a Western meal of roast chicken with fried rice, and a mix of local vegetables in season.

The waiter poured wine.

Renata took her glass and sat back in the thick leather seat. She crossed her legs.

"Ray, I really don't know much about you, and here we are at this fantastic restaurant. Tell me about yourself."

He pulled out a silver cigarette case, offered her one and lit both, then leaned back, exhaling. After tapping the ash into a silver ashtray, he clasped his hands behind his head.

"My hometown is named Moose Jaw, in Saskatchewan, Canada."

"A town named for the jaw of an animal? How strange."

"Not the strangest place-name in Canada, either. The town is about ten thousand people. Winters are harsh, summers are hot, and the mosquitoes are terrible, but it's great farming country."

"You told me you wanted to see the world. But is there more to it? I mean, why you left home?"

A hint of a frown appeared briefly. "I couldn't stand Moose Jaw. Stifling boredom, nothing to do but square dance and shoot gophers. And our tiny Jewish community felt claustrophobic after eighteen years. We were not mistreated, but neither were we fully welcome." He took another sip of wine.

Their first course, a cold soup with lemon, cucumber, and dill, arrived.

Renata tried a spoonful. Delicious.

"How about you, Renata? I know you're a German Jew, but how did you get here?"

As Renata shared her family's harrowing escape from Germany, Ray listened with increasing distress. He reached for her hand when she described the border guard who'd threatened her.

"I'd never let anything happen to you. I'd punch him out. I'd strangle him," he growled.

She retrieved her hand gently. "To the Nazis, we Jews are worthless, not even human. My father intervened and lost a tooth for his troubles. We were lucky he didn't lose his life." She dabbed her lips with a snowy napkin. "My entire family, other than the three of us, are still there." Her voice wobbled.

"What can they do now? Can they escape?"

The server removed the empty soup bowls and brought two small dishes of sorbet to cleanse the palate.

Renata tasted the cold, sweet froth before replying. It was inconceivable that Jews in German territories were starving, yet this bounty still existed. She lowered her spoon.

"Those still there have very few options. They are watched constantly, and I've heard Austrian Jews are being rounded up and shipped to some kind of work camps in Poland. We tried to talk our relatives into coming with us, but they had a hundred excuses."

Ray, one elbow on the table, drummed his fingers on his cheek. "You know that pretty much every country has turned back boatloads of Jews. Including Canada, unfortunately."

Renata nodded.

"But," he continued, "if you were, say, married to a Brit, you could move to England with him, right? Or a Yankee, or even one of us Canucks."

She looked up, saw his eyes widen.

"Is that the plan of the young women here?"

She decided to treat the comment lightly. "You're right. Most of us here would love to marry one of you foreign sailors. You don't happen to be in the market for a wife, do you?" She glanced at him sideways, eyes open wide, hoping the effect was coquettish.

One waiter removed the sorbet dishes while another delivered their main courses, steaming and aromatic.

He grinned. "Perhaps. I've been here three years now. I've met hundreds of women, had romances with a few. I expect to get married some time, have a family, settle down."

Sirens ruptured the conversation, instantly followed by screams. Ray stood in one fluid motion, and pulled out Renata's chair.

"Come on, we have to get to shelter." He called to a frantic waiter. "Where should we go?"

"The basement, sir. Reception," the waiter called over his shoulder, as he swept through the room, gathering other diners.

Ray took Renata's hand and they ran. Two frightened servers held open doors hidden in the ornate molding, and gestured people through. Everyone clattered down concrete stairs, Renata cursing her high heels. Below was a large storage room, where shelves in rows held jars, barrels, and casks of wine.

The maitre d' bellowed instructions.

"You may stay anywhere, but please do not sit on barrels or boxes. They contain food you may want to eat later." That comment garnered a few chuckles. "Don't bump the shelves. You don't want to knock anything over. No smoking, please, and remain calm."

Ray and Renata huddled together, looking without success for a comfortable place. The floor was their only option, so Ray spread his white jacket on the concrete floor to allow Renata to sit on it.

The drone of aircraft, muffled by the concrete surrounding them, raised the tension level. A few women were weeping. The men held their women, although the dark looks on their faces betrayed anxiety underneath.

The dull thud of explosions began. The sounds of ak-ak fire and aircraft fighting above them was a front row seat to a play no one wanted to attend.

Time stretched like a frigid winter's night, before the all-clear sounded and they were allowed upstairs. The restaurant was undamaged, but customers flowed outside, ignoring unfinished meals now cold on the tables.

"What shall we do now?" asked Ray, gazing at the dusty street, seeing no visible damage.

"I want to make sure my parents are all right," Renata said. "Would you please take me home?

"Yes, of course. We'll have to walk."

Renata's shoes squeezed her toes as they hurried to her apartment.

The closer they came, the more alarmed they were at the crushed buildings, debris, and volunteers working frantically to rescue those trapped in the rubble.

Around the last corner, her worst fears were realized. Their apartment building was gone, reduced to a pile of stones and broken beams. She broke into an awkward run with Ray at her side.

"Mama! Papa! Where are you? Ray, I have to find them. They must be here. I need my family!" Her belly felt lanced with icy daggers.

At the wreckage, she began tugging at enormous stones that would not budge.

Ray lifted some, then put his hand on her arm. "Renata, think for a second. The worst case is that your parents are under that rubble. But what if they are not? Let's check with the authorities."

His comments made sense, but it was hard to listen when she wanted to rip the stones apart. She felt like King Kong, full of rage and ready to destroy anything in her way. She clenched her fists and ground her teeth.

"All right, but we're not taking too long. If we can't find them, they must be under here." She wiped her face, smearing dust across her cheeks, and wiping her hands on the torn skirt of her silk dress.

Ray led her to a hastily created rescue coordination center, which consisted of a rickety table, two firemen, and local men with picks and shovels coming and going, all in a state of high alert.

She approached the fireman in charge. "My parents were in that building! Please help me!"

"Their names, Miss?" he asked, not unkindly.

"Dr. and Mrs. Lowenthal. I'm Renata Lowenthal. We lived in number twenty-three."

He shook his head slowly. "I'm terribly sorry There were a few survivors, but I don't have names yet. Check the Red Cross tent in the next street."

"Ray, let's go!" She caught his hand and ran in the direction the fireman had indicated. She thought her brain would explode.

The next block was worse. Flames and smoke billowed from the ruins. People, some injured, wandered around, dazed. Renata recognized no one.

The Red Cross tent, in the clearest part of the street, had a long queue snaking outside it. Renata had no intention of joining the line, so she headed straight to the tent, only to be yelled at by others already in the line.

"Hey, who do you think you are?"

"We're all taking our turn here, you take your turn, too!"

Ray said for her ears alone, "This could get nasty. Do as they say, and I'll see if I can get any news for you."

Reluctantly, Renata returned to the end of the line, to gibes and jeers. She folded her arms in defiance, at the same time realizing they had a point.

Ray disappeared, his uniform allowing him access the others could not obtain. Five minutes later he was back. "They think your parents are safe inside."

Renata squealed and threw her arms around him. "Oh, thank you! Thank God!"

"But you can't jump the line, or you'll start a riot. Keep your voice down and listen." He shook her shoulders and thrust his face into hers. "Look at me, Renata."

She raised her eyes to his.

"They are going to find your parents and let them know that you are out here. Wait your turn to see them, then tomorrow we can figure out what to do. Can you calm down, now? I'll wait with you."

She nodded her head, but could not speak. She could barely breathe. They were safe!

Ray stood with his arm around her shoulders.

Her mother would be angry about another refugee tent. Renata bit her lip. What if they were injured? Where could they go? Where was Dusty? At least her studio…oh, no, the studio! Could it have been bombed, too? That would be the last straw. But now, seeing her parents was the priority. Tomorrow she would find out if her studio still existed.

She kept her thoughts to herself and leaned on Ray's shoulder. His arm felt good around her. Her shaking subsided.

An hour of shuffling got them to the front of the line, and minutes later she and her parents held one another in a vice-like embrace.

Renata wanted to hold on forever. "Ray and I were in the basement of the restaurant. How did you escape?"

"We were at the Corniche for coffee when the raid started. We hid in the coffee shop basement, and when we got back, we learned we had no home," said her father.

"What about Dusty?"

Her parents exchanged glances. Karl coughed. "He was in the building. I'm so sorry."

Grateful as she was for her parents' survival, Renata felt an aching loss at the death of the innocent, lovable creature. She squeezed Papa's hand and mentally planned hideous punishments for the Italian bombers.

"We need to look for him," she said.

"Tomorrow, when it is light." Karl's practicality was maddeningly correct.

"Now we are homeless again." Lea's relief was giving way to anger. "What are we going to do?"

Ray said, "Mrs. Lowenthal, tomorrow I will help you find a new place to live. Can you manage here for tonight?"

Lea looked at Ray, as if seeing him for the first time. "We can manage. Some help would be most welcome. Thank you, and thank you for looking after our daughter."

"She was very brave. You should be proud of her." He squeezed Renata's arm. "But I must get back to the base and see what orders we might have now."

After a night of fitful sleep and bad dreams in cramped quarters with virtually no privacy, Renata announced she was heading out to look for Dusty, and to see if her studio was still standing. "Then, I'll check out apartments for rent and see what is available."

"But what will you wear? Your pretty dress is in rags," said Lea, touching the shredded silk tenderly.

"It's all I have. Maybe the Red Cross will have some other clothing later. Have you heard anything?"

"No." Her mother shook her head. She brushed dust off her shoulders and sighed. "I can't believe we're going through this again."

Karl ran his hand through his hair, so it stood up in cockeyed shards. "Losing your home gets very tiresome." He put an arm around his wife and scratched his beard.

Renata hugged him, alarmed at the chalky hue of his skin. She kissed his cheek and left.

Damage to the city was not as bad as she had feared. Their section had taken the worst hits. Fire trucks, Army rescue crews, and citizens were still searching for survivors in the rubble.

She asked the crews if any small dogs had been rescued, but they shook their heads and continued working.

Renata stood by the wreckage of her building and shouted as loudly as she could, "Dusty! Dusty! Come!" There was no response. She repeated calling the little dog at the other end of the building, but again, she heard nothing.

Then, just as she was leaving, feeling defeated, she heard it. A faint yipping from under the rocks.

"That's him! Did you hear that? That's my dog!"

She raced to the rescuers and urged them to follow her. In minutes, three men were hauling off bricks and lumps of concrete to find the trapped animal, whose yaps were getting louder. Others came to join the rescue.

Half an hour later, they unearthed the little cave where Dusty, incredibly, had found shelter. More amazing yet, a three-year-old child was with him. She was barely conscious, covered in cuts and bruises, but she was alive. The men stared in astonishment.

"If not for your dog," said the leader to Renata, "we would not have found this little one alive. Your dog is a hero."

Renata scooped a very dusty Dusty, and held him tight, while the rescuers retrieved the child and sent her to hospital.

Another crew member brought a bowl of water, which the dog lapped eagerly until it was gone. Renata didn't want to leave him alone again, even with her parents in the tents, so with him in her arms, she walked quickly toward her studio and…she stopped and choked. The Gallérie! What if all her completed works were gone? In her broken heels, she hurried down the hill, across some twisted tram tracks. Dusty nestled into her, and didn't seem to mind being bounced along.

At last the Gallérie came into view, undamaged. She closed her eyes with relief. If only the studio was in one piece, she could continue working. She refused to contemplate that bombing attacks might scare off art customers.

Complete devastation had leveled the surrounding block, but the studio building looked only mildly damaged. Barricades surrounded it, but Renata slipped behind and made her way to the door.

It would not open. Looking up, she noticed the lintel had settled. There were cracks in the concrete that had not been there before. Cursing under her breath, she looked for another entrance, around the back. That door hung off its hinges, but she got in. She smelled spilled linseed oil soaking into the wooden floors. Dust clogged her nose. Easels lay on the floor. Canvasses, paintbrushes, and opened tins of paint created their own dystopian work of art on the floor. Renata picked her way through the mess to her studio space, as Dusty licked her cheeks every time she stopped.

As she expected, her wet painting was ruined, but she retrieved her brushes, replaced the closed paint tubes on a shelf she shared with two others, and left the spilled paint to dry on its own. *Not a complete disaster*, she thought with satisfaction. Some cleaning and a few more colors, and she could get back to work.

On her way back, she remembered Ray's promise to help them find a new apartment. She wondered if he meant it. No point relying on a man, she decided, detouring toward apartments close to the water. But the usual "to let" signs were replaced with "no vacancy." Snorting with disgust, she returned to the temporary camp, where Ray was speaking with her parents.

"...there aren't many, but I got you in for a month at least." He noticed Renata and Dusty and reached out a hand to her. "Here you are! And Dusty? How on earth did you find him?"

Karl and Lea fussed over the dog while Renata told them the story. When she mentioned the child, Karl interrupted.

"So Dusty is the dog that saved the child? I helped the Red Cross treat her. They told me about the dog, and they found the child's parents too. Wow, Dusty, you are quite the pooch!"

Lea said, "I'll see if anyone has some food scraps we can give the little guy."

"How is the little girl?" asked Renata.

"Coming along. Her parents were planning her funeral, and now they are ecstatic!" Karl shook his head and grinned. "Miracles do happen."

"How about your studio, Renata?" asked Ray.

"It survived, but there's a lot of cleaning to be done. What were you talking about when I arrived?"

Ray replied, "Military housing. The family housing units aren't fully used, so I got you an apartment for a while."

"Wonderful!" She hugged him. "Mama, Papa, isn't he the best?"

"I would say so," said Karl.

Lea murmured agreement, but her warm smile said much more.

Within a day, they were in the apartment, which was furnished, but had no bed linens, nor, of course, any clothes. Dusty scampered around inside, happy to have a bowl of water.

"The Red Cross is handing out any clothes they can find, but we have to line up near the tent to get any. Meanwhile, we'll have to put up with being a little smelly," said Karl.

"I will go, if you'll watch Dusty, Papa." offered Renata.

Her father nodded and smiled.

A day of waiting produced one change of clothing (minus underwear) and two scruffy towels. It was a start.

Chapter Fifteen

Sofia's Wedding, 1940

Hamish and Sofia married on October eighth, 1940, after the worst of the damage was cleared and most families resettled. The groom wore his uniform, the bride wore a dress her mother had made from several lace tablecloths. Dresses and suits, loaned from those who had not been bombed, adorned those who had. The fifty in attendance at the synagogue, included a portion of the Greek community, several men from the base with their girlfriends and wives, a Greek rabbi, Ray and Renata, and Renata's parents. Isabella was there with an officer Renata did not know.

A bagpiper led the bridal party into and out of the synagogue, but the Greeks took over the dinner and dancing with a joy and fervor that obliterated the stress of war for an evening.

Renata, a bridesmaid and the only non-Greek, joined in the fun and laughter, but she gave up on the round dances and sat beside Ray.

"Ray, come dance with the men," urged Sofia, visiting their table, as the Greek men circled in a dance that blended Jewish and Greek cultures.

He shook his head. "I'm waiting for the foxtrot and jitterbug. Or a square dance, if you have one coming."

Sofia laughed and slapped him lightly on the shoulder. "Canadian men must be the worst dancers. At least promise me you'll dance when the Greek music is over."

"Sure, we will. Right now, we need to refresh our drinks, if you don't mind."

Renata slipped her hand into Ray's elbow and steered him towards the bar.

Fresh drinks in hand, they wandered toward Lea and Karl, who were deep in conversation with Captain Crutchley and his wife.

"Well, if it isn't that slug, Ray Stern," said a female voice behind them.

As they turned to see who was speaking, Isabella slapped Ray across the face as hard as she could. "You bloody worm, ditching me for this bitch!" She pushed Renata backwards.

The room was instantly silent. Shocked guests watched the spectacle with open mouths.

Ray grasped Isabella's wrists. "Hey, get your hands off her! What the hell do you think you're doing?"

"Let her go, Ray." Renata's voice was smooth as snakeskin. She sauntered close to Isabella and drew a gloved finger slowly along her cheek, then gripped her chin hard.

"Listen to me, honey. You lost. Get lost. You don't deserve him." She pushed Isabella's face to one side, picked up a glass of water from a table, and took a sip.

Isabella spat she-dragon fire. "You cheated on me! Fuck you! Fuck you both!" She pulled away from Ray as a couple of burly Marines approached.

Her stunned escort seemed paralyzed with shock.

"Now, Miss, if you'll come quietly. This is no way to act at a wedding," said a Marine.

Isabella tugged her dress back into place, spat again at Renata, and allowed the Marines to escort her out.

"Gee, I'm so sorry, I had no idea…" faltered Isabella's escort. "I'd better go see to her." He disappeared.

"Are you all right?" Ray took Renata's hand and rubbed the inside of her wrist. "I had no idea you could be that feisty."

She was not only all right, inside she was cheering her victory, without Ray ever knowing there was a battle. "I'm fine. I expected a reaction, just not here. Did she do that kind of thing when you and she were dating?"

"Not that bad, but she does have a temper." He led her toward the bar. "I think we need another drink after that."

"Agreed."

She sipped a gin and tonic, enjoying Ray's arm around her waist and his lips close to her ear. She looked around the room. "Oh, listen, they're playing jazz. Ray, you promised!"

They left their drinks on the bar and glided onto the dance floor. The band launched into "In the Mood," a new song by the American Glenn Miller, and the guests went so wild, the band was forced to repeat it twice. Renata gyrated, Ray flipped her over and under, a little risky on the crowded floor, but they managed with no broken bones.

Afterwards, a server rushed gin, tonic, and water to the exhausted musicians.

"Let's go out for some fresh air, shall we?" suggested Ray.

Renata, panting, fanned herself. "Good idea. Where to?"

Outside was cool and quiet after the sweaty intensity of the hall. Ray led her to the waterfront, the most scenic part of town and one of their favorite places. Fishing vessels tethered to the dock bobbed and swayed. Beyond lay military vessels at anchor. The reflection of the moon on the water, scattered into bright jewels, danced on the waves sloshing under the jetty. Seaweed floated near their feet, where a seal was nosing around for fish.

Renata inhaled the salt air and put her hand on Ray's shoulder, elated at the opportunity Isabella had handed her. He pulled her close. His lips brushed her head. A moment later, they were wrapped in each other's arms, steamy kisses complementing the mist rising from the water.

Ray ran his hands up and down her back, cupped her buttocks, then massaged her slowly, up to her neck.

Her heart was pounding. She unfastened the brass buttons of his uniform and slipped her hands inside, easing the jacket off his shoulders.

He took a moment to fold and place it on the pier, then helped her sit down. They dangled their legs above the water, where spray sifted over them with each wave. The seal swam over to inspect them, then rolled onto its side and slid beneath the surface.

"It was a nice wedding, wasn't it?" Renata leaned back, arms propping her; she turned her face to him. He kissed her once more, a lush kiss, his tongue probing hers, one hand cradling her face.

"It was a nice wedding because you were there," he

murmured, dropping moist kisses all over her face. His hand traveled down her neck, traced a muscle to her collarbone, then to her throat, then slowly, slowly, down to her breast.

She inhaled sharply. It felt so delicious. She arched into him, wanted more.

He fondled her breast through her clothing, bringing her nipple erect, and leaned in to nibble on her ear.

Her breathing grew faster. She felt moisture between her legs.

"You're taking advantage of me, you demon," she complained, unconvincingly.

"I know," he whispered, easing down the zipper at her back. He pulled the dress off her shoulders, and unhooked her bra, far more than he had dared with her before. "And you love it. I dare you to disagree. By the way, I love your breasts."

He caressed them, squeezing the nipples, sending urgent messages to other parts of her body. She closed her eyes, moaning softly. He leaned over her and took one breast in his mouth while massaging the other.

The noise of a passing car distracted them.

"Ray, we can't do this here. What if someone comes?" Yet she allowed him, wanted him to continue. His other hand reached for her thighs, and slid slowly upwards.

A sudden Klaxon in the street startled them apart.

"You're right, I'm so sorry. Here, let's get your dress on. Turn around." He stopped.

She heard a sharp intake of breath when he saw her back.

"What the hell happened to you, Renata?" His fingers traced the fading scars.

She turned, and saw horror in his eyes. "A Nazi police officer whipped me for painting decadent art."

"Holy shit." He looked dazed. "Does it hurt?"

"It was agony at the time, but it doesn't hurt any longer. You see why we got out of Germany."

He pulled her to him, zipped her dress, then wrapped his jacket around her shoulders.

"You're safe with me. And respectable again."

She laughed nervously, aware of the distended front of his

pants.

"Let's go somewhere. I'm tired of being respectable."

"You took the words out of my mouth."

"Your apartment?"

The officers' quarters were deserted. Inside Ray's suite, they undressed each other slowly. Ray kissed each newly exposed piece of skin, even her scarred back, which he touched tenderly, running a finger along each scar, then kissed it.

She undid his belt and zipper. He stepped out of his pants, sloughed off the shirt.

When her dress was on the floor, he unhooked her bra and slid it off her shoulders. Suddenly they were naked, skin on skin, mouth on mouth. He carried her to the bed and lay beside her, stroking her body, kissing her everywhere. She loved the firmness of his muscles, the clutch of hair on his chest, his tanned skin, but she was nervous at what was to come.

"I'm a virgin, Ray. Please be gentle with me."

"Don't worry. I want you to remember this night with pleasure, not pain."

She panted, hoping it would not hurt too much, as he touched her most intimate places in ways that set her on fire. A groan escaped her lips.

Ray reached for a condom from his bedside table, rolled it on, then continued to explore every part of her body.

When at last he pushed inside her, she cried out in pain, then delight, and fell back on the pillows, gasping with exhaustion. She smiled at him. "Thank you. Now I won't die a virgin."

He laughed.

Renata reached for his cigarettes and gave him one. They lit up and lay propped on the pillows. Ray folded one arm behind his head.

"You seemed to enjoy that." He gave her a salacious grin. "Not bad for your first time."

"You weren't exactly miserable, either." She exhaled, watching tendrils of smoke curl above her head.

"I thought I fooled you."

She punched him lightly on the arm, before he extinguished the cigarettes and cuddled into her, spoon-style. They slept.

Ray banged the shrilling alarm clock. Five hundred hours.

He shook her shoulder. "I gotta go to work, honey. Rise and shine."

Renata rolled over and pulled the pillow over her head. "No, it's too soon, can't we sleep some more?"

He lifted the pillow and tickled her. She shrieked, jumped up, and swatted him. They crowded into the tiny shower together, scrubbing each other, tempted to try sex.

"Okay, okay, enough," said Ray. "The thought of being late for the Vice-Admiral's briefing is too terrifying to contemplate." He jumped out and dressed.

"Must be bad if it's worse than wasting that." She gestured at his erection.

He slapped her bottom and she yelped.

"Want some breakfast? I have to be at work in an hour," he said as he buttoned his uniform.

Renata nodded. She toweled her hair and put on last night's rumpled clothing. She was elated, excited, feeling better than she had since…Hans came to mind. She and Hans had only kissed, and as a new non-virgin, she realized what they had missed. She pushed the thought away, and hummed a little tune while pouring a cup of coffee.

Renata and Ray ate toast and eggs, drank another cup of coffee, and planned the day.

Ray worked until six.

"Why don't you come to my apartment after work, Ray? My parents would love to see you, and Mama enjoys having another man to cook for." She swallowed the last of her coffee and put down the mug. "I have to be at the market sketching soon, but I'll clean up here so you're not late."

"You're a sweetheart, thanks." Ray gave her a swift kiss after finishing his coffee. "I'll be there around eighteen thirty hours."

After a day of sketching and a little painting, with Dusty her steady companion, she returned home to find Ray already there.

He was in civvies, finishing a minor repair to the balcony railing with her father. A year ago, her father would never have asked for help.

"What's for dinner? It smells marvelous, Mama. And here's my money for today."

Lea accepted the cash, put it in a jar on a shelf, and returned to stir a sizzling frypan. "Ray brought cod and scallions. The man is a marvel."

"He's not too bad." Renata gave him a hug and a brief kiss, then greeted her father. "I hope you had a useful day, Papa."

"Very much so, thanks to this young man. He has plenty of news on the war, and we have time to talk over a smoke."

"The war, always the war," grumbled Lea, stirring the scallions.

The men chuckled as they put away their tools and washed their hands in the kitchen sink.

Ray beckoned Renata close.

"What is it?" she whispered. "Is something wrong?"

"No, silly girl. I just want a proper kiss, not one of those weak, preacher's wife excuses." He tilted his face toward her.

"All right, then, here you are!" She planted a long, powerful kiss on his lips, then released him, coloring when she saw her parents watching.

"Much better." Ray draped his arm over her shoulders.

Once they were seated, Lea ladled a magnificent fish stew into bowls.

"Renata, get the bread, please, and Karl, do we have more wine?" Lea's voice verged on sharpness.

She was jealous, Renata realized with dismay, as she set a fresh loaf on the table.

Papa served the wine while Mama returned the pan of stew to the counter, wiped her hands on her apron, and seated herself.

Papa chanted a blessing. Renata, stealing a sidelong glance

at Ray, saw he bowed his head respectfully.

"Please, eat," urged Mama, taking up a knife to slice thick slabs of bread for everyone.

"Mmm, this is delicious, Mrs. Lowenthal," said Ray.

As they ate, Karl addressed his daughter. "How did your painting go today, my dear?"

"Very well, Papa. I finished one today, just a few touches added. Now it's drying, so I'll start another tomorrow. I sold half a dozen sketches, too."

"Do you have any plans for tonight?"

Renata glanced at Ray.

He responded with a grin. "I thought we'd go see that new motion picture with Charlie Chaplin, *The Great Dictator*. I hope it's as funny as I've heard."

"Me, too." She and Ray also might take advantage of the dark theater to create their own bit of romance.

"Best we see it before I ship out in two days." His voice was casual, but his words dropped a blanket of tension over the group.

Renata tried to hide her shock.

"We won't be gone long." Ray smiled, but no one was buying his cheer.

"I hope not," Renata commented with false levity.

Once the stew was finished, Lea served a strudel and Karl poured the wine, but Ray's news put a damper on the conversation.

Renata gathered up the empty bowls and took them to the kitchen. She and her mother washed dishes, while the men sat on the balcony, smoking and talking.

Renata watched them through the door. Did she love Ray? She wasn't sure. The men would soon be gone, and her opportunity lost. Perhaps she should marry him, and live in Canada. The thought of living well again, was nearly as arousing as sex, and her mother would be satisfied with a Jewish son-in-law. She wiped a plate, then a chipped wineglass. Lea talked nonstop, but Renata barely listened. She kept glancing at the men. They were comfortable with each other and that was a big plus. Mama, difficult as she was to please, seemed quite smitten by him. What more could she ask?

Chapter Sixteen

Changes, 1940

It was December. The men had been in and out on convoys to Malta, and had waged a massive battle at Taranto in Italy, where the *Illustrious* and her colleagues destroyed the Italian fleet at anchor. The victory raised everyone's spirits after a disheartening year.

Ray spent all the time he could with Renata, much of it in bed.

Her period was late. They had been casual about the use of condoms, which she intentionally had not pressed. He'd mentioned long ago that he expected to have a family someday, but now she regretted their focus on sex, and the dearth of serious conversation. She still wasn't sure she loved him. But in wartime, liking him was enough; it had to be, and it would get her what she wanted, provided he took the news like a gentleman. If he proved not to be a gentleman, she was in deep trouble.

She went through her improved wardrobe and selected a suit he liked—a navy blue jacket with a peplum and slim skirt. She added a cream blouse and a coat against the winter chill. Winding her hair into the fashionable coils the film stars wore, she mulled over the situation she had created. A glance in the mirror, a quick application of some rouge and lipstick, and she was ready.

"Goodbye, Mama and Papa! Ray's ship is in and we're meeting for lunch," she called as she headed out the door, wanting to avoid conversation. Surely, if she could see Renata's eyes, her mother would read her secret.

She enjoyed the cool salt air and sunshine on her face on the walk to the Corniche. It was possible to forget there was a war here, provided she avoided looking at the bombed-out section to the east. She ordered coffee and a newspaper, determined to appear confident despite her nerves. Italians were in Egypt at Sidi Barrani—practically next door—and editorials begged for an offensive. She pursed her lips and turned to the arts section, now decimated along with so many buildings. Poor old Pécard, she mused. His living gutted. Hers, too. Regardless of today's outcome, she would somehow support her child and parents, but could she manage the shame she would experience if Ray rejected her?

"Hello, darling. Have you been here long?" He bent over and kissed her cheek.

She wound her arms around him, and kissed his willing mouth.

He grinned. "Can't complain about that welcome."

"I hope not. Just enough time to read my latest reviews. It seems I'm still doing quite well in the art world." She grimaced. "I wish. At least I can still sell postcards."

A waiter took Ray's order of coffee and scones.

"Brave girl. You do amaze me." He reached for her hand and they laced fingers.

"I'm not sure you would manage with someone who did not amaze you."

The waiter returned with coffee, scones, and marmalade. Renata split a scone, spooned marmalade onto it, and took a bite. "These are marvelous!"

Ray did the same. "This is one food the Brits get right." He sipped his coffee. "You had something to tell me. Nothing bad, I hope."

She put her scone on the plate and glanced away, her smile gone.

"Renata, what is it? Are you ill?"

Taking a deep breath, she took his hand. "No, I'm not ill, but something has happened that will change us one way or another."

He puckered his eyebrows.

Renata continued, her voice shaking. "You know that sometimes when we had...relations ..." she lowered her voice and swallowed. "We didn't always use protection." She looked at him, pleading with him to understand.

His eyes widened. "Hell, you're in a family way."

She covered her eyes and, despite intentions not to do so, began to weep. "I'm so sorry. I never intended for this to happen." She even believed it at that moment.

Scones and coffee forgotten, Ray drummed his fingers on the table, lit a cigarette and inhaled deeply. His mouth was a tight line. "How long have you known?" He blew out a torrid cloud of smoke.

"I suspected two weeks ago but now I'm certain. I've missed my monthly twice." She looked at her hands. "What are we going to do?"

"I'm not sure what YOU are going to do, but I'm leaving right now." His voice chilled her. He tossed coins on the table and left her in a puddle of tears and cold coffee.

The waiter brought two napkins and slid them beside her elbow.

"No rush, Miss. Just take your time." He scooped up the money.

She lit a cigarette with guilty, shaking hands. She closed her eyes, inhaled, then slowly exhaled the bluish smoke. Again. Again. Again. The waves, the skirl of the seagulls, the vapid chitchat from other tables, slowly calmed her.

She stubbed out the cigarette, and headed to Sofia's. She would explode if she didn't tell her best friend.

"Renata! Come on in, I'm making a cup of tea. Join me, won't you?" Sofia's zest bubbled over Renata's misery.

The women sat at the table with tea and biscuits between them. Renata noted changes Sofia had made since her marriage: wall decorations, fresh paint. It looked like the home of a married couple. She sighed and stirred sugar into her tea.

Sofia took a mouthful of tea. "Now, love, what's up? You don't look yourself today. Have you and Ray had a spat?"

Renata nodded. "You might say that. I'm going to have a baby."

"A baby! That's fantastic! Congratulations!" Sofia jumped up to hug Renata, then stopped. She put both hands on her friend's shoulders. "Oh, no. He's not happy about it?"

"Not at all. But it's a baby, and it's ours, so we must look after it, mustn't we?"

"Of course, you must, and you'll be wonderful parents. Not every child comes when the parents want." She paused. "I was conceived before my parents married."

Renata stared at her. "You were? Were they happy about it?"

"Not at first, but they knew they had to get married. They told me it was quite the scene when they told my grandparents. Grandfather wanted to beat Papa!"

"Oh, dear!"

"But when they told them they wanted to get married, it all worked out. And here I am." She spread her hands and grinned.

Renata leaned her chin on her hands. "Ray is furious. I hope he talks it over with his friends. Hamish, do you think?"

"I doubt it. He knows what Hamish would tell him."

"I don't know his Navy friends well. I'll give him a week to ask me to marry him. If he doesn't, I'll tell my parents and his CO. Then we'll see some fireworks."

"Renata." Sofia's voice softened. "Do you want to force him to marry you? Do you think that kind of marriage can be a happy one? You need to think further ahead than the birth of your baby, dear."

Renata pushed back her chair and walked to the kitchen window, shoulders tense. "I am, I am! You know what people will think of me, a mother with no husband. A fallen woman! And my baby a bastard all his life. No man will marry me if I have an illegitimate child, and how am I ever to get out of Egypt without a husband?"

Sofia hugged her, patted her back, murmured soothing sounds.

Renata clung to Sofia's ample shoulder until her shaking ceased. "Thank you. No one else knows but you. Please, can you not tell Hamish until I get things sorted with Ray?"

"Of course, our secret. Anytime you need to talk, come over."

"I will. And you're right, Sofia. I can't force him, but by God, I want him!" She realized it was true as soon as she spoke.

"Things will work out, dear. You'll see."

Focusing her energy on painting, each day Renata finished one canvas, sketched another, and polished off five postcards. To hide her morning nausea from her mother, she left the apartment early, and returned at dinnertime, sufficiently exhausted that her parents expressed concern about her health. If they noticed Ray's absence the past ten days, they said nothing.

Paints and brushes put away, works-in-progress covered, she headed home in the fading light, no longer able to thrust away thoughts of the baby, Ray, and her self-induced vulnerability. She would have to tell her parents.

She trudged upstairs and opened the door, then froze.

Ray was there with her parents, a sheepish smile on his face.

Her heart pounding, cheeks hot, she stepped tentatively into the room. "Ray!"

He walked slowly toward her, arms outstretched. "Come here, Renata."

She needed no further encouragement. Dropping her bag on the floor, she ran and wrapped her arms around his neck.

He lifted her and twirled her around, as he buried his head beside hers and whispered. "I'm sorry I was such a blighter. Can you forgive me?"

For an answer, she kissed him, oblivious to her parents' presence.

He lowered her to the floor, kept one arm around her, and together they faced Lea and Karl.

"Doctor and Mrs. Lowenthal, I'd like permission to marry your daughter."

Renata gasped. Her parents stood, mouths open.

"You have our permission," said Karl slowly, "provided she wishes to marry you. Do you, Renata?"

"Yes, Papa, yes, yes, yes!"

Ray held her tightly.

"Then it is settled," said Karl. "Lea, do we have brandy?"

Lea produced brandy and four glasses, which she filled with

a trembling hand.

Karl distributed them and cleared his throat. "To our beloved daughter, Renata, and our future son-in-law, Ray. We wish you health and happiness, wealth and wisdom, for many years. Congratulations."

He raised his glass and the others followed suit. Everyone hugged everyone else.

"Dinner will be ready in a few minutes, Ray, if you can join us." Lea fanned herself. "You have taken us by surprise, but a good surprise."

"Thank you. I accept."

Dinner of schnitzel, noodles, and soup was a cheerful affair, absent discussion of the war. Ray and Renata resisted attempts to draw them into a discussion of their wedding plans.

"We need to discuss the plans ourselves, if you don't mind," said Ray. "We haven't had time to do that yet, and the Navy has a claim on my time."

"Let's go out for a walk, Ray." Renata gathered empty plates and returned them to the kitchen. "After I do the dishes, I'll be ready."

Fifteen minutes later, they were walking hand in hand. Although Renata was buoyant, she was nagged by uncertainty about Ray, his decision, and how she should behave. She opted for humility.

"Ray, I was so frightened." She lowered her eyes. "Thank you."

He squeezed her hand. "I had no one to talk to, until I remembered the Navy rabbi, Rabbi Wiseman. He set me straight in a minute and told me to do my duty. I thought of my niece whom I have never seen. And my father taught me to treat women with respect, and be an honorable husband to the woman who would bear my children someday. I just never thought someday would come so soon."

Renata winced.

Ray chuckled. "Then I thought about you and me. We've had a great time together, and you are a smart woman. I think we can have the kind of life I want."

"Lots of men would walk away."

"Not if they have a Navy career they care about, they

wouldn't. And it was mostly my fault anyway. I'm over being upset, so let's just plan our wedding, shall we?"

She had been holding her breath. She exhaled slowly. "It must be soon. I'll be showing in another four weeks."

"Uh-huh. And I will be sent away on orders. I hope you don't want a big, fancy wedding."

She shrugged away the lifetime dream. "A small wedding is fine, but it must be a Jewish ceremony. I'll talk to Sofia's rabbi, and maybe we can marry at the same synagogue."

His eyes lit up. "Brilliant! Is two weeks enough time?"

"We'll manage. But you must know, Mama will be upset when she knows about the baby."

"Must you tell her?"

"She'll know the instant we tell her the wedding date."

"Then I'll speak with my captain tomorrow and see about the marriage license. We'll have the wedding on a Monday or Tuesday."

"Where will we live after the wedding, dear?" She tried the endearment, tasting it like sweet chocolate.

They stopped and faced each other, holding hands, unconsciously imitating the marriage ceremony to come.

"I'll apply for married quarters. It won't be fancy, but it will be ours."

Renata and Ray were joined in marriage on December seventeenth, 1940, by Rabbi Mizan, with Sofia and Chester standing up for them. Chester and Hamish signed the wedding contract, the *ketubah*, and Renata was also permitted to sign. Ray was in full dress uniform, except for a *yarmulke*, worn with his officer's permission. Renata wore a blue two-piece mauve dress with cutouts in the sleeves and skirt, and a hat to match. She circled Ray seven times under the *huppah*, with her parents on either side of her.

Magnificent ancient prayers, the vows, the rings, the broken glass…Renata had not appreciated until this moment, the splendor and depth of the wedding ceremony. And finally, the kiss. She was Mrs. Raymond Stern.

The guests cheered. The rabbi congratulated them and disappeared into the back of the synagogue. Chester had a bottle of champagne from a black marketer and Sofia brought baklava. All the guests toasted the bride and groom, then returned to work.

Clutching their marriage certificate, Ray took his wife's arm as they walked outside.

"I'm treating us to a taxi." He flagged down a vehicle and ushered her inside. They snuggled in the backseat and shared smiles, but remained bashfully silent until they were outside the married quarters.

He scooped Renata into his arms and carried her over the threshold of their new home.

"We only have a couple of hours, and that's the captain giving me a break on our wedding day. Everyone's doing double duty with those thousands of POWs. Even though I'm in the Navy, we still have to do our share."

"Then let's make the most of it." She tugged him toward the bedroom, slipping off shoes and unbuttoning her jacket along the way.

Ray grinned. "What my wife wants, my wife shall have."

They scattered clothing around the room, and in two minutes were making love with such noisy abandon that a neighbor pounded on the wall.

Mortified, Renata sat up and pulled the bedclothes around her. "I had no idea people could hear us. That's embarrassing."

He laughed and reached for her. "I'll bet she was jealous. Come here."

But she pulled away, the mood broken. "You have to get back to work. Any idea when you'll be home?"

His face fell, along with his arms. "Probably late tonight. You don't need to wait up if you're tired."

"I'll be up. It's our wedding night, after all."

Ray washed quickly and put on his uniform. Renata, wrapped in a towel, kissed him good-bye.

She looked at the gold band on her finger—on her left hand, unlike the German tradition of the right hand—then around the little apartment. It had a bedroom, a bathroom, and a kitchen including a small refrigerator. Inside were five bottles of beer, a moldy piece of cheese, and some oranges. A trip to the market was her first priority, and after that, she needed clothing from home. She searched through cupboards and drawers, and found money in his underwear drawer, noting that he kept his things in meticulous order. She left the marriage certificate on top of the bureau and grabbed her purse. After shopping, she headed to see her parents.

When she opened the door to her parents' house, she heard sobbing. Her mother. The sobs were different somehow, terrible, anguished. Her father had his arms around her, which seldom happened.

"What happened? Mama, why are you crying?" But Lea only shook her head.

Karl spoke for her. "It's Aunt Adele. She and her chauffeur committed suicide."

Renata screamed and collapsed onto the sofa.

"No, no, not Aunt Adele!"

They held each other, sobbing, until they ran out of tears. Finally, Renata felt able to read the letter.

> *Dear Tante Lea and Onkel Karl,*
>
> *I hope you and Cousin Renata are staying safe and healthy. I regret to bring you bad news, but things here get worse every day for Jews.*
>
> *A dreadful thing happened just this week. The Gestapo broke into Mother's house and stole the paintings she's had for generations. It broke her heart so badly she could not face another day, so she took her own life with cyanide. Her chauffeur took his own, too. They died in her automobile. She was dressed in her best, all her jewelry and furs. They're gone now, of course, stolen. We didn't dare have a proper funeral for her. I'm beyond heartbroken and cry all the time.*
>
> *We never hear from the men taken to the camps. There's no way to know if they are still alive. We struggle to find enough food. Our businesses are closed, our children banned from school, and the Reichstag speech a year ago,*

doubtless you heard about it, used the word Extermination.
I wish, wish, wish we had listened to you and left then! Now
all we can do is try to find food and keep hidden. The world
has gone completely mad. I may take my life, too, if it gets
much worse. Please, talk to the soldiers near you, tell them
this story. This is what they are fighting for.
    Much love to you all.
    Your niece,
    Ruth

The terrible letter burned Renata's hands. "She should have come with us. We could have saved her, saved them. It's our fault they died! We should have insisted." Renata paced the room like a caged panther. "Can we not help them, Papa? There must be something we can do."

"Our survival is the best we can do, I'm afraid." He and Lea stared at the wall.

"May I take this letter to show my friends? At least we can do as Ruth asked."

He handed it to her.

She packed her clothing into one large suitcase. Her father insisted on paying for a taxi. She felt guilty at such extravagance, knowing how her relatives were suffering.

Back at the apartment, she put her clothes away, then spent the afternoon reading and re-reading the letter. Although she and Hans had foreseen relentless persecution of Jews, the crushing despair in her cousin's letter was beyond Renata's worst nightmares. Touching her belly, she thought of the new life inside. A new Jewish life. Funny, she didn't feel that religious, but she felt protective of her Jewish baby-to-be, and determined to raise the baby as a Jew, and keep him or her safe.

Sighing, she put the letter aside.

It was satisfying to fill empty cupboards with food she could prepare. For dinner were latkes, string beans, and fish.

Ray arrived, waving papers.

"We're shipping out in three weeks, honey. Another Malta convoy." He pushed his cap back on his head. "I knew this was coming, but I hoped we'd have a few months together at least.

Come here."

He wrapped his arms around his wife of eight hours, who buried her head in his shoulder and stifled the fear that lay in the middle of her chest. She was a Navy wife now. She forced a smile.

"We'll make the most of those weeks, then, won't we? Don't worry, I'll be fine. Why don't you change, and I'll make dinner."

Over the meal, Renata shared Ruth's grim letter. "This is why we're fighting, Ray. There's a reason. It's not a few big poo-bahs fighting for land, like the Great War. This is pure evil."

He read it silently. "Whew! I never knew things were that bad." He glanced at her. "I'll tell all my men. The other officers, too. I'm glad your parents let you show me."

"Thank you, my love. Do you realize you are saving one Jewish family?" She smiled and touched the back of his hand.

"I hadn't thought of it that way, but you're right. The baby, too." He kissed her fingertips.

As Ray peeled the orange Renata handed him for dessert, he commented casually, "I didn't realize your family was wealthy."

"It didn't seem worth mentioning, since the way things are going, there'll be nothing left at the end of the war."

"I suppose you're right, but I hope not." He folded his napkin, then showed her a stack of papers he had brought home.

"Renata, you need these papers. How to apply for a passport, how to access my pay when I am away, and what happens if I am caught, injured, or killed."

Fear clogged her throat, but she listened carefully.

When he was finished, she sat on his lap, arms around his neck.

He nuzzled her neck. "I'll let you organize it, then."

"There's something else we need to talk about."

He furrowed his brow. "I think we've covered everything."

She rolled her eyes. "Everything except the baby, silly. What if he or she is born while you're away? I'm sure my parents will help, and I'll use the base doctor, but is there a special name you'd like for our child?"

Ray pursed his lips. "It seems such a long way off. Let me think it over, and I'll tell you if something comes to me."

"All right. After the dishes are done, would you like to repeat this afternoon's performance? Minus the noise and the neighbor?" She traced her fingers along his shoulders and smiled.

"Hmm. If I help you, the dishes will be finished faster."

The night before the departure, they saw Sofia and Hamish, Chester and his new date, Rachel. After dinner, with hugs, handshakes, and a few tears, they separated, conscious it could be their last time together.

Back in their apartment, Renata and Ray made love again, with the quiet desperation of the soon-to-be parted.

It was black outside at oh-three-forty-five when he left, duffel bags and kit in hand.

"Write to me, won't you, darling?" she said, kissing him one last time.

Chapter Seventeen

Time Apart, 1941-1942

January 10, 1941
My Dearest Wife,

    I am uninjured. Please don't worry. I'm taking as much care of myself and my men as possible.
    I hope you and our little one, are doing well. How are you feeling? No more sickness, I hope. Stay with your parents as much as you want while I'm away. Please give my greetings to them.
       All my love,
       Ray

Renata folded the letter and tucked it into the pocket of her dress, annoyed with the censors for blacking out what had happened. At least, as he said, he was not injured. She missed him more than she had imagined possible. The apartment was lifeless without his cockeyed grin and his arms around her.

As she stood, she felt a faint fluttering in her womb. The baby! She sat down suddenly, wondering for the first time what the tiny stranger inside her would look like. What he or she would smell like, feel like. A new emotion overwhelmed her: love. She knew, without a doubt, at that moment, that she would willingly give her life for her baby.

Excited, she picked up her handbag and rushed out of the apartment, dirty dishes forgotten.

Lea dabbed her eyes and patted her daughter's slightly swollen tummy, then brought out a quiche and insisted Renata eat a slice. "You're eating for two now, you know."

"I don't want to turn into a blimp, Mama." But she ate dutifully.

She wiped crumbs from her mouth and took her mother's hand. "Mama, can I ask you something? When I felt the baby move, I fell in love. I mean a head-over-heels, crazy love." She lowered her eyes. "Could that be how you felt about Solomon?"

Sadness passed across Lea's face, but when she looked up, she smiled through glittery eyes.

"Oh, yes. And, even though you must have thought for years that I did not love you, I feel that way for you, too. Now you understand." She drew Renata to her and the two generations united, finally, in their motherhood, stood in a long embrace.

> *January 30, 1941*
>
> *Dear Ray,*
>
> *I felt the baby move for the first time yesterday! I'm not sick anymore, and you can see roundness in my belly. I am sewing maternity clothes and will wear them proudly. And if anything threatened us, I would take on a wolf with my bare hands to protect our baby.*
>
> *My British passport arrived. I feel much safer, with a country to call mine.*

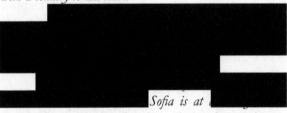

> *Sofia is at tending the wounded, but I see her each time she is on leave.*
>
> *Mama and Papa send their best wishes. We are praying for your safety. Write soon.*
>
> *Love,*

Your wife, Renata

February 16, 1941
Dear Renata,
  You'll be seeing me soon, but the ▮▮▮▮▮▮▮ ▮▮▮▮▮▮▮▮▮▮▮▮▮▮▮▮▮▮▮▮ A few days at most.
  The ▮▮▮▮▮▮▮▮▮▮ did a great job in the desert, didn't they? Chin up, we'll see more victories the longer this goes on.
  Love,
  Ray

March 10, 1941
Dearest Ray,
  How I miss you! The week together was heavenly, but now I am praying for your safety.
  Papa is not well. It is his heart, and there is nothing to be done but avoid exertion. It hurts to see him getting weaker. I tell him he must see his grandchild, hoping that will give him the strength to carry on.
  The baby and I are doing fine. Wasn't it fun to see my growing tummy? I'm beginning to waddle, Sofia says, although she's expecting too, and can hardly criticize. She's retired from nursing, so we spend time together whenever we can.
  I'm still painting but my legs hurt when I stand for long. Papa will make me an easel I can use while sitting, which should help. The Gallérie canceled all art shows for the foreseeable future, so although I'll miss the income, I have time to finish new paintings before the baby comes.
  ▮▮▮▮▮▮▮▮▮▮▮▮▮▮▮▮▮▮▮▮▮▮▮▮▮▮▮▮
  Stay safe, my love.
  Renata

April 22nd, 1941

Dear Renata,

Thinking of you all the time, and I'm adjusting to the idea of having a little one. I certainly don't want him (or her) to grow up in a world like this. The sooner it is over, the better, but we have a long way to go yet.

It's impossible to keep track of all the battles, but I'm sure you heard of ▮▮▮▮▮▮▮▮▮▮▮

▮▮▮▮▮▮▮▮▮ *The Admiral gave a stirring speech, saying, "Navy must not let the Army down." We* ▮▮▮▮▮▮ ▮▮▮▮▮▮▮▮▮▮ *whenever we can.*

Pray for us all.

Ray

June 1st, 1941
Office of the Admiralty
Dear Mrs. Stern:
This is to notify you that your husband has been promoted to Commander and re-mustered to the Canadian Navy. His pay packet will reflect the promotion. He is now enroute to London and will work for the Canadians there. You may write to him at this address:
Cmdr. Ray Stern RCN
FOB 86229
Canadian Naval
Headquarters, London,
England

Sincerely,
The Secretary of the Navy

Sofia insisted on coffee at Pâtisserie Délices and collected Renata at ten o'clock. The two women giggled at their ballooning figures.

Renata ordered tea and a crumpet. "What's the news with Hamish?" She stirred milk into the tea and took a sip.

"He can't really tell us anything. Frustrating, even though I understand why."

"Ray's letters are so blacked out by the censors, I'm going crazy worrying about him."

"I'm worried sick about Hamish, too. What if something happens to him?"

"Come on, girl, it's only war." Renata covered her friend's hand with her own. "We don't know if we'll have tomorrow. One day at a time, love, one day at a time."

"I suppose you're right." Sofia sipped her coffee. She put down the cup and started crying. "I just have this feeling that something terrible is going to happen."

Renata moved around the table to hug her friend, but their bellies got in the way and they ended up giggling.

Finally, Sofia sat down again. "We didn't solve anything, but you made me feel better. Are you painting today?"

"Yes, I'm heading to the studio. Same time tomorrow?"

"Absolutely."

Restless, Renata stayed that night at the apartment. Her legs were swollen from standing most of the day, so she laid on the sofa with her feet up. Turpentine fumes had given her a headache. A nap would help.

A few hours later she was awakened by a monster in her gut. Her belly had tightened into a hard lump the size of a medicine ball. It didn't hurt, exactly, but it took her breath away until it subsided. She barely had time to take a few normal breaths and get a glass of water, when the tightness came upon her again, twice as strong. Holding the counter, she barely managed to avoid falling. And this time, it hurt.

She staggered into the hallway to the telephone. Her father answered.

"Papa, the baby's coming."

"Get a taxi to the hospital and we'll meet you there."

The taxi driver gaped wide-eyed at his hugely pregnant passenger, obviously in labor.

Gasping, Renata maneuvered her bulk into the backseat with the bag she'd packed weeks ago. "Just go. I'm fine."

He crammed the gearshift into first, and the taxi leaped forward, hitting every pothole, rock, and rut on the way. Renata gritted her teeth as wave after wave of pain clutched her.

The driver screeched into the emergency entrance and held out his hand for the fare. Her father, bless him, ran up, paid the driver, and helped her into a wheelchair.

Nurses flocked around her like anxious pigeons, cooing and clucking, and Renata lost all sense of time and location. Her world narrowed to her body, determined to expel the foreign creature it had sheltered for nine months. Nothing else mattered. Hours passed.

"Papa, I need to go to the bathroom."

"Nurse, in here! She has to push!"

The internal exams had become routine. The nurse peeled off her rubber gloves and smiled.

"You're ready, dear. We'll take you into the delivery room now, but your parents must wait outside."

Intense lights and green walls were all she remembered. She had to push, over and over, with only short breaks in between powerful contractions. The doctor urged her on. A nurse mopped her sweat-soaked face.

Finally, someone announced they could see the head. It happened quickly after that. A huge push and the head was out. A second push and the baby slithered out of her onto a waiting blanket.

"A little boy, Mrs. Stern. Congratulations."

A nurse cleaned him and then laid him in her arms. She smiled, thinking that she'd loved him before, when he was smaller than an apple, but now, seeing her firstborn child, she loved him even more. She unwrapped the little mite. His eyes, indigo blue, sought hers. His tiny hands flailed in curious arcs, but gripped her finger tightly when she touched them. Her baby! She had given birth to a new human being. Cradling his head, she kissed the downy hair, felt the perfection of his shell-like ears. His rosebud lips turned to her hand when she stroked his cheek.

The nurse standing beside her, smiled. "Your first, Mrs. Stern?"

Renata, speechless with wonder, could only nod.

"That's his rooting reflex, looking for a nipple. You'll want to be nursing him straightaway. Here, let me show you how."

With practiced efficiency, the nurse brought the baby's mouth to Renata's nipple.

Renata gasped as he latched on and began to suckle. He was strong!

The nurse showed Renata how to use a pillow to support the baby, how to unlatch his glue-like grip, and how to switch sides. "Only a few minutes each side today, then. You'll increase just a little each day. Your milk will come in in a few days. By then you should be almost an expert!"

Renata had not expected the cramps that came with nursing.

"That's nature's way of helping you get your figure back, dear," said the nurse. "It will last a week or so. Let me take you to your parents."

Two orderlies wheeled her to a ward, where Karl and Lea greeted their first grandson with tears of joy. Lea crooned to the baby and rocked him. Karl brought out his seldom-used camera and took a photograph

Renata watched them, overwhelmed with the responsibility the baby brought. Her family was growing.

"Papa, we need to send a telegram to Ray. Tell him about the naming at the Bris. Mama, would you let Sofia know when you get home?"

"Of course, darling." Mama kissed her, and Papa handed the baby to the nurse, who bundled him off to the nursery.

She ushered the grandparents out, and dimmed the light. "Sleep now, Mrs. Stern. We'll look after him until the morning."

But Renata was already asleep.

July 18th, 1941

Dear Ray,

    You are a father! Your son was born on July sixteenth, and he's the image of you. We'll have the Bris, on July twenty-fourth. I'll send a photo and his name, as soon as I can. I'm madly in love with him.

    Love,

    Renata

August 15, 1941

Renata,

    The baby, such good news. I'll watch for the photo. I am terribly busy with the ███████████ *They think I know what I'm doing, so they throw new assignments at me as though I'm a dart board. I will send letters whenever I can.*

    Love,

    Ray

September 22, 1941

Dearest Ray,

    Our little one is growing fast. I named him Thomas Karl, and he is well healed from the circumcision now. He guzzles down my milk so quickly and my breasts are monstrous. Too bad you're not here in person to see them. (Naughty smile.) Tommy has begun to smile, and his laugh is a wonderful sound. Here's his photo.

    Stay safe.

    Love,

    Renata

November 30, 1941

Dear Renata,

    Thank you for the photo of our little boy. He is a good-looking lad, isn't he? I must say, having a child changes one's perspective. Children are completely dependent on their parents and so vulnerable in this war.

    I'm ▓▓▓▓▓▓▓▓▓▓▓▓▓▓▓▓▓ *Not easy when you know some* ▓▓▓▓▓▓▓▓▓▓▓▓▓▓▓▓▓▓ *but Hitler's days are numbered, believe me.*

    As always,

    Ray

A telegram arrived December fifteenth.

    CMDR R STERN INJURED DEC 1 STOP IN CDN HOSPITAL WATFORD LONDON STOP REQUESTS NO VISITS FULL STOP

December 16, 1941

Dear Ray,

    I received a telegram that you're injured and I'm going out of my mind with worry. What happened? Will they discharge you? I desperately want to see you.

    The ▓▓▓▓▓▓▓▓▓▓▓▓▓▓▓▓▓▓▓▓▓ *all over, but at least you weren't in them. Hamish is in hospital with an arm missing. Sofia visits every day. I forgot to tell you they have a little girl named Margaret.*

    Thank God, the Americans are in now.

    Tommy sends a baby kiss. I send wife kisses. You and he are the two most important people in my world.

    Love,

    Renata

Chapter Eighteen

Changes, 1942

Balancing the baby on one hip, Renata swirled her cup and swallowed the last of her coffee.

"Mama, would you mind watching Tommy for a couple of hours, so I can get some work done on my painting?"

"No, of course I don't mind." Lea reached for the baby with a smile. He went to her, flailing his legs in excitement.

How her mother had changed since Tommy's birth. Renata could not quite believe it, but with her newfound comprehension of motherly love, it made sense. Mama had let go of Solomon, now that she had a new little boy on whom to lavish her affections, which was also a huge help for Renata.

Her father was finally practicing medicine under the table to make ends meet, but each day he came home, his complexion was worse.

He sagged into a chair, short of breath from climbing the stairs, as Renata was preparing to leave.

Lea was upset and alarmed. "Karl, you can't work yourself to death like this. Renata is working again, so would you please stop?"

"Please don't tell me what I must do. I am still the head of this family." His words were firm, but his voice was weak.

Renata put an arm around his shoulder, which grew bonier by the week. "Papa, Mama will look after Tommy, so I can paint. Don't worry, I'll soon be making as much as I was before he was born."

"You are a mother now. You shouldn't be working."

She knelt beside his chair. "The world has changed, Papa dearest. I'm working because I must. Your value is in far more than whatever money you can earn. Let it be." She kissed the top of his head and decided to drop in at Sofia's on her way to the studio.

Sofia hadn't combed her hair and the sink was full of dirty dishes. The smell of unwashed nappies wafted from the bathroom, and Margaret was wailing in her crib.

"Sofia, what's wrong? I've never seen your place like this. I'll get Margaret and make us a cup of tea." Renata scooped up the baby, one sniff telling her why the child was crying. Once she had a clean nappy, the baby was all smiles for Auntie Renata.

When the tea and crackers were on the table, Sofia started talking.

"I don't know if I can go on, Renata. This is harder than anyone told me it would be." She wrung a well-used handkerchief and wiped her cheeks. "Since Hamish was injured, he's a different person. He can't stand Margaret crying, so he left for a walk. What am I supposed to do? I have two children now, not one."

She took a bite of biscuit and washed it down with tea.

Renata bounced Margaret on her knee and dangled her keys for the child. "I'm so sorry, Sofia. Will he be able to go back to work? In an office job?"

"The doctors say yes, but not yet. His stump needs to heal, but between you and me, that's not his biggest injury."

"What do you mean?"

"He has nightmares, and is afraid of loud noises. Hamish never had a temper before. He was the sweetest, most patient person I've ever met. The doctors call it 'shell shock.'"

Renata's thoughts went to Ray, who had not answered her letter of months ago. She would ask her father about shell shock.

"I can't solve Hamish's problems, Sofia, but I will do your dishes and watch Megs, so you can have a bath. Go on, right now."

Sofia's pale smile was all the thanks she needed.

Once she was bathed and dressed in clean clothes, Sofia

took Margaret from Renata and gave her a warm hug. "Thanks. Now I can face the day."

"You can come over to the studio or to my parents' anytime, if you need a bit of space. Ask Hamish's doctor about his behavior. Surely there is something they can do."

"I hope so." She shifted the baby to her other hip. "Have you heard anything from Ray?"

Renata sighed and shook her head. "I don't know what else to do. I've sent him letters every week since I got the telegram, but nothing. All I can do is carry on and hope to hear from him soon."

Sofia put an arm around Renata. "I'm sure you will. Stay strong, dear, and if you need me, just call."

Thanking her friend, Renata slipped out the door.

It was later than planned when she arrived at the studio. Her newest painting reflected her experience of motherhood—a murky, powerful image of an Egyptian mother carrying her infant away from firebombed buildings, the look on her face angry and determined.

Once she added the finishing touches, Renata swirled her paintbrush in the bottle of turpentine, wiped her fingers on a rag, then hung her paint-spattered smock on a hook. She took a critical look at the canvas, which she intended to put into her next show, whenever that might be. It would do. Next, she created seven scenic postcards, which she'd ask Rachel to sell for her, along with others she'd created last week.

Time to go home. Her engorged breasts needed Tommy. She hummed a tune along the way.

At her parents' apartment, Renata dropped her bag on a chair near the door, and spied Tommy with her mother. "Tommy, come see Mommy!"

The child crawled toward her with saliva running down his chin, and a fifty-kilowatt smile on his chubby face. He gurgled and cooed with delight.

Renata swept him into her arms and planted kisses on his tummy. He squealed and flapped his legs.

"Shall we play peekaboo?" Renata hid behind her hands in

the timeless baby's game.

Tommy giggled every time she reappeared, until it was time to nurse him.

She put the baby to her breast and felt her milk let down. She relaxed. Nothing could spoil this most intimate duty of motherhood. She closed her eyes, thinking of how her life had changed in a year.

Her father arrived, his eyes warm at the sight of the drowsy child, milk dribbling from the corner of his mouth. Renata laid Tommy in his arms, then kissed her father on his cheek.

"Renata, there's a letter here for you," Lea said, indicating the plate near the door. "I'll take the baby, if you like."

"No need, Mama, Papa has him now."

She disappeared into the bedroom and slit open the envelope. It was from Ray, at last.

> *January 3, 1942*
> *Dear Renata,*
>
> *Sorry I haven't written sooner. I've been going through treatments for burns, and progress is slow. It's my face. I'm horribly disfigured. I cannot bear to look at myself in a mirror or I vomit from the monster I have become. You and Tommy would scream at the sight of me. Under the circumstances, I cannot expect you to spend five minutes, let alone the rest of your life with me. Terminating the marriage seems the kindest thing to do. I know you will find another man worthy of your love. I will have a lawyer draw up divorce papers for you to sign, and of course, you will retain custody of our son.*
>
> *I'm so sorry. You are the best thing that ever happened to me.*
> *Sincerely,*
> *Ray*

"Mama? Papa? She stumbled from the bedroom in shock, and dropped the letter in her father's lap. He scanned it and handed it to his wife. She read it, and sat down as if pushed into the chair.

The trio regarded one another in silence.

"Oh, dear," whispered Lea.

"Poor bastard," added Karl, who never swore. "Burns are the worst, and the scarring can be horrific. I've seen people with ears and noses burned off...."

"Stop it, Papa!" Renata squeezed her eyes shut, trying to block out the image. "But he has a wife and child. He can't just throw us away!"

She paused, remembering her conversation with Sofia. "Papa, Sofia said Hamish is acting oddly, too. She thinks it may be shell shock. Have you heard of it? Could it be affecting Ray, too?"

"Possibly. If he has shell shock, he won't be making good decisions."

"What can be done for him?"

Karl twisted his mouth and shook his head. "We don't know much about treating the mental problems of soldiers. After the Great War, men were afraid of noise, had terrible nightmares, some became violent. There were suicides, too."

"If I can find him, speak to him, do you think I can convince him that he's making a terrible mistake?"

Lea shifted in her chair. "Renata, if he is as disfigured as he says, you need to consider that maybe he's right."

"What?"

"If it's as bad as he says, you could never go anywhere without people staring. You would have few friends. He would have a terrible time getting work again. Is that the life you want?"

Renata sat back in her chair, feeling slightly ill. Could she look at him without wincing? What about sex? She could not shake off the macabre thought.

Lea put Tommy to bed, and made tea.

Renata took a cup and headed to her bedroom. The hot beverage calmed her a little.

In just four years, she had escaped almost certain death in Germany, and achieved a brief rebirth of her artistic career, now stalled by the war. She'd held onto the hope of Hans in the face of impossible barriers, then let him go—mostly—when she married Ray. And now she had a child who would never see his father, if she signed the promised divorce papers. A marriage that had barely started. And a handsome husband who was now, in his own words, a monster.

Remembering the delight of their lovemaking, she wondered if Mama had a point, ashamed as she was to admit it. Could she look at her injured husband without flinching? Could she bear to have him touch her? Would kissing even be possible?

She stared out the window at clothes drying on the opposite balcony.

All she had were Ray, Tommy, and her parents. Ray, alone and devastatingly injured in a hospital, thousands of miles away. *Oh Ray, I can't believe you look as horrible as you think you do. I want Tommy to know his father. All we have in this world is each other. We are a family, aren't we?* Her eyes swam with tears.

But tears would not solve her problem. She wiped her face before returning to the living room. She had to start somewhere.

"Papa, do you have any writing paper?"

Mama said, "Renata, are you sure? Remember what I said."

"I remember, Mama. Papa, the paper?"

He found some in a drawer and handed it to her.

She unscrewed the top of the fountain pen and began.

March 18, 1942

Dearest Ray,

 Thank you, my love, for writing. The letter just arrived today. You have no idea what a relief it was to get anything from you, bad as the news was. But I don't care if your face is burned. You are the father of my child, my husband. We are a family. I don't know how, but I'm going to London. Once I see you, maybe you'll believe we can still make a future together.

 All my love, from your faithful wife,

 Renata

After blotting the letter and addressing the envelope, she ran to the post office to catch the last collection of the day.

Part II: The Search

Chapter Nineteen

Renata put the telegram and the letter from Ray in her purse, collected her hat and gloves, and headed to the Navy base, which was crawling with Allied personnel from six or seven countries. She arrived at the Cecil Hotel.

Armed patrolmen at the gate asked her name and business, an increase in security since her last visit. She handed them her passport and marriage certificate.

"Which way to the personnel office?"

One patrolman raised the barrier, the other returned her papers.

"Ma'am," he said, touching his cap, "past those two buildings, then left."

With a nod and a tight smile, Renata passed them. In the distance, she saw stevedores working with Allied sailors to haul boxes, load trucks, and move equipment into some unfathomable order. She picked her way across the road to Personnel. Inside was a young ensign in spotless whites, his black hair visible below his cap. His face was scabbed where he'd cut himself shaving.

"Good morning, Miss, how may I help you?"

"It's Ma'am, thank you." Renata drew her mouth into a line. "My name is Mrs. Stern, and my husband is Commander Ray Stern. I must find out where he is."

"Is he not receiving his mail?"

"May I speak with your commander? This is rather personal."

"The Commander is a very busy man. I'll need more information, so fill out this card and I'll see what I can do." He passed her a pencil and a pre-printed card. She started to fill it out, but by the fourth line, she was simmering.

"Why in hell do you need to know my birthdate? Get me the Commander, right now!" She threw the pencil down and glared at him.

The ensign, little experienced with feisty women, tried again.

"Uh uh uh, well Ma'am, I'm s-s-so sorry, that's just the rule. If you want to see the Commander, we n-n-need to know why."

"I TOLD you why, you little vermin! I need to find my husband!" Renata slammed her hand on the counter and glared at the unfortunate, daring him to defy her.

"One moment, let me see if he is available." He darted down the hallway, and returned minutes later.

"Please follow me, Mrs. Stern." He opened the gate and led her through.

Renata allowed herself a tiny smile of satisfaction and nodded. She tucked her handbag under her arm and followed him, her heels tapping on the marble floor. The ensign opened a door, ushered her in, then closed it with a soft click.

Around fifty, with a rugged, weathered face and splotchy nose suggesting too much rum, the Commander was smoking a cigarette—into his second pack of the day, Renata guessed from the overflowing ashtray and the nicotine stains on his fingers. His office was lined with wooden file cabinets. On the desk behind a nameplate were a telephone and a stack of folders. In the center sat a single file folder, closed, and a pen, perfectly aligned.

"Mrs. Stern, I am Commander Deschanels." He pointed to the chair. "Sit down, please." He leaned back, stroked his large gray mustache, and appraised her with icy blue eyes. "Now, how may I assist you?"

Renata sat and crossed her legs. She removed her gloves while collecting her thoughts. How to explain so she didn't sound as desperate as she felt?

"Commander, thank you for taking time to see me," she began. "I can see you are terribly busy."

The Commander's mouth twitched; he gave a brusque nod and sucked on his cigarette.

"My husband is hospitalized in London and I need to reach him."

"Mrs. Stern, this is wartime." He spewed smoke sideways and spoke with a patience reserved for small children and imbeciles. "Travel for family reunions, even with an injured serviceman, is strongly discouraged." Deschanels shifted his weight in a squeaky oak chair and flipped a pen back and forth between two fingers.

Renata took a deep breath.

"My husband has been badly burned, and says he doesn't want me or our son anymore. I must see him." Her nails dug into sweaty palms.

His eyebrows rose half an inch. "Do you have the letter?"

Renata handed it across. He read it and frowned.

"What is his name, rank, and division?"

"Commander Ray Stern. He was re-mustered to the Canadian Navy and is working in London."

Deschanels punched a button on his intercom. "Ensign, here, now!"

Seconds later, the ensign entered and snapped to attention. "Yessir."

Deschanels gave him Stern's information, with instructions to bring his file, and be quick about it.

He turned back to Renata. "There is probably nothing I can do. Your husband isn't the first man to think his wife won't want him once he's a cripple."

Renata was shocked. This happened to other women, too?

"How long have you and Commander Stern been married?"

"A year and a half. We have a baby, Tommy." Renata's voice shook.

Deschanel appraised her, stubbed out his cigarette, reached for another and lit it. He muttered to himself, "Now where is that damned ensign?"

The ensign reappeared with a tea tray and a folder. He placed both on the commander's desk, poured tea, then plopped two sugar cubes into a dainty china cup with Naval insignia, and handed it to his senior officer.

While Deschanels held his teacup with one hand and flipped open the file with the other, he glanced at the hovering ensign.

"Hell, Ensign, pour some for the lady, too." He returned to the file, scanned the contents, then looked up.

Renata accepted tea from the shame-faced ensign and smiled at him beatifically.

"He sailed on the *Illustrious* in the fall of 1940, which I assume you know."

Renata nodded.

"After the Battle of Taranto, *Illustrious* headed to England. Stern's logistics work has been exceptional, based on these notes. I don't have any more information since he left this theatre, but there's no way for a civilian to get to London, unless you have some clout with the Admiralty. Do you?"

"No." Renata was crestfallen. "What about one of the merchant ships? Surely there are some passengers. I won't be any bother, and my baby is quiet."

Deschanels leaned his elbows on the desk and clasped his hands together, cigarette between his fingers. "Mrs. Stern, allow me to paint the picture for you. The Merchant Navy is shipping armaments, food, and supplies to the various theatres as quickly as it can. The return ships have raw goods, food, and fuel for Britain. Civilians must be approved, their travel necessary for the war effort. We haven't had a woman aboard for six months now. A child, not since war was declared, and for each convoy, we are losing anywhere from twenty to eighty percent of the ships to Jerry."

Renata gulped. "What about an aeroplane?"

"Impossible, I'm afraid. Those are few and far between, for high-level politicians on Top Secret missions. It's very risky, at any rate. The Sahara Desert is an active war zone with no roads and extreme weather. Quite impassable. I'm sorry."

He closed Ray's file and stood, hand extended, the interview at an end.

Renata shook his hand and left, discouraged.

Pondering her dilemma, she meandered through town. Although the Merchant Navy seemed out of the question, perhaps one could be persuaded somehow. At a café, she ordered an espresso and sat to think. The heat of the sun and the hot drink calmed her a little. London. And travel with a baby, in wartime. Was it the right thing to do? How could she take Tommy? Alternatively, how could she possibly leave him behind? But how could she not go to Ray?

A ship around the Cape was the only possibility she could think of, but how she would find one to take her, she did not know. It was time to talk to Sofia.

Hamish answered her knock.

"Come in, Renata. Sofia's not here, though. She went to the market for a few things and should be back in a quarter of an hour. Would ye like some coffee?"

Trying not to look at the empty sleeve on his left side, Renata nodded her thanks when he placed a mug of coffee in front of her, then excused himself to get Margaret.

He returned with his curly-headed daughter in his arm. "Any news from our Ray lately?" Margaret grabbed at his beard. "These wee ones, much as we love them, they do try your patience, don't they?"

She smiled and nodded, noticing his shaking fingers. There was tension in his voice that had nothing to do with Margaret. "I received a letter from Ray, and as long as Sofia is out, I wonder if I could ask you a few questions."

She handed it to him.

"Aye, lass." He read the letter quickly.

Renata saw a cloud pass over his face.

"Whew! And I thought I was hard done by! Poor man. What are ye planning to do, then?"

"That's just it, Hamish. First, I don't know if he's burned as badly as he says. Second, he's never seen his son. And third, is it possible that he's not thinking straight because of his injury?"

Hamish drew his mouth into a straight line and looked out the window.

"Ah, Renata. Ye've no idea what battle does to a man." His eyes glittered. He smiled at the baby, his mouth a tight line, and bounced her on his knee. "I can't describe it to someone who's nae been there, but normal life, like my bairn here, seems like a dream, while fire and death and blood are the only reality." He paused. "I'm fair certain Ray is going through the same thing. I've put Sofia through plenty of worrying, too, but she's a bonnie wife, so bloody patient."

Renata reached out her hand and touched his shoulder. "Hamish, she loves you so much. Thank you for telling me." She hesitated, but had to ask her next question. "Were you worried that she wouldn't love you with an arm gone?"

A look of anguish crossed his face.

"Aye, I was, that. She's told me a thousand times she loves me just as much. At first, I didn't believe her, but now I'm beginning to."

"My mother said I would cringe every time I saw Ray's burned face. I almost believe her. I don't know what to do."

"Now lassie, don't you go believing that. He loves you and he needs you. Do you love him?"

Before she could reply, the door opened, and Sofia walked in carrying two heavy shopping bags. She took in Hamish and Sofia sitting at the table, and Margaret on her father's knee.

"Renata! If I'd known, I would have put off my shopping trip."

The women hugged. "Is Hamish being a charming host?"

"Of course, but Margaret wins the prize for cutest. Anyway, I need to go."

"What's the rush? Come, sit down again. Hamish, I bought a tin of biscuits, if you'll put a few on a plate for us."

Tea and biscuits later, Sofia read Ray's letter, her hand over her mouth.

"The poor man. But poor you, too, what a dreadful letter. What are you going to do?"

"I want to go to London, to convince him we can still be married, but the problem is finding a way. The Navy turned me down, and the Merchant Navy isn't allowed to take passengers not needed for the war effort, and especially not children. It's dangerous. Sofia, would you leave Margaret to travel to London if Hamish was hospitalized there?"

Sofia shook her head slowly. "I have no idea. No one should have to decide between their husband and their child." She turned to

Hamish. "Thank God you are here."

"And thank the good Lord you are, too, or I dinna ken what would become of me." Hamish hugged her with his remaining arm.

"My mother will look after him, but what if I'm gone for a long time? A year? Tommy won't know me when he sees me again." Despair spread like a cold fog in her lungs.

Sofia gripped Renata's shoulders. "Now, you listen to me. This is wartime. The usual rules don't apply. If you love your husband, you move heaven and earth to keep your family together."

Yes. Her family. Her husband and child. Renata's uncertainty dissolved. She did love Ray. Only the faded memory of Hans had prevented her from acknowledging it. Lowering her head onto Sofia's shoulder, she could only whisper, "Thank you."

Chapter Twenty

The Merchant Marine, March 1942

Two days later, after purchasing mangoes and oranges at the market, Renata walked to the civilian docks, a part of town with a scurrilous reputation. The military dock was a model of organization and cleanliness compared to the utter bedlam before her. Squalling camels and bleating donkeys protested their loads. Small Egyptian and darker Abyssinian men swarmed like ants, shouting in their native languages, although she heard English curses.

Renata picked her way through dung, straw, and cargo bins bursting with cotton bales. Warehouses, a hodgepodge of wood and concrete, lined the wharves, their corrugated iron roofs too rusty to reflect sunshine. Furtive glances and lewd grins followed her. One man licked his lips. She averted her eyes, disgusted.

A lopsided sign hanging on a door proclaimed, "Shipping Offices: Maracanth Steamships."

Renata smoothed the front of her skirt and pushed the door open.

Assailed by the odor of stale tobacco and urine, she covered her nose. No one was around, but a window with a bell and a handwritten sign said in Arabic, English, and French: "Ring bell for superintendent." Renata tapped the bell. Nothing happened, so she hit it again with more force and sat on a bench to wait.

Ten minutes ticked by. She smashed her hand down on the bell, the noise reverberating around the small room. She heard scuffling.

A man appeared holding a clipboard. He was short and

wiry, with a full black beard and well-worn Egyptian native dress. He looked at Renata. His jaw dropped, as did the clipboard, which hit the concrete floor with a clatter. He raced back to wherever he had come, chattering loudly in what Renata assumed was Arabic. Several urgent voices mingled, and the volume sank to a more normal level. A door swung open and a white man appeared. His clothes were cleaner than the other man's, but a long way from the spotless uniforms of the Navy officers. Tall and handsome, his leathery skin lined from years in the sun, he pushed a smudged maritime cap high on his forehead. A lock of curly hair sprung loose over his left eye, and a stubby pencil sat over one ear.

"Well, Miss, whatcha doin' here? Are ya lost?" He winked at her and grinned.

Hearing his American accent, Renata's eyes widened.

"I'm looking for passage to England," she said, holding her chin up.

"Zat so? Huh, well, not sure we can help you, kiddo. The military takes all our space, for people and cargo." He retrieved the pencil from behind his ear and tapped it on the counter.

"I can pay." As soon as she said it, she realized it was not true. She thought of Mama's sapphire-and-diamond set that Papa had hidden somewhere. *Did she dare ask him?*

"Sorry, lady, no can do. You can't afford what I'd hafta charge you. I gotta get back to work. You go on home. Go on, get outta here before one of these savages gets the wrong idea." He turned to leave.

Renata grabbed the back of his jacket. "No! Don't go! My husband is badly injured. Please..." Heat suffused her face.

The man turned back, his eyes narrow. "The Navy is your best source of help, honey. Something else going on, problems in paradise, that sort of thing?"

Renata clenched her fists and moved closer. "You get me and my baby on a ship and I'll make it worth your while," she growled through gritted teeth, not sure what she was offering.

He appraised her thoughtfully, the hint of a grin twitching the corner of his mouth. "Lemme talk to the captain of a ship I have in mind. Come back tomorrow afternoon and I'll have more info. But no baby. We ain't takin' a baby along."

She frowned. "I'm not going without my baby!"

He shrugged and turned to leave, whistling a tune.

She leaned over the counter, her voice raised. "Tell me how much!"

There was no response.

She pounded continuously on the bell for a good twelve minutes until the Egyptian showed up and handed her a piece of paper, which read:

£100, you only. If the Captain agrees. See me tomorrow if you're still interested.

A hundred pounds! He may as well have asked for ten thousand. She was shaking, furious with herself as well as that smarmy, good-for-nothing creep.

The Egyptian disappeared again. Just as she turned the door handle, she heard the office door open.

"Hey, now, don't leave with hard feelings, darlin'. Just a business proposition."

She poked him in the chest. "You don't give a damn about anything but your precious money. I'm sorry I bothered." Her hand was on the door knob.

He grabbed her wrist. She writhed and pulled, her chest heaving, but his grip was tight. His other hand wandered over her body from neck to thigh and he brought his mouth to her ear.

"I can get you a place, sugar, but no kid. Take it or leave it." His tongue slipped in her ear, then he released her and left, slamming the office door behind him.

"Damn!" she slammed her fist on the wall. She steamed out of the ramshackle building and scorched a trail home, rubbing her wrist.

Eyes down, the bag of fruit hanging over her shoulder, she nearly bumped into her mother wheeling Tommy in his pram.

"Here, Mama, I'll take Tommy. I bought some fruit." She handed the shopping bag to her, and took over pushing the pram. The simple activity helped slow her breathing.

"How did it go at the dockyard today?"

"The place is disgusting. I met a man who said he could possibly get me on a boat, but there's no way he will take Tommy. I'm to return tomorrow to find out details." She chewed the inside of her mouth, thinking of the nonexistent funds she would need.

"You'd leave Tommy behind? How could you even consider it? I assumed you'd take him with you."

"Of course, I want to, Mama! I don't know if I can. I don't know what other choice I have if I want to win Ray back." She gritted her teeth, pushing the pram up the slight incline.

She glanced at her mother who had paled slightly. Renata hoped she was thinking of what it took to leave behind a living child, let alone a dead one. "If you have a better idea, I'd love to hear it."

Lea stared into the distance. They walked a few hundred meters before she replied. "The only other option is to agree to Ray's terms, and that's very hard. I'd hate to have a divorce in the family. If you want him back, you must go. You need to be sure that's what you want, because this journey will be even more dangerous than the one we took to get here."

"That's pretty much what Sofia said, too. But Mama, I need to be sure you don't mind looking after Tommy. I may be gone for a year or more, there's no way to know. Please be honest with me, if it's too much."

"Whatever you decide, Renata. I'll look after him. You know he means a lot to me and he will be as safe here as anywhere. Assuming all goes well, eventually we can join you."

"I'll do my damnedest to make that happen."

Renata carried Tommy upstairs while Lea parked the pram in a small storage area.

"I got a chicken this afternoon, Renata," called Lea up the stairs. "Get it into a pot, and there are parsnips and herbs to add."

"I will, after I feed Tommy." Sitting on the divan, she smiled at the baby as he reached for her hair. That smile would launch a thousand ships, she thought, kissing the top of his head and loosening a breast for the child, who kicked his legs, panting at the sight of the nipple until she slipped it into his mouth. She could not imagine leaving him behind. But she loved Ray, too. Sofia and Hamish helped her see that. Despite his new appearance, she would find him and make a home for them.

Lea headed for the kitchen, making as much noise as possible with the pots.

"I'll be there in a few minutes, Mama. No need to be upset, I said I would make the dinner."

Tommy fed, Renata sat him on the floor with a pot and a spoon, which he banged enthusiastically. She reached for a cooking pot, expertly cut the chicken into pieces and added parsnips, onion, garlic, and salt. Minutes later, it was on the stove, simmering.

Whistling outside announced her father's arrival.

Renata greeted him with a beaming Tommy beside her, still beating a tattoo on the pot.

"How was your day, Papa? Did Frau Schneider have her baby yet?"

"It was a difficult birth, but the little girl is in her arms and all should be well." He gave Renata a light hug and peck on the cheek. "I feel guilty working without a license, but the medical care is so poor, and there are not enough doctors." He put his medical bag on the floor, hung his jacket on the hook by the door, and eased himself onto the sofa.

"And how are you, my daughter? Any closer to finding your husband?"

"Possibly. I have a lead on a passage to London on a merchant ship for me only."

"That's outstanding. When does it leave?"

"It's not definite. I return tomorrow to see if the captain will take me. It's not according to the rules, but, for enough money, one can do anything." She paused. "As you know, we have none. They told me the fare is one hundred pounds. I have no idea where we can find it."

Karl sighed and stared at the ceiling. "So, the black market works for shipping people too?"

"It seems so."

"We have one source of money left." He looked at her meaningfully.

Renata gasped. "But you wouldn't sell Mama's necklace, would you?" Even though it was exactly what she had been thinking.

Overhearing, Mama burst into tears. "No, Karl, for God's

sake! It's all I have left."

Karl bowed his head. "Renata and Tommy are all we have left, Lea. We have a son-in-law who needs our help. Can you deny him?"

Renata's throat prickled with guilt, as she watched resentment, sorrow, and finally, resignation, play out on her mother's face.

Lea whispered. "If you must, then. But if possible, keep the earrings."

"You are very brave, my dear. Thank you." Karl kissed her gently on the cheek.

Tommy was fussing. Lea picked him up and played a bouncy game with him on her knee until he was giggling. Renata checked the pot on the stove, relieved that the crisis was over.

"Dinner's ready. Please come sit down." She served the soup into matching bowls, a gift to her mother from one of her commissions, after listening to endless complaints about mismatched dishes.

How can I leave them? Renata wondered, gazing at her confused mother, her aging father, and her miraculous baby. *I should wait until the war is over, then find Ray and win him back.* But she knew if she did not try now, the marriage was lost.

She tried the soup, then gave Tommy a taste. It dribbled at the corners of his mouth, his face a study of concentration. Then he opened his mouth for more and everyone laughed as Renata obliged him.

Leaving Tommy would be the hardest thing she had ever done.

The American was ready for her when she arrived.

"Okay, honey, here's the scoop: The captain will take you for a hundred pounds—half now, half when you board." He shook his head and raised a palm as she began to object. "I know it's a lot, but you're a big risk to him and the ship. Also, he'll expect you to work on board. You'll only have a day's notice once he gets his sailing orders. Then, you just gotta get that pretty little backside here two hours ahead. Clear?"

"Where am I supposed to get that kind of money?"

He raised his eyebrows, crossed one ankle over the other and leaned back against the counter, picking at a fingernail. "Not my problem. Tomorrow, or no deal. And I want a show of real appreciation from you. You know what I mean, honey. A little ass will ensure you a spot."

She blanched. "Go to hell, you lecherous devil!"

"Feisty, too, ain't ya? Okay, gal," he raised his palms in concession. "Come on, shake on it."

After this, there was no turning back. Leaving her child and parents, heading deeper into the war with no idea when, or if, she would see Tommy or Ray again, was another crazy wartime decision. She took a deep breath, extended her hand and shook.

Over dinner, she broke the news to her parents.

"He doesn't know the day yet, but he's promised me. I have to pay him tomorrow."

"Do you know where the convoy is going?" Karl asked.

"London, I assume. I have to check daily at the dock, and I'll have one day's notice, so I'll keep a suitcase packed and ready."

"You're leaving me with the baby so soon?" asked Lea.

Renata's stomach tightened. "With all my heart, I don't want to, but I don't see any other way. Are you sure you don't mind?"

"I love him like my own, but you're still nursing him. Wait until he's weaned, at least. And what if you don't come back? I need papers that name Papa and me as his legal guardians."

Tears sprang to Renata's eyes. She looked out the window. But her mother was right. "The longer I wait, the worse my chances of finding Ray."

Tommy burst into tears for no apparent reason. Renata pulled him onto her lap and undid her dress. The family laughed at his instant excitement at the sight of his mother's breast. The tension broken, Lea picked up the dinner dishes and put them in the sink.

Karl remained beside his daughter. "You know, Renata, if you decide to stay, none of us would be unhappy. Especially this little one." He stroked Tommy's downy head. "Stay, if you want to." He pulled a handkerchief out of a pocket and dabbed her eyes. "It is your decision, and don't worry about the money, all right?"

She leaned her head on his shoulder. "Papa, dearest Papa, Ray is my family now as well, and I can't abandon him. But leaving Tommy is breaking my heart. Do you understand? Am I crazy?"

"No, my dear, you're not crazy. Often, we do things we don't want to do, but we hope we're doing them for good. This is like our escape from Munich. Many times, in Tolumbat, I thought I had made a terrible decision, but now, hearing what is happening to our relatives in Germany, I see it was right. This decision is like that. You can't see the outcome, but it is your destiny."

"Will you manage financially without my art? I'll share my wife's allowance with you for Tommy's care."

"We'll manage somehow. You need some for yourself, don't forget."

She shifted Tommy to the other breast. "When I need money, I will work in London. Papa, the more I think about it, the worse the idea seems, but I can't give up on Ray. Do you think Mama will..." She choked.

Karl put a hand on her shoulder. "She will be a good mother to him while you are gone. I think she is a mite jealous that you have a son and she does not, but there's no question she loves Tommy."

Renata leaned close to her father. Tommy, between them, burped and sighed contentedly.

"Thank you, Papa. I will miss all three of you so much. I love you."

"I love you, too."

Chapter Twenty-one

1942, Finally

Her decision made, it remained only for Renata to pack her suitcase and squeeze in as much time with Tommy as she could. She weaned him onto a bottle. A lawyer friend of Karl's wrote a statement of guardianship that she signed.

Into her suitcase went the warmest clothes she could find. News clips of English rationing reminded her to take scarce items: silk stockings, soap, tinned food. When she retrieved her diary from its hiding space under the bed, her fingers touched the bundle of unsent letters to Hans. She would keep the diary, but what should she do with the letters, wrapped in a scrap of pink ribbon? *Where was Hans? Did he still think of her?* She reminded herself that she was married to a husband who needed her. Hans was part of a life long gone, a dream, a childhood fantasy. Best she burn them.

She took them to the small incinerator outside used by everyone in the building. A sluggish fire was burning. She undid the ribbon and let the letters float into the flames one at a time. With surprise, she realized she was not terribly sad. Ray was her husband, her love, her future. She brushed ashes off her fingers and left.

For weeks, she made the daily walk to the dockyard. Her nerves were raw. The pandemonium was familiar; the odor of the office no longer made her gag; the wiry Egyptian was no longer surprised to see her.

"You come see boat ready? I get Mister Shipper for you, you wait here, he come back quick."

The shipper, whose name she had intentionally not learned, breezed into the waiting room with his arms wide, beaming. He tossed the stubborn locks off his face.

"Good news! You'll be sailing tomorrow on the *M.V. Georgic*, which is heading around the Cape to Southampton or Liverpool. You won't know which until the last couple of days. Are you ready? She sails at sixteen hundred hours. Come on, give me another hug, darlin', you'll be on your way soon!"

He wrapped Renata in a vice-like embrace, and ran his hands down her back to her buttocks, squeezing lightly. She struggled to escape, while excitement and terror churned in her belly. She felt nauseous.

"I'm going to be sick," she stammered. "Where's the bathroom?"

"Aw, shit, lady—oops, I mean, shoot, pardon my language—there's a bucket in our office. Not very nice for a lady, though."

Renata staggered outside and vomited into a corner. The shipper offered his dirty handkerchief. Lacking options, she wiped her mouth, then gave it back to him.

"Sorry." She gulped. The smell of dung and diesel fuel was not helping. "Tomorrow, by two o'clock, right? I'll bring you the money." A lump rose in her throat.

Renata raced home as quickly as traffic and her feet allowed. Her stomach felt better, but her tangled emotions were like a ball of yarn batted about by six kittens.

"Mama! Papa! Tomorrow's the day!" she shouted breathlessly. "I have to be there at two o'clock."

There was no answer. Panting, she threw the door open and glanced around. There was the suitcase, where she left it. Then she remembered her father had a patient. Her mother and Tommy had gone to the market.

Renata began dinner. This would be her last dinner with her family for a very long time. She wiped her eyes with the back of her hand while she chopped onion and eggplant.

Twenty minutes later, Lea returned with Tommy and a basket of bread, fruit, and some hard-to-find beef. She handed Tommy to Renata, and took the food to the kitchen.

"I'm leaving tomorrow, Mama," Renata said. She and her mother put the food away together. "The convoy leaves at four o'clock and I have to be there by two. I want this to be a nice dinner.

Anything special you want me to cook?"

Lea answered, "Yes, that pot roast, if you don't mind adding the carrots and onions."

Renata bounced Tommy on her hip. He was chewing on a spoon, his current favorite toy.

Lea put one hand on the counter. "So, this is really going to happen?"

"Yes." Renata heated the pot, added oil and the beef, turning it over to ensure all sides were browned, wondering how much detail to share. Her one-handed kitchen skills were superb.

Karl's footsteps dragged up the staircase.

Renata, anguished, would not hear that dear sound again for a long time. She handed Tommy to his grandmother, wiped her hands on her apron, and gave her father a bear hug, the instant he opened the door.

He returned the embrace, then held her at arms' length. "You have some news today?"

"Oh, Papa. I leave tomorrow." A wail escaped her, and she threw herself into his arms. "I must be out of my mind!"

He held her tightly for what seemed an eternity.

Lea called them to dinner.

Dinner was delicious, but Renata, holding Tommy on her lap, could barely eat. She struggled to stave off tears throughout the meal.

Lea tried to cheer her. "Try not to worry about us. You have prepared as much as possible. Tommy will be fine."

"Thanks, Mama." She squeezed her mother's hand. "It seems so unreal."

Papa leaned toward her. "I hope you are safe. We hear such terrible news about the U-boats."

"Good thing I know how to swim. Both of you, here's a deal: I won't worry about you if you won't worry about me."

They looked at one another, shook their heads, and began to chuckle at the ridiculousness of it all.

"All right, we're all allowed to worry. Just not too much." Renata managed one more piece of carrot. "I will write, I promise." She stood to clear the table.

Lea brought a bottle of wine and glasses. Soon they were

giggling and recounting memories of their time in Tolumbat. Lea changed Tommy's nappy and brought him to Renata, who kissed his cheek and sat beside her father again. They played with the tot, who had two teeth and was trying to climb on anything he could reach. Renata suspected he'd be talking before she saw him again. Impending loss permeated her, a sadness so profound that the light seemed dim, her vision unclear.

Chapter Twenty-Two

The M.V. Georgic, 1942

At two o'clock the next afternoon, Renata, her suitcase bumping her leg, followed the shipper to the quay.

As they passed each ship, Renata wondered if it was the one, but her companion strode on, dodging the ubiquitous ropes and dung, forcing her to hurry.

Past the fourth ship appeared a smaller vessel. Gray, like the others, but with a substantial coating of rust, dents along one side, and portholes so murky they may never have been cleaned. Two smokestacks spewed thin streams of black smoke. A faded red cross in a white circle took up most of the side, and a ramp angled up the side of the ship from the dock. The ship's name, *M.V. Georgic*, was barely discernible.

It looked to Renata like a passenger vessel. How fortunate it would be if there were other passengers to talk to.

"Have you heard of a Q ship?" asked the shipper.

"No. What's that?"

"It's a ship that looks like something it ain't. This one looks like a hospital ship, but she'll be carrying wheat, cotton, and guns."

"But why?" asked Renata, confused.

"Sweetheart, even Jerry isn't supposed to bomb hospital ships. This one will have a better chance of getting through. She has an important cargo, and she can defend herself if she's attacked. The last convoy lost most of their ships, so every gun counts."

"Oh." Renata's heart fluttered as she contemplated weeks on this rusty tub. "What if it sinks?"

"A ship is a 'her' not an 'it,' and get that right if you don't want to upset the Cap," warned the man. "If she sinks, you might survive, and you might not. Keep your clothes on when you sleep, in case there's a night attack, and always have your life jacket handy. Them U boats are constantly prowling for prey."

Renata swallowed. Her palms were sweaty. "I'm ready. Let's go."

"Not so fast, sweetheart. Money first." He extended his palm.

Renata dug in a pocket for the bills, the balance owed. She dropped it in his hands and he unfurled it, counted, then smiled.

"Good girl. I'll take you aboard."

She wrestled her suitcase up the ramp, the shipper behind her, in case she fell.

At the top, a skinny man in dirty civilian clothing took the suitcase and offered a rough hand to Renata as she stepped onto the ship.

"I'm done here, sweetheart. Good luck." With a tip of his cap, the shipper trotted down the ramp and out of sight.

She was strangely reluctant to see him go.

The skinny man turned without speaking and headed across the deck. Renata trotted to keep up with him.

Not a single surface of the ship was clean. Fine red dust covered everything. The decks were worn oak. Lifeboats hung in their racks, but their condition did not inspire confidence. The ship creaked as it rocked. Sailors rushed about, preparing for departure.

She had little time to observe, when the skinny man opened a door and gestured her inside.

"Watch your step, Ma'am. Lift your feet."

She stepped over the ledge into a dim interior smelling of tobacco and rum.

"Here she is, Cap'n." Skinny put the suitcase down and left, closing the door behind him.

As Renata's eyes adjusted to the light, the captain came into focus. He was seated at a tiny table, a glass of rum in one hand, a cigar clamped in his teeth. His dark beard and hair were neatly trimmed. He wore his worn uniform casually, jacket unbuttoned, no tie, his cap on the desk. His round belly strained against his belt. He looked at her with amusement, his blue eyes twinkling.

Renata swallowed.

The captain rose slowly, took the cigar out of his mouth and set it on the ashtray.

"So, here y'are," he drawled, in a voice so deep it sounded like the bottom of a mine. "I'm Captain Smith and you'll call me Captain at all times. Meals are at oh six hundred, twelve hundred, and eighteen hundred hours. Jimmy, who brought you in, will show you to your cabin and the mess hall. The head is just around the corner to the left. Daytime, you work with the kitchen crew; dinners you have with me in the officers' mess. You any good at cooking?"

Renata nodded, then found her tongue. "Yes, Captain, sir, I can cook."

"Good. Make yourself useful and you'll have no complaints. You'll find I'm an easy man to work for, provided you follow the rules. Break my rules, I come down hard. Clear?"

"Yes." Renata licked her lips.

"We sail in twenty minutes." He rang a bell, then approached her, swaying slightly.

She wondered how much rum he had drunk.

He reached for her hair, and ran his fingers through her curls.

Renata's heart beat wildly. This was not part of the deal.

"Pretty. Long time since I've had a pretty woman."

He belched, and the odor of rum and tobacco made Renata wrinkle her nose and turn her head.

The captain pressed her against the door and held her head with both hands, so their noses almost touched. "There's lots of time on a voyage. Time to get to know each other really well."

His smile sent chills down her spine.

"Jimmy will be here in a sec to take you to your cabin." He opened the cabin door and walked out, leaving Renata shaking. *Why did I do this? I should go home to my baby! I'm so stupid, stupid, stupid!*

But the ship shuddered to life, the engine pitch increased, the floors vibrated. It was too late.

Jimmy burst in.

"Okay, Mrs. Stern, follow me." He picked up her suitcase and headed down a corridor with several doors. She noticed railings on either side of the hallway, and narrow, rounded doors that ended six inches above the floor. She made a mental note to be careful of doorways.

"Right in here, Ma'am." Jimmy opened one of the doors into a tiny cabin, gestured for her to go ahead, then followed, and placed her suitcase on the bed. "Would you like to see the mess now? Or do you want to settle in?"

She opted to see the mess, to learn more about the *Georgic*'s layout. He dropped the cabin key into her hand.

"Right-o, then, this way. Once we get up to our convoy speed, you'll be glad of these railings. The Canal is a piece of cake, but the Indian Ocean can be rough. Might have a stop in Capetown. Shore-leave would be nice, but we've precious little of that these days. I'm hoping there's no torpedoes waiting for us in the Atlantic. Well, here we are. This here's the men's mess, where you'll eat breakfast and lunch. Tea and dinner in the officers' mess. Don't be surprised if you're alone there. If we're busy, the officers eat whenever they can."

"Am I the only passenger?"

"For this trip, yes. Usually we have up to ten, but with all the sinkings, not many want to try."

Renata shivered.

The mess was occupied by a dozen or so sailors huddled in a corner over plates of food.

"The officers' mess is just up here, if you'll come this way." Jimmy led her into a smaller, well-appointed room.

There were twelve seats around a large oak table that had some papers strewn on top. One wall was covered with officers' certificates; the other had a bookcase full of nautical books. Light streamed through a porthole.

"Thank you, Jimmy. Is there anything else I should know?"

He looked both ways before responding, *sotto voce*. "Captain's got a bit of a roving eye, if you catch my meaning. Keep your cabin door locked. If you need a hand, there's a bell pull in your cabin. I'll come when you call."

Her instincts were accurate, then. "Thank you, Jimmy, and let me know if there's anything I can do for you, will you? Post a letter, that sort of thing? I'm to be working in the galley, so if there's any special food, I'll keep some for you if I can."

He nodded, touched his stained cap, and disappeared.

She found her way back to her cabin, making a few wrong turns. From the outside deck, she saw the ship navigating the harbor entrance, which she had heard lacked a submarine net. The *Georgic*, belching black smoke and sounding its horn, inched past the breakwater. She looked behind and saw the rest of the convoy following.

There were no directional signs, but she identified the bridge, the captain's likely location. She tried another door that led into what was obviously intended to be a passenger lounge, but found sailors sitting on benches, surrounded by guns facing portholes. She noticed that the walls could be taken down to expose the guns. Some sailors whistled and leered. She glared at the offenders, then approached a quiet one.

"Can you tell me how to find the galley? I'm supposed to help cook."

He pointed toward a stairwell at the back, while some of the others laughed and shared knowing looks. "Downstairs, Miss, second door on the left."

Renata thanked him, turned to the others, and hissed, "Keep your eyes to yourselves, boys. None of you do a thing for me."

They watched her in startled silence.

The staircases were metal plate with raised bumps for traction. At least the staircase and hallway were clear of junk.

The smell of cooking led her to the right place on the second level. She knocked, but no one answered, so she opened the heavy door and stepped in.

The galley was compact and in decent condition. Pots and pans hung neatly on hooks suspended from the ceiling. The large grill was clean, and three enormous pots simmered on the gas stove. Shelving, fitted with railings and ridges to prevent things from falling, contained mugs, dishes, and cutlery. Even the counters had raised edges. A bucket stood in front of the oversized sink, and three tea towels hung from a drying rack on the side. Through a small open porthole, fresh sea air and sunlight streamed in. From the galley, she could see the mess hall Jimmy had shown her, now empty.

Renata took a tentative step. Whoever worked here cared about his workspace enough to keep it clean. She lifted a lid off one of the pots. Fish stew, and she was hungry, but did not dare try it without someone's permission. Eighteen hundred hours was two hours away.

Another door opened and the cook, she assumed, entered. He was of average height with curly brown hair, a bit of a beard, and thick glasses. He was about thirty years old and overweight, but then again, Renata had never met a cook who wasn't. He looked like the kid others beat up at school.

"Who the hell are you?" he growled.

"My name is Renata, and I'm traveling to England. The captain said I'm to help you in the kitchen. I hope that's all right with you, Mr....?" Renata smiled and offered her right hand.

He ignored her, turned to the pots, lifted a lid, and gave the soup a stir. Satisfied, he replaced the lid and turned to face her, arms crossed.

"Let me tell you something, lady. Cap'n has had more people like you on board this rusty bucket o' bolts than you can shake a stick at. I don't know your story and I don't wanna know it, and if the Cap says you must help me, I have to allow you here. But unless you are willing to work the way I want it done, it'll be best if you stay out of the way. You ever serve a meal for sixty guys?"

"No. I cooked for my family; that's me, my parents, my..." she hesitated to give personal information. "But I'm willing to learn and I work hard."

The cook looked at her, lips pursed. He leaned on the counter and squinted. "Right. Here's what I'll let you do: start peeling potatoes for dinner. I have thirty pounds that need peeling in an hour. Think you can handle that?"

Renata blanched. The task sounded difficult, but she was determined to show this arrogant man that she was up to the worst tasks he could throw at her. "Of course. And what shall I call you?"

"No one on this ship uses their real names, gal. Call me Soupy. The potatoes are in a storage locker outside that door. The bucket here's for peelings. When it's full, heave them over the side, through that porthole, there. Quarter the peeled potatoes and put them in this pot." He indicated another gigantic pot on a hook. "Here's a paring knife, and an apron."

She put on the apron and dragged the sack of potatoes into the galley. She pulled a stool from under the sink, gathered bucket, sack, and pot close to her, and went to work.

An hour later, her hands were raw, she had several nicks on her left hand, and she had emptied the bucket of peelings twice. Her back and buttocks hurt from sitting on the low stool. Her wrists and arms hurt; her shoulders hurt. She picked up another potato and peeled it. Then rinsed. Then quartered it and put it in the pot. Repeat. Repeat. Repeat. She never wanted to see another potato again.

Soupy bustled about, making biscuits and pastry for savory pies. Another sailor came in to set out the plates, bowls, and cutlery for the meal.

An increase in the engine's pitch indicated they were on the open Mediterranean, picking up speed. The rolling motion was more noticeable, but so far, her stomach did not object. Soupy, wiping his hands, inspected the peeled potatoes, then checked the sack to see how many were left. It was about a quarter full.

He shook his head slowly, then looked at a bedraggled Renata. "Well, Renata, you didn't finish all the potatoes, did you?"

She shook her head and lowered her eyes, missing Soupy's mischievous look.

"But actually, you're the best worker I've had, so congratulations, you and I are gonna be partners for this voyage! Good work!"

Renata looked up in surprise, and smiled slowly.

Soupy grinned at her. "We only need three-quarters of a sack for dinner, so you did the right amount." He winked. "You can quit peeling. Wash your hands and I'll give you something else to do."

"I really didn't think I could do any more." Renata felt like hugging him, but instead she went to the sink to clean potato juice and blood off her hands.

The next hour was hectic. Soupy showed her how to fill the pies, bake them, and store them in a large warming oven until the sailors arrived. She put out butter, made coffee and tea, wiped tables. She realized she was enjoying the fast pace and the tempting smells.

A bell sounded at eighteen hundred hours. Moments later, scores of feet clattered down the metal staircase and barged into the dining room with raucous greetings.

"Hey, Soupy! What's for dinner tonight? Got any of that pork and beans we love?"

Soupy waved at them through the opening between the galley and dining room. "Fish stew, lads, and savory pies, biscuits, boiled potatoes. How does that tickle your fancies?"

It was a cheerful jumble of sounds: dishes and cutlery jangling and the rough talk of sailors. They ate speedily, dumped their dishes in bins, and left. Just like a hurricane, Renata observed.

She helped Soupy clean up, and then slowly climbed the stairs to her cabin.

The bed was built into the wall, with sides that prevented the sleeper from rolling out. Every inch of space had a use: a hook for clothing, cupboards, a tiny fold-down table, drawers. Unpacking her things would be convenient, but if they encountered trouble, her suitcase must be ready to move, so she unpacked only the toiletries she needed daily. The waterproof oilcloth money belt under her clothing, she would not remove at all. The shipper had said to sleep in her clothes. Or was that Jimmy? No matter, she decided it was good advice. She found a Mae West life jacket under her bed within easy reach.

The "head," supposedly, was in the corridor, so she explored again, trying each door. Finally, one opened into a cramped space that was toilet and shower in one, with a drain in the center of the floor, a small shelf for toiletries, and toilet paper in a drawer. So much for long, luxurious showers. She washed her face and hands and brushed her teeth.

After pulling the blackout drape over her porthole, she flipped on the small reading light over the bed. There was nothing to do, no entertainment, no radio, no books. Tomorrow she would see if the ship had a library. For now, sleep beckoned.

When she awakened they were past the Suez Canal, into the Red Sea. She breakfasted in the mess hall. No one spoke to her, although there were catcalls and whistles. Soupy needed her assistance to prepare the noon meal of boiled eggs and Welsh rarebit, a slice of bread covered in cheddar cheese, broiled in the oven until the cheese bubbled and formed a thin crust.

"Nice work, Renata," he said as they cleaned up. "You're used to hard work, aren't you?"

She nodded. "Yes. But I must eat dinner with the officers tonight. I don't want to offend anyone."

"Yeah, you can help me with dinner prep, but not service. They eat the same food, it's just served on nice china."

Once dinner prep was done, Renata excused herself. In her cabin, she changed into a clean dress, but kept it modest with no jewelry or makeup. She was jittery, praying there were other officers there besides the captain, who made her skin crawl.

At seventeen fifty-six, she walked into the officers' mess, her head held high. Three men she had not met stood and introduced themselves: Lieutenant Jones, Chief Warrant Officer O'Leary, Sub-Lieutenant Marshall.

She shook their hands. "I'm Mrs. Stern. May I sit here?"

"Of course," said Jones, "More fellows are arriving shortly. We talk, smoke, and drink too much, but we don't bite."

She sat between Jones and Marshall.

Two more officers drifted in, talking incomprehensible Navy lingo. One sat on Renata's other side and the other across from him. No sooner were the men seated, when the captain walked in. The men stood to attention. He waved them to sit down but noticed Renata.

"At ease, men. Move over, and let me sit near our guest."

Before Marshall could move, Renata interrupted.

"No, thank you, Captain. Lieutenant Marshall was explaining his job to me, and it's quite fascinating." She smiled at Marshall, hoping he would play along.

The captain raised his eyebrows but said nothing.

Marshall launched into a detailed description of the maintenance required to keep the vessel running. Renata interjected what she hoped were intelligent questions, and the men joined in as the steward entered with steaming plates of food.

The captain, outmaneuvered for the moment, finally spoke over soup. "So, Miss Stern, is your room satisfactory? Jimmy taking good care of you? We missed you here yesterday."

"The room is fine, thank you, and Jimmy has been very kind. But it is *Mrs.* Stern, Captain." She peered at him to make her point. His eyes flickered, but he gave no other sign acknowledging the correction.

A few glances bounced around the room as the others watched the interplay. Renata forced herself to eat, but her stomach was in knots and her mouth was dry. The physical distance from the captain provided her with safety for the moment, but she knew her strong woman persona was no match for his physical strength, should he decide to use it.

"Gentlemen, I think *Mrs.* Stern is the most attractive passenger we've had in many months, don't you agree?" He looked around the table.

"Better-looking than us," mumbled Jones, his mouth full of pie.

Marshall added, "Since none of our passengers for months have been female, you are correct, Captain." He smiled and speared Welsh rarebit with his fork.

Renata's cheeks flushed. Her temper ran at a slow boil.

"I'm not sure why my appearance is of interest to you supposed gentlemen," she snapped. "I doubt you comment on your male passengers' appearance. I'm here because of a family emergency, and I'd appreciate it if you'd stop this kind of talk." She wiped her mouth with her napkin, rose, and stormed out, slamming the door behind her.

She remained in her cabin the rest of the evening, writing letters home, including little drawings for Tommy, and a letter to Ray and another for Sofia. As she prepared for bed, she heard a soft knock at her door.

"Who is it?"

"It's Captain Smith. I apologize for my boorish behavior at

dinnertime, and assure you it won't happen again."

"Thank you." There was a pause, no retreating footsteps. "Good night."

"I was wondering if I could make it up to you by offering you a glass of sherry in my cabin?"

"Kind of you to offer, but if you'll excuse me, I've had a very tiring day."

"Perhaps tomorrow, then?"

"I don't think so."

Finally, she heard him leave. She double-checked the lock on her door, then settled down to a restless sleep. She awakened twice, checked the lock on her door each time, and tried to sleep, despite her pounding heart.

The days blurred. She had only a vague idea where they were. Soon to round the Cape, she heard. Once they reached the dangerous Atlantic, the ships would be closer, making it easier for the escorts to patrol the perimeter. Every day, the captain plied her with compliments, offered drinks, asked her into his cabin. After polite rebuffs failed, she told him to leave her alone, and look for a woman in the next port.

Shortly after the turn north into the Atlantic, they sighted a German destroyer, which meant a U-boat was likely in the vicinity. The convoy escorts coordinated an attack, visible from the deck where Renata watched, her heart in her mouth. The enemy, damaged, retreated.

After the battle, she turned toward the galley and her afternoon chores. In the empty corridor, the captain's arms snaked around her and pulled her close.

"Get your hands off me!"

"Hey there, settle down, I just want to talk to you. Do you know how long it's been since I had a conversation with a woman?"

"I don't care! Let me go!"

He gripped her arms like a vise and tried to kiss her. She twisted her head away. Holding her wrists together, he clamped his other hand on her face. His mouth covered hers. The foul smell of his breath, and his tongue pushing down her throat made her gag. Screaming was impossible. She bit his tongue, hard, and tasted blood.

"You bitch!" He backhanded her across the face and redoubled his grip on her arms. "You do that again, you'll get hurt. And no one's around to hear you."

She aimed a kick at his knee but missed.

"Feisty, aren't you? I like a woman with spirit."

"You bastard, let go of me!" she hissed as the hand on her mouth slipped momentarily. His grip tightened as she struggled to get loose. He thrust her inside his cabin and locked the door, panting, his eyes reptilian, salacious.

She looked around for anything she could use to defend herself, but he had planned this well. The place was immaculate. She backed up to a wall, breathing hard, trying to think.

"You don't want to do this," she panted. "You know it's not right."

He lunged for her.

She dodged him.

He snagged her by the wrist, pinioned her arm behind her back with one hand, and with the other, tore her dress from top to hemline.

She screamed, hit him with her free hand, but he barely noticed.

He retrieved a piece of rope from under the bed.

"Leave me alone, you bastard!" she screeched, thrashing and kicking, her blows as useless as snowflakes against artillery. In twenty seconds, he bound and tied each hand to a corner of the bed. Despite her flailing, he ripped off her panties, and from somewhere produced another rope. She landed a strong kick on one shoulder, but he gripped her ankle and tied that leg down, then the other. She was spread-eagled on the bed, naked, helpless, and wailing. He struck her viciously across the face.

"Shut up!"

After dropping his pants, he thrust into her with all his strength, grunting like a pig.

The pain was excruciating. Renata screamed again and again, but as he had assured her, no one heard.

Sated, he rolled off her, dressed himself slowly and meticulously, and splashed water from a tiny sink onto his face.

Renata, still bound, lay there gasping, with pain and horror and revulsion, watching him. Liquid trickled between her legs. Her face flamed with humiliation and rage.

Finally, tying his tie, wearing a fresh uniform with knife-edge creases in the pant legs, he addressed her in a tone one would use to announce a trip to the grocery store. "I'm going to let you go now. If you speak a word of this to anyone, I will tell them you seduced me. They'll believe me; they've seen it before. Will you be quiet?"

She gulped and nodded.

He loosened her bonds, then disappeared.

After some persistent wriggling, she slipped her hands from the ropes and untied her feet. She had nothing to wear but her torn dress. Exploring cabinets and cupboards, she put on a dressing gown, stuffed the ruined dress and panties into a corner, and left. She wanted no clothing to remind her of this hour.

She showered for half an hour, washing his stench from her skin and stanching the bleeding from between her legs, but she could not erase the bruises on her face, and the pain inside. Would she ever feel clean again?

Once dry and dressed, she threw the dressing gown overboard, hobbled to her cabin, and wedged a chair under the handle. Any noise in the hallway set her heart racing. She curled into a tight ball on the bed but could not stop the tears of fury, shame, and guilt. Pounding the bed with her fists, she cursed the captain, the ship, and her own stupidity. She felt hollow, dry as an ancient log, with nothing left inside. What had she done? She must have led him on somehow. Was it her clothes? How could she face Ray after this?

Wasted, she finally fell into an uneasy sleep, but wakened repeatedly, shaking and soaked in perspiration.

The long night finally ended. Exhausted and longing for some sanity, she rang for Jimmy, who took one look at her and offered to escort her to the galley.

Soupy looked up from mixing eggs. "Jesus, what happened to you?"

"Fell down the stairs." She lifted a palm. "I'm okay, don't

worry. But I will not be taking dinner at the officers' mess any longer. May I eat with the enlisted men, instead?"

"Sure, no problem." He frowned. "Something happened, didn't it? And not a fall down the stairs. You want to talk about it?"

"No, I don't." She avoided eye contact. "Please don't ask again."

She went through the motions of cooking, setting the tables, and when Soupy was not looking, she took a sharp knife from a drawer full of so many, he wouldn't miss one.

The convoy was approaching Europe. It had lost one ship so far but to Renata, the Nazis were a remote threat compared with the captain. Although she saw him once in passing, he merely touched a hand to the tip of his cap and said, "Good day, Mrs. Stern." The thought of him made her nauseous; the sight of him made her furious. She kept the knife in her clothing, and would not hesitate to use it.

She heard with relief that they would dock in England in four days, barring enemy attacks. She dreamed of Tommy, and Papa, and the captain tying her down, nearly every night. She wondered for the five-hundredth time if she had done the right thing. To give up Tommy for this? Ray had damned well better want her back.

Chapter Twenty-three

Battle, 1942

Two days later, in the middle of the night, a Klaxon sounded "battle stations." Putting on her warmest clothing and life preserver, and at the last minute slipping her diary into the money belt and the knife into her coat pocket, Renata hauled her suitcase toward the center of the ship. She found a nook among the huge vents and squeezed herself into a space where she could watch.

Men ran and shouted, and *Georgic*'s guns roared to life. In the dark, the battle was impossible to follow. Two ships in the distance exploded and sank into the murky water. Freighters, she guessed, from the lack of fuss with which they died. Flak filled the skies and drifted onto the deck, igniting small blazes which crew members rushed to extinguish. Fires on other ships produced mountainous clouds of dense, acrid smoke, which cloaked both convoy and enemy. Shouts, screams, the roar of massive guns, and ear-piercing blasts forced Renata to cover her ears as she readied herself to move, listening for the ominous whistle of incoming shells.

An explosion in the fore section sent flames shooting hundreds of feet high, and a colossal shudder vibrated through the ship. A shell had found its target: the forward smokestack, and crates of ammunition beneath. The forward end of the ship was gone; it listed sharply as it took on water, and the sailors' shouts gained a note of desperation.

Renata wrapped her coat around her and rose. The *Georgic* would not last. No longer moving, it tilted forward and then to port.

She startled a crew member.

"What should I do? Where should I go?"

"The abandon ship order has been given, Miss. Lifeboats, this way." He gestured with one arm and supported her with the other. Walking on the tilting deck through black smoke and ashes, unable to see or breathe, they held onto railings, stanchions, anything to keep from sliding into the flames. They climbed aft and to starboard, stumbling over debris.

The port lifeboats were underwater, but one of the starboard lifeboats was in the water and pulling away. A steady young officer handed out life preservers, but some of the crew, chased by rapidly spreading flames, jumped into the ocean without life vests. Parts of the ocean were ablaze and one unfortunate screamed as he landed right in the inferno. Renata turned from the grisly scene.

The men jostled and shouted for a place on a lifeboat, but Renata's arrival created a minor sensation. They opened a path for her. One of the men handed her into the boat, but tossed her suitcase overboard. It caught fire and sank.

She felt nothing. She was alive. Her hand rested on the hidden money belt.

Once the lifeboat was full, others began winching it into the ocean, a dangerous undertaking from a listing ship. The men used the oars to keep it from the ship's side.

A sudden wave dashed the lifeboat against the hull, knocking sailors off their perches, and the lifeboat plummeted into the water, forward-end-down.

Renata screamed. Oily water closed over her head and all she could think of was never seeing Tommy or Ray again. She kicked mightily and surfaced, thanking God for her Mae West.

The water was not frigid, so she looked for something to hang onto. She spotted Soupy.

"Soupy! Soupy! Over here!"

He waved and thrashed toward her, pushing aside flotsam.

"Are you okay?" he asked.

"Yes. You?"

"I think my arm is broken. We need to get a boat."

They looked around, supported by their life jackets.

Two more lifeboats launched, but that was all. Men threw themselves into the water and swam as fast as they could away from the ship. The *Georgic* rolled onto its side, and slid to a quick, quiet death in the murky Atlantic, sucking anything nearby with it.

Noise dwindled, except for the cries of men in the water.

A junior officer directed a lifeboat towards the cries. They hauled three aboard without much difficulty.

Renata noticed a fourth man, blackened beyond recognition, thrashing and screaming hysterically.

"Let's see if we can calm him down, Soupy," she said.

He nodded. They splashed toward the suffering man, Renata in the lead. When they drew close, they saw why he was hysterical—one of his arms was missing and he was bleeding profusely. Half his face was charred black. For one long second, Renata wondered if this was how Ray looked.

"Over here! Over here!" screamed Renata, waving frantically to the lifeboats, busy rescuing other survivors.

The injured man lost consciousness. Soupy, gasping and gray-faced, caught up to her.

"I have a belt we could use as a tourniquet, but I can't get it," Soupy said. "Can you reach it?"

It was awkward with the life jackets, but she managed, choking as the dirty saltwater washed over her.

"He's bleeding less," she said, once the belt was tightened on the gruesome stump. Wiping the man's face, she took a closer look beneath all the filth. She gasped; her blood curdled.

"It's the captain, Soupy." She moved an arm's length away. "I can't touch him, after what he did to me." One hand went to the knife in her pocket.

Soupy stared at her. "I knew something happened to you. Bloody old goat. I think he's done that to every woman on his ship for the past three years."

She held the point of the knife to the unconscious man's throat. "He's bleeding to death, but God, I'd like to help him along to hell."

Soupy sloshed between her and the captain. "Hey, hey, calm down. He's a goner, anyway. God will handle him now." He put his good arm on her shoulder. "Okay?"

She nodded, her chest tight, and lowered the knife.

Soupy panted faster and faster. "I may be a goner, too. It's more than my arm."

Renata dropped the knife and waved her hand frantically at the nearest boat.

"Over here! We need help!" She held Soupy close with one arm, but he began drifting into unconsciousness. "Please, Soupy, come on, stay awake!" She patted his cheek rapidly.

He opened his eyes but could not focus.

A lifeboat shone a searchlight on them, and a lookout called, "We got another three here, Chief! Two look pretty bad!"

Sailors easily lifted Renata onto the overloaded boat, but the unconscious captain and semi-conscious Soupy were dead weights.

One sailor reached the captain's remaining hand and held fast. The other two reached for his clothing. The little boat threatened to capsize, then he rolled inside, vomiting, moaning. Salt water, oil, and blood filled the bottom of the boat.

Wondering why he, of all the men, had to be saved, Renata withdrew as far away as she could, her teeth chattering with cold. The satisfaction of seeing her attacker gravely injured warmed her briefly, but it was like milk going sour. Revenge was not sweet.

Next, Soupy rolled into the bottom of the boat and Renata knelt beside him. Now that he was out of the water, she could see his injuries were severe: a large gash in his stomach bled profusely. She wadded what she could gather of his shirt and pressed it into the wound.

"Soupy, please, come on, Soupy. You can make it." His hands were cold, his breathing sporadic. She rubbed his hands, and whispered to him over and over, willing him to fight for his life, while the chief got the boat moving.

Renata glanced around. Other lifeboats continued picking up men. Fiery patches of oil lit the hellish scene of burning corpses bumping into debris, spreading the flames. Survivors, faces blackened, held onto floating pallets and scraps of lumber.

Dawn silhouetted the corvette and the destroyer, still mopping up after the battle. A spotlight from the destroyer found the exhausted survivors, and lowered a ladder to assist them. Navy medics hauled Soupy and Captain Smith up in stretchers and they disappeared from Renata's sight.

Aboard the destroyer, Renata thanked a sailor for the warm

blanket wrapped around her, and for the mug of steaming tea. The infirmary bed was the most wonderful thing she had ever seen. Moments after finishing the drink, she was asleep.

When she awakened, she forgot where she was and had no idea of the time or day. She tried on sailor's clothes left at her bedside. She giggled hysterically at the thought of wearing the ill-fitting clothes in public, then burst into tears.

A young nurse pulled aside the curtain. "Good afternoon, Ma'am! How are you feeling?"

She sniffed. "A little emotional right now, I'm afraid. I'm sore all over, but all right, considering. What time is it, please?"

"It's sixteen hundred hours. Would you like tea and something to eat?"

"That would be marvelous." She paused. "The others on my lifeboat—are they all right?"

The nurse put a hand on her shoulder. "Everyone survived, except the man who lost his arm and the young man who came in with him. Were they special to you?"

Renata closed her eyes, and swayed a little. Her friendship with Soupy had made the voyage bearable. Her face flushed with shame, as she recalled him preventing her from murdering the captain. She would never forget him.

The nurse steadied her around the waist. "Here, come sit down. Sorry to give you such a shock. Who were they?"

"The man with the missing arm was the captain. He was not a good man," she said bitterly. "But the other fellow was Soupy, the cook, and he was my best friend. I can't believe he didn't make it!" No more tears came, just a cavernous ache in her gut.

The nurse held her, patting her arm.

Tea, soup, biscuits, and jam appeared minutes later, and after eating, Renata recovered a little. "Where are we, nurse? When do we dock?"

"We'll be dropping you off at Southampton three days from now, in the afternoon. Is there anyone I can contact for you?"

"No, but I must get to London. How far away is it?"

"Not that far in miles, but with the bombing, petrol shortages, and so forth, it could take you a day or two to get there. While you're here, I suggest you get as much rest as you can."

She accepted the nurse's advice, and returned to her bed for a nap. The rocking motion of the ship was so soothing…

She was in the mess hall of the ship. Four Nazis were taking turns assaulting her while the captain looked on, laughing. The laughter grew wilder and wilder; her screams grew louder and louder as water slowly covered the floor.

"Wake up, Mrs. Stern, it's just a bad dream, love."

Renata awoke to the nurse shaking her shoulder. She sat up with a start and pulled the blanket tight around her neck. "Where are the Nazis? Did they capture the ship?" She was shaking, and clasped the nurse's hand so tightly that the poor woman winced.

"No, dear, you're on a British ship and safe. Dreams can be very intense after such an experience. Do you want to tell me about it?" She sat beside Renata on the bed.

Telling about the rape and the sinking ship was the last thing she wanted to do. She shook her head slowly, staring into the distance, willing the ghastly images to fade. "I'll be all right once I get to London. But thank you. I could use a hot drink, though."

"Tea?"

"Thanks."

But the dreams returned. Sometimes the captain was beating her, and the Nazis were laughing. One time Soupy was being whipped. She dreamed she was killing the captain with a knife, and her hands and face were soaked with his blood. She dreaded going to sleep, knowing the punishment that awaited her in that shadowy land. Whatever happened in England had to be better than this.

Ray faded in her mind. She clung to images of sweet little Tommy, laughing and drooling, and wondered why she had been permitted to live.

Chapter Twenty-four

England, 1942

Relentless bombing had reduced Southampton's dock area to mountains of broken stone, wood, and glass. Rubble and dust disguised still-standing buildings as set pieces from a dreary, long forgotten world. The grayness of everything—buildings, roads, clouds, even the people in their shabby clothing—chafed Renata's damaged spirits.

Her immediate problems were finding her way to London, and finding a place to stay.

Busses stopped at the intersection nearby, taking on and disgorging passengers intent on errands. Each bus displayed the places it was going, but the unfamiliar names were useless to a stranger. Street signs were painted black to foil any invading force. This was not a place for outsiders.

A sudden breeze whipped dirt into a chilly dust devil, which stung her bare skin. Finding a new coat was high on her checklist.

She crossed to the bus stop, a popular one, based on the number of people who were already queuing since the last bus's departure. She smothered a grim smile at the Brits' capacity to maintain order in the middle of chaos, while she debated which person to approach. A young man in the Army. A business man clutching a leather briefcase. A mother with a young child in tow. An elderly woman wearing a maroon scarf, holding a lightly filled shopping bag.

The old woman looked kindly.

"Excuse me, Madam, can you tell me which bus I catch for

London?"

The woman scowled. "What's that accent? Ye sound German, lass, and if that's so, ye'd best be off to jail. Be glad I'm not calling the coppers." She spat at Renata's feet, tightened her scarf under her chin and stepped onto the next bus.

Renata recoiled.

The other passengers glared at her, but after the bus pulled away, the young soldier remained, a puzzled look on his face. "I'm curious, Miss. Sergeant Blakely, by the way." He extended his hand.

She shook it, then accepted the cigarette he offered. "Renata Stern. Just arrived on the ship over there." She gestured behind her toward the destroyer at its berth.

Blakely twisted his mouth. "Really. You expect me to believe that? Where'd you come from?"

"Egypt. Our convoy was attacked off Spain, and that destroyer rescued most of our crew, plus me." She flicked her ash onto the pavement. Why should she have to explain herself to a stranger? Aware that he would be looking for spies, she maintained eye contact and kept her voice even. "Can you help me find my way to London?"

"I might, but I need some proof you're who you say you are."

Wordlessly, she handed over her passport. He examined it, then handed it back.

"Too strange to be a lie. I've to return to my barracks, but I can point you in the right direction." He extended his arm northeast. "You've to take the second bus that arrives here, in about half an hour, if you're lucky. It will take you to the train station. Do you have any English money?"

"I have money, but I don't have a coat, only what I'm standing in. Is summer always this cold here?"

"The fare should be a few shillings, plus the train fare, which you'll buy at the station. There's supposed to be a fare chart inside each bus, but half the time they're missing. Be sure to keep your ticket until you get off, because inspectors can hop on anywhere and demand to see it. And, yes, summers here are usually cool."

More people had gathered, huddled into their coats, which Renata eyed enviously, rubbing her arms in a futile attempt to keep warm. Unbelievably, it was June.

A bus came into view, its gears grinding, and pulled into the curb.

"Not this. The next one. Good luck." Sergeant Blakeley boarded and disappeared.

Hunger pangs gnawed at her, but she dared not leave and had no idea how long the trip to London would take. How annoying that she failed to ask such a basic question.

The second bus came from a different direction about forty-five minutes later. With a dozen others, Renata climbed on board. She hoped a seat near the front would be warmer than the back of the bus, which was open to the elements.

The conductor, an affable elderly gent, carried tickets in various colors attached to a rack. He exchanged pleasantries and snippets of gossip with many of the passengers, as he made his way to the front of the bus and Renata.

"Righto, Miss, where to?"

"London, please. I understand this bus will take me to the train station."

He raised his eyebrows. "You've a long journey ahead. That'll be one shilling, if you please." He handed her the ticket and turned to his next fare once she paid him, but she gripped his sleeve.

"Please, I'm new here. Can you tell me how long it will take, and what train I will need?"

He frowned. "You'll get off at Winchester station. Could take half an hour today. At Winchester, you'll catch the train to London, but track conditions are unpredictable. The train may be delayed, or shunted to a side track to let troops and supplies through. You probably won't get there until later tonight. But once you're in range of the tube, you can get off anywhere. Where are you heading?"

"The Canadian hospital, in Watford. Do you know where it is?"

"You don't want to go all the way into London, then. Watford is north." He gave her detailed directions that left her utterly confused.

She shook her head. "Thank you, but I think I'll continue into London for tonight, and find Watford tomorrow."

"Very sensible."

Catching the train in Winchester went smoothly, and she dozed as soon as the train pulled out of the station. The conductor's announcement for each station jostled her awake at irritatingly regular intervals.

A few hours' journey in peacetime became a full day. The train stopped several times near bomb craters and fire hoses, which snaked across roads where firefighters contended with multiple blazes from the previous night's raids. Ambulances carted away the injured and dead. Volunteers combed the wreckage for survivors. She stared at the bizarre sight of a milkman carrying bottles of milk down a rubble-filled street.

Twice the passengers were shunted to another train. Once they sat motionless in the country for two interminable hours.

By the time the train wheezed to a stop in London, it was late. Much darker than the Alexandria blackout, she noticed. Visibility dropped to nil, with the occasional slit of light immediately followed by a voice shouting, "Hi! Close off that light right sharpish!"

Dizzy from hunger and thoroughly chilled, Renata staggered off the train, at a loss as to her next move, until she saw a small café at the back of the station.

A cheery waitress plunked down a pot of tea and a mug, with apologies for the lack of milk. "Menu today's mutton stew, just a bit left, if you fancy it." She pursed her lips. "Where's your coat? Aren't you cold?"

"Mutton stew sounds divine, and yes, I'm cold. I lost my coat on a sinking ship."

The waitress stared. She left to deliver the order and returned minutes later with a steaming bowl of stew that consisted of fatty lumps of tough mutton, a few cubes of potato, and bits of shredded cabbage.

Renata spooned it down gratefully, feeling the hot liquid warming her insides. The mug warmed her hands. She took her time sipping the hot tea and mulling over what to do next, while her shivering gradually subsided.

When the woman returned with the bill, Renata took a chance. "I'm new to town and wonder if you know a place that would put me up for the night, until I can find my own lodgings."

Concern filled the waitress's face. "Oh, dear, love. Let's see. The Red Cross is your best bet. They put up the people who've lost their homes, so I expect they could find you a cot. Hold tight a minute and I'll ask the supervisor."

She returned shortly with a matronly woman wearing a bilious green uniform, with a "WVS" insignia.

"Here, love, this is Mrs. Fitzsimmons. She'll see to you."

Mrs. Fitzsimmons sat beside Renata and appraised her. "What is your name, Miss?"

"It's Mrs. Renata Stern." She repeated the story of her journey, showed her marriage certificate and passport.

Mrs. Fitzsimmons' eyes narrowed. "That certainly sounds like a German accent, Mrs. Stern."

Not again. Renata tightened all her muscles to stop her shaking. "You're right, but I am not a spy. I'm a Jew who escaped from Hitler, and I hate him just as much as you do."

"Of course, that's exactly what a spy would say, isn't it? But we can't have you out on the street, so please come with me to the Red Cross station just down the lane. I expect they can find you a coat, too."

She rose and strode out the door, leaving Renata fumbling with her money belt to pay for her food. Outside, Mrs. Fitzsimmons stood waiting for her, frowning.

"You must keep up. It's very easy to get lost in the blackout."

"I'm sorry. I had to pay my bill." Renata shivered anew in the evening chill, but Mrs. Fitzsimmons kept up a fierce pace, which soon had blood flowing into Renata's arms and legs as she trotted beside her, dodging rubble, garbage, and stray dogs.

The Red Cross was in a church basement. The room was full of Army-style cots and people: women, children, the elderly. Some were sleeping, but those awake were clearly traumatized, judging from their wide eyes and blank stares. None paid the slightest attention to Renata and Mrs. Fitzsimmons, who knocked on a side door.

A Red Cross nurse opened it, and grasped the situation immediately, but her welcoming smile faded when Mrs. Fitzsimmons spoke.

"She's German, this lass, apparently married to a Canadian.

Keep a close eye on her, and we'd best notify the authorities." Mrs. Fitzsimmons left abruptly.

The nurse, at least, had a kindly smile. "What's your story, then, dear? I'm Nurse Heather."

Renata had never before been called "dear" and "love" by strangers, and although she was sick of repeating her story, she was too tired to object. "Renata Stern. I was bombed in a convoy. I arrived in Southampton more than a day ago, and have been making my way here since, but I lost all my clothes, everything except what's on my back. I'm desperately tired and cold. And I'm not a spy. I'm here to find my husband, who's been injured."

Her teeth chattered.

"We'll get that all straightened around in the morning, Mrs. Stern. In the meantime, take this bed." Heather patted an empty cot in a corner, and wrapped a blanket around Renata's shoulders. "I'll be back in a minute with more clothing."

Renata stretched out on the cot and was asleep in seconds.

Sirens woke her in the middle of the night. Family groups clustered in the basement shelter, where the Red Cross nurse walked through, calm as a summer breeze, assuring them they were as safe here as anywhere. The percussive thud of explosions began far away. The noise grew and grew until Renata could hear the whistle of the bombs falling through the air before they exploded. She covered her ears and huddled under her blanket. Memories of bombings in Alexandria and on the *Georgic* mingled with the shuddering walls and deafening blasts outside.

Watching mothers trying to comfort their terrified children, Renata thought of Tommy. At least he wasn't enduring this horror. She wondered if the bombers reached Watford, and what they did with patients during raids.

The attack drifted away, leaving an uneasy calm. The all-clear sounded. Volunteers came in and chattered urgently to the nurse, who was preparing for more arrivals needing medical attention.

Deciding there was nothing she could do, Renata closed her eyes and surrendered to sleep.

It was light when she awoke, astounded that she had slept so long. She stared at newly bombed out people drinking tea from chipped mugs, waiting their turn for first aid. No one paid her any attention when she collected her tea and a bun. Heather was bandaging a little boy's head and hands, talking in soothing tones. The little chap had tears streaking down his dirty face. No one in the group was touching him or speaking to him as a parent would. With a jolt, Renata wondered if he'd lost his parents last night.

Wrapping the blanket around her shoulders, she edged toward the nurse, who was finishing the bandages. Nurse Heather patted the boy on the shoulder and lifted him onto the floor.

"Good lad, you'll be fine in a day or two. Would you like tea and a bun?"

Large tears wobbled over his eyelids and dribbled down his face. His chin quivered. He shook his head.

"No thank you, Nurse. When can I see my Mummy? I want my Mummy."

Tears threatened Renata, too, hearing the child's lonely agony. Was Tommy suffering like this? Suddenly, she wanted to hug this little boy and tell him his mother would soon be back, but she knew it would be wrong to give him false hope. Instead, she addressed Heather.

"If he's alone, I'd be happy to take care of him for a while." She smiled encouragingly at the child.

With a frown, Heather surveyed the room, and the others clamoring for her help, then looked back at Renata with a short sigh. "Oh, thank you, if you don't mind. His mum is…" Heather gave a brief shake of her head. "Anything you can do to get him to eat and drink. Poor wee mite."

Renata squatted down to the child's eye level.

"Hallo, young soldier, you've had a very bad time, haven't you?"

The child nodded slowly, warily.

"Do you know, I have a little boy about your age? He's a long way away, and he probably feels like you do right now."

He blinked, and looked her in the eyes for the first time. "What's his name?"

"Tommy. And my name's Mrs. Stern. What's your name?"

"Davey. Do you know where my mummy is?"

"I don't, Davey, but you know, she'd want you to have something to eat and drink. I have a cot over there. How about we get your tea and bun and eat together?" She offered her hand.

He stared for a long time, then slowly reached out and took it. She squeezed gently.

"Are you cold? I have a blanket we can share."

Twenty minutes later, Davey had finished his bun, drunk his tea, and was sound asleep on Renata's cot, snug in the blanket.

Renata stood without disturbing him. She needed to talk to Heather about the Watford hospital.

Heather had her hands around a huge mug of tea and was sitting in a corner, her duties caught up for now. Unaware of being observed, for a moment, her deep anguish and unbearable fatigue were exposed.

Renata cleared her throat.

Heather smiled out of her weariness and patted the chair next to her. Renata sat down.

"Thank you, Mrs. Stern. You were just what he needed, pour soul, and I'm convinced no spy could be so tender to that young lad. There's a telegram gone to his grandparents in Lancashire to come and get him." She shook her head. "It gets hard to bear. I expect you know."

"We had a few bombing raids in Egypt, but nothing like this. The Egyptian King absolutely refuses to black out his castle, which tells you it's not all that dangerous in the city. But the lads out in the desert and on the sea, that's a different story." She paused. Her suffering on the *Georgic* would never leave her.

She saw how the relentless grind of death sapped Heather's strength, yet hardened her resolve. She admired Nurse Heather very much.

"My husband's in the Canadian Hospital at Watford. Would you know how to get there?"

The nurse's eyes closed briefly, as if from some terrible memory, but she smiled, that forced smile people make when they'd rather cry. "It will take you a few hours to get across the city. There's not one straight route."

With a pencil and paper, she wrote directions, including

tube stations and bus stops. "Be prepared. The routes can change after a raid. You might have to walk partway. When are you planning to leave?"

"Now, if you can manage young Davey. But I wonder if you have a spare coat I could use?"

Heather disappeared into her office and returned with a gray coat, drab, not too clean, but serviceable.

"Thank you. One more thing. May I come back here tonight? I have nowhere to stay. Or if you have other suggestions…"

"You may come back, but we have a five-day limit for everyone. You understand. Tomorrow, let's talk it over, shall we?"

The trip to the Canadian Hospital was as challenging as Heather had warned. The tube stopped at Maida Vale, past Wembley Station, blocked by an unexploded bomb that had penetrated far enough to plug the line. The passengers climbed up, directed away from the crater, inches from the staircase.

Renata took a bus next, which nearly knocked the passengers off their seats when it rolled over fire hoses aimed at a blazing storefront. How commonplace destruction had become. Peace would seem strange, once this war ended.

The bus came to the end of its line, and the passengers were told they would have to walk to the hospital. Renata did not mind. The damage was less extensive this far from the center of town. Walking was calming.

She declined to join the conversations of the others. Instead, her mind was going over what she would say to Ray. She wanted to tell him she would not give up on him, she loved him, they had a wonderful little boy, but as the moment drew closer, her courage faltered. She slowed down. The final block to the hospital entrance, she felt like a prisoner being led to execution. Then she remembered that many of her family were facing that exact experience, and she flushed with shame.

The brick-and-stone building had a look of solid practicality, with little ornamentation. She pulled open the door, and gagged at the smell of antiseptic. Above the desk of a pert nurse who looked about eighteen, hung a sign reading, "Admissions and Visitors." The nurse smiled. "Welcome to Canadian Hospital. How may I help you?"

"I'm here to see my husband, Ray Stern, in the burn unit."

After flipping through lists and charts twice, the nurse said, "I don't see anyone listed here by that name."

"But you must! I received a letter from him when he was admitted."

"One moment, I'll go speak with Matron." The nurse disappeared down a corridor and into an office.

Renata didn't know what to think. Had he died? Was he moved to another hospital? On a ship again? Perhaps he was in a rehabilitation center close by. She kept an eye on the door.

Eventually the nurse reappeared, followed by a fearsome-looking woman carved out of an ancient Norse legend. Steely hair, steely frown, steely walk. Why wasn't she on the front lines? The Germans would be helpless against this battleship of a woman.

The nurse introduced them. "Please come this way."

She ushered Renata into a small room with three chairs and a desk. Renata was sweating. This did not look like a room where good news was dispensed. The nurse left and closed the door.

Matron's voice matched her physique: booming, low, commanding. "Now, Mrs. Stern, I understand you believe your husband is here."

"Yes, Matron, he sent me a letter." She handed over the letter that, along with her passport, had survived the sinking.

Retrieving a pair of reading spectacles, Matron perused the letter quickly. "This letter was written six months ago. What took you so long to get here?" She glared at Renata.

Renata felt like a schoolgirl being scolded, and gritted her teeth. "I was in Egypt. It's not easy to arrange passage from there."

Matron cleared her throat and a flush crept up her face. She was not used to being wrong, Renata realized.

"He is not here now. I reviewed the list of patients with Nurse Kingsmith to be sure. However, I checked the past records. He was here, but he checked out two months ago."

Renata's mouth dropped open. "I've been travelling for months to find him. Do you know where he is now?"

"I'm afraid we are not informed as to the eventual situations of our patients, although I can tell you he did not pass away in our care. Now, if you'll excuse me." Matron rose and left, leaving the door open.

Renata uttered a single long scream.

Kingsmith ran in. "What's wrong?"

But Renata was past hospitals and nurses. Ignoring the young nurse, she pushed her way out of the room, and left. Determined not to cry, she stormed to the bus stop and rode to the tube station, fuming.

It was a half-mile walk from the tube to the shelter. Wrapped in her own thoughts, she did not see the young soldier coming her way. He must have been similarly preoccupied, because they bumped into each other hard enough that Renata fell. He offered a hand to help her up.

"I'm so sorry, Miss, I wasn't watching…" his voice trailed off as their eyes met. "Renata?"

"Hans? *Oh, mein Gott!*"

Chapter Twenty-five

England, 1942-43

Renata and Hans clung to each other, laughing and crying.

"What in bloody hell are you doing here?" He spoke English with no German accent when they finally pulled apart.

"What are you doing here? And a British uniform? What on earth are you up to?"

"Shhhhh." He put a finger to his lips. "Come, we can talk at a café I know."

He took her elbow and guided her easily along the streets. He was the same, yet not.

She stole glances at him. The boy was gone; this was a man with well-defined jaw, a determined brow, and a five-o'clock shadow. His eyes were the same brilliant blue, but lines at the corners and a certain heaviness about the lids suggested perpetual weariness. She wondered if he noticed similar changes in her.

He steered her to an isolated table near the back of a tiny café. The touch of his hand on her back was electric.

"Sit down facing the wall. I don't have to remind you what language not to speak, do I?"

She shook her head. This Hans was used to giving orders and expecting obedience.

A waitress wandered over, teapot in hand. She filled the cups on the table. "What'll it be, loves? Looks like a happy reunion here. Charmed for you both, I'm sure. We have eggs and toast today, or a bit of kippers, if you fancy them."

"Eggs and toast would be lovely. And we'd appreciate any

privacy you can give us." Renata winked solemnly at the waitress, who widened her eyes, then nodded in collusion.

"Right you are, Miss. Right back with the eggs and toast." She returned to the kitchen with a smirk on her face.

Renata giggled and whispered, "She thinks we're having an affair." She looked at him more seriously and touched his hand. "I thought I would never see you again. I can't believe it is really you, Hans."

He interrupted with a hiss. "Don't call me that. I'm Henry now. It's very important, do you understand?"

She lowered her voice to a whisper to match his. "Of course. I won't give you away. But you owe me a bit of an explanation, don't you think? What are you up to?"

He sat back and sipped the tea, then smiled at her, but not that intimate smile they used to share. It was as if he needed to get to know her again, to see if he could trust her.

With a shock, she realized she felt the same way.

He kept his voice low. "I'll give you the short version. When I arrived in Switzerland, I went to the British Embassy and offered my services. Naturally, they were suspicious, but I convinced them I was serious. They sent me over here to train. I've been back and forth so many times I've lost track."

"What do you do?"

"I can't tell you details. Let's just say it's extremely risky and extremely important."

Renata gasped. "So, you're, you're a..." She could not bring herself to say the word.

He nodded. "The worst is not ever feeling like yourself. Always pretending, even when I'm here, because many would turn on me if they knew my background. Always watching my back. And then to see you, a face from home." He shook his head. "It's a miracle."

The waitress brought the food. She dawdled a bit, but they remained silent until she left.

"Ha—Henry." She held his hand under the table while the eggs cooled. "You have no idea how much I missed you, especially since I couldn't write. It is a miracle, finding you in this beastly city."

"I missed you, too, but it was safer for me to push thoughts of you out of my mind. Your turn now. How did you get here? And why?"

"I've something to tell you…Henry." The name felt strange on her lips. She took a deep breath. "I'm married, and I have a little boy."

She noticed the flicker of disappointment and hurt, quickly covered. She pulled her hand away from his and drank some tea to cover her embarrassment. "My husband is in the Canadian Navy. He was injured and in hospital here at Watford. Do you know the place?"

"I've heard of it but never been there."

"After a terrible voyage, I went there today, but he's not there. No one can tell me where he went. He was badly burned, you see, and sent me a letter assuming I couldn't love him, and wanting us to divorce." She could not believe she was having this conversation. "I thought that if I could see him and convince him that he's still lovable, we might save our marriage. He's never seen his son." She blew her nose into her handkerchief, still feeling Hans-Henry's hand on her back. "Now I feel like I've given up my son, and for what?"

"Who's looking after him?"

"My parents."

"You are some amazing woman, finding your way here all alone." He leaned toward her and spoke softly. "I want to kiss you so badly I can hardly stand it."

She squeezed his hand and smiled wistfully, then gently shook her head, although her heart was fluttering and her pulse racing. "It would be wrong."

"You're right. We've too much catching up to do, to think of misbehaving."

He dropped her hand and tackled his egg. He kept his voice friendly but casual, toning down the sexual undertones flickering between them.

They swapped stories all afternoon. The waitress refilled their tea and took away the remains of the tiny meal. It felt surreal, talking with Hans/Henry about Ray and Tommy. She felt numb all over and tingly at the same time. The relief of a familiar face after months of strangers left her giddy with joy. And for it to be Hans, of all people. She tried to squelch the arousal growing each time she looked at him.

The sun cruised toward the horizon and the waitress announced closing time in fifteen minutes.

"We'd better leave." Henry stood and pulled out her chair, helped her into her coat, and dropped money on the table. They walked outside, the door slamming shut behind them. "Where are you staying?"

"In a Red Cross shelter, but they will only allow me four more nights. Then I have to move on, I've no idea where."

Henry stood facing her and took both her hands in his. "Come and stay at my place. I have room, and it's warm."

The invitation hung between them. To hold him in her arms, to feel his lips on hers, to be touched and caressed and loved once again after months of fear; she wanted him so badly she was sure he could hear her pounding heart. She saw the need in his eyes, too. Without a word, she took his hand and they walked, sweaty palms conducting sparks between them.

He pushed open the door to his bed-sit and let her in. Her throat was dry, yet other parts were decidedly moist, and she was shaking like a leaf. To come all this way for Ray, then to betray him? What kind of wife was she? And yet, Ray had rejected her and disappeared. Did she owe him fidelity, especially in the wild uncertainty of war?

"Any port in a storm," some of her friends would say if they knew, but an old friend was hardly any port.

She took in the bed-sit in one slow pirouette. A narrow bed, a chair, a shabby sofa for two. A microscopic kitchen in the corner, and one window that faced another brick wall.

Henry pulled the blackout curtain across the window, then lit a lamp on a table that served the bed and the easy chair. He removed his coat, hung it in a small armoire jammed between the bed and the window, then turned to her.

Slowly, he removed her coat, draped it over the sofa, and pulled her to him.

Any lingering resistance dissolved into his warmth. Tilting her head up, he brought his lips to hers in the gentlest of kisses.

Suddenly, she put her arms around his neck and drew him close, pressing her mouth to his. Their lips parted, and she felt his tongue, probing, playing, teasing.

She fumbled feverishly with his buttons while he undid her dress and dropped it to the floor. He picked her up and carried her to the bed, their lips still melded together. Moments later they were naked, limbs entwined, weeping with joy and sorrow, frantic to stop the pain of their lives with these stolen minutes. He cupped her breast and brushed the nipple with his thumb, smiling as it rose in response.

"Renata, you pleasured me for years without being anywhere near me. You have no idea how much I longed to feel you. With that, he licked the nipple, then drew it into his mouth and suckled her. She moaned and arched into him.

"Hans...don't make me call you Henry here, will you?" she gasped.

He shook his head, sucking harder.

"I hope you don't think I'm a bad woman."

Flattening himself on her, he traced a finger down the side of her jaw, to her collarbone, down to her waist. "I rather like you being bad."

Raising himself, he continued his exploration of her body down her thigh, then back up to the mound between her legs.

She gasped, closed her eyes as he probed with his fingers, exploring and rubbing the little nub that sent shocks to the rest of her body. She felt herself floating, disappearing, feeling only the exquisite pleasure of his touch. She reached for him and felt his readiness.

And then, when she thought she could not bear another moment, he slipped inside her and rode her, made her heat rise with each thrust, deeper and deeper. She wanted him, had always wanted him, and then he exploded inside her as the wave crested over her. Writhing and gasping, she arched again and again, feeling each aftershock, feeling his hardness inside. He uttered a single long, low moan, then lowered himself and rolled them sideways, still connected. He smiled and lifted a curl off her face. He was panting and bathed in sweat and she loved the stickiness and heat of him.

"Woman, girlfriend of my youth, you are far more in person

than my wildest imagination dreamed. You are amazing." He kissed the tip of her nose.

"You are amazing, too, for a kid with no experience." She chuckled and poked him in the ribs, prompting an "Ow!" and "Nasty woman!"

Seconds later, they were wrestling, until Henry grabbed her wrists in jest. She froze and screamed. "No! Get off me!"

He complied, confused. "What's wrong? We were just playing around."

She was shivering, the mood of the evening gone. She ran to the sink and heaved.

Henry leapt to help her; offered her a towel.

"Don't ever do that to me again."

He wrapped a towel around his waist and backed off, frowning. "Renata, what the hell? What happened to you? I would never hurt you, you know that. Did Ray...?"

Covering her eyes with one hand, she slumped onto the chair, spent. How could she tell him? She curled into a ball. He crept toward her and spoke soothingly, softly.

"Whatever happened to you, you can tell me. I'm here. If you want, I'll hold you, but if not, I'll stay here. Just tell me how I can help." He kept talking, until she opened her eyes.

He brought her a clean, damp flannel.

She wiped her face and sat up. Was this what sex would be like from now on? Ruined by the captain? In that case, he had won, and that she could not live with. She raised her arms to Hans.

Hans lifted her onto his lap and gently cradled her, rocking slowly side to side. "You don't have to tell me if you don't want to," he whispered, "but if Ray hurt you that way, he doesn't deserve you."

She shook her head. "It wasn't Ray."

They moved to the sofa, still draped in towels, he with an arm around her.

"It happened on the *Georgic*." She told him the whole miserable story, including the captain's death the night the ship sank. "I didn't know I would react that way. What if I can never enjoy sex again?"

"If he wasn't already dead, I would find him and kill him,"

said Henry, his voice quaking with anger.

She had no doubt he meant it.

They sat in silence for a time. It was he who broke it. "Does it feel any better now that you've told me?"

Renata considered. "You know, it does, at least a little. It helps that someone else knows, but it will never go away completely." She turned and kissed him on the cheek. "Thank you for getting me to talk about it."

She stood. "I'd better get back to the Red Cross shelter. They are supposed to give me my ration books today, and I can't eat yours."

"I agree. Ration books taste terrible."

She punched him lightly on the arm.

Hans said, "I'll walk you. We could hear sirens anytime."

He left her at the shelter, promising to see her the next evening at the café.

"Oh, hello, Mrs. Stern." Heather's cheery greeting snapped Renata out of her muddled feelings. "I've ration books for you. Here's the one for food, one for clothing and other things."

Heather explained the ration system. Coupons were a different color for each week, limits on butter, eggs, sugar, and more but no limits on vegetables. "It doesn't matter much, though," she added, "since we never have much selection. Usually turnips and cabbages."

Renata wrinkled her nose. Dolmades, dates, and fresh oranges were a few thousand miles away. No wonder everyone in England was skinny.

The next day was Heather's day off. Her replacement was an imposing woman whose stern face suggested a military background, or possibly a school headmistress. Well past retirement age, Mrs. Livingstone, her steely gray hair wound into a bun, and exhaustion etched into her face, smiled at Renata.

"Heather gave me the lowdown on your situation, Mrs.

Stern. I understand you went to see your husband yesterday. How did that go?"

Renata sighed and crumpled into a nearby chair. "He wasn't there. Matron said he'd been discharged months ago, and they didn't know where he'd gone."

Mrs. Livingstone nodded, a slight frown on her face. "Most upsetting. Didn't he write and tell you?"

"Even if he had, I wouldn't have received the letter because I've been traveling from Egypt for the last few months."

"Oh, yes, Heather mentioned your voyage. Quite remarkable." She shifted her weight to her other foot. "You realize you have only two more days in the shelter, correct?"

"I know." She considered telling the woman that she had met a longtime friend, but decided against it as too risky. Better to ask for help. "Do you know anywhere I can find housing? I hope to not be here too long, I'm willing to work, and I can pay rent."

Mrs. Livingstone hesitated and tapped one foot on the floor. She looked away, then back. "Right-o, I have a small chesterfield that you're welcome to share if you don't mind cramped quarters and rations. Do you have a ration book?"

Relief. "Yes. Heather gave me them yesterday." She picked them up from under her blanket.

"This week is blue. You can use them for clothing, food, and so on, and instructions are printed on the inside cover, right here. If you have money, you can buy more from the skivs—...the black market, although of course that's illegal." She winked.

"Thank you very much."

"Let's get you to my flat, shall we? You look as though you'd enjoy a bath. Where's your luggage?"

"The ship I was in sank, so I lost all my luggage."

Mrs. Livingstone reacted as though it was perfectly normal for a stranger to arrive from Egypt, with no luggage and a tale of a sunken ship. Her stern features clearly did not reflect her warmth and generosity.

"Come along, then, let's see if I've a few extras. Are you hungry?" She called another volunteer to take her place at the desk.

They walked four blocks, passing demolished buildings and a few scruffy children with haunted faces.

"Eh, loves, a bit peckish, are you?" The children nodded. "Right then, the shelter around the corner, you know the downstairs place? Tea's at four o'clock and you're all welcome."

The listless children perked up and smiled.

On the second story of an old Victorian, attached to a row of homes that dissolved into a pile of rubble at the end of the street, was Mrs. Livingstone's flat. The place was tiny but immaculate—floors swept, shelves dusted, things put away. The single room had a hot plate and a small gas water heater built above the sink. A curtain separated Mrs. Livingstone's sleeping space from the rest.

"Here, sit down and relax. I don't doubt you're feeling a bit ragged."

Mrs. Livingstone produced a small plate with a bit of cheese, a biscuit, and a half slice of spam, and set them in front of Renata, who dropped her head into her hands.

"There, there, dear, don't worry, it'll all be better tomorrow," soothed her hostess, an arm around Renata and a handkerchief in her hand. "If you want to talk about it, I'll be glad to listen, but you needn't if you don't want to." She rubbed Renata's shoulder.

It reminded her of Hans rubbing her back. Renata looked at her benefactress. "I'm so sorry. It's your kindness that has me undone, Mrs. Livingstone. I've had such a terrible time."

"Don't mention it. Do you think you can eat now?"

Instantly ravenous, Renata finished the food, even the Spam, which was certainly not Kosher, in seconds. The tea, weak but hot, she drank gratefully.

Mrs. Livingstone found some clean clothes, and escorted Renata to a bathroom shared with four other tenants. A claw-foot tub had a hot water meter on the wall above the taps, so each user paid their own. Explaining how to use the meter, Mrs. Livingstone continued.

"Soak in the bath as long as you like, but keep your ears open, and if you hear anyone, get out quickly. Here's a towel, rather thin, I'm afraid. We haven't had new towels in ever so long. Soap is rationed, so go easy. Anything else you need?"

"No, thank you. This is perfect." The memory of the luxurious Castile soap lost in her suitcase surfaced for a moment, then sank.

Renata eased gratefully into the hot water. She scrubbed herself from head to toe, washed her greasy hair, then soaked until the water cooled. Back in the flat, she washed her clothes in the chipped kitchen sink and hung them on a line strung across the room.

"Now, regarding air raids," said Mrs. Livingstone, "we don't get many anymore, but if there is one, I go to the office where we met. It's a bit far, but it's much safer than other places closer by. Can you find your way back there?"

"I think so."

"Good. We'll set you up with a gas mask tomorrow."

Renata, drowsy after food and a bath, nodded sleepily. The chesterfield looked so inviting. She stretched out and slept.

Sirens woke her. Mrs. Livingstone was gone. She had missed her meeting with Hans. She threw on her coat and raced to the café, bumping people hurrying in the opposite direction to tube stations and shelters.

Of course, the café was closed. Shoulders sagging in disappointment, she turned to go back. A hand grabbed her from behind and she pulled away, twisting, ready to fight. "Get your hands off me!"

"Renata. It's me."

"You bloody fool, don't ever grab me like that again!" She tried to slap him, but he pulled her close and kissed her. Her pounding heart now had another reason to beat madly.

"We need to get out of here," he whispered.

"I can hardly go to the shelter with you, and your apartment isn't safe. What do you suggest?"

Bombs began falling in the distance.

"There's another shelter I use sometimes. Come on."

They raced through the streets, skidding inside as someone closed the door, mere seconds before explosions rattled the building. Hans indicated that she should move to the opposite corner of the room, where she found a spot on the floor and sat. The people around her did not react to her arrival, focusing instead on the booms, crumbling buildings, and smoke that continued for over an hour. Sleep was impossible.

Once the all-clear sounded, everyone emerged, scattering to their homes to check the night's destruction. Hans' flat was still in one piece. Inside, they clung to each other.

"I go to work today, and I may be leaving for a while," he whispered as he covered her face with gentle kisses. He led her to the bed. "I want to see you naked again."

Moments later they were making love desperately, hungrily, bathed in sweat, hoping to preserve this moment in all the uncertainty of war.

Afterwards, she spooned against him. "I don't know if I can bear losing you again. Must you go?"

"I must, if we are to win this war." Still naked, he led her to the sofa and sat her on his knee, then wrapped an old quilt around them. She curled into him like a child.

He nuzzled her neck.

She whispered, "When we arrived in Egypt, I wanted you terribly, especially after your last letter."

"You're finally getting what you wanted," he said, "even if it was a long time coming."

He stretched on the sofa and pulled her full length on top of him. He ran his hands through her hair and grinned.

"I've been longing for a good screw to forget the war, even for half an hour."

"Me, too," she said uncertainly. But was that what she wanted, really? The sex was marvelous release, but she thought of Ray and Tommy. Sweet baby Tommy, giggling and clutching at her. How could she even contemplate the treachery she had already committed?

Renata pushed herself up on one elbow.

"Hans, I need to tell you some things. Once we got to Tolumbat, the refugee camp, I wanted money, and I found a way to make that through painting." She played with the hairs on his chest. "But bombs damaged my studio, and no one wanted to buy art. My mother was miserable, and you know how she could be."

Hans nodded.

"I decided I needed a husband who could get me out of

Egypt. Mama was pushing me to marry."

"I know you're married, darling…"

She put a finger to his lips. "I deliberately got in the family way, so Ray would marry me." She peeled herself off him, awaiting judgment. "That must sound terrible."

His voice was noncommittal. "Desperate times, desperate measures. Did you love him?"

"I liked him a lot. He was fun and smart and good-looking. I grew to love him, though." She sat up, pulled the quilt around her bare shoulders. "Now I've lost him and who knows if I'll ever find him. I don't know when I'll see my son again. There's no one here who would care if I died in an air raid except you, and no one to tell my parents what happened."

She looked at him. "Hans, I'm scared. I don't know if I made the right decision coming here. I don't know if I'll ever find Ray, and I don't know if I'll still be able to love him even if I do find him. And this…" she gestured around the tiny flat. "Finding you here in London, was like the answer to a prayer. The sex has been amazing…" Her voice trailed off. How to tell him?

She coughed gently. "But it seems sordid, somehow. I don't want to sneak around, calling you another name, not knowing when I'll see you next."

Disentangling himself from her, Hans wrapped himself in a towel and went to the kitchen. "I'm making tea, lousy as it is, re-used tea leaves, you know. Want some?"

He raised the kettle in her direction and she could see the fire in his eyes.

"Sorry, I shouldn't have said that. Yes, tea will be fine." She walked to the bed and dressed.

He handed her a chipped cup and sat at the table, gesturing for her to do the same. His expression was hurt, distant.

"What the hell are you doing here, Renata? You trick a man into marrying you. You travel halfway around the world to find that husband, who doesn't want to see you. You leave your son and parents, risk your life, endure horrors. You find me against all odds and, yes, I admit I wanted you desperately, but you didn't put up resistance the way a truly married woman would have. Now you're implying you don't want me, either. Who are you? What happened to that girl in Munich who wanted fun with a little danger mixed in? Does it matter how many people you hurt on your quest to get whatever you want next?"

He slammed the flat of his hand on the table and stood up, his back to her.

Shocked into silence, Renata sat motionless. His words stung like nettles. Was she really that selfish? Isabella came to mind, against whom she had schemed to land Ray for herself. Regret over leaving Tommy flooded her. She tried thinking of Ray but could barely remember his face, as it used to be, anyway. She glanced at Hans' back, his hunched shoulders. Continuing this affair would be a betrayal of Ray, but also of Tommy, Mama and Papa, and all they had sacrificed to get her to London.

Hans' reaction floored her. He seemed to expect her to continue this little affair. At the most, they would have stolen moments together. This was not the life she wanted. She needed to salvage some self-respect.

Quietly, she retrieved her coat, then put her hand on the doorknob. Her eyes stung.

"I need to go, Hans, and perhaps it's best if we don't see each other again. You want the girl I used to be, not who I am. Good-bye." She stifled a sob.

The door was open before Hans reached her, but he stopped short of taking her in his arms. His face was contorted in pain. "You're the only woman I've ever wanted, Renata."

She put a finger on his lips. "Shhhhh." Her hand caressed his cheek. "Live."

He would have had to be blind not to see the agony on her face.

It took every ounce of will to walk down those stairs and out of his life.

The Red Cross shelter was empty midday, other than Mrs. Livingstone and Nurse Heather, who were setting out blankets and sorting bandages. She walked in, determined not to show the anguish ripping her insides to shreds.

"Good afternoon, Mrs. Stern," said Heather. "Tea? Just made some fresh."

"No, thank you. I'll be happy to help you with whatever needs doing." She hung her coat on a nail, and set to washing dishes before the night's arrivals.

They worked for a time in silence, while Renata grappled with Hans' painful words. It had never occurred to her that she was hurting others, but he was right. She had hurt Tommy most of all. Once they were reunited, who knew if she could ever heal whatever wounds she had caused in his baby soul? Had she hurt Ray? Brutal honesty forced her to admit that trapping a man in marriage was wrong, and possibly one reason he didn't want her to come to him.

She sighed, stacked the dry cups on a shelf, and put the spoons in a rough wooden box.

"We're done now, dears," said Mrs. Livingstone. "Renata, best you go to the shops and use those ration coupons for some food, soap, and clothing. A sturdy pair of shoes would be helpful, if they have any."

Heather added, "I'm heading there myself, if you'd like to come along. I'll show you how it works."

"That would be lovely, thank you."

The women put on their coats and left.

The ration portions were shockingly small, but Renata returned to the flat with butter, an egg, tea, a tin of spam, and a pair of gloves. No shoes were available.

She and Mrs. Livingstone managed tea with the egg and spam, and Renata offered to do the washing up.

Later, settled on the sofa with a newspaper, the women looked at each other; Renata, with embarrassment, and Mrs. Livingstone with curiosity. The latter spoke first.

"If you don't mind my saying so, dear, you seem dreadfully preoccupied today. Is something on your mind?"

Renata sighed. "Mrs. Livingstone, if you're up to it, I could use your advice."

"Certainly, dear." She set her teacup down on the table.

Renata opened her mouth to speak three times, but the right words would not come out. Instead, she heard herself say, "My husband was not at the hospital, and I don't know where he is.

Where could I go to find out?"

"I should think the Admiralty would be the place. I'll show you how to get there tomorrow, after a good sleep."

They yawned simultaneously, then laughed. Mrs. Livingstone disappeared behind the curtain to her tiny bed. Praying for no more bombs, Renata loosened but did not remove her clothing, then lay down on the sofa, unable to get Hans and Ray out of her mind. Snoring issued from behind the curtain, and sleep eluded her. She found herself counting specks on the ceiling and lumps in the sofa, wishing she had never left Egypt, while realizing she could not quit now.

Chapter Twenty-six

The Admiralty, 1943

The next day, after an hour of riding the underground, two buses, and asking for directions twice, Renata stood outside a gray marble building with the imposing Admiralty Arch, big enough for buses and parades to march through. Uniformed men and women streamed in and out with briefcases, gas masks, and serious expressions.

Inside, past security, a receptionist directed Renata down a hallway, past portraits of admirals from centuries past, to a large room alive with the clatter of typewriters and voices. Telephones rang insistently.

A second receptionist inquired how she could help.

"My husband was discharged from the Canadian hospital in Watford, and I need to know where he went."

"Oh, the Canadians, sorry love, you'll need to go across the hall for them." The woman pointed, then returned to her typewriter.

Across the hall, in a smaller room, were different uniforms and Canadian accents

"Hi, I'm Private Sutcliffe, can I help you?" offered a brash, freckled young man.

Again, Renata told her story.

"Just a sec, I'll look him up for you." Private Sutcliffe disappeared between cliffs of filing cabinets that threatened to topple their contents any second. Ten minutes passed, before he reappeared.

"Upstairs to room three-ten. They'll take care of you."

Renata trudged up the heavy oak staircase. The double doors of room three-ten led into a waiting area crowded with women, children, and fussy babies. Two children pushed small toy trucks around the floor, making motor noises. She wove her way to the desk where a uniformed woman fielded phone calls and juggled files. The woman held out a clipboard holding several pages with carbon paper in between.

"I need your passport, name, husband's name and rank, and marriage certificate. Press hard, you're making four copies."

Renata sat down and filled out the form, trying to ignore the children and their mothers who made almost as much noise trying to keep them quiet. When she stood up, she nearly tripped over a little boy, and bit her tongue to keep from snapping at him. She scowled at the mother, who grabbed the child's arm and pulled him out of the way. Then, guiltily, she thought of Tommy.

"I'm sorry," she said to the red-faced mother.

"Very good," said the receptionist, reviewing Renata's completed form, "but you've a bit of a wait here, over an hour."

"Andrews, Mrs. Andrews," she called, and an exhausted-looking woman in a drab dress and tatty sweater followed the employee through the gate.

Renata took her chair and settled in to wait.

Two hours later, someone called her name. Inside, the office was filled with the soprano clatter of thirty or so typewriters, bells chiming when the women reached the end of each line and slammed the carriages back. She was escorted to one of the private offices that bordered the room.

A female officer whose nameplate said, "Carter," offered her a seat while she took the file from the receptionist. She took her time reviewing it before looking at Renata.

"How may I help you, Mrs. Stern?"

Renata cleared her throat. "I just arrived from Egypt, where my husband and I were married. I need to find him." Her voice wobbled.

Carter frowned and lifted her hands. "Mrs. Stern, our men are off fighting, and we can't send women into war zones. You don't look like a stupid person, though, so why are you really here?" She folded her hands together on the desk.

Renata took a deep breath. "Several months ago, I received notice that my husband was injured and in Watford hospital. Shortly afterward I got a letter from him, but it wasn't what I expected. He wanted to divorce me."

Carter took notes as Renata recounted the story and shared Ray's letter with her. When Renata had finished, the officer sat back in her chair and folded her arms.

"I can find out where your husband is. If he's on a ship, you can't go there, obviously. But at least you can re-establish communication."

Renata nodded. "Thank you."

"Please wait here." Carter left Renata listening to the office noise and staring at a photo of a young airman on the desk. Ten minutes passed.

"You're in luck, Mrs. Stern. He has a shore job, logistics and supplies. He was placed in Ottawa initially, but now he's in Esquimalt, on Canada's west coast." She pushed a piece of paper across the desk. "Here's his latest address."

Renata tucked the paper in her pocket.

"You can go to Canada, if you like, as a war bride, all expenses paid, but the voyage is still dangerous."

"I was hoping to get to him this month or next."

"More likely to be a year, I'm afraid. Best if you find something useful to do between now and then. We're sending hundreds of women overseas."

Renata gasped. A year?

"But this is a special case, isn't it? I doubt many of the other brides are looking for a badly injured husband who said he wants a divorce. Is there any way you can get me in sooner?"

Carter looked at her thoughtfully, tapping a pencil on the desk.

"I'll see what I can do. If a space comes up, I'll be in touch right away." She reached across the desk and shook Renata's hand. "Best of luck to you, Mrs. Stern."

Renata walked out of the building in a fog. A year? Did Carter mean what she said?

Helping Nurse Heather and Mrs. Livingstone became Renata's

full-time job. She rolled bandages, made soup, comforted children. There were far fewer raids as the Allies turned the tide of the war, but no one let their guard down.

Finding paper was a challenge, but the backs of old posters gave Renata a medium for drawing. She entertained the young with cartoon sketches. As much as possible, she recorded the sights she saw, and hoped that someday she could show them to her parents and Tommy.

Four months after her meeting with Carter, a letter from the Canadian Naval Office arrived, giving her an appointment a week following.

Private Sutcliffe greeted her again. "Mrs. Stern, good to see you again. Commander Stern is in the west coast fleet HQ." He whistled appreciatively. "Quite the guy you got there."

When Sutcliffe brought out a map, her heart sank. A hostile ocean and a continent—over seven thousand miles—stood between her and Ray. Esquimalt was built around the Navy shipyard adjacent to Victoria, the capital city of British Columbia, located on Vancouver Island.

"The war bride program can take a while. I had an aunt came over from Canada to be with her husband. Took her nearly a year, but someone has pulled some strings for you."

"What?" She gripped the arms of the chair, unsure she had heard correctly.

He smiled. "Yes, you heard me. You'll be sailing within a few weeks. Follow me." Sutcliffe picked up her file and escorted her to another office, this one marked, ironically, "Family Reconciliations." He opened the door and gave her file to the receptionist.

"Please take a number, and have your marriage certificate ready." The cheery female voice belonged to a plain, heavy-breasted blonde in a snug uniform. She handed Renata a card with the number eighty-five stamped on it, and told her to take a seat.

Fifteen women sat on wooden benches, looking tired, bored, and anxious. One had three children who clamored for attention and food. Another was knitting. Two were biting their nails and three were dozing.

Renata sank into her chair and noticed the wall clock said quarter to ten. The tapping of typewriters, the pervasive buzz, people coming and going, created a soporific sound cocoon. Her eyelids drooped; her breathing slowed.

At three o'clock her number was called, and she walked into an open area, with six broad oak desks, five of which were occupied by busy secretaries.

Behind the sixth desk sat First Lieutenant Evens, according to his name badge. Evens's uniform was rumpled and had a stain on one sleeve. He was clean-shaven with a pleasant, open face and fine features. In a previous lifetime, Renata would have found him attractive, especially when he gave her a warm smile and a firm handshake.

"Yes, Mrs. Stern, so you want to go to Canada, do you? Let's see what we can do to get things moving along for you. Let me see your marriage certificate first, please."

Renata handed it over, along with her passport.

He walked Renata through the application process. She must be packed and ready to go with two days' notice. Memories of the *Georgic* surfaced momentarily. Her convoy would sail out of either Liverpool, Glasgow, or Southampton, and she would receive a telegram telling her where and when to report. There were hostels in each city for the war brides, run by Red Cross Escort Officers, women who would chaperone them on the voyage, and give them the final embarkation details. She must not under any circumstances divulge to friends, family, or strangers, when and from where, her convoy would be leaving. That included her husband.

Renata nodded.

Once she arrived in either via Halifax or New York, she would board a train to Toronto. There she would change trains, and continue with the five-day rail trip to Vancouver. A ferry would take her to Vancouver Island. All paid for by the Canadian government.

Renata could not believe her luck. "Would it be possible to stop in Moose Jaw, Saskatchewan, where my husband's family lives?" she asked.

Evens nodded. "Sure, Moose Jaw is on the main rail line. I'll have you issued an initial ticket to Moose Jaw, and then one from Moose Jaw to Victoria. The dates are open, so check with the ticketing clerk ahead of time, once you get there. Any other questions?"

She shook her head, dazed at the speed with which change was happening.

"Then we're all set. Here is your war bride travel form. Don't lose it, whatever you do. And if you change your address, be sure to notify us right away."

"Thank you, Lieutenant. You've been so kind." Renata left, exhausted but eager to leave war-weary Britain.

Chapter Twenty-seven

The Wait, 1943

Knowing she had only weeks to fill rather than a year cheered Renata no end, despite the suspicion she encountered with every new person who heard her speak. A few spat at her and accused her of being a spy. The irony of Hans, a real German, spying for the British, made her want to scream at them that they didn't understand, she was doing all she could, and she hated Hitler as much as they did.

One priority was to catch up with letters home, and give them Ray's new address.

April 1, 1943
Dear Mama and Papa,

Ray is in Canada, not England. It's hard not to feel discouraged, with another ocean to cross and the entire North American continent, but I'm on the list for the War Brides program, so I can travel there and join him. I don't know how long it will take, but I'll let you know when I am allowed. Mrs. Livingstone has promised to forward any letters you send to this address. I'll give you Ray's address when I arrive, assuming all is well.

Everyone is required to help the war effort. Sometimes I work at the soup kitchen, feeding those who've lost their homes in the bombing, and sometimes I help search for survivors. The worst are the children, who are horribly injured or lost their mothers. I cry almost as much as they do, thinking of Tommy. Can you possibly send me a photograph of him?

We hear on the BBC that Monty is beating Rommel. What good news! Now if only the Allies can capture Italy.

How are you all? Please write soon, and kiss Tommy for me.

All my love,
Renata

May 20, 1943
Dear Renata,

We were so relieved to receive your letter and hope you are on your way to Canada by the time you receive this. We're very proud of all you are doing. Here, things have quieted down a lot since Rommel was defeated. We are all breathing much easier and daring to enjoy life a little.

Tommy is growing so quickly. He chatters away all the time, has learned some colors, and loves the hobby horse I found for him. It was in rough shape, but I painted it and he is perfectly happy.

Mama is doing well caring for him and is very protective of him. Perhaps a little too much, but I'm not a mother so I'd best not judge. As for me, my heart continues to act up, so I am unable to treat as many patients as I would like, but we manage in the smaller apartment. Sorry, dear. We couldn't afford to keep the big one.

Lots of love,
Papa

June 19, 1943
Dear Mama and Papa and Tommy,

Did you know the clothing rations here are so restricted, that the women cut the hems off their dresses to make new clothes for children? They look rather daring with short hemlines, and the children look as though they are dressed in bits of old quilts. I saved enough coupons to buy a new winter coat, which I will need in Canada.

I've done a little drawing of where I'm living for

*Tommy. Please explain it to him. I'll send for him as soon
as I can. I would do more drawing, but paper is virtually
impossible to find. There's no shortage of charcoal. (Sorry,
that is a bad joke.)*

*There are hardly any air raids here now, thank
goodness.*

Goodbye for now,
Renata
*PS: Flour mixed with sawdust tastes terrible. I
shall never eat another cake as long as I'm here.*

July 2, 1943
Dear Renata,
*It has been a most difficult time. Two weeks ago,
I found your father at the foot of the stairs, dead. His heart,
of course. The shock put me in bed for a week and Tommy
is beside himself. Sofia looked after him for two weeks, but
he's back now. The worst is money. We have none. Can you
please send us some through the post office?*

*I'm sorry to give you the news this way. He loved
you so much. I wish you were here.*
Mama

Renata clutched her chest and staggered to a bench, gasping.
Never to see her father again! Never to hear his voice or feel his
arms around her. She sat in a stupor until a stranger walked up and
said, "Are you all right, luv?"

"My father is dead," she moaned, not caring that the
stranger saw her agony.

"Let me see you home, then. Where do you live?"

But when she looked up, she saw a man who reminded her
of the captain.

"No, thank you, I'll be fine." She pulled her coat around her
and got up.

It was Hans she needed; Hans who knew her father and
mother, and had helped them to the train station that night. Without
stopping to think, she walked to his flat and knocked. There was no

answer.

She pounded until an old biddy in the basement unit stuck her head out the door and hollered, "Leave it alone, Miss! 'E's gone again. Can't keep track of 'im from one week to t'other."

Renata slumped to the step and leaned her head against the door.

She must have dozed. Footsteps climbing the steps penetrated her subconscious. She looked up to see Hans gazing down at her, hands on his hips, an unreadable expression on his face.

"Well, well, if it isn't the very person who didn't want to see me again." He reached out a hand and helped her to her feet. "What is it this time?" His voice was not angry, but not exactly welcoming, either.

She handed him the letter. "Papa's gone."

Ten minutes later she was seated on his sofa with a cup of chicory coffee in hand. Hans was careful not to touch her. He seated himself in the armchair and leaned forward, elbows on knees, mug in hand.

"I'm sorry about your father. He was a good man. How's your mother taking it?"

"You read the letter and that's all I know, but she's never taken loss well. She wants money and I don't have any. All I get is the wife's allowance from Ray's pay, and that's skimpy enough, since I'm already sending her as much as I can to care for Tommy."

"And your other plans?"

"I'm registered for the War Brides program, for travel to Canada. I should hear any day."

"Sounds like you've made up your mind to stick with your husband."

"I have, having come this far. Can you imagine what an idiot I'd look if I gave up now?"

"Your mother might appreciate it if you went back."

She clapped a hand over her mouth. "I'm ashamed to say I never thought of going back. Hans, I'm so tired of decisions. I want someone to tell me what to do."

"I certainly won't. You're perfectly capable of making decisions. Look at what you've decided so far."

Perhaps he was mocking her, perhaps not, but she sensed under his cynical tone, that if she accepted Ray's proposed divorce, Hans would take her back immediately. No more harsh decisions, only bring her family to England after the war, maybe even sooner. She looked away.

It had been a mistake to come. Already she felt the magnetism between them, despite what had turned into a bit of a quarrel, and felt hot at the thought of them making up, preferably in bed.

"I thought a lot about what you said the last time I was here." She wrapped her arms around herself. "You were right. I've hurt everyone in my path, including you and a few you don't know about. Starting now, I want to do the right thing."

He raised his eyebrows, nodding for her to continue.

"Decisions you make for the wrong reasons can turn out to be right. I believe that. Do you?"

He shrugged slowly, but he was listening, his eyes on her. "Perhaps. What do you mean, particularly?"

She shifted in her seat and set the empty cup on the floor. "I married Ray to get out of Egypt, not because I loved him. He gave me a graceful exit if I want to take it. But perhaps I can make it turn out right."

She looked deep into Hans' eyes, felt a stirring in her groin. It took every ounce of strength to stay seated across the room from him. She owed him honesty, at least. "Hans, I will only say this once: I loved you, even when my mother and friends were telling me to forget you, even when I first married Ray and had his baby. I wrote dozens of letters to you that I never posted. But I don't want an affair with a man living under an assumed name." She dropped her eyes; her hands were tight-knuckled, white. She shivered. "I want my family together again. That's all that really matters in this crazy world. We need to learn how to live in peace, raise children, go on picnics. Normal life, with no bombs and no Hitler and no more young men dying. You can't give me those things."

Hans dropped his head into his hands. "Letting you go twice is more than I can bear." He looked up, pain in every line on his face. "Please stay."

She shook her head. "I can't."

Her chest was tight when she gathered her coat and went to the door.

"Thank you for suggesting I go back to my mother, but I can't afford the fare." A wisp of a smile crossed her face. "Goodbye, Hans."

He grabbed her hand and pulled her to him for one last passionate kiss. Then she ran out, took the steps two at a time while he called her name. She raced to her flat, afraid if she looked back, he would be there.

She had the flat to herself. She wanted to cry, but refused to indulge herself. There was nothing she could do about the ache in her chest, though. Best to focus on doing, not feeling. Covering her eyes, she recited the Kaddish for Papa, feeling isolated, with no fellow Jews to share her sorrow.

Numbness spread throughout her brain, but she had things to do. Mulling over her mother's money worries, she remembered the sketches she'd done in the market. Too bad her mother couldn't do some, too.

She looked up. Why couldn't Mama do artwork again? Her own painting supplies were still there.

She found a pencil and paper.

> *Dear Mama,*
>
> *My heart is broken. Poor, dear Papa! And me not there to share our grief. Who sat shiva with you? A friend suggested I return home, but I have no money, even if passage was available. I will honour Papa on my own. I know we need ten to recite Kaddish, but I hope God understands when I say it myself, and I promise I will recite it monthly until Yahrzeit. God willing, we will be together by then.*
>
> *I will send you a little more of my allowance, but it won't be enough. I have an idea, though. What if you were to sketch postcards like I did? It is easy work, my supplies are still there, and you'd earn lots if you sell to the sailors and soldiers who are always looking for a souvenir*

from Egypt.

But dear Papa. I will love him forever.

How is Tommy doing? Please tell him I love him and will see him again but I don't know when.

All my love,

Renata

Dear Sofia,

I'm writing to you, but please share this with Rachel and Alicia as well, since I can't afford stamps for three letters. You know that my father died. I'm devastated. Please look in on Tommy and Mama, if you can, and let me know how they are doing.

Mother is short of money, so if you could spare a little now and then, she'd be grateful. I suggested she start doing sketches, and if the moment is right, perhaps you could encourage her as well.

I miss you, and there are days when I'm sure I did the wrong thing. I hope that soon I'll find Ray and we can be a family again.

Love to you all,

Renata

She posted the letters the same day and felt a little better. At least she had done something that could help, if Mama was receptive. Next, she went to the bank and arranged to send a little more money to her each month. It left her short. No matter, she was getting good at scrounging. As she gathered bits of clothing and a battered suitcase for her upcoming voyage, she debated whether to write to Ray. Perhaps he would be angry at her for coming and would tell her to stay, and that she could not permit. But on the other hand, he might have second thoughts about divorce, if he knew the effort she had made thus far. Westward, she was determined to go. Nothing else mattered now.

Chapter Twenty-eight

Voyage, 1943

The cool, wet British fall brought yellow and gold everywhere, making even the ruins look cheerful. Renata stood at the sink in Mrs. Livingstone's flat washing dishes when a delivery boy arrived on a squeaky bicycle. Her hands shook as she took the telegram from him. She dried her hands and sat down, heart thudding, and slit the envelope with her nails.

DEPART CHARING X STN PLATFORM B SEPTEMBER 24 0900 HRS STOP

She retrieved the booklet Lieutenant Evens had given her and read the instructions again. *Charing X* meant sailing from either Liverpool or Glasgow. She tossed her apron across a chair, put on her coat, and flew to the Red Cross shelter.

"Mrs. Livingstone, Mrs. Livingstone, I got the telegram!" she shouted, waving it over her head.

The others clustered around, congratulating her with handshakes and hugs.

Mrs. Livingstone walked her outside. "Bloomin' marvelous, dearie! When do you leave?"

"On the twenty-fourth. I'll need to go to the bank and get some money. Oh, Mrs. Livingstone, I can't believe it! I'm so excited."

They caught hands and the two broke into a little street dance.

Less than forty-eight hours later, Charing X station echoed

with the noise of steel wheels, porters' dollies, and feet. Renata promised to write, and Mrs. Livingstone pressed a spam sandwich into her hand for the journey.

At Platform B, a uniformed woman with a clipboard checked off names of arrivals.

"Renata Stern."

The woman flipped over a few sheets of paper, and ran her finger down the list until she found "Stern, Renata." She put a checkmark beside it and said, gesturing behind, "Into that room, love."

The stuffy room held about two hundred women and perhaps twenty-five children and infants. She received another envelope and stood in line for tea and sandwiches. Some of the children were whining, and the smell of a dirty nappy permeated the air. Other women trickled in, and a few minutes later, the one with the clipboard came in and closed the door behind her.

Someone tapped a spoon against a cup and the room quieted.

"Welcome, ladies! I'm going to be your chaperone for our journey to the dock. Which one, will become obvious soon enough. In the envelope are your train ticket and boarding pass for the ship. A few rules."

She ticked them off on her fingers. "One: If you don't have children with you, please help those mums who do. Two: Speaking with other train passengers is strictly forbidden. Three: You will be staying in a hostel prior to boarding your ships. Please obey their house rules. Usually just one night, but delays sometimes happen."

Some of the women snickered. Delays were constant in wartime.

"If you're at the hostel more than one night, you may find conditions a little crowded, so your patience is appreciated. Now, we're going to board the train. We have coaches just for you, so follow me, and we're off."

The chatter started up again. Renata picked up her suitcase and looked around for women with children who might need a hand, but couldn't see any without helpers.

Half an hour later, they pulled out of Charing Cross station. The train headed north, chugging slowly until it was clear of the city. It was difficult to tell that the countryside was at war. Every available field was ready to harvest; cows and sheep chewed their cuds, children played, and houses stood intact.

In Renata's compartment, one mother bounced her baby on her lap. The tot giggled, and saliva dribbled onto his jumper. Renata, thinking of Tommy and the time she was missing with him, had a lump in her throat. She hoped he would remember her.

Three hours later, they disembarked at Liverpool. Buses ferrying the women from the station to the hostel, detoured around collapsed buildings, and craters holding unexploded bombs.

At the hostel, Red Cross Escort Officer Olive Bown greeted the women. "Welcome, dears. There's dormitories on the second, third, and fourth floors; beds are first come, first served. Dinner is at one o'clock, so as soon as you're settled, come back down here and we'll see you fed. Tea is at six o'clock, breakfast at seven o'clock. Curfew is ten p.m. Be careful of your money and your papers as thieves are anxious to get their hands on them."

Renata carried her suitcase to the second floor, but it was full, so she continued up another level. The room contained two rows of iron-framed beds, with thin linens and one gray blanket each. She put her suitcase on one at the end of the row and sat down, wondering what to do next.

The room soon filled. Claiming beds beside and opposite her were two bubbly young women, who introduced themselves as Maisie, from Huddersfield, a small town in Yorkshire, who was heading for Calgary, Alberta; and Lily, from Birmingham, who was bound for Montréal, Québec. Their accents were a strain for Renata to understand, but there was no mistaking their excitement about their forthcoming adventure.

Renata told them she was from London.

"Coo, wun't the bombing dreadful there, luv? 'Ow'd ye manage?" Maisie asked.

Shrugging, Renata said, "It's unbelievable what you can get used to."

"Birmingham took it in the neck too. Me Mum and me brother was both killed when our house took a hit," said Lily.

The other two offered murmurs of sympathy. They returned to the dining room and swapped stories over the meal.

Mrs. Bown addressed them again with more details about their departure.

The next morning, the women and children, with their suitcases, boarded busses for the short trip to the harbor.

It was a nightmarish sight. Rusted hulks of sunken ships jutted up from the water at crazy angles, while active shipping lanes wove around and through the rubble over oily water. Renata grew uneasy. They were thousands of miles from safety with another cold, dangerous ocean to cross.

Boarding proceeded onto the *Britannic*, which was also taking some injured troops home to Canada. She shared a cabin with Maisie, but Lily was on a different ship.

As soon as they had deposited suitcases in their cabins, they headed on deck. Maisie and Renata watched the submarine nets open and the convoy take shape under the eye of the corvettes and destroyers.

When the first meal was served, Renata decided she was already in a different country.

The women gasped and cheered as the stewards brought out platters of roast beef swimming in broth. Beets and parsnips. Huge servings of fresh mashed potatoes dripping with butter and gravy. They devoured the feast; many had seconds. Dessert was apple pie, the flaky moist crust made with real butter and real flour instead of paraffin and who-knew-what-else. The women moaned with the kind of pleasure that in a peaceful world would be reserved for the bedroom.

Renata sunk her teeth into a plum and closed her eyes, feeling the sweet juice in her mouth, remembering the plum tree in their garden in Munich. "Maisie, if Canada is anything like this, I'm going to love it."

"Right, you are, luv! I've been peckish for three years. I wonder if all the meals will be this good."

The relative peacefulness of the voyage worked some healing on

Renata's bruised soul, despite a nagging seasickness that would not go away. She walked around the deck several times a day, noticing the sailors signaling from one ship to another with semaphore flags and lights. The crew treated the women with respect, calling them "ma'am," opening doors for them, and best of all, feeding them so well that they noticed their clothes getting tight.

The one thing there is on a voyage is time. Endless hours with nothing to do but watch the flying fish and the corvettes, bobbing at the perimeter of the convoy. Time to think, time to talk.

Maisie and the others confessed themselves nervous about the upcoming meetings with their new in-laws.

"'Ow about you, Renata?"

"You've had letters from your new families, haven't you?"

They nodded.

"I've had nothing. I don't know what that means, but either they are upset at the thought of a daughter-in-law, or they are very unfriendly."

"You don't know, dear," said Maisie. "Perhaps they've been ill, or traveling, or…" her voice petered out.

Maisie, Renata had learned, was almost unbearably optimistic.

Another woman named Betty said, "I assume they know he's married."

Renata stared at her. Was it possible Ray had not told his parents? That made more sense than other explanations. "I think you've found it, Betty."

She drummed her knuckles on the table, thinking of all she had not told her new friends about Ray: his injury, his divorce papers. They jealously assumed she was reuniting with her husband, while their husbands were still in Europe fighting.

She should have written to her in-laws as soon as she was married, but she had left it to Ray, and men were notoriously bad letter-writers. It was a good thing she was going to Moose Jaw to see them, but it could be more of a shock than she had anticipated.

Canada, they learned, produced vast quantities of newsprint and paper, and there was enough on board that Renata, speaking to the kindly steward, persuaded him to part with a few dozen sheets and some pencils she quickly put to use, sketching her friends, the ship, even some of the sailors, who paid her for them as gifts to wives and mothers.

Eight days later, after hearing "battle stations" twice, losing one small ship, rescuing its crew, and watching corvettes kill the sub with depth charges, the welcome cry of "land ho!" came from the watch. To have crossed the Atlantic safely in 1943 was no small feat. As they clustered on deck with their suitcases, the women hugged and exchanged addresses.

They disembarked at Halifax's Pier 21 into a cold, drafty metal shed. Canadian Red Cross volunteers circulated, offering mugs of tea, coffee, and cocoa.

Clearing customs completed, the women were escorted to a warm room, where they were served another excellent meal.

"Blimey, that was a treat," sighed Maisie, as she wiped her chin with a serviette.

"It wun't 'alf bad," agreed Lily, who had rejoined them.

"I wonder if everyone in Canada eats this well," said Renata.

"Let's just 'ope our lads is doing a great job of knockin' off them huns, so's everyone back 'ome can eat this well again," said Lily.

Lily's comment sobered them. Still, Canada welcomed them with open arms, and for the time being, they were optimistic.

After a night in another Red Cross hostel, they boarded a train for Toronto. Canadian trains were completely different from their British cousins—longer, wider, designed for immense journeys of thousands of miles, not short hops of a few hundred.

Renata felt sick on the train, too. "Travel sickness" advised the porter. "Sit facing forward."

It helped.

In Montréal, they said farewell to Lily and promised to write.

They arrived at Toronto's Union Station after sunset. They could see nothing but city lights, which none of them had seen since 1939, such a magical sight that adults and children squealed with excitement and clapped their hands. Renata's mouth had been open in wonder since they landed in Halifax.

Several of the women would be living in Toronto, and others departed for places in Ontario with very English names like Stratford and Waterloo, but still others to places with names impossible to pronounce, such as Penetanguishine and Kapuskasing. The little group of brides was breaking up, and there were many tearful good-byes and address-exchanges.

"All aboard for Winnipeg, Calgary, and Vancouver," shouted the conductor the next morning, minutes before their next train snorted and glided out of the station. Engines belched smoke and wheels squealed as they gained traction.

On and on and on they went, soothed by the rhythmic clacking of the rails. They rode through prosperous farm country where farmers harvested crops, and trees blazed glorious fall reds, oranges, and yellows.

The train stopped at Sudbury, which the conductor told them was the site of the world's largest nickel mine. Vile smoke from the smelters had killed most plants and animals in the area. Renata was glad when they departed the godforsaken place.

The Canadian Shield wilderness was more rugged and remote than anything in Europe. They passed over countless bridges, through tunnels and cuts that had only been touched once by human hands. Tiny towns were separated by scores, even hundreds of miles. The ancient, primeval land quieted them. On and on, the train continued through the night.

Renata crept into her berth, made up by a black porter, and kept private by heavy green curtains. She was lucky to have a lower berth with a window, so she left the blind up, even though outside was total darkness. She drifted into an uneasy sleep, cradled by the swaying train. Dreams of the captain, the shipper, and Tommy, woke her twice.

Once the train crossed into Manitoba, the scenery changed instantly from rugged, rocky forest to flat farmland. Towns were marked by tall, narrow buildings with the town name painted on them, along with "Manitoba Wheat Board." Once they learned the buildings were grain elevators, spotting the elevators and reading town names became the newest way to pass the time.

Occasional glimpses through the window showed farmland as far as the eye could see. Renata had heard about the Rocky Mountains and wondered how far away they were, and if there were any in Moose Jaw.

Towns rolled by, with quick stops at each. Before long, the conductor announced Regina, a major stop. The train wheezed to a halt, spewing smoke and steam. Renata and Maisie got off to stretch their legs. They purchased a cup of coffee at the cafeteria and watched people bustling in all directions. Porters carted stacks of suitcases and trunks. A small train of funny-looking baggage carts jiggled to the train, and Renata watched three young men load trunks, parcels, and suitcases onto the carts, which were then pulled by a small tractor to the baggage room.

Many of the men wore cowboy hats and walked as though they preferred to ride a horse. One chewed on a long piece of straw.

Maisie pointed at him and she and Renata giggled. "It's just like the cinema."

Renata nodded, grinning.

"All aboard for Calgary and Vancouver!" cried the conductor.

Renata felt more and more nervous as her moment of truth approached. "I'm scared, Maisie. What if they don't like me?"

"Aw, tsh! 'Course they'll like you! And if they don't, then you just drop me a line and you can come and live with me." She gave Renata a quick squeeze.

It was brave talk, considering Maisie didn't know what her welcome would be either, but she didn't have a husband who had asked for a divorce. They swapped addresses. Renata promised to look Maisie up if she were ever back in Calgary.

Three stops and two hours later, Renata stood on the wind-blown platform of the Moose Jaw station, suitcase in hand. The train carried off her only friend, its whistle blowing mournfully. She had never felt more alone.

Chapter Twenty-nine

Moose Jaw, 1943

A harsh wind stung her cheeks and sprayed grit into her eyes the moment she stepped from the train. Renata pulled her coat tight, then wrestled her suitcase through the station to the street. Shielding her face, she paused a moment to look around.

To the left and right, an unpaved street ran parallel to the railway track, disappearing into the yellow gauze of both horizons. A rancher chewing on a piece of straw sped his battered truck westward, spewing dust into the air. Renata coughed and turned away. Straight ahead, red brick buildings lined Main Street, with advertisements on the walls and neon signs out front, proclaiming a café, a hotel, and assorted retail shops. Vehicles lined both sides of the street. It was nothing like Europe. Wild and untamed, was more like it. And no bombed buildings anywhere.

A few teens rode their bicycles in the aimless circles of youth. At one corner, a clutch of women swapped gossip, stealing glances at the stranger.

Squaring her shoulders, Renata headed across the street to the Exchange Café and opened the screen door. It slammed shut behind her, admitting a chilly gust of wind. A middle-aged woman wearing a white uniform, polished a table and filled the serviette holder.

She smiled. "Hi, honey. Just arrived on the train? Pick any table and I'll be right there."

Suddenly Renata did want something to eat, anything to fortify herself for the meeting to come. She slid onto the seat and pulled out the plastic-covered menu tucked behind the salt, pepper, and sugar. The menu was plain, but the pies—apple, saskatoon, rhubarb, and chocolate cream—sounded mouthwatering.

When the waitress reappeared, Renata ordered a slice of apple pie and coffee.

"Do you want cheese?" asked the waitress.

"On the pie? Is that customary here?"

"So, where are ya from, honey? Yeah, we love cheese on our apple pie. Ice cream is good, too, if you don't like cheese." She poised her pen above an order pad, and shifted her weight onto one leg, waiting.

"Very well, I'll try the cheese. Do you by any chance have cream for the coffee?"

Cream was nonexistent in England.

"Loads of cows down the road at Kientz's dairy, so we got all the cream you want. I'll get your pie and coffee right away." The waitress disappeared into the kitchen.

Renata glanced at the only other occupied table.

Two angular old men with leathery skin, wearing fleece-lined jackets and crushed cowboy hats, each held a mug in one hand and a cigarette in the other. They stared at Renata, the look that small-town people give to strangers that says, *You don't belong here.* The moment Renata met their gaze, they returned to their coffee and a discussion of the going price for hogs.

She retrieved her notebook from her bag and found the Stern family's address just as the waitress reappeared with coffee and pie.

"Thank you, that pie looks delicious. Do you know they put paraffin in pies in England, because they have no butter?"

The waitress's jaw dropped. "That's just terrible!" She shook her head in disbelief. "Doesn't it poison people? The paraffin?"

She put the coffee down beside a jug filled with thick cream.

Renata's mouth watered. "No, but it tastes awful." She dribbled some cream in the coffee and took a sip. "Ah, that's so good. And may I ask you a question or two? I'm looking for a family here, but I haven't met them, and I need directions to their house."

"Sure, go ahead."

"It's the Stern family. They have a son, Ray, in the Navy, and another son in the Air Force, and one daughter."

"Uh huh, you mean Jean and Sheldon Stern. Everyone calls them Ma and Pa, because they're always looking out for the women whose husbands are off fighting. I hear Ray is some big-shot Navy officer or something, out in B.C. The daughter, Karen, she's the music teacher at the high school and performs quite a bit."

"That's them. How do I get to their house? Are there any taxis?"

"No, Moose Jaw's pretty small. Just go five blocks west, to Fifth Street, then turn right. Three more blocks and you'll see number three thirty-two, a two-story clapboard. Blue railing and door. Only one on the block."

Renata finished the pie, paid her bill, and dragged the suitcase outside. Before she headed west as the waitress directed, she noted a hotel on the corner—the Churchill, just in case.

The sun dipped toward the horizon and the temperature dropped with it. The belligerent west wind stung her face. Her arms ached from hauling the suitcase, but soon she stood before the blue door. Her heart pounded, and she was perspiring despite the frosty temperature.

She knocked. A large dog inside barked and footsteps approached.

Someone opened the inner door and looked through the screen while the dog snuffled and panted nearby.

"May I help you?" an elderly woman asked.

"I hope so. I have come a very long way to meet you. Are you Mrs. Jean Stern?"

"Ye-e-es," drawn out. "And who are you, Miss?"

Renata took a deep breath. "I am your daughter-in-law, Renata. I'm Ray's wife."

The screen door opened, revealing a short woman of about sixty-five with rosy cheeks and short, curly gray hair. Her worn housedress and apron were dusted with flour. Irritation filled her face.

"Ray isn't married. What are you talking about?" She turned inside the house and yelled, "Sheldon! Come down here! It's about Ray."

Renata felt light-headed, and reached a hand to the railing

to steady herself. Betty was right. Thank goodness, she'd had time to mentally prepare for this moment.

Rapid footsteps clattered down the stairs, and Ray's father appeared. An older version of Ray, he had a full mustache that draped over his mouth, and wrinkles around his eyes that hinted of laughter and sun. She was sure he could hear her pounding heart.

"Come in, Miss." He escorted Renata to the kitchen and offered her a seat.

The excited dog, clearly of mixed parentage, hovered, nudging her knee. She patted its head tentatively. Satisfied, it retreated to the floor and lay there, thumping its tail.

Mrs. Stern sat opposite, dabbing her forehead with a damp cloth. She tapped Sheldon's hand. "She says she and Ray are married. You tell her, Sheldon. Ray's a single man." She twisted her hands.

"Now, Miss," said Sheldon slowly, "you'd better tell us your story. I'll get us a glass of water. Mother, calm down, I'm sure there's a good explanation."

He filled three tall glasses, then set them on the table. He scraped a chair out, folded himself into it, and waited for Renata.

She swallowed. "My name is Renata Stern. Ray and I were married over two years ago, in Alexandria, Egypt. We have a baby, Tommy, who is nearly two now. I have our marriage certificate," she handed them the document, "and a picture of Tommy, and Ray and me, and my passport. I'm your daughter-in-law."

She spread photos and passport on the table.

They gaped at the certificate, picked up the photos, and stared at the wedding band on Renata's finger.

Jean kept shaking her head. "I can't believe he got married without telling us. And we have a grandson?"

Sheldon stroked his mustache and patted her back. "There, there, Mother, it'll be all right," he soothed.

Renata liked him instantly.

She waited while they poured over the photos. A dog yapped outdoors, rousing the Stern's dog. Children ran on the street, laughing and yelling. Wondering if they would accept her, Renata's nervousness grew. The silence dragged on.

Finally, Jean blew her nose and spoke.

"I'd like to hear about the wedding, please."

Renata described their first meeting, courtship, wedding, her pregnancy, and Ray's departure. She described her joy at Tommy's birth, and her devastation at the news of Ray's injury. She showed them the letter from Ray requesting a divorce because of his disfigurement. An hour later, she rested her case.

Sheldon scratched his head. "We know about his injuries. He spent a month here with us, recovering, before the Navy ordered him to Esquimalt."

"How…how badly is he burned?" Renata wasn't sure she wanted to hear the answer.

The intense look she received told her more than words.

Sheldon cleared his throat and seemed to have something in his eye. "Well, Miss…I mean, Renata, he's not the same as he was. Many of the men coming home are not the same."

Jean was on the verge of tears. "I hardly knew him. He's my son and I'll always love him, but…"

"…his appearance is very different, is that what you mean?" Renata spoke as gently as she could. How would she feel if it were Tommy?

"Yes. Terrible what war does to young men." Jean bunched her fingers and stared at the wall.

"Do you think I'm doing the right thing, going to see him?"

Sheldon answered. "He thinks he is ugly now, and to be honest, many people will view him that way. Ray was always a bit vain. You may have noticed."

Renata nodded.

"Now that he's not handsome, he doesn't think anyone can love him. But if you can, and you convince him of it, it will be a step toward healing his soul." Leaning forward, he reached out for Renata's hand. "You may be the very thing he needs. You must love him very much to have made such a journey."

His tenderness took Renata's tension down a few notches. "I do love him. I want a life with him and our son."

Sheldon collected the water glasses and put them in the sink while talking over his shoulder. "Renata, you are welcome to stay with us for as long as necessary. Our home is simple, but we have ample to share. And please, call us Ma and Pa."

Renata wanted to give him a kiss, but she settled for a hug.

"Thank you. I will gladly stay until I leave for Victoria."

Ma took Renata upstairs to Ray's old bedroom while Pa retrieved her suitcase from the yard. Noticing old photos of Ray on the bureau, she picked them up one at a time, fascinated. Ma described them to her. Ray with a pair of skates on an outdoor rink. Ray in the old swimming hole at the river. Ray hunting gophers. The family celebrating Shabbat.

Then Ma offered Renata a bath, which she accepted gratefully. She soaked away the grime and fatigue of the journey in an immense tub of hot water, then returned downstairs.

Ma served a supper of roast lamb, latkes, and string beans. Renata savored every mouthful. Once the table was cleared and dishes done, they headed to the parlor again.

Ma said shyly after they were seated, "We'd love to meet Tommy someday when the war is over."

"What are your plans, Renata?" asked Pa.

"I know he is in a place called Esk—something. I don't know how to say it."

"Es-kwy'-malt."

"Yes. I want our marriage back and I want to raise our child together, if I can convince him that I still love him."

Just then the screen door slammed, and Karen arrived.

"Hi, Ma and Pa!" Books thudded onto the kitchen table. "The rehearsal was tough but in the end…" She walked into the parlor and froze, open-mouthed.

Pa made the introductions. Ma retrieved Karen's dinner from the oven. While Karen ate, Renata repeated her story to her sister-in-law, who plied her with questions.

Finally, she begged off, pleading exhaustion. Upstairs, she studied Ray's photographs, climbed into his bed, and slept.

She dreamed of Ray. She was alone, Tommy was with her mother, and Ray stood at a distance. She begged him to take Tommy, but he refused, and her mother backed away. She tried to reach her mother and Tommy, but could not.

She awakened in a sweat that turned to shivering. She

burrowed into the bedclothes, but sleep eluded her, and the travel sickness had not gone away.

After breakfast, Renata begged Ma not to contact Ray until after she arrived, so she would not lose the element of surprise, which she felt she needed, under the circumstances. Reluctantly, Ma agreed.

Karen, excited to have another female in the family, chattered with Renata about fashions, men, and music. Moose Jaw lacked all but basic shopping, so when Karen saw Renata's war-weary wardrobe, she insisted on a trip to Regina.

"Calgary's even better, but it's too far," she said as they boarded the train for a day excursion.

Department stores were a revelation to Renata. She loved the endless space in Eaton's and The Hudson's Bay. They purchased fabric for dresses, a new pair of shoes each, and a coat to replace the drab, worn thing from London. Milkshakes delighted her. She discovered that French fries were the chips she'd enjoyed in England.

Karen went on about a British airman she liked named Jack, who was in Canada for training. "He's just such a dreamboat," she gushed, hands clasped in excitement. "His family lives on a farm in England somewhere, or maybe it's Scotland."

Renata tired of the mindless prattle. How could she have been one of those girls in Egypt, so long ago? After years of life and death struggles, it seemed so silly. But, dependent as she was on the goodwill of the Stern family, she joined in the conversation with a smile.

"We had dances on the base in Egypt, and lots of men eager to spend their money on us."

"I think maybe Jack's the one, but I'd have to move, wouldn't I?" Karen sipped her coffee. "Was it hard to leave your family?"

Renata paused. "Terribly hard. And I left twice, from Munich and Alexandria. But my mother and son can come to Canada, once the war is over. Egypt isn't an ideal place for people who don't fit into the local culture."

"What's it like to have a baby?"

"Frightening, but the most marvelous thing in the world. Do you think you'd like to have children?"

"Yes, someday. Two boys, two girls, and a bulldog would be

perfect." Karen sprinkled vinegar and salt on her French fries, and munched one thoughtfully.

"Do you want to live in England?" asked Renata, curious.

"Well, not right now, of course, with all the bombs and death and everything. Maybe afterwards. All the local boys here are off fighting, so for girls who want a husband, the Brits are our best bet."

Reflecting that she herself was much like Karen two years ago, oblivious to the demands of marriage and motherhood, Renata felt like the big sister even though Karen was older. She finished her milkshake in silence.

"Time to go; the train's due in about twenty minutes." Karen paid the bill and the women headed to the station.

Two days passed. Ma was polite but cool, accepting Renata's help in the kitchen and around the house, avoiding talk of Ray.

Renata listened to Karen practice the piano, and spent time with her friends, but with Pa she had her most meaningful conversations. He was supportive, practical, and best of all, thrilled when Renata expressed her determination to raise Tommy in the Jewish faith.

"Renata, we are one of only five Jewish families in Moose Jaw. We need more, to make it more comfortable here. Ma, she's always been so proud of Ray. To be honest, he is her favorite, but don't tell Karen I told you so or I'll deny it. To see him damaged, then find out he was dishonest with us, well, it hurts her. Give her some time." He leaned back and puffed on his pipe.

"What if Ray won't take me back? I'm here with no family or friends."

"We are your family, my dear."

"Thank you, Pa, but what if we divorce, and Ray remarries?"

Pa stared at the ceiling and blew a smoke ring upwards, reminding her of Papa and Ray blowing smoke rings on their balcony. She couldn't decide if the memory was sweet or painful.

He cautioned, "Don't put the cart before the horse."

It took Renata a few seconds to decipher the unfamiliar figure of speech.

She sighed. "You're right, of course. I need to go see him as soon as possible, so tomorrow I'll get my train ticket, and with luck, I'll leave in two days' time. Ma can mail him a letter then, if she wants to. You've been so kind."

Pa stood up and pulled her to him in a fatherly bear hug. Tears sprang to her eyes as she remembered Papa.

Chapter Thirty

Victoria, 1943

Passengers, eager for a view of Canada's most English city, crowded the forward deck of the ferry *Princess Marguerite*. Gasps went up when they rounded the bend to the Inner Harbor where, among the sailboats and fishing boats, a gigantic "Welcome to Victoria" sign was fashioned in flowers on the lawn. The stately Empress Hotel, wrapped in ivy, and the Parliament Buildings with their green oxidized copper cupolas and gray stone walls, looked as if they sheltered secrets and ghosts from bygone eras. Horse-drawn carriages clip-clopped up and down the streets, the drivers expounding points of interest to their passengers.

The other passengers *oohed* and *aahd* over the city's beauty, but Renata had shivers and a queasy stomach, and her heart boomed inside her chest like a bass drum. The chilly drizzle didn't help.

Onshore, she purchased tea and toast and thought about her next move, as if she hadn't thought of anything else all the way from Moose Jaw. After the third cup of tea, no brilliant new strategy emerged. She had to go to his home. Dropping a few coins on the table for a tip, she picked up her suitcase and flagged a cab.

Other than a bright blue bridge with massive weights on the east end, Renata noticed nothing about the ride. Her focus was trying to keep the toast in her stomach.

Ten minutes later, the taxi deposited her on Dunsmuir Road in front of Eight Fifty-two. She handed over the last of her money. The taxi sped away.

The yard was unkempt, and a shutter on the main window

hung at a cockeyed angle. For a man as meticulous as Ray, the messy yard was odd. She wondered what she did not know about his injuries.

To be convincing, she had to give not the slightest sign, no twinge, no wince, that Ray's looks disturbed her. Would she know it was him? Pasting on a smile, she climbed the steps and rang the doorbell. A minute later, the door opened.

The man who answered was dark-haired, which was the only thing she recognized. Her smile froze; it took all her self-control not to scream. The left side of his face was an angry red patchwork of skin grafts, and his left ear was missing. A patch covered the left eye, presumably gone, and the left side of his mouth had no lips, which twisted his face into a perpetual sneer. Equally shocking, his clothes were dirty, and he reeked of smoke, perspiration, and alcohol.

"Whaddya want?" he snarled, swaying slightly.

Swallowing and gritting her teeth, she recovered and extended both her hands. Her smile was weak. "Hello, Ray."

He stared, then gasped. "Renata?"

She nodded. "I got your letter, but I couldn't go through with a divorce without seeing you."

Finally, he found his voice. He clung to the doorknob for balance. "Good heavens, how on earth did you get here?"

"It's a long story. I've been trying to reach you since I received your letter." She peered around him, trying to get a glimpse of the house. "May I come in?"

He shuffled back and held the door for her.

"Sorry, just such a...surprise. Come in."

The odor of garbage assailed her, and the place looked worse than anything she had seen in Tolumbat or London. Newspapers and piles of magazines were scattered everywhere. Dirty clothes hung over the worn sofa and piled on the floor. Dishes with moldy food scraps were stacked on the oak desk beside the telephone. The floor was barely visible.

She could not disguise her revulsion. She covered her nose and picked her way over the clutter, looking for a place to sit. He rushed to remove newspapers from the sofa.

"My, uh...I haven't had time to keep the place up. If I'd known you were coming..." he trailed off.

She felt like screaming but knew she must not. She was breathing quickly, frantically, searching for the right words. This was what she had endured so much for? This wreck of a man in his wreck of a house?

"It's all right." It wasn't. She tried hard to smile at him. "I was worried I'd never see you again."

"Renata, why are you here?" he asked, his voice harsh.

She cleared her throat, attempting to keep the pain out of her voice. "Do you remember our wedding ketubah? Our promises to each other?"

"Look at me, I'm a monster. No one can stand to be around me now."

"The people you work with must be able to stand you."

"The Navy? Good grief, no! None of them can look me in the eye I have left."

Renata felt slammed. "Then why did they pay for me to come here? They told me you are a commander doing some kind of supply job."

"All right, all right, I'm on sick leave, but they don't want me. And you'll leave tonight if not sooner. It would be better if you did."

He pulled a cigarette out of the package in his breast pocket and lit it, then seated himself behind the desk on a crooked chair.

"I'm not leaving, Ray." She took a deep breath. "I love you."

They were the hardest words she had ever said. She held out a hand to him, but he cowered like a beaten dog. Better to let him come to her. She sank slowly into the faded sofa and waited, chilled.

He paced the room, chain-smoking. Eventually, he sat down across from her. He leaned forward and clasped his hands on his knees.

"I didn't want you to see me like this. Hell, I don't want anyone to see me. I am a grotesque who frightens little children. Our own son would run away, screaming, if he saw me. Do you deny you felt like screaming when you first saw me? I saw it in your eyes."

She shook her head slowly, horrified and heartbroken. If she had known it was this bad... But she was here. There had to be a way to bring old Ray out of the prison of his flesh.

In her handbag, she found the latest photo of a dark-haired smiling boy holding a wooden truck in one hand and an orange in the other. "Here, I brought you another picture of Tommy. He looks like his father."

"No thanks." He pushed her hand aside.

She left the photo on a pile of books, and got to her feet.

"I could use a cup of tea. If you'll point me in the right direction, I'll make some for both of us."

Since there were no clean cups available, and the sink was piled high with half-eaten meals clinging to dishes, she opted to clean instead. She scraped plates, bundled the garbage outside into a trash can, and found dish soap underneath the sink.

It felt like scaling a mountain, but the pile of dishes shrunk. There were no clean tea towels, so she let the dishes drip dry while she collected dirty laundry from the living room, kitchen, bedroom, and bathroom, and deposited it by the basement door. Six or seven loads, she estimated.

There was no sound from the living room. She peeked in to see Ray, still smoking, gazing out the murky window.

"Ray?"

He turned but said nothing.

"Can you show me where to find the tea?"

He sighed and rolled his eye, found tea crammed on a shelf with other tins and boxes. The kettle was on the stove, along with numerous pots, the contents of which were in various stages of decomposition.

Renata hauled the offending pots to the sink, filled the kettle, and turned on the burner.

"You don't have to do this, Renata." There was an edge to his voice.

"If we want tea, yes I do." *Since you clearly haven't been doing shit in this place for months.*

"I've been managing okay."

She faced him, cheeks blazing.

"You call this managing? This is a pigsty! We lived better than this in Tolumbat!" She folded her arms with a thump. "Ray Stern, Commander, RCN, you are a damned disaster, and I'm not talking about your face. This filth disgusts me far more than your scars."

She returned to the sink, furiously scrubbing food-encrusted pots, not caring what Ray did, wishing she had never come.

He stood by silently, watching.

The whistle of the kettle interrupted her. She made tea. A quick check of the icebox revealed nothing fit for human consumption, so they would drink it without milk.

"Can you clear a spot for us?"

He slid clutter to one side of the table. "Here, is that better?"

She ignored his sarcasm, brought the cups and teapot over, poured the tea, and sat waiting for it to cool. Ray blew the steam off his cup and took a tiny sip. Tea, the time-honored British ritual to solve all problems.

Searching her mind for a neutral subject of conversation, she finally decided on art.

"I began sketching again while I was in London. Can you imagine what the worst problem was?"

"Finding paper, I'll bet." He swallowed a few mouthfuls of tea and wiped his mouth with the back of his hand. "I was there, remember?"

She nodded. "I used cardboard, old posters, anything. But there was no shortage of charcoal. Burned wood everywhere. Messy, though."

The hint of a smile crossed the good half of his face.

She smiled back.

"You were always determined, weren't you?" he said. "Nothing ever got in the way of you getting what you wanted. I suspect you had your sights on me when I was still seeing Isabella."

Heat suffused her face. She shook her head. "I'm ashamed of that, but not sorry about the result."

"Still?" His eyes locked on hers.

She could not falter, must be honest. "I hope so. I need some time to..."

"Get used to my horrific face?" His voice inched up a couple of notches.

"Not just that. You've changed inside as well, and that's the worst part. I can get used to your face, but I can't get used to someone who has given up on himself."

He slapped her across the face, knocking her off the chair.

"What the hell do you know about it, little Jewish princess? Daddy not doing enough for you these days?"

Her gaze drilled into him as she got up. "Papa is dead. Mama has been raising our son for the past two years."

She stormed out of the room, but there wasn't much space to hide in the tiny house. A pack of cigarettes and lighter were on his desk, so she helped herself to one and stood by the window, smoking, trying to calm down. There was no movement in the kitchen, so once the cigarette was finished, she stubbed it out and went in search of him.

He was still at the table, his head down on his hands. Flummoxed by the weirdness, she hesitated, then barely touched his shoulder.

He flew up, threw off her hand, and ran out the back door, but not before she saw the wetness on his face. Poor bastard, what had he gone through?

Much as she wanted to, she knew following him would not work, so instead, she continued cleaning. Once the dishes were done, she made space for them in the cupboards. Empty boxes, half-eaten donuts, scrunched paper bags all went in the garbage. With satisfaction, she stacked the clean dishes on clean shelves and turned to the next task: clearing every horizontal surface.

Old newspapers going back months went outside. She filled one trash can and started on the next, wondering what day was garbage pickup, or if they had to burn it. Empty food cans. Unopened mail, most of it advertisements. She tossed the advertisements and set aside the real mail for him to attend to whenever the mood struck, which she hoped would be soon.

Slowly, the home began to emerge. Still dirty, but much less cluttered. She had not found mops and brooms, but at least she could see the worn linoleum in the kitchen, and the scuffed hardwood in the living room.

When she glanced at the clock sitting on a shelf in the living room, she was stunned to realize that two hours had passed. No wonder she was tired and hungry, but where was Ray? Minutes later, he came in, shivering, having left without his coat while the flaccid autumn sun rationed its rays.

He found a clean glass, filled it with water, and leaned against the counter. His eye twitched while he scanned the cleaned room. "I'm sorry, Renata. I haven't been myself lately."

No kidding. She tried again, reaching out to him. This time, he allowed her to lay her hand on his arm. "You're my husband. I forgive you. Can we start again?"

She asked him to tell her what had happened. He shook his head, looking out the window.

"I don't talk about it. Unless you've been in combat you can't understand the fear and horror. You wouldn't have a clue."

She stood, hands on hips. "Actually, Ray, you are wrong. I've known plenty of fear and horror. I was flogged with a riding crop. I was raped on the boat that took me to London. I was on that boat when it was torpedoed, burned, and sank. I saw men jump to fiery deaths in a burning ocean, and came close to drowning myself. Oh, I know fear. You think it was easy for me to come here and beg you to take me back? To love me again?"

Her voice wavered, and she turned away. "I'm going back to cleaning."

She returned to the kitchen and was soon elbow-deep in soapy water. Scrubbing the dishes helped her calm down.

Fifteen minutes later, she heard footsteps behind her.

Ray joined her, produced a clean dish towel, and began drying dishes. He cleared his throat. "Uh, I'm sorry, Renata. Really sorry. You suffered for me and I'm so ashamed."

He reached for another clean pot and wiped it dry.

Renata held her breath.

He continued. "After what you've gone through, I owe it to you to tell my story, if you still want to hear it."

Drying her hands on her skirt, Renata turned to him. "Of course, I want to hear. Shall we sit down?"

He led her back to the living room sofa, avoiding her glance.

"What happened, Ray?" She sat beside him and took his hand.

He took a deep breath.

"I was on a ship that had just docked when the first bombs started falling. The ship's crew had all guns blazing, and managed to knock one enemy out of the sky. We all cheered at that, but an instant later, a bomb landed amidships and blew everything to hell."

Ray stood and paced. "I was barely far enough from the damage. Everyone closer was killed outright. I felt fire on my face, but a young sailor in front of me looked worse than I felt, and his leg was badly broken. I managed to drag him to safety before I collapsed. I woke up later in the hospital. It would have been better if they had just left me."

When he looked at her, she saw pure agony on his damaged face.

She went to him and put her arms around him.

For the first time, he returned her gentle embrace. "We've both suffered, Ray," she whispered. "Can we help each other heal? No one should have to go through this kind of thing alone."

He nodded, then went to his bedroom and returned with a handkerchief. After blowing his nose and wiping his face, he laughed, a wry cackle. "Now on top of ugliness and a bruised ego, I've turned into a weakling, crying in front of my wife."

Renata shook her head, and stroked his scarred cheek. "It's all right. What happened with the Navy?"

"They sent some idiot to assess whether I was ready for work. The young officer could not look at me, and made excuses to get out of my ward."

She held his face in her hands and gazed into his eye. "And when you got here, you decided to stay inside and never go out?"

He blushed and nodded, twisting out of her reach.

"You're not on sick leave, are you? The Navy put you on permanent disability. Nobody wanted to force the disfigured commander back to work, because they didn't want to see you either."

He looked up. "How did you know?"

"Just a lucky guess." She tugged him back to the sofa. "There's more to my story."

She described getting permission to sail to Canada as a war bride. Of meeting Hans, she said nothing. He was in her past, and she needed to focus on the wobbly present. When she mentioned meeting Ma and Pa, Ray was stunned.

"Never in my wildest dreams did I imagine you meeting them. I came to Esquimalt, to get away from their pity." He paused and rubbed his chin. "I suppose I should ask how they are."

"Worried, especially your mother, although your sister doesn't let much bother her, does she?"

He snorted. "You might say that. She's a flighty woman, if ever there was one."

Cheered, Renata nodded. "But Pa is a dear. I hope we can see them again soon."

He shrugged. "Maybe. Hey, look, enough talking. Are you hungry?"

"I've been hungry for hours now, but you don't have anything to eat in this place, unless there's a pantry you haven't shown me."

"I suppose cold beans out of a can won't do?"

She smiled. "That's more like it. You always had a joke or two ready. If there's a grocery store close, I'll go pick up something, if you have some money."

She prepared the meal of salmon, turnip, and potatoes, while he remained in the living room reading a newspaper and listening to a local radio station. After the openness of their earlier discussion, she felt him distancing himself again. Although encouraged by his honesty, she suspected there were other demons he was battling. They were in uncharted territory and she had no one to help her. Touching his damaged face, looking at him directly was hard enough. She tried to imagine how she would feel if she were disfigured, and realized suicide would be a reasonable option.

The meal was quiet.

"I'd forgotten what good home-cooked food tastes like." Ray cleaned the plate, pushed back from the table and smiled, then stopped and touched his face.

"It's all right," said Renata. "Your smile isn't the same, but I know you're not making faces at me."

She popped a piece of juicy salmon into her mouth. "Let's go for a walk after dinner. I need some fresh air, and you should get some too."

"I don't go for walks anymore."

"You can't hole up in here forever."

"Why not? I hate stares.

"Because if we're going to be a couple, you need to live in

this world, not just this house. Come on, I'll be with you and you can cover part of your face with a scarf."

"Who says we're going to be a couple? Just sign those divorce papers and be on your way."

She glared at him. "You said you didn't like your parents' pity, but you know what's worse? Self-pity. Now get your coat."

The Ray she remembered would not have accepted orders from her, but he meekly retrieved their coats from the hall closet.

She adjusted his scarf to hide the missing ear and twisted mouth and asked him to look in the mirror when she was done.

He grunted assent, pulled on his gloves and they were off, after he looked around to make sure no one was in sight. He accepted Renata's proffered hand.

She nodded, smiling encouragingly. "If they see you with me, they'll know it's all right. You should wear your uniform, so they will know you were injured in the war."

She heard his choppy breathing and felt his hand shaking, but there were few people out in the quiet neighborhood after dark.

They passed another couple. The husband tipped his hat to Renata, who nodded. The wife's eyes darted to Ray, then back to Renata, who saw sympathy, not horror, in her eyes.

A young man rode by on a bicycle, ignoring them.

They continued for six blocks and turned back.

Ray thanked her as he hung up their coats. "I've become a hermit, and I'll go mad if I stay inside much longer. Perhaps I'm a little mad already." He looked around the tidier living room. "You've been here less than a day and already the place is transformed." He kissed her awkwardly on her forehead.

"Thanks. Now, we have dishes to do. If you want to help, that is."

She headed for the kitchen and collected plates, not expecting Ray to join her, but he did. The kitchen was clean in ten minutes.

"Would you like some brandy, Renata? I think we both deserve it." He produced a bottle and two glasses, which they took to the living room. The liquid seared her throat, warming her in seconds.

"Cheers, Ray."

He raised his glass. "Cheers."

The awkwardness dissolved after the first glass, but it felt like a different courtship to Renata, more like de Villeneuve's fairy tale, "Beauty and the Beast," instead of "Cinderella." It would be vital to get Ray out a little more. She doubted they would ever have large numbers of friends, but she could not cope with him staying home all the time.

They shared more stories of their time apart. She was voluble; he, laconic. Nevertheless, it qualified as a conversation. Updates on Sofia and Hamish. Pranks the sailors played on one another. Papa's gradual decline. The evening wore on, and with it, Renata's energy flagged.

"I need some sleep, Ray. I've been up for twenty-four hours."

"All right, it is getting late. But now," he glanced in the direction of the bedroom, "we come to a test. Will you share my bed?"

There was only one possible answer. Her stomach tightened, but she made herself smile. "Of course, provided you bathe first."

It was the fastest bath on record, after which he took her suitcase into the cramped bedroom and watched while she undressed. Images of their early lovemaking, her tempestuous affair with Hans, and the rape swirled in her mind. She found herself shaking and cold in her flannel nightgown, so she jumped into the bed and pulled the covers up around her chin.

"I'm nervous, Ray. We haven't done this for a long time."

"Just like riding a bicycle, so I'm told." He slid in beside her, naked, and reached an arm across. "But I don't like nightgowns. Take it off."

"I'm cold."

"I will warm you in no time."

Left without excuse, she removed the nightgown and dove back into bed, wondering if she could go through with sex. It was a good thing he had no eye to see the misgivings written on her face. Perhaps if she closed her eyes. But as soon as she did, Hans was before her. She opened them again.

Ray's hand found her breast and caressed it gently, then more urgently. She gasped when he dragged his nails across her belly, making it flutter. There was no doubt he was ready; she felt his hardness against her. Sliding his fingers between her legs, he pushed her legs apart, then rubbed her until she was panting, and, without thinking, she wrapped one hand around his manhood and squeezed. It was his turn to gasp.

He slipped inside and began thrusting, slowly, then faster and faster until they both cried out, then collapsed in one another's arms, in tears.

She didn't dare question what her own tears were for.

"I don't need to ask if that was good for you, do I?" he asked after he'd found two bottles of beer in the icebox and brought them back to the bed.

Shocked at her ability to be aroused despite his appearance, it dawned on Renata that ugly people, presumably, enjoyed sex, too. Now she knew how. Appearance didn't matter; it was more about the partner's ability to give pleasure. She smiled, a genuine, deep-down smile, for the first time.

"No, you don't. You didn't have any trouble, either." Unconsciously she laid her head on his chest. He brought his arm around her and held her close.

The beer forgotten, they fell asleep in each other's arms.

Chapter Thirty-one

Victoria, 1943

He woke her licking her nipples. Startled, she responded willingly enough, and they spent the next hour making love. It almost felt like they were back in Alexandria, discovering the joys of the flesh with each other for the first time.

However, her sense of relief was tempered when he announced it was time for his morning radio program, and he would bathe later. The bathroom was too small for two, so she waited for him to wash before running water for her own bath. She soaked until it cooled, wondering what to do. Her confusion grew once she was dressed and saw him slumped over his desk, dozing, while the radio blared news of Allied victories in Italy.

When she shook his shoulder, he mumbled, "Go 'way."

"What's wrong, Ray?"

He lifted his good eye and fixed her with a baleful glare. "Are you shittin' me?"

She hissed at her own stupidity. "Is there some money for me to get more groceries, so I don't have to run to the store three times a day?"

He pushed onto his elbows and leaned his head in his hands. "Money. She wants money. Shit." He pulled open a drawer in the desk and handed her twenty dollars. "This better be enough for a week, gal."

She took the money. By the time she had her coat on, his

head was down again.

Some vague fear prompted her to look in the bathroom, for what she didn't know. The towels were hung, the tub was empty. Wondering if they needed bathroom cleaner, she pulled open the medicine cabinet.

It was full of pill bottles. She opened one bottle, which was half full. Morphine, said the label. Another bottle, from a different doctor. Morphine. And another, and another. She closed her eyes and leaned on the wall, feeling sick.

As she walked to the grocery store, she wondered where she would find help. Maybe a pharmacist would know. She selected food, paid, and bagged it.

"Is there a chemists' nearby?" she asked the clerk.

The woman squinted at her. "Chemist? You mean drugstore, honey. From England?"

Renata nodded, her lips tight. She was in a hurry.

"Up the street and turn left. You'll see the Rexall on the corner."

The pharmacist, a white-haired man in his sixties with thick glasses, had two suggestions after hearing Renata's story.

"Morphine? You need to get him to his doctor. Hard to treat, I understand. Hide all the morphine or better yet, throw it away where he can't get it, but don't expect him to be happy about it."

"How would he have gotten all he has?"

He shrugged. "Pretty easy for him to go to different doctors with the same complaint and get multiple prescriptions. We see people we think are addicts sometimes, but there's no central registry and we aren't allowed to deny a doctor's prescription. Sometimes I tell the doctor. Sometimes they listen, sometimes they don't. Sorry I'm not much help."

"You have been very helpful, thank you."

It was a start, but disposing of the morphine would be tricky with Ray in the house all the time.

Ray was still dozy when she arrived home. Making no attempt to be quiet, she cleaned out the icebox and put away groceries. She made a mental note to ask Ray where he ordered ice, once he was conscious.

While storing shampoo and sanitary supplies, it occurred to her that she couldn't remember her last monthly. With all the coupling she and Ray had done, there would be no surprise if she had conceived again, but when she worked backwards, she realized with shock that her last period had been in London. Two months, nearly three months ago. All the travel sickness… she should have realized.

She closed her eyes. She was carrying Hans' child. She leaned against the counter, clenching her fists. Her mind felt like a cloud full of rain it had not yet dropped.

Ray must think it was his, or she would have to leave. Maybe she should leave anyway. Things here were not exactly cozy. Her thoughts returned to the stash of morphine pills. A few extra and he would never wake up. Would it really be so bad? He had expressed a desire for death a few times already. Helping him along wouldn't exactly be a crime, would it? Then she could write to Hans, get Tommy and Mama back, and…

She shuddered. Was she really thinking of murdering her own husband? Face burning with shame, she returned her attention to the kitchen.

She located an ancient percolator in a cupboard she had not yet tackled, and put it on the stove with some fresh ground coffee. The aroma was heavenly. When it was ready, she poured herself a cup with shaking hands, and added a dollop of cream.

It tasted as good as it smelled, but did not solve the quandary she was in. If she could get Ray to stop using morphine, then get him cleaned up, find a job, maybe this marriage would survive. It had impossibility written all over it. If she could get a job until the baby came, they would have enough to live on for a few months. Then, maybe, he would be ready to quit the morphine and look for work. Or maybe he'd throw her out of the house, and she would be alone in a foreign land with an infant.

She must tell Hans. But Ray?

She heard a noise from the living room, and he wandered in, scratching his head and armpits.

"I thought I smelled coffee."

"You did. Would you like some?" She poured it for him while he sat down. "Hungry? I could make you some toast."

"You don't have to do all this for me, you know." He stirred a spoonful of sugar into the coffee.

"I didn't have to travel from Egypt, get shipwrecked, survive bombing in London, and come across the Atlantic and Canada, either. But I did." She put bread into the toaster, found butter and jam.

"I wouldn't have done all that for me."

She noticed he slopped a bit of coffee with unsteady hands. She flipped over the toast, watched it carefully, then took it out, spread butter and jam, and divided it onto two plates.

"Here you go."

They ate their toast in silence. She felt taut as a violin string, afraid she would snap.

"More coffee?" she asked.

He held out his cup; she refilled it. Interesting how he said he didn't need her, but he was sure acting like he did.

She dusted crumbs off her fingers and slurped her drink. "Ray, I need to ask you something."

He looked at her.

"Why do you have all that morphine in the bathroom?"

His expression changed from bored to wary. "The doc gave it to me for pain. You can't imagine the pain I went through."

"Um-hm. I've heard that burns are the very worst sort of pain." She swirled the last of her coffee in the cup and swallowed it. "I didn't realize you're still in that much pain."

He shifted sideways on his chair. "Not anymore, but I like to have it around in case."

"Ray." Her voice sharpened. "How often are you using? How many pills a day?"

"Hey, what are you, my doctor? Just some now and then, whenever I need it."

"You had some this morning after we had sex, didn't you? You didn't seem to be in pain while that was going on."

He stood suddenly, sending the chair flying backwards.

"Mind your own business, why don't you? Leave me alone!" He went into the bedroom and slammed the door.

Being alone gave her time to think. After washing the dishes, she ventured into the basement. Dingy and cobwebby, it had rough wooden shelves along the walls, full of boxes, contents unknown. The concrete floor had a drain in the middle. Clotheslines were tacked between floor joists. Instead of a washing machine, she found a washboard and two huge square tin tubs on stands, which would make six loads backbreaking work. Instead, she sifted through the piles for towels, underwear, and a few changes of clothes for each of them. A conveniently located tap filled the tubs.

While she scrubbed clothes, she planned. Ray's pills must be disposed of in a place he could not find. She would flush the pills down the toilet, and leave the empty bottles in the cupboard, except for one. He'd need a few pills to get used to the idea that there would be no more.

Ray would not interrupt her while she was in the bathroom with the door locked. She smiled grimly, and headed outdoors to hang the clean washing.

But she had heard of addicts getting ill and mean when they were denied their drug, and she didn't want to be alone with Ray then. She thought of Maisie in Calgary, Ma and Pa in Moose Jaw. Maybe Pa would be willing to help. She couldn't expect Maisie to come all this way for someone she had never met, and anyway, Renata needed a man's strength.

The laundry snapped in the breeze once she got it on the line that ran the length of the yard. It would dry quickly while the sun lasted.

Inside, she checked the bedroom door. Still closed. A good time to write. She found paper, envelopes, and a fountain pen in the desk and decided to write to her mother first.

Dear Mama and Tommy,

I arrived in Victoria, Canada, which is a very beautiful city. Ray has a small house. His injuries are rather shocking, but so far, we are doing as well as can be expected. We'll send for you the instant the war is over.

Love,
Renata

Dear Ma and Pa Stern,

I arrived yesterday and met Ray. He is worse than I expected, and I don't mean his face, although that's bad enough. He is addicted to morphine. You cannot imagine the condition of the house when I arrived. It was my first clue that something was seriously wrong. He never goes outside, eats food cold out of cans, and hoards newspapers. At least he allowed me to clean, and it looks better now, but he took morphine this morning, then slept for several hours. When I confronted him with my suspicions, he got angry and locked himself in the bedroom. Sorry to bring you this news, but I need your help.

Pa, is there any way you could come here? I want to help him, and that means getting rid of the morphine. He's going to go through a terrible time then, and I am worried for my own safety. I understand if you can't, but I need someone strong and sensible here, and I don't know anyone else to ask.

Please reply as soon as possible,
Your daughter-in-law,
Renata

And now, the hardest.

Dear Hans,

Please forgive me for breaking my own rule that I not contact you, but you'll see why in a few lines. I've been here with Ray for over a month now. It has been terribly difficult and many days I want to run away. We have some serious issues to resolve, one of which is that I'm expecting another baby, and Hans, it is yours. I was sick so much on the trip from London, but I put it all down to travel sickness, and I was too preoccupied to notice my monthlies had stopped. I don't expect you to do anything, even if you

could right now, but you will soon be a father. Regardless
what happens between Ray and me, your child will be loved
and cared for.
> *Always,*
> *Renata*

She addressed envelopes and found stamps in a drawer. Grabbing her coat, she ran to the mailbox near the grocery store, and posted them. It would take a month for Hans and Mama to get theirs, but Ma and Pa would have theirs in less than a week. She could not throw away the morphine before she heard from Pa.

Pa arrived three weeks later. Renata met him at the dock, since Ray was still reluctant to be seen in public. Renata used the time alone with Pa to update him on the plan: destroy all but a few of the pills tomorrow morning.

Ray knew his father was coming, but not why.

He greeted his father with a smile as huge as his face could manage, and a handshake.

"Glad you could come, Pa. Now, you can tell me all about Ma and Karen. Renata, could you make some coffee?"

"Nice to see you, son. Glad your wife asked me." Pa settled comfortably in a kitchen chair.

Renata brought coffee and cookies, then made dinner while the men chatted. Ray had perked up, and she was happy for him, especially knowing he was heading into a very rough week.

They ate, played a few rounds of cribbage, went for an evening walk. Pa would sleep on the sofa, where Renata had set up sheets, a pillow, and a blanket. She grew jittery as the evening wore on.

Ray asked, "Hey, honey, something the matter?"

She shook her head. "No, just tired. Do you mind if I go to bed now?"

"Nope. Good night." Ray kissed her on the lips.

"Good night." Pa dipped his head, his look transmitting his agreement to go ahead with their plan.

Ray slid between the sheets long after she was asleep.

Next morning, Pa asked Ray to show him the neighborhood while Renata announced she would take a long bath.

The instant the men were out the door, she turned on the taps. While the bath filled, she began emptying pill bottles into the toilet. She worked feverishly, flushing the toilet and replacing caps on the pill bottles. Seventeen bottles in all, plus one with four pills that she kept. Once the pills were gone, she turned off the taps and climbed into the tub, enjoying the last few minutes of peace she was likely to have for the next week.

She was in the kitchen making soup for lunch by the time the men returned.

"Did you enjoy your walk?"

"Very nice neighborhood," Pa commented, "but while I'm here, how would you feel about me giving the yard a once-over?"

Ray ground his jaw. "Pa, I'm embarrassed it looks so messy. But if you really want to…"

"Tea's ready." Renata set a tray on the kitchen table and poured, giving the men no polite option but to sit down and drink it with her. Renata's pulse was racing. She cleared her throat.

"Ray, I have something to tell you. Two things. First, we are going to have another baby."

"Wonderful, son, wonderful! Congratulations!" Pa clapped him on the shoulder.

Ray's jaw dropped. "But you've only been here two months!"

"Yes, but we've been very married, haven't we?" She gave him a seductive smile.

He blushed. "Wow. Okay. But you mentioned two things."

"This one is harder. Remember when I asked you about the morphine?"

His eyes narrowed.

"You have part of one bottle left. The rest of it is gone."

"What the hell? Fuck, Renata!"

"Language, Ray, language," Pa interrupted.

"You have no business doing that! It's my body, my health, you have no right!" Ray picked up his cup of tea and threw it across the room.

It smashed into a million pieces, leaving a trail of tea

spattered across the floor, and a dint in the wall. Renata shrunk into her chair, but he grabbed her by the neck, hauled her to her feet, and pressed her to the wall, screaming, his scarlet face an inch from hers.

"You waltz in here, turn my life upside down, get pregnant, and you take away my one escape? You bitch!"

Pa pulled Ray's arms, trying to separate the two.

"Now, son, she's your wife. Let's sit down and talk it over."

Ray was panting, still furious, but he allowed Pa to take him to his chair.

Renata sagged. Shaking, she sat down, and moved her chair closer to Pa's.

Pa spoke first. "I know you're angry, son, and I understand why. But you need to listen to Renata for a few minutes. And I will not allow you to lay a hand on her, is that clear?"

Ray was seething. But he nodded.

She clasped her hands to stop the shaking. "I knew something was wrong, more than the burns, when I got here. In Egypt, you were the tidiest man I had ever met. The messy house was bad enough, but you were dirty, your clothes hadn't been washed in forever. Then I saw all the pills, and I asked a pharmacist and two doctors. They told me you are a morphine addict, and it is very common in people who were given a lot of morphine in the hospital. But it's ruining you as a person. I'm trying to save your life, here, Ray."

"I don't want you to save my lousy life!"

"There are still some pills left in one bottle, so space them out. You will get very sick as your body adjusts, and you may need to go to the hospital."

"No! No hospitals!"

"Pa and I are going to help you through it."

He got up, running a hand through his hair, and paced the room. "What the hell have you done?"

He headed to the bathroom and opened the cabinet door. They could hear him opening bottles and dropping them on the floor. He began throwing them. Shattering glass echoed through the house.

"You fuckers!" he roared. Next thing he was outside, running down the street.

With Pa's help, she cleaned up the mess, noting that the bottle with the pills was intact. Ray had no coat so would not last long outdoors, but she was afraid of what he would do next.

"He's in a bad way. I'm glad you wrote." Pa said. He hugged his daughter-in-law.

"You see why I couldn't do it alone."

He nodded.

"My only other option was to leave. I can't live like this."

The front door crashed open and Ray stormed in, ignoring them. He went to the bathroom and they heard him fiddling with the medicine cabinet.

Renata and Pa exchanged glances.

From the bathroom, Ray went to the bedroom and shut the door.

Ray had taken the remaining pills, and was soon in a deep sleep.

Pa offered to stay in the bedroom with him.

Renata declined. "I'll leave the bedroom door open. If you hear anything strange, come in."

"I will. Be careful, now, I don't want you hurt, too."

"Good night, Pa. Let's leave the kitchen light on, shall we?"

"Fine with me. Good night, Renata."

She was awakened hours later by Ray moaning and thrashing around.

"No, no, need my pills. Get me my pills, will you?" He tapped the flat of his hand on her shoulder. "Pills, please, I need more!"

He was sweaty.

She held his hand as Pa came in rubbing his eyes. She shook her head at him.

Ray sat up suddenly. "Where the hell are my pills?" He was first angry, then pleading. "My pills, please, don't do this, get me my pills."

Renata kept her voice steady. "There are no more pills, Ray. You're going to feel strange and sick for a few days, but we're here to help you through it. Life will be much better without them."

"NO!" He aimed a fist at Renata's head

Pa, with lightning speed, deflected the blow. "Stop it, Ray! You're a little out of your head right now."

Pa and Renata stayed with him until dawn, when he complained of a headache and began crying.

"Just let me die, Pa. I'm such a mess. Go away, Renata. You can find someone better than me. Just go away and leave me alone." Ray sniffed constantly and the pile of dirty handkerchiefs on the floor grew.

"We're not leaving you alone, Ray," said Renata. "Pa and Ma want you alive and so do Tommy and I. You remember, your son, Tommy?"

At mention of his faraway son, he focused, swaying, on Renata.

"We have a son? How come you never told me?"

"I did tell you, you've seen photos. He needs his father. Come on, Ray, you can get through this."

Renata and Pa took turns sitting with Ray, taking him to the bathroom, sponging down his sweat-covered body and rubbing cramped, aching muscles. Eating was difficult. They managed to get some broth into him, but Renata and Pa needed more substantial meals, so she made a pile of sandwiches and left them on the counter, so they could eat anytime.

The worst was to come.

"I'm gonna be sick," Ray announced, but before they could get him to the bathroom, he vomited and lost control of his bowels at the same time. The stench was hideous, the bed awash in excrement.

Renata propped him up with one arm and Pa took the other.

"We're taking you into the bathroom, so we can clean you up, Renata said.

"Come on, son. It's going to get better soon."

Ray began to laugh, but instead vomited in the hallway.

Pa said, "Let's sit him on the toilet, Renata, then one of us can clean him and the other can clean the bedroom."

"Right."

They arranged Ray on the toilet, just in time for another

round of diarrhea.

"I'll clean him, Pa. Just remove the dirty bedding and put it downstairs. We don't have time right now to wash it, and I may just throw it out."

Ray curled onto his thighs and wailed. "I'm so cold, I feel awful. Put me out of my misery, please, someone."

Thankful that she had washed towels before all this got started, Renata ran hot water into the sink and lathered soap onto a washcloth.

"I'm washing your back now, Ray, then I'll dry you off. One bit at a time, but I need to clean your privates, too." She reached over and flushed the toilet. "Give me your arm. That's good, now the other one." She worked methodically, focusing on the vomit that had settled in his chest hair, on his face, and the creases of his groin.

Ray's eyes were half-closed, but he cooperated, even bending over the tub when she told him to.

Never had she expected to have to clean a grown man's soiled behind. Gritting her teeth, she scrubbed, rinsed, and dried him. *If this wasn't love,* she told herself, *it had to be stupidity.* She threw a large dry towel over his shoulder and looked at the man she had married. Unexpectedly, warmth spread through her breast. She wrapped her arms around him and kissed his forehead.

He looked at her and laid his head on her belly.

Pa returned, announcing that the bed was re-made. "I found an old chamber pot in the basement. We can keep that in the bedroom in case you have a sudden need, Ray."

"I don't care, just let me die," he moaned.

"Here we go, back to the clean bed." Pa and Renata helped him into bed, whereupon he immediately curled into a ball.

Half an hour later, he sat up abruptly. "Everything hurts. I gotta shit again."

This time they got him onto the chamber pot in time. The stool was liquid, beyond foul, but the bed was still clean. He fell asleep when they tucked him back into bed.

When Pa and Renata were out of the bedroom for a few minutes, he took her aside and asked quietly, "You sure you signed up for this, honey?"

Her eyes filled. She'd been thinking the same thing for the

past three days. She shook her head slowly. "He's all I've got, Pa. I came this far, what else can I do?"

"Come here, girl." Pa wrapped her in his arms. "Don't cry now. You are the bravest gal I ever met, and Ray is damned lucky to have you. I'll give him a piece of my mind if he ever says anything against you."

She looked up at him through her tears. "Pa, you are the best."

"Let's grab a bite while we have a minute."

They managed some time at the kitchen table and finished the last of the sandwiches before Ray called out, needing the chamber pot again. While Pa helped him; she cleaned the kitchen. Her lips were a tight line as she slapped the dishcloth on the table, shoved the chairs under the table, and heaved garbage into the can outside. She hoped this would end soon. It was hard to stay awake.

"Hey." Pa came into the kitchen. "He's dozing. We should nap while we can. You want the couch?"

They had been trading the couch and the floor since sleeping with Ray became impossible. She accepted the couch, while Pa arranged himself on the floor.

Ray's withdrawal gradually eased a few days later, just when Renata thought she could not possibly stand it any longer.

When she awoke, it was dark, although the kitchen light remained on. How had she slept this long? She heard shuffling from the kitchen, although Pa was still sleeping. Whipping the blanket off, she stumbled around the corner and ran into Ray making coffee.

"Hi, honey." He smiled easily. "Want some coffee? I'm hungry, thought I'd make some scrambled eggs if you're interested."

"You're—you're better?" She touched him tentatively, as though examining an ancient artifact subject to disintegration.

"I began feeling better about two in the morning. No more bouts of the runs, the cramps stopped. My head still hurts, but nothing like before."

He looked her over. "You look terrible." Suddenly he laughed. "Can't believe I said that, knowing how I look. Come here,

Renata."

He gathered her in his arms.

"Ray, I love you. What you've been through…" She shook her head and squeezed his shoulder gently. "I'm here. Truly."

And she knew, finally, that it was true. She would do anything to save him.

Pa staggered into the room rubbing his eyes.

"Whoa, somebody's feeling human again, I think." Pa clapped a leathery hand on his son's shoulder.

"Good morning, Pa. I feel pretty foolish. Did I hurt anyone? Say anything stupid?"

"You didn't hurt anyone, but some of the things you said don't bear repeating," said Renata. "Let's get those eggs going."

Over eggs and toast, Pa announced it was time for him to head back to Moose Jaw, if that suited them.

"So soon?" asked Renata. "But the whole trip has been work. Can't you take a few days to do some sightseeing before you go?" She would have preferred him to stay indefinitely, suspecting Ray was not completely out of the woods yet.

Ray added, "Pa, you've done so much for me. At least allow us to treat you like a guest for a couple of days."

Pa raised his hands in defeat. "Okay, okay, I know when I'm outnumbered. I'll arrange the ticket for three days from now. Satisfied?"

They nodded.

Victoria's downtown reminded Renata of Europe. Its charming stone and brick buildings housed government offices, shops, and restaurants. Renata's favorite was Roger's Chocolates, a tiny shop wedged between two larger ones, which sold a tempting variety of handmade chocolates she could not resist. Pa purchased a small box for Ma, and Ray insisted on a large box of hand-picked goodies for Renata.

"Oh, Ray, you'll make me fat! But since I'm eating for two, I'm not going to say no."

On day two, they took a bus to the famous Butchart Gardens, which was another test for Ray. His scarf and his family were the only screen he needed. Renata noticed his self-consciousness fading.

The third day arrived much too quickly. They saw Pa off on

the *Princess Marguerite*, from which he would catch the train home.

Renata felt bereft. "I'll miss him. He's a wonderful man, and I'm trying hard not to be a crybaby."

Ray pulled her close while they waved to the disappearing ferry. "You and he saved my life. Did you notice something?" Ray gripped her elbows and backed up.

Confused, she shook her head.

"I'm outside! We're in public and I'm not hiding my face. Sure, I've had quite a few stares, but I don't care."

"You're right. How could I miss it? And we've had fun." She leaned in to kiss him, ignoring the glances of two passersby.

"I can think of more fun to be had at home, my girl. Let's go."

Back home, Ray picked her up and carried her to the bed, where they spent the rest of the afternoon making love, dozing, and making love again. Eventually, her bladder forced her up, and then, when she was washing her hands, Ray came behind her, kissing her hair and caressing her naked breasts. She turned to his embrace. This was the old Ray, back at last.

"I will never forget what you and Pa did for me, my love," he said, nuzzling the back of her neck. "I was in trouble, but I couldn't admit it."

"I have you back, now, darling. The only thing I ask is that you never touch that stuff again. Can you do that?"

He leaned back, and their eyes met.

"I knew a lot of boys at Watford who got hooked on morphine, just like me, and none of us would admit it. We used more and more and more. All those pills you threw out, they'd last a real patient a few months. I'd go through them in a week."

"Oy vey."

"A few vets came to our ward to talk about morphine. They'd all been addicted and had quit, but it was hard. The craving is what got to them." He tilted her chin up. "Do you understand what I'm telling you?"

"That you will want to use it again. But I don't understand why."

"It gives you a feeling that you can escape anything you don't like and float in a dreamy world where nothing matters."

"I could have used something like that a few times over the past few years. Good thing I didn't. Is there anything I can do when you are tempted to use it again?"

He considered, twirling a lock of her hair in one finger, grinning that lopsided smile at her.

"Guess."

She slid her hands down his belly and touched his swelling organ. "This?"

He sighed and closed his eye.

Chapter Thirty-two

Calgary, 1945

The Canadian Pacific Railway station in Calgary teemed with returning soldiers, and loved ones anxious to greet them. Balloons and boxes of chocolate were high on the list of gifts; excitement was the prevalent mood. Renata regretted bringing baby Dorothy along, but Ray paved a way through the crowd for them, his parents, and Karen, here to greet Tommy and Lea. Everyone agreed it was important that Tommy meet his sister at the first possible opportunity.

Arranging visas and passage for Lea and Tommy had been less difficult than expected because a for-once cooperative government was determined to reunite families separated by war as quickly as possible.

The move to Calgary, necessitated by the utter lack of non-military positions once Ray began looking for work again, had been a good one. He found a job as a manager for a shipping company. Proud owners of a new home in the Crescent Heights neighborhood, they had made friends with neighbors, planted a garden, and were saving for a car. Renata and Maisie rekindled their friendship, and the families got together frequently. In fact, Maisie, her husband, and their two children had a picnic planned with the Sterns once the new arrivals were settled.

Moose Jaw was too far for daytrips to see Jean and Sheldon, but close enough for occasional visits. Renata taught art at Mount Royal College a few evenings each week, and two of her paintings hung in local galleries.

Ray had never questioned Dorothy's parentage, despite her "early" birth. Renata had received no reply from Hans.

Although far from the wealthy lifestyle they had dreamed of in Alexandria, they had something of more value: contentment.

The public-address system announced the arrival of the ten o'clock train from Medicine Hat and points east. Renata's stomach fluttered. Would Tommy recognize her? It was unlikely, but she wanted it so much. And how would her mother be?

Passengers streamed in, greeted with hugs, kisses, and tears. It was hard watching them and not crying with them, Renata discovered as she waited, holding the squirmy toddler who would have much preferred to be put down. She scanned the flood of passengers.

"There they are!" she shouted and pointed. Lea, she recognized, although she had aged ten years, but the handsome four-year-old beside her took her breath away. "Tommy! Mama! Lea! Over here!"

Ray elbowed through the crowd and reached them first, and Renata noticed the shock on Mama's face when she saw him. Tommy hid and cowered behind Lea.

Finally, they stood face-to-face, did the introductions. They hugged, kissed, spoke kind words, but Mama's voice shook, and she couldn't look Renata in the eye.

"Are you all right, Mama?" Speaking German, Renata put her hands on her mother's shoulders and squeezed gently.

"We're exhausted. I'll be so glad when we stop moving." Lea held Tommy by the hand. "Alexandria after the war wasn't the same. The Brits left, and the Egyptians became quite nasty to Jews. I don't know if we'd have survived there much longer."

"You're safe now. Wait until you see our house." She squeezed Mama's arm and turned to the children. She squatted in front of Tommy with Dorothy, and took his other hand. He lowered his head and puckered his child-red lips.

"Tommy, I am your mother, and this is your sister, Dorothy. Can you say hello to her?"

"Hello." His voice was flat. He turned to Lea.

"Can we go home now?" His English had a slight German accent.

Ray crouched beside him. "Tommy, I'm your father. We're going to your new home now. These are your other grandparents, Grandpa and Grandma Stern, and your Aunt Karen."

Jean offered a balloon, which Tommy accepted gravely. Karen gave him a stick of horehound candy and showed him how to peel back the cellophane wrapper. The taste brought the first smile to his face.

"I can't wait to show you your new bedroom," Renata said.

Tommy nodded, sucking on the sticky candy.

Aware the child must be exhausted and a little frightened by these strangers acting so familiar with him, Renata opted for time-tested mother's techniques. "We'll get you something to eat, and we have some toys for you to play with."

He perked up at the mention of toys, and allowed himself to be carried by Ray, first to the baggage claim, where they arranged to have two suitcases and a trunk delivered that afternoon, and then to the bus stop.

"Here we are. Welcome home." Ray unlocked the door and ushered everyone in. Tommy headed for a toy box in one corner of the living room, while Renata showed Mama around.

"We have three bedrooms, so the children will share, and the third is for you. They aren't large, but they are big enough for a bed and a bureau."

Mama nodded, and dropped her handbag on the bed in her new room. She looked up at her daughter and smiled tentatively. "Your home is so nice, dear. To have my own room after all this time…and a bathtub…you have no idea."

A few tears splashed down her face.

"It's your home, now, too. Would you like to freshen up?"

"Yes, please."

"Here are some towels, then. Come into the kitchen when you're ready."

Jean was deep into a loaf of bread, making tuna sandwiches. Sheldon and Ray were chatting and keeping an eye on the children.

Lea tiptoed into the room and dried her face, as Dorothy

was watching Tommy build a tall castle with wooden blocks. He placed each block meticulously, and had a stack of eleven, when Dorothy swatted it, scattering blocks every which way. She squealed with glee, but Tommy turned purple.

"Mama, look what she did! She broke my tower!"

Both Renata and Lea, face still wet, ran to him. Tommy threw himself into Lea's arms. "Mama, I don't like her! Do we have to stay here?"

Renata, Lea, and Ray froze.

Renata's disbelief rapidly turned to fury. "Tommy, I am your mother. Lea, tell him. Right now."

"Renata, I'm sorry. I can explain..."

"You're explaining why you told my son that you are his mother? What kind of explanation can you possibly have for that? Tell him the truth, this minute."

Ray, Sheldon, and Jean disappeared with Dorothy into the kitchen.

Her voice shaking, Lea took Tommy to a chair and sat him down on her knee. "Tommy, my dear, I have something important to tell you."

The child pouted, and tears filled his eyes.

"I am your grandmother, not your mother. This lady, Renata, is my daughter, and she is your mother." Tears overflowed onto Lea's cheeks as well.

"No!" Tommy scowled and folded his arms. "I don't believe you."

Lea spoke with effort. "It's true. And Ray, the man in the kitchen, is your father."

"But Papa died!" Tommy pulled himself away and stood against the wall.

"Papa was your grandfather."

Where was the script for this? Of all the disasters that could have occurred, this was one Renata had not anticipated.

Painful memories surfaced. The ghastly voyage from Egypt to London. The struggle to find Ray. Letting Hans go. Fighting for Ray's life and sanity, all to reunite her family, and now? Renata sank to the floor, her heart broken for her own suffering, and even more, the misery she saw in her little boy's uncomprehending face.

"Tommy…"

He turned his face to the wall and hunched his shoulders. "I'm not listening to you! Go away!"

"I know you love your grandmother, Tommy, and that is a good thing. But I love you, too, because I am your mother."

He turned to her. Doubt filled his face. His lip wobbled, and tears trickled down his cheeks.

Renata held her arms out. "Come here, Tommy."

Lea tensed.

Slowly, he stood, and took three steps toward Renata, then stopped and looked at Lea.

"Tommy," Renata continued, "it is all right if you don't love me now. You can't love a person you don't remember. But I promise you, I will do all I can to make you happy. One day, I will tell you the whole story of how hard I fought for this very moment. Maybe then, you will come to love me and your father."

She waved Ray into the room and gestured for him to join her on the floor with the children.

"Can I still call her Mama?" the child asked, pointing at Lea.

All three adults shook their heads. Ray said, "You must call me Daddy, and your mother Mommy, but your grandmother Lea you must call Nana. Can you do that?"

The child threw himself at Lea, but she stopped him and held him at arm's length. "No, Tommy. These are your parents now."

Renata noticed the word, "now" as though Tommy were being adopted. She wanted to scream at her mother, but smiled instead. "Tommy, we have always been your parents, but I can see why you're confused. Parents love us and keep us safe. And while I was away, Nana was like a mother to you for four long years."

Tommy's face was scarlet, and he was panting, trying to reach his grandmother, fists straining to reach her. "Why don't you love me anymore? Why don't you want me?"

"I do love you, but you are not mine. Go to your parents." Lea stood abruptly and disappeared into her room, slamming the door shut.

Tommy followed her, wailing and thumping on the door.

Ray handed Dorothy to Renata, and followed his son. Crying escalated to screaming. Ray appeared with Tommy in his arms fighting to get down.

"What should we do?" he asked Renata quietly, struggling to contain the violent child.

She shook her head. "We need him to calm down first, then we'll figure it out. Why don't we put him in the backyard and let him play in the sandbox? We can keep an eye on him through the kitchen window. Maybe Karen or Pa will play with him."

"Okay, Tommy," grunted Ray, "we have a sandbox in the backyard with plenty of toys. We're going to let you go out there, and when you feel better, you can have something to eat."

An hour later, a much calmer child accepted milk, crackers, and cheese from Renata, and agreed to walk to the playground with Ray, Karen, and Sheldon. There had been no sound from Lea's room.

Jean had remained quiet since they arrived home, and had focused on making lunch and doing dishes with Karen's help. Now she looked at Renata, reached out, and patted her hand. "This must be very hard for you."

"Thanks for being here." Renata forced a smile. "It's not what I expected at all, but you know what it's like when one of your children changes."

"I can understand your mother, too. Go to her. You need to sort this out."

Renata tapped on Lea's bedroom door and went in. Lea's eyes were red, and her face was wet.

"Mama, I..." began Renata, but her mother interrupted.

"I am so sorry, so sorry!" She gulped for air.

"Why, Mama, why?" It was impossible to keep the anger out of her voice.

"Once he started talking, Mama was his first word, and it was easier to let him keep calling me that." She glanced into the empty backyard. "After your father died, Tommy started asking questions. I didn't have the heart to tell him the truth. And if something had happened to you, he would have been mine, anyway."

Feeling the dig, Renata admitted to herself that there was

some justification for her mother's behavior. Her anger faded. She sat beside her mother on the bed.

"I'm sorry, too, Mama."

Her mother raised her eyebrows.

"I'm sorry I left. I'm sorry I left Tommy behind, I'm sorry I didn't realize what it would do to you and to him. Or to me." She took her mother's hand. "I learned, Mama. I know what it is to feel unloved and alone like you did."

Lea nodded and looked down.

"I learned some other things, too, Mama." She paused and folded her hands in her lap. "I never realized how selfish I could be."

Mama's eyebrows shot up, but she remained silent.

"Someone I met on my journeys told me. I realized that leaving Tommy with you was selfish, even though it turned out Ray really did need me. I'm sure you can think of a hundred other examples."

"You got with child on purpose, so Ray would marry you. There's nothing much more selfish than that."

Renata winced, remembering her mother's pressure to marry. Was it worth bringing up? "*Touché*, Mama. But we are here, and so is Ray. Let's let the past be the past, and start again."

Lea looked up at her daughter, eyebrows raised in a question mark. "How?"

"I'd like to show you some sketches I made. Would you like to see them?"

Minutes later they examined a half-dozen cardboard and charcoal sketches of London while Renata shared some of the horrors she had experienced.

"Was it as bad as the newspapers said?" asked Lea.

"Much worse. Yet I survived."

"You suffered, too. I never realized, despite your letters." Lea shifted, a slight flush coloring her cheeks. "I think perhaps I'm a little selfish, too."

The two women looked at each other for twenty seconds, then began giggling. Giggles turned to laughter, laughter turned louder and longer, and soon they both had tears on their faces, but this time, the cleansing tears of forgiveness.

They embraced, warmly this time.

"Oh, I forgot," said Mama. "I have a letter for you. Two, actually." She dug in her handbag and handed the wrinkled envelopes over.

Renata ripped one open. It was from Sofia.

> Dear Renata,
> I'm so happy to hear that your mother and son will soon be with you in Canada. My new address is at the bottom of the page. Hamish and I are settled in Greece, along with my parents and our three children. Hamish misses Scotland, so we're planning a trip there as soon as we can save enough money.
> Some sad news, though. I looked up the Moustakis for you. The shop is still there, same name but a different owner, not Jewish, of course. All the Jews are gone. The Moustakis were taken away. The same thing happened to the Pontecorvos, I heard from Isabella since she returned to Italy. The horror of it all weighs heavily on us, but we are determined to rebuild not only our cities, but our faith.
> Your mother told us you have another baby, a girl. That's wonderful! Do write, I miss you very much.
> Love,
> Sofia

Handing the letter to her mother, Renata bowed her head. Six million dead Jews was more than the mind could comprehend, but people she had known, family, friends, helpers, all gone. Jews would mourn forever. She and Ray needed to find a synagogue and reconnect with their faith.

The second letter had vaguely familiar handwriting. Her heart skipped a beat when she saw it was from Hans.

It was dated 1944, August, over a year ago.

> Dear Renata,
> By the time you receive this letter, I will be dead. I am suspected of betrayal by the Germans on whom I am spying, and that never ends well, especially when it is true. I wanted you to know that what we had, in the midst of all

the horror, sustained me long after you had gone, and kept me sane in my darkest moments. And our baby! By the time you receive this, the little one will have arrived, and it is the deepest sadness of my life that I will never hold him or her, or you, again.

I hope you found Ray, and I hope the two of you have a good life together. Be happy, my dearest. Do not weep for me. I am happy to give my life, so others may live.

All my love,

Hans

It was impossible to follow his injunction not to weep. She wept for Hans, his selflessness, his courage, his love, and his child, who would never know whose she was.

"Such a waste, Mama, so much death. I feel guilty being alive."

"We all do, my dear. All we can do is live as well as we can. Come, the others are back."

Arm in arm, the women returned to the kitchen where Ray was buttering crackers.

"It was fun at the park, Mama…I mean, Nana," said Tommy, his smile fading with his mistake. Renata's mother had raised a child who wanted to please. "And I have another grandpa. He pushed me on the swing."

He looked up at Sheldon, who smiled and mussed the child's hair.

Nana Lea beamed. "Good boy for remembering." She sat at the table and helped Dorothy with her cup of juice.

Renata wrapped her arms around Ray's neck and kissed his damaged skin.

He smiled and nuzzled her. "Did you and Lea sort it out?"

She nodded, hinting at more details to come. "All right, who's ready for a story?"

"Me!" yelled Tommy. Dorothy banged her empty cup on the table.

"Come on, then."

Renata scooped up Dorothy and went into the living room, where she selected four children's books from a pile. The adults and Tommy followed. With Dorothy beside her, Renata sat on the sofa. Ray joined them, while Lea took the old armchair. Sheldon and Karen brought in kitchen chairs. Tommy stood between his parents, hesitant, until Renata opened the first book and began to read; then he came close, wanting to see the pictures.

"Um, M-mommy…" He hesitated. "Can I sit with you and…Daddy?"

"Of course." She seated him between herself and Ray.

By the story's end, both children were nearly asleep. Renata and Ray carried them to their beds and tucked them in, turning on a little musical lamp they had bought. Seeing the two together, Renata was overpowered by love for her children and her husband. She leaned on his shoulder.

He kissed her cheek. "I can't believe this day has finally arrived, thanks to you."

"Me, neither. Finally, I have what I've always wanted. My family together. And we are safe." She wrapped her arms around him. "But there's something else I must do, for Tommy. Would you mind entertaining the family for a little while?"

"Of course not."

Ray announced lemonade for all, and led the others into the now shady backyard. Renata stole into their bedroom for pen and paper. She began to write.

"The young woman drew rapidly, sketching the old man on his knees in the street with blood running down his face…"

Notes

World War II is such a richly documented period of history that one hardly supposes there is much about it that is not written down or photographed somewhere. Yet, I learned many surprising facts in my research for this book.

For example, I learned that the mass exodus of Europeans to Egypt and Syria was far less documented than, for example, the exodus of Jews to Palestine. Because refugee camps in Egypt and Syria were not created until 1942, I modified that date to fit the needs of my story. I lengthened and changed dates of the bombings of Alexandria for the same reason.

I was fortunate to have eyewitness accounts and family stories that included the European refugees in Alexandria, Egypt; London during the latter part of the war, and convoy voyages. I bolstered these accounts with historical photos, books, and websites, which provided me with rich details of settings I have not had the opportunity to visit.

All ships in the book, were real vessels operating in the theatre in which I placed them. I took some liberties with the M.V. Georgic, which was indeed damaged during the war, and later repaired, minus one of its original two smokestacks. However, it was not sunk in the Atlantic Ocean, but in the Mediterranean. The Royal Navy keeps an excellent archival website on convoys and navy battles during WWII, which I drew from, in my description of activity in the Mediterranean theater of war.

The War Brides program operated much as described. Convoys heading for Canada would dock at either Halifax, Nova Scotia, or New York City. The destination of convoys was a closely guarded secret, the better to confound the U-boats and German warships.

My intent is to keep this book as true as possible to real events. Nonetheless, it is a work of fiction, and I trust my readers will forgive my occasional variances from the truth. Any errors are my own.

About The Author

Ann Griffin comes from a family of adventurous women. An immigrant twice (to Canada and to the USA,) she understands from personal experience the challenges of being uprooted, either by choice or not, and remaking a life in a new place.

Ann writes historical fiction, flash fiction, and short non-fiction. She has published articles in the journal of the British Home Child Advocacy and Research Association, and guest blogged for the award-winning writers' blog, Writers in the Storm.

Ann and her husband divide their time between Mesa, Arizona, and Toronto, Canada.

Connect with Ann Griffin

Facebook: facebook.com/anngriffinwriter
Twitter: @anngborn2write
Website: anngriffinwriter.com

Did you like this book? Please leave a review!

Would you like Ann to speak to your book club or other organization?
Contact Ann at info@anngriffinwriter.com and she will be pleased
to arrange it.